CHAOS

Patricia Cornwell is recognized as one of the world's top bestselling crime authors with novels translated into thirty-six languages in more than 120 countries. Her novels have won numerous prestigious awards including the Edgar, the Creasey, the Anthony, the Macavity, and the Prix du Roman d'Aventure. Beyond the Scarpetta series, Cornwell has written a definitive book about Jack the Ripper, a biography, and two more fiction series among others. Cornwell, a licensed helicopter pilot and scuba diver, actively researches the cutting-edge forensic technologies that inform her work. She was born in Miami, grew up in Montreat, NC, and now lives and works in Boston.

www.PatriciaCornwell.com

@1pcornwell

Facebook.com/Patricia.Cornwell

1pcornwell

ALSO BY PATRICIA CORNWELL

Patricia Cornwell

CHAOS

HarperCollins*Publishers*

HarperCollins*Publishers*
1 London Bridge Street
London SE1 9GF

www.harpercollins.co.uk

First published in Great Britain by HarperCollins*Publishers* 2016

2

First published in the United States by William Morrow,
an imprint of HarperCollins*Publishers* 2016

A catalogue record for this book is
available from the British Library

ISBN: 9780008150631

This novel is entirely a work of fiction.
The names, characters and incidents portrayed in it are
the work of the author's imagination. Any resemblance to
actual persons, living or dead, events or localities is
entirely coincidental.

Printed and bound in Great Britain by
Clays Ltd St Ives plc

MIX
Paper from
responsible sources
FSC™ C007454

FSC™ is a non-profit international organisation established to promote
the responsible management of the world's forests. Products carrying the
FSC label are independently certified to assure consumers that they come
from forests that are managed to meet the social, economic and
ecological needs of present and future generations,
and other controlled sources.

Find out more about HarperCollins and the environment at
www.harpercollins.co.uk/green

To Staci
—In Memory of Tram—

THERE IS LOVE IN ME THE LIKES OF WHICH YOU'VE
NEVER SEEN. THERE IS RAGE IN ME THE LIKES OF
WHICH SHOULD NEVER ESCAPE.

—Mary Shelley, *Frankenstein*

CHAOS

From the Ancient Greek (χάος or kháos)

A vast chasm or void

Anarchy

The science of unpredictability

PROLOGUE

BEYOND THE BRICK WALL bordering Harvard Yard, four tall chimneys and a gray slate roof with white-painted dormers peek through the branches of hardwood trees.

The Georgian building is a welcome sight no more than fifteen minutes ahead as the crow flies. But walking wasn't smart. I was foolish to refuse a ride. Even in the shade it feels like an oven. The atmosphere is stagnant, nothing stirring in the hot humid air.

Were it not for the distant sounds of traffic, the infrequent pedestrian, the vapor trails overhead, I might believe I'm the only human left on a post-apocalyptic earth. I've never seen the Harvard campus this deserted except maybe during a bomb scare. But then I've also not been witness to such extreme weather in this part of the world, and blizzards and arctic blasts don't count.

New Englanders are used to that but not temperatures edging past a hundred degrees Fahrenheit. The sun is molten in a bone-scrubbed sky that the heat has bleached the blue out of as I've heard it described. *The greenhouse effect. Global warming. God's punishment. The Devil's in his workshop. Mercury in retrograde. El Niño. The end times.*

These are some of the explanations for one of the worst heat waves in Massachusetts's history. Business at my headquarters, the Cambridge Forensic Center, has gone through the roof, and that's the paradox of what I do. When things are bad they're normal. When they're worse they're good. It's a gift and a curse that I have job security in this imperfect world, and as I take a shortcut through the center of the campus in the stifling heat, I tweak the talk I'm going to give at the Kennedy School of Government tomorrow night.

Cleverness, a play on words, provocative stories that are real, and maybe my sister Dorothy isn't the hopeless tool I've always believed. She says that I have to be entertaining if I'm to get an auditorium full of jaded Ivy League intellectuals and policy makers to listen. Maybe they'll even walk around in my shoes for once if I share the dark side, the underbelly, the scary basement no one wants to enter or acknowledge.

As long as I'm not expected to repeat insensitive jokes, certainly not the ones I constantly hear from the cops, rather dreadful slogans that end up on T-shirts and coffee cups. I'm not going to say *our day begins when yours ends* even if it's true. Although I suppose it's all right to quip that the more dire the straits the more necessary I am. Catastrophes are my calling. Dreadful news gets me out of bed. Tragedy is my bread and butter, and the cycle of life and death remains unbroken no matter our IQ.

This is how my sister thinks I should explain myself to hundreds of influential students, faculty, politicos and global leaders tomorrow night. In my opinion I shouldn't need to explain myself at all. But apparently I do, Dorothy said over the phone last night while our elderly mother was ranting loudly in the background to her thieving South American housekeeper, whose name—no kidding—is Honesty. Apparently Honesty is stealing vast amounts of jewelry and cash again, hiding Mom's pills, eating her food and rearranging her furniture in the hope she'll trip and break a hip.

Honesty the housekeeper isn't doing any such thing and never did or would, and sometimes having a nearly photographic memory isn't to my advantage. I recall last night's telephonic drama, including the parts in Spanish, hearing every word of it in my head. I can replay Dorothy's rapid-fire self-assured voice advising me all the while about how not to lose an audience since clearly I will if left to my own devices. She told me:

Walk right up to the podium and scan the crowd with a deadpan face, and say: "Welcome. I'm Doctor Kay Scarpetta. I take patients without appointments and still make house calls. Wouldn't you just die to have my hands all over you? Because it can be arranged." And then you wink.

Who could resist? That's what you should tell them, Kay! Something funny, sexy and non-PC. And they're eating out of your hand. For once in your life you need to listen to your little sis very carefully. I didn't get where I am by not knowing a thing or two about publicity and marketing.

And one of the biggest problems with deadbeat jobs, no pun intended, like working in funeral homes and morgues, is nobody knows the first thing about how to promote or sell anything because why bother? Well to be fair, funeral homes are better at it than where you work. It's not like it's part of your job description to make a dead person look presentable or care if the casket is pretty. So you have all of the disadvantages of the funeral business but nothing to sell and nobody to say thank you.

THROUGHOUT MY CAREER AS a forensic pathologist my younger only sibling has managed to equate what I do with being a mortuary scientist or simply someone who deals with messes no one else wants to touch.

Somehow it's the logical conclusion to my taking care of our dying father when I was a child. I became the go-to person when something was painful or disgusting and needed tending to or cleaning up. If an animal got run over or a bird flew into a window or our father had another nosebleed, my sister would run screaming to me. She still does if she needs something, and she never takes into account convenience or timing.

But at this juncture in life my attitude is the two of us aren't getting any younger. I've decided to make a real effort to keep an open mind even if my sister might be the most selfish human being I've ever known. But she's bright and talented, and I'm no saint either. I admit I've been stubborn about acknowledging her value, and that's not fair.

Because it's possible she really might know what she's doing when she mandates that I should speak less like a legal brief or a lab report and more like a pundit or a poet. I need to turn up the volume, the brightness and the color, and I've been keeping that in mind as I polish my opening remarks, including cues such as underlines for emphasis and pauses for laughter.

I take a sip from a bottle of water that's hot enough to brew tea. I nudge my dark glasses up as they continue to slip down my sweaty nose. The sun is a relentless blacksmith hammering in twilight's fiery forge. Even my hair is hot as my low-heeled tan leather pumps *click-click* on bricks, my destination now about ten minutes out. Mentally I go through my talk:

Good evening Harvard faculty, students, fellow physicians, scientists and other distinguished guests.

As I scan the crowd tonight I see Pulitzer and Nobel Prize winners, mathematicians and astrophysicists who are also writers, painters and musicians.

Such a remarkable collection of the best and the brightest, and we are extremely honored to have the governor here, and the attorney gen-

eral, and several senators and congressmen in addition to members of the media, and business leaders. I see my good friend and former mentor General John Briggs hiding in the back, slinking low in his seat, <u>cringing</u> over the thought of my being up here. [Pause for laughter]

For those of you who don't know, he's the chief of the Armed Forces Medical Examiner System, the AFMES. In other words, General Briggs would be the <u>forensic surgeon general of the United States</u> were there such a position. And in a little while he's going to join me during the Q&A part of the program to discuss the Columbia *space shuttle disaster of 2003.*

We're going to share what we've learned from materials science and aeromedicine, and also from the recoveries and examinations of the seven astronauts' remains that were scattered over a fifty-some-mile scene in Texas . . .

I HAVE TO GIVE Dorothy credit.

She's dramatic and colorful, and I'm somewhat touched that she's flying in for the lecture even if I have no idea why. She says she wouldn't miss tomorrow night but I don't believe her. My sister's not been to Cambridge in the eight years I've headed the CFC. My mother hasn't either, but she doesn't like to travel and won't anymore. I don't know Dorothy's excuse.

Only that she's never been interested until now, and it's a shame she had to choose tonight of all nights to fly to Boston. The first Wednesday of the month, barring an emergency, my husband Benton and I meet for dinner at the Harvard Faculty Club, where I'm not a member. He is and not because of his FBI status. That won't get you any special favors at Harvard, the Massachusetts Institute of Technology (MIT) and other Ivy League institutions in the area.

But as a consulting forensic psychologist at the Harvard-affiliated McLean Hospital in nearby Belmont, my FBI criminal-intelligence-analyst husband can avail himself of the most marvelous libraries, museums, and scholars in the world anytime he wants. He can help himself to the Faculty Club to his heart's content.

We can even reserve a guest room upstairs, and we have on more than one occasion been given enough whiskey or wine during dinner. But that's not going to happen with Dorothy flying in, and I really shouldn't have said yes when she asked me to pick her up later tonight and drop her off at her daughter Lucy's house, which will get Benton and me home after midnight.

I don't know why Dorothy asked me specifically unless it's her way of making sure we get to spend a little alone time together. When I said yes I'd come and Benton would be with me, her response was "I'm sure. Well it doesn't matter." But when she said that I realized it does matter. She has something she wants to discuss with me privately, and even if we don't get the chance tonight, we have time.

My sister left her return flight open-ended, and I can't help but think how wonderful it would be if it turned out I'd always been wrong about her. Maybe her real reason for venturing north to New England is she feels the same way I do. Maybe she at long last wants to be friends.

How amazing if we become a united front when coping with our aging mother, with Lucy and her partner Janet, and with their adopted nine-year-old son Desi. And also their newest addition Tesla, a rescue bulldog puppy who's staying with Benton and me in Cambridge for a while. Someone has to train her, and our greyhound Sock is getting old and likes the company.

CHAPTER 1

MY SHOES SWISH THROUGH the hot dry grass, and sweat trickles beneath my clothes, down my chest, my back. I'm moving again, seeking shade as the sun settles lower and the slanted light shifts.

Every time I escape the glare it finds me again, the walled-in center of the Harvard campus a maze with its greens and lawns, its quadrangles and courtyards connected by paths and walkways. The stately brick-and-stone buildings draped in ivy live up to the stereotype, and I remember what I felt when I was given a tour at the age of fifteen. It's as if I'm back in time with every step I take, sweetly, sadly.

It was on one of my few trips outside of Florida during my senior year in high school when I began exploring colleges and what I might amount to in life. I'll never forget walking exactly where I am now and experiencing a limbic rush at the same time I was self-conscious and out of place. The memory is interrupted when I'm startled by a vibration, what feels and sounds like a large insect buzzing.

I stop walking on the piping-hot sidewalk, looking around, noticing a drone flying high over the Yard. Then I realize the buzzing is my own phone muffled by my suit jacket pocket, where it's tucked away from the heat and sun. I check to see who's calling. It's Cambridge Police Investigator Pete Marino, and I answer.

"Is there something going on that I don't know about?" he says right off, and the connection is pretty bad.

"I don't think so," I puzzle as I bake on the bricks.

"Why are you walking? Nobody should be out walking in this shit." He's curt and sounds irritated, and I'm instantly alerted this isn't a friendly call. "So what the hell got into you?"

"Errands." I feel on guard, and his tone is annoying. "And I'm walking to meet Benton."

"Meeting him for what reason?" Marino asks as our cellular connection continues to deteriorate from good to spotty, back to okay and then fractured before it's better again.

"The reason I'm meeting my husband is to eat dinner," I reply with a trace of irony, and I don't want a tense time with yet another person today. "Is everything all right?"

"Maybe you should be the one telling me that." His big voice suddenly booms painfully in my right ear. "How come you're not with Bryce?"

My chatterbox chief of staff must have informed Marino about my refusing to get back into the car at Harvard Square, about my *violation of protocol and reckless disregard for safety.*

Before I can answer, Marino begins confronting me as if I'm a suspect in a crime. "You got out of the car about an hour and a half ago, were inside The Coop for maybe twenty minutes," he's saying. "And when you finally exited the store on Mass Ave? Where'd you go?"

"I had an errand on Arrow Street." The sidewalks in the Yard form a brick spiderweb, and I find myself constantly making adjustments, taking the most efficient path, the quickest and coolest.

"What errand?" he asks as if it's any of his business.

"At the Loeb Center, picking up tickets for *Waitress,* the Sara Bareilles musical," I reply with forced civility that's beginning to waver. "I thought Dorothy might like to go."

"From what I hear you were acting as squirrelly as a shithouse rat."

"Excuse me?" I stop walking.

"That's the way it's been described."

"By whom? Bryce?"

"Nope. We got a nine-one-one call about you," Marino says, and I'm stunned.

HE INFORMS ME THAT his police department was contacted about "a young guy and his older lady friend" arguing in Harvard Square about 4:45 P.M.

This young guy was described as in his late twenties with sandy-brown hair, blue capri pants, a white T-shirt, sneakers, designer sunglasses, and a tattoo of a marijuana leaf. The tattoo isn't right but the rest of it is.

Supposedly the concerned citizen who called the police recognized me from the news, and it's disturbing that my clothing description is accurate. I do in fact have on a khaki skirt suit, a white blouse, and tan leather pumps. Unfortunately it's also correct I have a run in my panty hose, and I'll strip them off and toss them when I get where I'm going.

"Was I mentioned by name?" I can't believe this.

"The person said words to the effect that Doctor Kay Scarpetta was arguing with her pothead boyfriend and stormed out of the car." Marino passes along another outrage.

"I didn't storm. I got out like a normal person while he stayed behind the wheel and continued to talk."

"You sure he didn't get out and open the door for you?"

"He never does and I don't encourage it. Maybe that's what someone saw and misinterpreted it as him being angry. Bryce opened his window so we could talk and that was it."

Marino lets me know that next I became abusive and physically violent, slapping Bryce through the open window I just described while repeatedly jabbing him in the chest with my index finger. He was yelling as if I was causing him injury and terror, and to put it succinctly, what a crock of shit. But I don't say anything because of the uneasiness in my gut, a hollow tight feeling that's my equivalent of a red warning flag.

Marino's a cop. I may have known him forever but Cambridge is his turf. Technically he could give me a hard time if he wants, and that's a new and insane thought. He's never arrested me, not that there's ever been a good reason. But he's never so much as given me a parking ticket or warned me not to jaywalk. Professional courtesy is a two-way street. But it can quickly become a dead end if you're not careful.

"I admit I might have been a little out of sorts but it's not true that I slapped anyone—" I start to say.

"Let's start with the first part of your statement," Marino the detective interrupts me. "How little's a little?"

"Are you interviewing me now? Should you read me my rights? Do I need a lawyer?"

"You're a lawyer."

"I'm not being funny, Marino."

"I'm not either. A *little* out of sorts? I'm asking because he said you started yelling."

"Before or after I slapped him?"

"Getting pissy doesn't help anything, Doc."

"I'm not pissy, and let's be clear about who you're even referencing. Let's start with that. Because you know how Bryce exaggerates."

"What I know is supposedly the two of you were fighting and disturbing the peace."

"He actually said that?"

"The witness did."

"What witness?"

"The one who called in the complaint."

"Did you talk to this witness yourself?"

"I couldn't find anybody who saw anything."

"Then you must have looked," I point out.

"After we got the call, I cruised the Square and asked around. Same thing I usually get. Nobody saw a damn thing."

"Exactly. This is ridiculous."

"I'm concerned someone might be out to get you," he says, and we've been through this so many times over the years.

Marino lives and breathes his phobic conviction that something horrible is going to happen to me. But what he's really worried about is his own self. It's the same way he was with his former wife Doris before she finally ran off with a car salesman. Marino doesn't understand the difference between neediness and love. They feel the same to him.

"If you want to waste taxpayer dollars you can check the CCTV cameras around the Square, especially in front of The Coop," I suggest. "You'll see I didn't slap Bryce or anyone else."

"I'm wondering if this has to do with your talk at the Kennedy School tomorrow night," Marino says. "It's been all over the news because it's controversial. When you and General Briggs decided to make a presentation about the space shuttle blowing up maybe you should have expected a bunch of fruit loops to come out of the woodwork. Some of them think a UFO shot down the *Columbia*. And that's why the space shuttle program was canceled."

"I'm still waiting for a name of this alleged witness who lied to one of your nine-one-one operators." I'm not interested in hearing him obsess about conspiracists and the pandemonium they might create at the Kennedy School event.

"He wouldn't identify himself to the operator who took the call," Marino says. "He was probably using one of those track phones you can buy right there at the CVS. It's one of those numbers you can't trace to anyone. Not that we're done trying, but that's how it's looking, and it's pretty much what we're up against these days."

I pass through the shade of a huge old oak with low-spreading branches that are too lush and green for September. The early evening heat presses down like a flaming hand, flattening and scorching the life out of everything, and I switch my shopping bag to my other arm. My messenger-style briefcase also has gotten very heavy, packed with a laptop, paperwork and other personal effects, the wide strap biting into my shoulder.

"Where are you exactly?" Marino's voice is cutting in and out.

"Taking a shortcut." I'm not interested in giving him my precise whereabouts. "And you? You're muffled every other minute or talking in a barrel. Are you in your car?"

"What'd you do, take the Johnston Gate so you can cut through the Yard to Quincy Street?"

"How else would I go?" I'm evasive now in addition to being slightly breathless as I trudge along.

"So you're near the church," he says.

"Why are you asking? Are you coming to arrest me?"

"As soon as I find my handcuffs. Maybe you've seen them?"

"Maybe ask whoever you're dating these days?"

"You're gonna exit the Yard through the gate across from the museums. You know, at the light that will be on your left on the other side of the wall." It seems like a directive rather than an assumption or a question.

"Where are you?" as my suspicions grow.

"What I just suggested would be most direct," he says. "Past the church, past the Quad."

CHAPTER 2

I WALK THROUGH A BLACK wrought-iron gate in the brick wall bordering the Yard, and I look up and down Quincy Street.

On the other side of it the entire block is taken up by the recently renovated brick-and-concrete Harvard Art Museum that includes six levels of galleries under a glass pyramid roof. I wait near a line of parked cars glaring in angled sunlight that is slowly waning, and I check the time and weather on my phone.

It's still an oppressive ninety-three degrees at 6:40 P.M., and I don't know what I was thinking a little while ago. But I simply couldn't take it anymore as Bryce prattled nonstop while he drove along the river toward the Anderson Memorial Bridge, turning right at the red-roofed Weld Boathouse, following John F. Kennedy Street to Massa-chusetts Avenue.

I didn't think I could listen to one more word, and I instructed him not to wait for me as I climbed out of the SUV in front of the college bookstore, The Coop. Harvard Square with its shops and Red Line subway stop is always populated even in the most miserable weather. There's going to be foot traffic and a fairly steady panhandling pop-ulation 24/7.

It wasn't an appropriate place for Bryce to roll down his window and argue like a boy-toy lover with a lady boss mature enough to be a cougar. He wouldn't listen or leave me, and started sounding slightly hysterical, which unfortunately is his personality. He wanted me to state "for the record" why I no longer desired his assistance and to inform him "chapter and verse" if he'd "done something." He kept repeating that he just knew he'd "done something" and wouldn't listen each time I denied it.

The curious were watching like hawks. A homeless man sitting on the sidewalk in front of CVS, shading himself with his cardboard sign, stared at us with the beady eyes of a magpie. It wasn't exactly an ideal spot to park a vehicle that has OFFICE OF THE CHIEF MEDICAL EXAMINER and the CFC's crest, the scales of justice and caduceus painted in blue on the doors. The SUV's back windows are blacked out, and I understand the impact when one of our marked vehicles pulls up.

After I managed to shoo Bryce off, I shopped inside The Coop for gifts for my mother and sister. I made sure my clingy chief of staff really was gone when I finally emerged from the air-conditioning into the brutal heat, heading out on Brattle Street.

I swung by the American Repertory Theater, the ART in the Loeb Center, to pick up six tickets for *Waitress,* having reserved the best orchestra seats in the house. After that I backtracked on Massachusetts Avenue, cutting through the Yard and ending up where I am now on Quincy Street.

I pass the Carpenter Center for the Visual Arts on my left, and I must look like a holy mess. After all the trouble I went to before my ill-advised ride, showering in my office, changing into a suit that's now wrinkled and sweat-stained. I dabbed on Benton's favorite Amorvero perfume that he finds in Italy. It's the signature fragrance of the Hotel Hassler in Rome, where he proposed to me. But I can't smell the exotic scent anymore as I sniff my wrist, waiting at an intersection.

Heat rises in shimmering waves from the tar-smelling pavement, and I hear Marino's big voice before I see him.

"You know what they say about mad Englishmen and dogs going out in this shit?"

I turn around at the garbled cliché and he's stopped at a light, the driver's window open of his unmarked midnight-blue SUV. Now I know why the reception was so bad when we talked a moment ago. It's what I suspected. He's been cruising the area looking for me, talking to people in the Square. He turns on his emergency flashers and whelps his siren, cutting between cars in the opposite lane, heading toward me.

Marino double-parks, climbs out, and I don't think I'll ever get used to seeing him in a suit and tie. Smart attire wasn't designed with the likes of him in mind. Nothing really fits him except his own skin.

ALMOST SIX-FOOT-FIVE, HE WEIGHS two hundred and fifty pounds give or take thirty. His tan shaved head is smooth like polished stone, his hands and feet the size of boats. Marino's shoulders are the width of a door, and he could bench-press five of me he likes to brag.

He's handsome in a primitive way with a big ruddy face, heavy brow and prominent nose. He has a caveman jaw and strong white teeth, and he tends to explode out of business clothes like the Incredible Hulk. Nothing dressy and off the rack looks quite right on him, and part of the problem is he shouldn't be left to his own devices when he shops, which isn't often or planned. It would be helpful if he would clean out his closets and garage occasionally but I'm pretty sure he never has.

As he steps up on the sidewalk I notice the sleeves of his navy-blue suit jacket are above the wrist. His trouser cuffs are high-waters that show his gray tube socks, and he has on black leather trainers that aren't laced all the way up. His tie is almost color coordinated and just as unfashionable, black-and-red-striped and much too wide, possibly from the 1980s when people wore polyester bell-bottoms, Earth Shoes and leisure suits.

He has his reasons for what he wears, and the tie no doubt is woven of special memories, maybe a bullet he dodged, a perfect game he bowled, the biggest fish he ever caught or an especially good first date. Marino makes a point of never throwing out something that matters to him. He'll wander into thrift shops and junk stores looking for a past he liked better than the here and now, and it's ironic that a badass would be so sentimental.

"Come on. I'll drop you off." His eyes are blacked out by vintage Ray-Ban aviator glasses I gave to him a few birthdays ago.

"Why would I need a ride?" The entrance to the brick path leading from the concrete sidewalk to the Faculty Club is just up ahead, a minute's walk from here at most.

But he isn't going to take no for an answer. He steers me off the sidewalk, raising a big mitt of a hand to stop traffic as we cross the street. He's not holding me but I'm not exactly free as he guides me into the front seat of his police vehicle, where I struggle awkwardly with my bags while the run in my panty hose races from my knee down to the back of my shoe as if trying to escape Marino's madness.

I can't help but think, *Here we go again.* Another spectacle. To some it might look like I'm being picked up and questioned by the police, and I wonder if I'll be hearing that next.

"Why are you riding around looking for me, since it seems that's what you're doing?" I ask as he shuts the door. "Seriously, Marino." But he can't hear me.

He walks around and climbs into the driver's seat, and the interior is spotless and tricked out with every siren, light, toolbox, storage chest and piece of crime-scene equipment known to man. The dark vinyl is slick and I smell Armor All. The cloth seats hardly look sat on, the console as clean as new and the glass sparkles as if the SUV was just detailed. Marino is meticulous about his vehicles. His house, office and attire are another story.

"Did I tell you how much I hate the damn phone?" he starts complaining as he shuts his door with a thud. "Some things we don't need to be talking about on a wireless device that has access to every damn thing about your life."

"Why are you dressed up?"

"I had a wake. Nobody you know."

"I see." I don't really.

Marino isn't the type to put on a suit and tie for a wake. He'll barely do that for a funeral or a wedding, and he's certainly not dressing up in weather like this unless he has a special reason he's not saying.

"Well you look nice, and you smell good. Let me see. Cinnamon, sandalwood, a hint of citrus and musk. British Sterling always reminds me of high school."

"Don't change the subject."

"I didn't know we had a subject."

"I'm talking about spying. Remember when the biggest worry was someone riding around with a scanner," he says. "Trying to hack into your house phone that way? Remember when there weren't cameras in your face everywhere? I stopped by the Square a while ago to see who might be hanging around, and some snotty asshole college kid started filming me with his phone."

"How do you know it was a college kid?"

"Because he looked like a spoiled little brat in his flip-flops, baggy shorts and Rolex watch."

"What were you doing?"

"Just asking a few questions about what they might have seen earlier. You know, there's always the usual suspects hanging out in front of The Coop, the CVS. Not as many in this heat but they'd rather be free and footloose in the great unwashed outdoors than in a nice shelter out of the elements. Then the kid was pointing his phone at me like I'm going to shoot someone for no reason and maybe he'll get lucky and catch it on film. Meanwhile some damn drone was buzzing around. I hate technology," he adds grumpily.

"Please tell me why I'm sitting here because clearly I don't need a ride since I've already arrived at my destination."

"Yeah you don't need a ride, all right. I'd say the damage is already done." He looks me up and down, his sunglasses lingering too long on the run in my hose.

"And I'm sure you didn't pick me up just to tell me that."

"Nope. I want to know what's really going on with Bryce." Marino's Ray-Bans seem to pin me in my seat.

"I didn't know anything was—beyond his being more frazzled and annoying than usual."

"Exactly. And why might that be? Think about it."

"Okay, I'm thinking about it. Possibly because of the heat and how busy work has been. As you well know we've had an overload of weather-related cases, and he and Ethan are having trouble with that same abusive neighbor, and let's see . . . I believe Bryce's grandmother had her gallbladder removed the other week. In other words there's been a lot of stress. But who the hell knows what's going on with him or anyone, Marino?"

"If there's a reason we shouldn't trust Bryce, now's the time to spill it, Doc."

"It seems to me we've discussed this enough," I say over the blasting air-conditioning, which is going to chill me to my marrow because my clothes are so damp. "I don't have time to ride around with you right now, and I need to make some effort to clean up before dinner."

I start to get out, and he reaches for my arm again.

18

CHAPTER 3

STAY." HE SAYS IT as if he's addressing his German shepherd Quincy, who's currently not in the cage in back. As it turns out, in addition to being a failed cadaver dog, he's also a fair-weather man's best friend.

Named after the legendary medical examiner on TV, this Quincy doesn't venture out to any crime scene when the conditions are inclement. I suspect Marino's furry sidekick is safely at home right now on his Tempur-Pedic bed in the den with the air-conditioning and DOGTV on.

"I'm going to drop you off the last damn fifty feet. Sit and enjoy the cool," Marino says.

I move my arm because I don't like being grabbed even gently.

"You need to hear me out." He shoves the gearshifter in drive. "Like I said, I didn't want to go into it over the phone. We sure as hell can't know who's spying anymore, right? And if Bryce is compromising the CFC's security or yours I want us to find out before it's too late."

I remind Marino that we use personal proprietary smartphones and have the benefit of encryption, firewalls and all sorts of special and highly secure apps. It's unlikely that our conversations or e-mails can be hacked. My computer-genius-niece Lucy, the CFC cyber-crimes expert, makes very sure of that.

"Are you talking with her at all about any of this?" I ask. "If you're so worried we're being spied on don't you think you could take it up with her? Since that's her job?"

Just as I'm saying this my phone rings and it's Lucy requesting her own version of FaceTime, meaning she'd like us to see each other as we talk.

"What timing," I say right off as her keenly pretty face fills the display on my phone. "We were just talking about you."

"I've only got a minute." Her eyes are green lasers. "Three things. First, my mom just called and her plane is going to be delayed a little bit. Well, I shouldn't say *a little bit* even if that's how she described it. We don't know for how long at this point. And I'm not a hundred percent sure what's going on with air traffic control. But there's a hold on all outbound traffic at the moment."

"What's she being told?" I ask as my heart sinks.

"They're changing gates or something. Mom and I didn't talk long but she said it may be closer to ten thirty or eleven by the time she gets here."

It's nice of my sister to let me know, it flashes in my mind. As busy as Benton and I are, and she wouldn't think twice about making us wait at the airport half the night.

"Second, the latest just landed from Tailend Charlie." Lucy's eyes are moving as she talks, and I try to figure out where she is. "I haven't listened to it yet. As soon as I'm freed up from the nine-one-one bullshit call I will."

"I assume what was sent was another audio clip in Italian," I point out because Lucy isn't fluent and wouldn't be able to translate all or possibly any of it.

She says yes, that at a glance the latest communication from Tailend Charlie is like the other eight I've received since the first day of September. The anonymous threat was sent at the same time of day, is the same type of file and the recording is the same length. But she hasn't listened, and I tell her we'll deal with it later.

Then she asks, "Where are you? In whose car?" She's vivid against a backdrop of complete darkness, as if she's in a cave.

Yet her rose-gold hair is shiny in ambient light that wavers like a movie is playing in the background. Shadows flicker on her face, and it occurs to me she might be inside the Personal Immersion Theater, what at the CFC we call the PIT.

I tell her I'm with Marino, and that brings her to the third and most important point; she says, "Have you seen what's on Twitter?"

"If you're asking then I'm sure it's not good," I reply.

"I'm sending it to you now. Gotta go." And then Lucy is gone from the small rectangular screen just like that.

"What?" Marino is scowling. "What's on Twitter?"

"Hold on." I open the e-mail Lucy just sent, and click on the tweet she cut-and-pasted. "Well as you suspected, there appears to be a video of you talking to some of the usual suspects in Harvard Square."

I show it to him and can feel his wounded pride as he watches the distant figure of himself lumbering about, barking questions at homeless people loitering in front of various businesses. Marino herds one man in and out of the shade as this person tries to duck questions in a most animated fashion. The indistinguishable noise of Marino raising his voice while the man shuffles from pillar to post is embarrassing. And the caption is worse. *OccupyScarpetta* with a hashtag.

"What the hell?" Marino says.

"I guess the gist is that you're territorial about me and were asking a lot of questions because of it. I presume that's how my name ended up in the tweet." His lack of a response answers my question. "But I doubt it will do any real damage except to your ego," I add. "It's silly, that's all. Just ignore it."

HE ISN'T LISTENING, AND I really do need to go.

"I'd like a minute to clean up." It's my way of telling Marino I've had enough of being held hostage in his truck full of gloom and doom. "So if you'll unlock the doors and release me please? Maybe we can talk tomorrow or some other time."

Marino pulls away from his illegal double-parking spot. He eases to the curb in front of the Faculty Club, set back on acres of grassy lawn behind a split-rail paling.

"You're not taking this seriously enough." He looks at me.

"Which part?"

"We're under surveillance, and the question is who and why. For sure someone's got Bryce tagged. How else can you explain the marijuana tattoo?"

"There's nothing to explain. He doesn't have a tattoo of any description."

"He does. Specifically, a marijuana leaf, as it was referred to in the call," Marino says.

"No way. He's so afraid of needles he won't even get a flu shot."

"Obviously you don't know the story. The tattoo is right here." Marino leans over and jabs a thick finger at his outer left ankle, which I can't see very well from where I'm sitting even if I knew to look. "It's fake," he says. "I guess you didn't know that part."

"It would seem I don't know much."

"The marijuana leaf is a temporary tattoo. It's a joke from last night when he and Ethan were with friends. And typical of Bryce? He figured he could wash it off before he went to bed, but a lot of these temporary tattoos can last for the better part of a week."

"Obviously you've talked to him." I look at Marino's flushed shiny face. "Did he reach out to you?"

"I got hold of him when I heard about the nine-one-one call. When I asked him about the tattoo he sent me a selfie of it."

I turn away to look in the sideview mirror at cars moving past. It occurs to me that I don't know what Benton is driving tonight. It could be his Porsche Cayenne Turbo S or his Audi RS 7. It could be a bureau car. I was busy with the dogs, with Sock and Tesla, when my husband left this morning at dawn, and I didn't see or hear him drive away.

"The tattoo's a problem, Doc," Marino says. "It gives credibility to the phone call. It pretty much proves that whoever complained about you and Bryce disturbing the peace saw you—unless there's some other reason this person knows about the tattoo and what the two of you were wearing."

I recognize the sound of a turbocharged engine changing pitch, and I listen as it gets closer, louder.

"You're still picking her up tonight?" Marino asks.

"Who?" I watch Benton's blacked-out RS 7 coupe glide past slowly, downshifting, sliding into the space in front of us.

"Dorothy."

"That's the plan."

"Well if you need any help I'm happy to get her," Marino says. "I've been meaning to tell you that anything I can do, just say the word. Especially now since it's sounding like she's going to be so late."

I don't recall telling him that my sister was coming—much less who was picking her up at the airport. He also didn't just hear this for the first time when Lucy called a moment ago. It's obvious he already knew.

"That's nice of you," I say to him, and his dark glasses are riveted to the back of the Audi as Benton maneuvers it so close against the curb that a knife blade barely would fit between it and the titanium rims.

The matte-black sedan rumbles in a growly purr like a panther about to lunge. Through the tinted back windshield I can make out the shape of my husband's beautiful head, and his thick hair that's been white for as long as I've known him. He sits straight and wide-shouldered, as still as a jungle cat, his gray-tinted glasses watching us in the rearview mirror. I open my door, and the heat slams me like a wall when I step back out into it, and I thank Marino for the ride even though I didn't want it.

I watch Benton climb out of his car. He unfolds his long lank self, and my husband always looks newly minted. His pearl-gray suit is as fresh as when he put it on this morning, his blue-and-gray silk tie perfectly knotted, his engraved antique white-gold cuff links glinting in the early evening light.

He could grace the pages of *Vanity Fair* with his strong fine features, his platinum hair and horn-rim glasses. He's slender and ropy strong, and his quiet calm belies the iron in his bones and the fire in his belly. You'd never know what Benton Wesley is truly like to look at him right now in his perfectly tailored suit, hand-stitched because he comes from old New England money.

"Hi," he says, taking the shopping bag from me but I hold on to my briefcase.

He watches Marino's dark blue SUV pull back out into traffic, and the heat rising off the pavement makes the air look thick and dirty.

"I hope your afternoon's been better than mine." I'm conscious of how wilted I am compared to my perfectly put-together husband. "I'm sorry I'm such a train wreck."

"What possessed you to walk?"

"Not you too. Did Bryce send out a *be on the lookout* for a deranged woman with a run in her stockings prowling the Harvard campus?"

"But you really shouldn't have, Kay. For lots of reasons."

"You must know about the nine-one-one call. It would seem to be the headline of the day."

He doesn't answer but he doesn't need to. He knows. Bryce probably called him because I doubt Marino would.

CHAPTER 4

A BICYCLE BELL JINGLES CHEERILY on the sidewalk behind us, and we step out of the way as a young woman rides past.

She brakes in front of us as if she might be going to the same place we are, and I offer a commiserating smile when she dismounts, wearing sporty dark glasses, hot and red-faced. Unclipping the chin strap of her robin's-egg-blue bike helmet, she takes it off, and I notice her pulled-back long brown hair, her blue shorts and beige tank top. Instantly I get a weird feeling.

I take in her blue paisley printed neckerchief, her off-white Converse sneakers and gray-and-white-striped bike socks as she stares at her phone, then at the Georgian brick Faculty Club as if expecting someone. She types with her thumbs, lifts her phone to her ear.

"Hey," she says to whoever she's calling. "I'm here," and I realize the reason she's familiar is I met her about a half hour ago.

She was at the Loeb Center when I was buying the theater tickets. I remember seeing her as I wandered into the lobby to use the ladies' room. At most she's in her early twenties, and she has a British accent, what strikes me as a slightly affected or theatrical one. I was aware of it when she was talking with other staff and several actors at the American Repertory Theater.

She was across the room taping index cards of recipes on walls already covered with hundreds of them. In this particular production of *Waitress* members of the audience are invited to share their own favorite treats and tasty family secrets, and before I left I wandered over to take a look. I love to cook, and my sister loves sweets. The least I could do is make something special for her while she's here. I was jotting down a recipe for peanut butter pie when the young woman paused as she was taping up another card.

"I warn you. It's lethal," she said to me, and she had on a whimsical gold skull necklace that made me think of pirates.

"Excuse me?" I glanced around, not sure at first that she was talking to me.

"The peanut butter pie. But it's better if you add chocolate, dribble it over the top. The real stuff. And don't swap out the graham-cracker crust for anything you think might be better. Because it won't be, I promise. And use *real* butter—as you can tell I'm not into low-fat anything."

"You don't need to be," I replied because she's wiry and strong.

This same young woman is in front of Benton and me on the sidewalk along Quincy Street, holding her iPhone in its ice-blue case, clamping it back into its black plastic holder, and she accidently fumbles her water bottle, sending it tumbling. It thuds to the sidewalk, rolling in our direction, and Benton bends down to pick it up.

"Sorry. Thanks very much." She looks hot, her face flushed and dripping.

"You definitely don't want to be without this today." He returns the bottle to her, and she secures it in its holder as I notice a young man trotting through the grass of the Faculty Club.

Her rimless sunglasses are directed at him as she remounts the

Ƀ bike, steadying herself, the toes of her sneakers touching the sidewalk. He's dark and thin, in slacks and a button-up shirt as if he works in an office. Then he's in front of her, hot and grinning, handing her a FedEx envelope that's labeled but not sealed.

"Thanks," he says. "Just put the tickets in and it's ready to go."

"I'll drop it off on my way home. See you later." She kisses him on the lips.

Then he trots away, back toward the Faculty Club, where I gather he must work. She puts on her helmet, not bothering with the strap that's supposed to be snug under her chin. Turning to me, she flashes a smile.

"You're the peanut-butter-pie lady," she says.

"What a nice way to be characterized. Hello again." I smile back at her, and I almost remind her to lock her chin strap.

But I don't know her. I don't want to be overbearing, especially after being accused of yelling at Bryce and disturbing the peace.

"Please be careful out here," I say instead. "The heat index is hazardous."

"What doesn't kill you makes you stronger." She grips the flat riser handlebars, pushing down the pedals with long strong strokes.

"Not always," Benton says.

I feel the hot air stir sluggishly as she rides past.

"Enjoy the pie and the play!" she tosses back at us, and she reminds me of my niece, sharp-featured, bold and extremely fit.

I watch her bare legs pumping, her calf muscles bunching as she picks up speed, cutting across the street, threading through the same gate I used earlier. I remember being that age when the best and worst was before me, and I wanted to know everything up front as if my fate could be negotiated. Who would I be with and what would I become? Where would I live and would I make a difference to anyone? I speculated, and at times tried to force my life in the direction I thought it should go. I wouldn't do that now.

I watch the young woman's retreating figure getting smaller, more distant and remote as she pedals through the Yard, between the sprawling brick Pusey and Lamont libraries. I don't understand why anyone would want to know the future. I wonder if she does, and the conservative answer is probably. But the more likely one is absolutely. Whereas I don't anymore.

"What did Marino want?" Benton lightly, affectionately touches my back as we follow the sidewalk.

Up ahead on our left is the split-rail paling, and set far back is the brick-and-white-trimmed neo-Georgian building, two stories with a glass-domed conservatory. The four tall chimneys rise proudly and symmetrically from different corners, and ten dormers stand sentry along the slate hipped roof.

THE LONG WALKWAY OF dark red pavers winds through rockery and ornamental shrubs. The sun has dipped behind buildings, and the oppressive air is like a steam room that's slowly cooling.

Benton has taken off his suit jacket, and it's neatly folded over his arm as we walk past the bright pink bottlebrushes of summer sweet, purple mountain laurel, and white and blue hydrangeas. None of it stirs in the breathless air, and only a scattering of dark green leaves shows the slightest blush of red. The longer it's hot and parched, the more unlikely it is that there will be much in the way of fall colors this year.

As Benton and I talk, I do the best I can to answer his questions about Marino's intentions, explaining he was emphatic that he didn't want me out walking by myself. But I don't think it's his only agenda. I have the distinct impression that Benton doesn't either.

"At any rate," I continue telling the story, "he was out and about all the while he was on the phone, basically bird-dogging me while he pretended he wasn't. Then he drove me the last fifty feet, and that's where you found me a few minutes ago."

"The last fifty feet?" Benton repeats.

"It's what he mandated. I was to get into his car and he would drive me the last fifty feet. Specifically the last *damn* fifty feet."

"Obviously what he wanted was to have a private face-to-face conversation with you. Maybe it's true he didn't want to talk over the phone. Or he used that as an excuse. Or it could be both," Benton says as if he knows, and he probably does because it's not hard for him to profile Pete Marino.

"So tell me why you decided to go for a stroll all by yourself, dressed in a suit and carrying heavy bags?" Benton gets around to that. "Aren't you the one who warns everybody about the heat index—the way you just did with the woman on the bicycle a minute ago?"

"I suppose that's why there's the cliché about practicing what you preach."

"This isn't about practicing what you preach. It's about something else."

"I thought a walk might do me good," I reply, and he's silent. "And besides I had the theater tickets to pick up."

I explain that I also had gifts to find at the college bookstore, The Coop. The T-shirt, nightgown and handsome coffee-table book may not be the most original presents I've ever bought but they were the best I could muster after wandering the aisles. As Benton knows all too well, my sister is difficult to shop for.

"But that doesn't mean I don't know what she likes," I'm saying, and he isn't answering.

A popular musical and a peanut butter pie, for example, and Dorothy also will be very pleased with the skimpy Harvard tee that she can wear with her skimpier leggings or jeans. Her Ivy League shirt will be amply filled by her surgically enhanced bosom, and no doubt she'll inspire many scintillating conversations in the bars of South Beach and Margaritaville.

"And the Cambridge photography book is something she can carry back to Miami as if it was her idea," I explain as Benton listens without a word, the way he does when he has his own opinion and it's different from mine. "And that's exactly how my sister will play it when she shares pictures of Harvard, MIT, the Charles River with Mom. It will be all about Dorothy, which is fine if it means Mom enjoys her gift and feels remembered."

"It's not fine," Benton says as we pass through the deepening shadows of tall boxwood hedges.

"Some things won't change. It has to be fine."

"You can't let Dorothy get to you this way." His tinted glasses look at me.

"I assume you've heard the nine-one-one call." I change the subject because my sister has wasted quite enough of my time. "Apparently Marino has a copy but he wouldn't play it for me."

Benton doesn't respond, and if he's listened to the recording he's not going to tell me. Had he been made aware of it, he might have requested a copy from the Cambridge Police Department, citing that the FBI wants to make sure a government official wasn't misbehaving or being threatened.

My husband could come up with anything he wants to gain access to the 911 recording, and he's quite friendly with the commissioner, the mayor, pretty much everybody who's powerful around here. He didn't need Marino's help.

"As you may or may not know, someone complained about me supposedly disturbing the peace." It sounds even more bizarre as I hear myself describe such a thing to someone whose typical day involves terrorists and serial killers.

I glance at him as we near the proud brick building in the gathering dusk, and his face doesn't register whatever reaction he might be having.

"I assume Bryce told you about it after Marino confronted him, wanting to know exactly what happened in Harvard Square when he dropped me off," I add.

"Marino's feeling insecure about you," Benton says, and I can't tell if he's making a statement or asking a question.

"He's always insecure," I reply. "But he's also acting oddly. He was pushy about wanting to drive to the airport. He was overly interested in helping pick up Dorothy."

"I wonder how he knows she's coming here. Did you tell him? Because I didn't."

"Since we had almost no warning, I really haven't had a chance to tell hardly anyone," I reply. "Maybe Lucy mentioned it to him."

"Or Desi might have. He and Marino have gotten to be real pals," Benton says, and he can mask his emotions better than anyone I know but he can't fool me.

I can tell when something hurts him, and the blossoming relationship between Marino and Desi obviously does. I've worried it would as Marino spends increasing amounts of time with a mercurial and insatiably inquisitive boy whose genetics are largely unknown to us. We don't know what to expect. We can't predict who he might take after.

It should be Janet's late sister Natalie since it was her egg she'd had frozen when she was only in her twenties. Long before she did anything about it she was researching surrogate mothers and sperm donors. I remember her talking about being a single parent, and in retrospect it seems she had a premonition that her days on earth would be few. And they were. Seven years after Desi was born she would die of pancreatic cancer. It's such a shame she's not here to watch him change rapidly like a butterfly breaking out of its cocoon.

"Look, I get it," Benton is saying. "I'm not nearly as much fun as Marino. He's already taken Desi fishing, started teaching him about guns, given him his first sip of beer."

"Fishing is one thing but I'm not happy if Lucy and Janet think the rest of it is okay."

"The point is—"

"The point is that you don't need to be fun the same way Marino is," I reply. "In fact I'm hoping you might be a good example."

"Of what? A boring adult?"

"I was thinking more along the lines of a sexy brilliant federal agent who drives fast cars and wears designer clothes. Desi just doesn't know you yet."

"Apparently Desi does know me. Marino told him I'm a retired school principal, and Desi asked me about it. I told him it was a hundred years ago when I was just out of college and working on my master's degree," Benton says.

"Did you explain that when you were getting started, a lot of FBI agents came from educational and legal backgrounds? That in other words yours was simply a sensible career path?" Even as I say it I'm aware that it's too much explanation, and the well has been poisoned.

"There was no reason for Marino to bring that up except to make Desi afraid of me. Which is harmful and ill-advised because he's headstrong enough already. I've noticed that increasingly he doesn't like being told what to do."

"I agree he doesn't like to be controlled. But then most of us don't."

"Marino's goal is to be Good Time Uncle Pete while I'm the school principal," Benton says, and I watch the darkness settle heavily, hotly.

We've reached the wide brick patio arranged with wooden tables, red umbrellas, and potted shrubs and flower beds. On this last Wednesday of September, there shouldn't be an empty chair out here. But there's no one sitting outside the Faculty Club, no one in the world but us.

CHAPTER 5

THE ENTRANCE COULD BELONG to a private home, and that's what the Faculty Club has become to my FBI-profiler husband, who didn't graduate from Harvard. Benton went to Amherst just like his father and grandfather did.

A home away from home. A portal to another place where pain, fear and tragedy aren't allowed. Benton can spirit himself away to his immaculate neo-Georgian escape in the heart of the campus and pretend for a brief spell that there's no such thing as ignorance, bigotry, politics, and small-minded bureaucrats.

He can enjoy a cloistered retreat where everyone celebrates enlightened ideas and our differences, and there's no such thing as violence or aggression. Benton feels safe here. It's one of the few places where he does. But not so safe that he's not carrying a gun. I can't see a pistol but I have no doubt he has one in his briefcase, and his backup somewhere on his person. His Glock 27 or concealed-carry Smith & Wesson Model 19 that he won't leave home without.

We've stopped in front of flanking pilasters that are painted white, and there's a transom over the dark red door. I gaze up at the perfect symmetry of the brick facade, and my attention lingers on the multi-paned bay windows of the upstairs guest rooms.

"Maybe another time." Benton looks up too and knows what I'm thinking.

"Yes, I guess there will be no sleepover tonight, thanks to my sister. But if I had anything to change into I'd rent a room anyway right now and take a shower." I can almost hear the creaking carpeted old wooden stairs leading up to the second floor.

I remember the sound and feel of the fabric-covered walls, the cozy elegance and most of all the narrow beds where Benton and I don't get much sleep. Ours is a well-practiced ritual that we engage in regularly and don't talk about with anyone but each other. It belongs exclusively to the two of us, and I wouldn't call it a date but consider it more like therapy when we come here once a month, assuming the stars are properly aligned.

So often they're not, but when they are we get a welcome reminder that decency and humanity still exist in the world. Not everybody lies, steals, rapes, abuses, neglects, tortures, kidnaps and kills. Not everybody wants to ruin us or take what's ours, and we're so lucky to have found each other.

We walk into the chilled quiet of formal antiques, fine paintings and Persian rugs. Benton closes the door behind us, and we're surrounded by sconces and mahogany paneling, dark tufted leather furniture, and wide-board flooring. Fresh flowers are arranged on the entryway table, and tonight's menu is displayed on a Victorian oak podium.

I detect the layers of familiar scents, the cut lilies and roses, and beeswax with a patina of musty staleness, that are reassuring and part of an old-world charm that makes me think of poetry, cigars and rare leather-bound tomes. I could close my eyes and know where I am. The energy is different in here. There's a gravitas, a formality that should be expected in a place that's hosted heads of state and some of the most accomplished people in the world.

I pause in the entryway, in front of an antique oval mirror, running my fingers through my limp blond hair. I stare into the pitted glass at the tall handsome man behind me in pale gray, hovering over me like a breathtaking apparition.

"Do I know you?" I ask Benton without turning around.

"I don't think so. Are you waiting for someone?"

"Yes."

"What a coincidence. I am too. I've always been waiting for someone."

"So have I."

"Well not just someone. The right person." His reflection looks at me.

"Do you think there's only one right person for each of us?" I ask the mirror on the wall.

"I can only speak for myself."

We don't have a name for our little game, and nobody is wise to our delightful choreography of meeting as if we're strangers. It's refreshing, sobering but also good psychology if one can handle the truth. What would happen if we really were meeting for the first time right now in the entryway of the Harvard Faculty Club?

Would we notice each other? Would he still find me as attractive as he did the first time we met? It's not always the same for men when their wives get older, and some mates may say they're just as in love when they're not. It's brave to ask such questions and face the truth unflinchingly. What might we feel were we to meet now instead of decades ago when Benton was married and I was divorced and we worked our first case together?

There's no scientific method for answering such a question, and I don't need one. I have no doubt we'd fall in love with each other all over again. I'm certain I would have an affair with him that would result in my being called a home wrecker. And I wouldn't care because it's worth it.

Benton places his warm graceful hands on my shoulders, and rests his chin on top of my head. I smell his earthy cologne as we look at our reflections in the convex mirror, our faces Picasso-like abstractions where the silvered glass is eroded.

"How about some dinner?" he says into my hair.

"Will you excuse me for a moment?"

I check my shopping bag in the coat closet, and step inside the ladies' room with its formal wallpaper and vintage Victorian theater posters. I set my leather messenger-bag briefcase on the black granite countertop and dig out a cosmetic kit. I face the mirror over the sink, and the woman in khaki staring back at me is slightly shopworn and disheveled.

Actually there's nothing slight about it, I decide. I look like hell, and I take off my damp suit jacket and drape it over a chair. My bra has soaked through my white blouse, and I turn on the hand dryer and blast hot air inside my collar, doing what I can so I don't sit around in wet underwear. Then I dig out powder, lipstick, a toothbrush. I contemplate my appearance and what else I intend to do about it. Not much.

I can't reverse the effects of lousy sleep, of running myself ragged and walking in the extreme heat. I feel a touch light-headed, and I'm weary and hopelessly clammy. I need food and drink badly. I need a shower most of all, and I take off my ruined panty hose and toss them in the trash. I douse a hand towel with cold water, cleaning up, but there's no quick remedy for rumpled sweatiness.

It's as if I were soaked and agitated in a washing machine, and I notice I've gotten a bit thinner in recent weeks. That usually happens when I neglect to exercise, and I haven't been jogging for a while, certainly not during the heat wave. I haven't touched my TRX bands, and Lucy's been after me to go with her to the gym.

I powder my face, and shadows in the low light of a crystal chandelier accentuate my prominent cheekbones and nose, and the angle of my strong jaw. I'm reminded of what journalists say, almost none of it relevant or kind. I'm *masculine* and *off-putting*. Or my favorite unflattering line that's been recycled excessively in stories: *Dr. Kay Scarpetta is compelling in appearance with an inaccessible, secretive and domineering face.*

I wet my fingers and muss my hair. I give it a once-over with a volumizing spray. I brush my teeth, and dust my forehead and cheeks with a mineral powder that blocks ultraviolet light and doesn't cause cancer. I don't care that it's about to be pitch dark out. I do it anyway. Then I dab on an olive oil lip balm and find the Visine and a small tube of shea butter.

I feel much improved but as I survey my wilted suit and blouse, I can hear Dorothy's voice in my head as clearly as if she's inside the ladies' room with me. She'd say the same thing she'll probably say when Benton and I pick her up in a few hours. I have a terrible sense of style. I'm boring and sloppy. I get dirty and dress in stuffy suits like a frump or a man. She can't understand why I don't wear stilt-like heels, heavy makeup or acrylic nails and gaudy polish.

It's lost on her why I wouldn't emphasize my body parts, as she puts it, "especially since both of us were endowed with big knockers," she likes to boast about what's most important. I don't dress or conduct myself anything like my sister. I never have and couldn't possibly.

Ever since I can remember I've been incompatible with fragile female accoutrements and empty-headed attitudes. We simply don't get along.

BENTON IS WAITING FOR me, chatting with the hostess Mrs. P at her station.

He grips his black leather briefcase with one hand, and in the other he holds his phone, typing on it with his thumb. He slips it back in a pocket as he notices my return from the ladies' room, and I understand what's meant by one's heart leaping. Mine is happily jolted by the sight of him. It always is.

"A big improvement? Hmm?" He takes his glasses off, making a big production of appraising me, his eyes glinting with a playful light. "Do you agree, Mrs. P?" he asks her as he winks at me.

In her early eighties, she has a nimbus of wispy grayish-white hair, and round wire-rim glasses like a caricature of a prim and proper New England matron. Her face is doughy and wrinkled like dehydrated fruit, and her dress and matching jacquard jacket are a rose-trellis design in greens and reds that reminds me of a William Morris pattern.

Mrs. P tends to eye me curiously even when I don't look overcooked and disheveled, as if there's much she wonders about but isn't going to verbalize. Several times now her eyes have dropped down to my bare legs, and then she looks up quickly as if she's seen something she shouldn't.

"What do you think?" Benton asks her.

"Well I'm not sure." Her glasses wink as she turns her head back and forth like a tennis match, from him to me, looking at one, then the other, and the two of them have their shtick. "You know not to put me on the spot that way," she affectionately reprimands him.

Mrs. P's surname is Peabody, pronounced with an emphasis on the first syllable, a drawn-out PEE-b'dy, like the city near Salem. I've never addressed her by her first name, Maureen, and have no clue if those close to her call her that or Mo or something else. In the years we've been coming here she's simply been Mrs. P, and Benton is Mr. Wesley. If she refers to me by name it's Mrs. Wesley, although she's well aware of my other life where most everyone else calls me Dr. Scarpetta or Chief.

It's a sad secret that Mrs. P knows what I do and who I am even as she politely pretends otherwise. Not long after Benton and I moved to Cambridge, her husband was killed in a car accident literally in front of their house, and I took care of him. Now it's as if that never happened, and what I remember most about her husband's case is his widow Mrs. P's refusal to talk to me. She insisted on going over her late husband's autopsy report with one of my assistant chiefs, a man.

But then Mrs. P started at the Faculty Club in a day when things were very different for women. You could be on the faculty here and find yourself relegated to the ladies' dining room or discover there's no place in the dorm and you're not welcome in the same libraries or housing as your male classmates. When one of the greatest legal minds of our time, Ruth Bader Ginsburg, arrived for her first year at Harvard Law School she was asked to justify her taking up a seat that could be occupied by a man.

"I think you need your head examined if you go outside in this," Mrs. P is saying to Benton, and he widens his eyes, staring at her with mock disappointment. "You'll melt like a candle," meaning that's what she thinks I look like.

Benton says to me with a shrug, "I guess that's a no. Sorry, Kay. It would seem Mrs. P thinks you still look like something the cat dragged in."

"I would never say such a thing!" Mrs. P laughs her soft self-conscious laugh, placing three fingers over her pink lips, shaking her head as if my husband is the naughtiest human being on the planet.

She's quite fond of Benton, who of course is teasing both of us. If you don't know him it would be difficult to recognize because his humor is as subtle as a cobweb you can't find but keep brushing from your face. He knows damn well my appearance isn't greatly improved. I don't have hose on, and the leather insoles of my unstylish scuffed shoes feel as slimy as a raw oyster that's been sitting out for hours.

"Let's not rub it in," I say to him as Mrs. P gathers two menus and the thick black notebook, the extensive *carte des vins*. "I realize it wasn't your intention to have dinner tonight with something the cat dragged in."

"Depends on the cat." Benton opens his briefcase with bright springy snaps of the clasps.

He trades his sunglasses for bifocals, the kind you get in the drug-store. I shoulder my messenger bag again, and we follow Mrs. P into the north dining room with its tall arched windows and exposure to the front lawn, which is cloaked in darkness.

Our feet are quiet on deep red carpet as we pass beneath exposed dark beams in the white plaster ceiling, through a sea of white-cloth-covered tables beneath brass chandeliers with small red shades over their candlelike lights. We're the only guests so far, and Benton and Mrs. P chat amicably as she shows us to our usual corner.

"Not until closer to eight tonight," she's telling Benton that the Faculty Club is going to be quite slow until then. "We have two pri-vate dinners upstairs but not much down here. It's too hot, you know."

"What about power outages?" Benton asks. "Have they affected you?"

"Now that's trouble when it happens. The power goes out and stays out, and you can't stay inside but can't go outside either. Let's hope that doesn't happen again, especially not while you're in here trying to enjoy a nice quiet dinner."

Mrs. P then begins to update us on Felix the Cat. That's his real name but she just calls him Felix for short, and apparently Felix hasn't fared well during the heat wave.

"He did very poorly the last time the power went out, which was just yesterday at noon, at least that's what I found out later because I was here at the time. Where I live is one of the worst areas on the grid map or something like that," she explains to both of us. "And you know Felix is old with all the problems that go along with it. I don't always know if the power's out in the house, you see. I might be fine here and have no idea poor Felix is suffering with no air-conditioning."

"Maybe there's a neighbor or someone who can check on him?" I suggest.

"My neighbors are in the same boat if the power goes out," she says. "And my children don't live nearby. Now my grandson's working part-time here while he tries to make it as a musician, and he helps out when he can. But he's twenty-three and allergic to cats."

"Could you bring Felix to work?" Benton asks, and Mrs. P just laughs.

"Why couldn't you?" Benton is serious.

"Well I couldn't." She looks across the dining room, making sure no one else has come in.

CHAPTER 6

OUR CORNER TABLE IS to the right of a big fireplace framed by a burled-wood mantel that reaches from the carpet to the ceiling. Perpendicular to it the gold-damask-covered wall has been arranged with fine British, Dutch and Italian art that wasn't here when we were last month.

The new exhibit includes a seascape, a religious allegory, and a still life that has a skull in it. There are oil portraits of stern men in colonial dress, and powdered women with corseted waists too cinched to be anatomically possible without bruised ribs and crowded organs. I never know what I'm going to see from one visit to the next because most of the art is on loan from the surrounding Harvard museums, which hold one of the finest collections anywhere.

The paintings constantly rotate, and this appeals to Benton in particular because it's not dissimilar to how he grew up. His wealthy father invested in art and constantly moved priceless paintings in and out of the Wesley home, a brownstone mansion not so different from the Faculty Club.

How amazing it must be to pick a Pieter Claesz this week and a J. M. W. Turner or Jan Both the next. And maybe a Johannes Vermeer or a Frans Hals while we're at it, I think as I scan our private gallery, each painting illuminated by a museum light and framed in gold.

It's difficult to imagine growing up the way Benton did when I compare it to the minimalist and decidedly nonglamorous conditions of my Miami upbringing. He comes from Ivy League New England stock while I'm the only one in my second-generation Italian family who went to college. As hard as it was to have so little in every sense of the word, I'm grateful that when I was growing up I didn't get what I thought I wanted.

Benton was deprived in a different way. He got everything his parents wanted. He lived their dreams, and in many ways it only made him more impoverished and lonely. I imagine I was sad and isolated at times when I was a child. But what I remember most is feeling driven, having no choice but to learn to make do, whether it was the way I dressed, what shampoo I could afford or how long I could make something last.

I became adept at experiencing the world through books, photographs and movies because there was no such thing as a vacation or traveling anywhere for any reason until I finally began visiting colleges in my midteens. Benton on the other hand lacked for nothing except attention and a normal boyhood. He says he never felt rich until we met, and it's the nicest thing anyone's ever said to me.

He moves the table a little, angling it as he pleases, as if the dining room belongs to him. "I'm worried you're going to be cold."

"So far I'm all right. Other than the way I look."

"Which is beautiful. Always the most beautiful person I've ever known." Benton smiles at me as he pulls out my chair.

"I think you're made delusional by the heat." I sit down.

Scooting in closer to the table, I tuck my messenger bag under my chair, and we never position ourselves so that our backs are to doors or any other egress. We don't place ourselves in front of windows that might make us as conspicuous as fish in a bowl.

In fact we really aren't shown to a table as much as we're deployed to one. Benton and I locate ourselves where we can keep up our scan of what's around us, making sure nothing could surprise us from behind or through glass. In other words, in my husband's safe home away from home, we sit at dinner like two cops.

We couldn't relax if we didn't, and it's the little habits that are sobering. It's impossible not to be reminded that we belong to a small and special tribe. The tribe of the public servants who are traumatized.

"Are you sure you're going to be all right in the air-conditioning?" Benton asks as a waiter heads our way, an older man who must be new. "Would you like my jacket?" Benton starts to take it off, and I shake my head.

"I'm fine for now. I'll manage. Again I apologize for ruining what was left of our night."

"I don't know what you're talking about. You haven't ruined anything." He opens his white napkin and drapes it in his lap. "Well, maybe your panty hose. How did that happen by the way?"

"Oh my God. Is there anything I've not been asked today?" Then I feel irrepressible bubbles of laughter rising up my throat as Benton watches me quizzically.

"Is there something I'm missing?" he finally asks, but the waiter is waiting.

He stands by our table in his white jacket, starched and buttoned up, and he has the gaunt face and loose skin of someone once handsome who lost a lot of weight. He looks at Benton, the pen resting on the order pad. We'd like water before anything else, my husband says, and suddenly I remember my panty hose in the ladies' room trash and I'm amused again.

"I'm sorry." I dab my eyes with my napkin. "But sometimes I'm struck by the absurdity. To answer your question, I ran my hose just like any other woman, I'm sure."

"I doubt it." He's watching the waiter talking with the young man we saw out front a few minutes earlier, both of them checking on a big table set for a large party, fussing with silverware, repositioning the flower arrangements. "Usually your mishaps involve sharp weapons, body fluids, and blowflies," Benton adds.

"I ran my panty hose on a gurney, one of those cadaver carriers with a crank for raising and lowering. As I was helping lift a body off I got snagged, possibly on one of the casters."

"And then what?" and it begins to penetrate that he really is asking for a reason. "You didn't change into a new pair of panty hose," he says. "Why not?"

It's not a frivolous question after all. Of course nothing he asks really is even when he's being funny.

AT MY HEADQUARTERS, BRYCE is in charge of keeping certain necessities in stock including coffee, snacks, standard toiletries—and extra pairs of panty hose.

If he doesn't oversee the supply of such things there's a good chance they won't enter my mind because skirts and stockings aren't my friends even if I pretend otherwise. Given the choice, I wear my usual field clothes of flame- and insect-resistant cargo pants, the more pockets the better, and tactical shirts embroidered with the CFC crest.

And of course sturdy cotton socks and low-profile boots. I'm also partial to parkas, packable jackets, baseball caps, and I suppose it all goes back to those impressionable years in medical school and the Air Force. When I was getting started I lived in scrubs and BDUs, and if I had my way I still would.

But since I'm often summoned to testify in depositions, in court and before lawmakers, I have to keep other accoutrements on hand that are appropriate for a director and chief who can influence the type of body armor our soldiers wear or whether someone should land in prison.

"I go through several pairs of hose a week at work," I'm explaining all this to Benton. "And I suppose Bryce hasn't been shopping much in this heat. Or maybe he's been too busy with his own dramas to bother ordering things online. So yes, I wasn't happy when I discovered I had nothing to change into after I ruined my hose. But I don't know why it didn't enter my mind to stop in the CVS myself at Harvard Square and pick up another pair so I'm not sitting here bare-legged. I suppose that's yet another miscalculation on my part."

"Then what you're saying is Bryce has been letting you down, and you were upset with him even before he drove you to the Square. When you realized you had nothing to change into, that was the catalyst." Benton slides his reading glasses out of their case. "But the fuel load was already laid."

"And what fuel load might you mean?" I smooth my napkin over my skirt and am reminded of how badly I want to get out of these clothes.

"I think you know."

What he's leading up to is my family—specifically my reaction to my sister's uninvited and unexpected visit, and I glance at the time. I'd planned on heading to Logan by nine thirty but now I'm not sure what to do. Lucy says Dorothy might be late. Well it would be nice of my sister to let me know so Benton and I don't race away from here and end up sitting outside the baggage area for hours.

"Bryce stopped by my office around four thirty to give me a ride to The Coop, to take me on any errands and then drop me off here," I begin recounting what happened this afternoon. "And that was fine except he wouldn't stop talking. I honestly couldn't take it."

"Talking about what?"

"That's very difficult to reconstruct when it's Bryce. It seems he's convinced I don't feel the same about him, that I don't like him or want him around, and this predates today's incident with the panty hose. Lately I've gotten the impression he has some strange notion that I've distanced myself and am thinking of firing him or who knows what."

"Based on?" Benton slips on the reading glasses, parking them low on his straight narrow nose, his hazel eyes finding me over the top of the frames.

"Based on his repeated questions about what else he'd done wrong. He kept asking that when he was arguing with me in front of The Coop."

"Were you arguing or was he?"

"I've always heard it takes two."

Benton laughs. "It doesn't when it's him. Bryce is pretty good at playing both sides of the net."

"I didn't argue. I just resisted and denied, telling him I needed to go. He was so worried about the broiling heat, and here I was standing out in the middle of it because he wouldn't leave me alone."

"So in other words, he's reacting to you." Benton picks up the thickly bound wine list that was on top of his menu.

"As usual but it's more extreme, it seems."

"This may shape up to being one of those unfortunate situations that's all about bad timing." Benton turns several thick creamy pages, glancing at wines. "I hope not. But it was bad timing for you to get out of sorts with him while a detractor, possibly a stalker, was watching. Normally we could let it go, dismiss it as a deranged rambling. But the marijuana-leaf tattoo is a problem. If it wasn't for that detail I wouldn't give any credence to someone calling in what sounds like a completely frivolous complaint. I wouldn't even bother listening."

"What are you saying?" I reply. "And how did you know about the tattoo?"

But Benton turns another page in the wine list. He doesn't answer.

"Are you suggesting that you've listened to the nine-one-one recording? Is that what you're telling me?" I ask him next.

CHAPTER 7

THE WAITER HAS RETURNED with a bottle of still water, and we're quiet as he fills our glasses.

We say nothing unless it's related to appetizers and how lovely it is to have the dining room all to ourselves for as long as it lasts. Benton always gets the crab cakes with grilled scallions and pickled banana peppers, and I usually indulge in the lobster bisque with lemon brown butter.

But it's too hot for either, we decide, and instead we pick the Mediterranean salad with heirloom tomatoes and crumbled feta. I ask if we can substitute purple onions for sweet ones and have extra dressing on the side with crushed red pepper to add a kick. I order another bottle of water, this one sparkling with lots of lime. The instant the waiter has moved on I return to what Benton was saying.

"What do you mean you wouldn't bother?" I ask. "Your wife is the subject of a police complaint and you wouldn't bother to pay attention? Even if it's chickenshit?"

"This wouldn't be the first time unstable people have spotted you in public and called the police and the media." Benton turns another page in the wine list, and the light catches his gold signet ring engraved with his family coat of arms. "You're recognizable, Kay, and people associate you with sensational crimes and disasters. I could tell you otherwise but it wouldn't be the truth. So yes." He glances up at me. "I might not have paid attention or as close attention as I should have."

"You've listened to the recording." I won't let him evade the question. "I'm going to keep asking."

He silently reads the wine list, and I can see his eyes moving up and down a page of white Burgundies. I'm not sure why. The most he can have is a glass. In a while he has to drive, and I think of Dorothy and get only more adamant with Benton. I can't seem to help it.

"I want to hear the recording," I tell him. "Do you have a copy? And I'm not interested in the transcript. I want to hear the bastard lie about me."

"Marino should play it for you," Benton says as he turns pages back and forth between different types of wines. "I assume he's investigating your egregious disturbance of the peace just like any lead detective worth his salt would spend his time doing."

"I told you he wouldn't tell me scarcely anything the person said. He wouldn't discuss it in detail, and legally I can push this, Benton. I have a right to face my accuser, and in this case the accuser is the person who's lying about me on that recording. I want to hear it for myself—with my own ears. There are no legal grounds for withholding that recording from me unless you think I'm implicated in a federal crime. And last I checked, disturbing the peace wasn't."

This is exactly what Benton wants me to do—to threaten him in a confrontational offended way that doesn't really reflect my true feelings. What I mustn't do is treat him like my husband when it comes to this particular matter, which ironically he wouldn't know about in the first place if we weren't a couple. He needs to be Special Agent Benton Wesley this moment and I need to be the Chief, and we've been down this road many times.

He turns another page in the *carte des vins*. "I think we should have white wine," he says. "But it depends on what you want to eat. We'll have just enough to taste and cork the rest for later, after we finally get home."

"It would take nothing more than a Freedom of Information Act request. But it's stupid to make me go through that. I was thinking about fish. Something light." I open my menu without picking it up as he reaches down next to his chair and finds his briefcase.

He places it in his lap, and I hear the bright snap of the locks again.

"Remember what my eighth-grade teacher said to me?" He pulls out his wireless headset in its zip-up case. "Good ol' Mr. Broadmoor . . ."

"Who declared that one day you're going to get what you ask for and be sorry," I finish the anecdote for Benton, one he repeats often when he's sure it applies to me.

"It won't be pleasant and I'd rather spare you." He unzips the small black case. "But as you know, the laws about nine-one-one recordings are rather murky in Massachusetts. There's no statute that tells me you can't listen. You're right about that."

He hands the headset to me and I put it on. He places his phone in the middle of the table, and touches several prompts on the display. I hear static and clicking in stereo. Then:

"Nine-one-one, what is your emergency?" The dispatcher is a woman, and I recognize her voice from the chronic radio chatter in my life.

"Hello. It's not exactly an emergency but I think the police should know that one of our esteemed public servants is disturbing the peace in front of God and everyone in Harvard Square."

The caller's voice is mellow and flows at a rhythmic slow pace, bringing to mind someone pulling taffy. It's as if the person is stoned or putting on an act, and I remember what Marino said about not being able to tell if the caller is male or female. I'm not sure either.

"What's the address of your emergency?" the dispatcher asks.

"I don't know precisely but I should think a good way to describe the Square is it's the area around the T station."

"Is there an address of a business you can give me?"

"No." The caller coughs several times.

"What number are you calling from?"

"It's my cell phone so it's not going to tell you my location. You won't be able to confirm anything about me like that . . ."

At this point the caller becomes abusive and argumentative in his slow, languid way, and I think of him as a *him*. But I honestly can't say because the voice is low and husky in a pleasant range somewhere between a baritone and a tenor.

As I listen to him describe what he allegedly witnessed it enters my mind that my so-called shit fest with my "boyfriend" isn't something that was happening while this witness who's a liar was on the phone with the dispatcher. What he says seems too rehearsed to be happening in real time, and instantly I'm suspicious he's reporting his made-up story after the fact.

"Do you know where the female subject is now?" The dispatcher is asking about me in the recording as I stare down at the white tablecloth and listen carefully through the headphones.

"No, but she's a C-U-Next-Tuesday if I ever saw one, and I sure as hell wouldn't want her showing up at my damn house if somebody died. Jabbing her damn finger, slapping the fool out of some poor sissy kid who looks like a real loser. I can't imagine what sort of bedside manner a nasty bitch like that would have . . ."

"Where are you?" the dispatcher asks as the caller coughs and clears his throat again. "Are you outside?"

"With the birds and the bees. Of course I'm outside! How the hell else could I be reporting something that's going on outside in the elements right before my very eyes?"

This goes on until she lets him know the police are on their way, and she asks the caller's name.

"You don't need my name, lady, what you need is to pay attention to their names. You hear me?"

"I need a name so the police can find you—"

"Don't try that shit with me. I know what you're doing. You're going to cover this up just like you do everything about the damn government, and it's time for the intolerance and fascism to end . . ."

THE VILENESS GOES ON for almost a minute total, and it's difficult to hear such awful things about me. My anger spikes. I take off the headset, returning it to Benton.

"It would seem this individual has a personal problem with me for some reason." I'm shaken and incensed, and it's the only thing I can think to say.

"Is the voice familiar?" Benton's eyes don't leave mine.

"No it's not. What time was the call made?"

"Twelve minutes past six." His stare doesn't waver as the meaning hits me.

June twelfth or six-twelve is my date of birth. Usually I would assume this is nothing more than a coincidental overlap with my personal life except for a not-so-minor problem. Six-twelve P.M. is also the exact time Tailend Charlie has been e-mailing his recorded threats to me since September 1.

"So it was almost an hour and a half after the fact." I reach for my water glass. "Bryce and I were talking in front of The Coop at closer to four forty-five. Are we sure there's no way the time could be faked?"

"I don't see how, Kay. The time stamp is on the nine-one-one recording."

"Then the call was definitely made after I'd left the Square. At six-twelve I'm certain I was walking through the Yard. That's also in the ballpark of when Marino reached me on my cell phone."

"Can you check?" Benton indicates my phone on the table.

I pick it up and look at the incoming calls. "He tried me first at six-eighteen," I reply. "I remember what building I was walking past when my phone vibrated, and it was him."

"What this suggests is he must have been contacted the instant the police got the complaint about you," Benton says, and I don't know if he's asking or telling.

"Don't forget Rosie's always been a little sweet on him. They dated a few times. She probably didn't waste a minute getting hold of him."

"Rosie?"

"The dispatcher," I remind him. "I recognized her voice. Her name is actually Rosemary but Marino calls her Rosie."

"Which brings me back to the same question. Was there anything familiar, anything you noticed about the voice you just listened to in the nine-one-one call? Anything that struck you?" Benton looks down at his phone, but the screen has gone to sleep and there's nothing to see but a glassy black rectangle.

He unlocks it and the displayed video file reappears with its frozen PLAY arrow.

"Beyond how arrogant and hateful the person sounded?" I'm thinking hard. "Nothing struck me, not really."

"It sounds like you're not sure."

I look up at the plaster ceiling and replay the 911 audio clip in my head. "No," I decide. "It's unfamiliar, just a normal pleasant voice. I'm not sure what else to say about it."

"And you're equivocal again." Benton's not going to tell me why he thinks that.

It's not his style to lead the witness even if the witness is his wife, and I take another drink of water as I think for a moment. He's right. I'm uncertain, and then it occurs to me why.

"It's too uniform, too homogenous," I explain what I've been picking up on but couldn't identify. "There aren't the variations I might expect. There's something stilted and unnatural about it."

"In other words it sounds artificial or canned. Fake, in other words," he says, and I wonder if this came from Lucy. "We can't tell if it's synthetized." He answers my unspoken question about my niece. "But Lucy agrees that it's strangely consistent from one comment to the next. She says that if it's been enhanced or altered—"

"Wait a minute. If you got the audio file from the police, then how could it have been altered?"

"Lucy introduced the idea of a voice changer similar to what gamers are into. There are a lot of these apps on the market, although not the quality of whatever this person used. The typical voice disguised by software tends to sound obviously fake like a poor animation. It's within the realm of possibility the caller has proprietary highly sophisticated software that changes your voice as you speak into the phone—"

"And it sounds different from your usual voice but normal to whoever's on the other end." I finish his thought because I already know what's next.

Benton asks if I think it's possible that my cyber-stalker Tailend Charlie is the one who called 911 and lied about me.

"Indicating this individual is stepping things up," my husband adds. "Escalating whatever his game is, and we know without question that Tailend Charlie is technically sophisticated."

"Let's hope that's not who placed the nine-one-one call because it would suggest he was in close proximity to me today," I reply. "And I've been hoping whoever the cyber-bully is he's not in Cambridge. Preferably he's on the other side of the planet."

"It strikes me as a little too coincidental that you began getting the e-mailed threats only a week ago, all of them altered audio clips. And now this," Benton says.

"So tell me, Mr. Profiler." I press my leg against his, and the fabric of his suit is smooth and cool against my bare skin. "What do you have to say about someone who calls nine-one-one to report your wife for being a C-U-Next-Tuesday?"

CHAPTER 8

MALE. AND NOT OLD. But not young," Benton says. "I doubt it's a student unless we're talking about a mature one."

"As in a graduate student?"

"Don't know, forties at least," he replies. "Older but not so old as to preclude this person from moving about freely in all sorts of weather. More like someone from the homeless population around the Square but that doesn't mean it's what we're dealing with. He's educated but could be self-educated.

"He probably lives alone, probably has a psychiatric history. And he's intelligent, way above the norm. He's antigovernment, which means anti-authority, and yes, I'd say there's genuine hostility toward you. He's the sort to overidealize relationships and even assume ones that don't exist." Benton ticks all of this off like a grocery list.

He doesn't even have to think about it.

"Could it be someone I know?"

"Yes. But it's more likely you don't. Possibly you've never met."

"Marino thinks this person was using a prepaid phone, a TracFone, something that isn't traceable," I reply. "And that makes sense if you don't live the sort of life that involves monthly phone bills, et cetera.

But how does that fit with using some sort of voice-changing software that has to be installed?"

"It would seem to me that you could install software on just about any type of smartphone and still use it with prepaid cards."

"Yes. And we associate such things with homeless people but there's something else I'm sure you've considered . . ." I start to say, but the waiter is back with our sparkling water and lime.

Benton raises his hand to signal we'll fill our glasses ourselves. When the waiter drifts away I mention the Obama Phone, a rather irreverent reference to a government program for low-income people that provides a free cell phone with unlimited minutes, texting and all the rest.

"That's typically the sort of device we're talking about in the homeless population we find in area shelters and out on the streets with their cardboard signs," I explain as Benton listens. "But you have to apply and register for an Obama Phone, for lack of a better word. And I would think that if the person who called in the bogus complaint about me was using such a thing, then the number would trace back to the carrier."

"SafeLink," Benton says, and I can tell he's already thought about it. "It's one of the biggest and most popular noncontract cellular services."

"But if the phone is part of a government program?"

"That would be the difference. You have to be registered. You have to enroll to qualify, and you have your own account." He picks up the bottle of water and refills our glasses.

"That's exactly what I'm getting at," I reply with a nod. "So Lucy possibly could have traced the phone that made the nine-one-one call if the person were part of this program."

"Yes she could," Benton agrees.

"Then the witness who's such a fan of mine wasn't using an Obama Phone," I summarize, and Benton just stares at me.

He knows that I'd rather the crank caller was using an Obama Phone, and that's the bigger point. I'd prefer to take my chances with someone who truly might be a regular at the Square, perhaps some disenfranchised person who's unpleasant and unstable but not harmful. What I don't want is to be on the radar of an experienced criminal. Especially one sophisticated enough to create software that sends all of us down the wrong path.

If we can't recognize evil, then we can't say for sure it's not in our midst. Whoever made the call, whoever Tailend Charlie is, even if they're one and the same? The miscreant could be right in front of us. And there's no thought much scarier than that. It would be devastating to learn that the person who lied about me to the police is someone I know. It would be worse if whoever is sending me death threats in Italian is someone I care about and trust.

"Who called you about the nine-one-one recording?" I ask Benton. "How did you get involved by the way?"

"Well I'm married to you. Start with that. But Bryce called me as I was finishing up a meeting and about to head out of the office. The lamb or the halibut? You decide. I'll have what you're having."

"I'm going to try the halibut with brussels sprouts. How did you get a copy of the recording? I can't imagine the Cambridge police gave that to Bryce."

"They didn't. I think we should go for a Burgundy. A Chablis *premier cru*."

"The 2009 Montée de Tonnerre." We've had it before, and the wine is refreshingly clean and pure with a chiseled finish.

"Very good," Benton says, and he's not going to tell me if he got the 911 audio clip from his friend the police superintendent, and I'm not going to ask further because I'm not sure I want to know.

THE WAITER IS BACK with our salads, and both of us order the pan-seared halibut with brussels sprouts for our main course.

I ask for sides of spaghettini vegetables and wild mushrooms, and we order the Chablis. Then we wait in silence until he walks away again and can't overhear our conversation, and I'm beginning to get the sense that he's lingering. But only a few people have started to trickle in, and he's probably bored.

"By the way, in case you didn't know, we issued a new terror bulletin a few hours ago," Benton says to me, and he means the FBI has.

"It's hard to keep up with them. I just make it a habit to assume we're on high alert all of the time. Anything specific?"

"Just that it's something major, and there's reason to suspect we're talking the East Coast. Hopefully not Boston again but there's a lot of chatter out there about it and also D.C."

"Thanks for passing it along." I look at him because I feel him watching me closely. "Is there something else? Because you look like you have a question. I can practically see it in a bubble over your head."

"Maybe I shouldn't say it."

"And now you have to after a loaded comment like that."

"All right. I'm wondering if it's possible that Bryce is acting a little loosely wrapped because you are."

"I'm loosely wrapped? I don't believe I've heard that before. I've heard a lot of things including very vulgar things, but never that."

"Let me ask you an important question. If Dorothy wasn't suddenly coming to town, do you think the incident at Harvard Square would have happened?"

"No. Because I wouldn't have had to bother with gifts or theater tickets."

"That's not the only reason, Kay. She's coming here. She didn't ask, she told, and as usual you accommodated. You paid for her ticket and even offered her a room in our house."

"Which fortunately she declined because she'd rather stay with Lucy." I feel anger rising like heat from a lower level of my psyche, a region of my inner self that I don't approve of and might just hate.

"I have a feeling the person she'd rather stay with is Marino," Benton says. "But only if he lived in a penthouse."

I set down my glass too hard, and water slops over the rim. I watch the white tablecloth turn gray where the water soaks in. Then Benton uses his napkin to pat dry the mess I've made while I stare at him in disbelief.

"What are you talking about?" Noticing Mrs. P lighting a candle with an electric match several tables away, I try not to look upset.

I don't want it to appear that I'm fighting with someone else. I realize how thin my skin is right now.

"I mentioned it when all of us were in Miami last," Benton says as our waiter reappears with two glasses and the wine.

I think back to our most recent trip this past June, and remember that Marino and Dorothy started driving together to pick up takeout food. He rented a Harley and took her for a ride, and I recall Benton making a comment. When I'm with my family in Miami and also dealing with Lucy, Janet and Desi, I can be very distracted. But it's also true that what Benton is alluding to is something I wouldn't want to notice. I wouldn't want it to be true. I can't think of much that's more frightening than the idea of Marino and my sister together.

The waiter slides out the cork with a soft pop, and hands it to Benton. He lifts it to his nose and watches as a small amount of the pale cold Chablis is poured.

"You do the honors." He hands me the glass, and the wine is sharply clean, waking up my tongue.

Benton nods for the waiter to pour us each a taste.

"Happy Wednesday." Benton touches his glass to mine in a toast, and this is the second time in the past hour that I've felt that an insect is in my clothing.

My phone vibrates in my jacket pocket.

"Now what?" I set down my glass as I check who's calling. "Speaking of . . . It's Marino again."

After all that's gone on, even he wouldn't interrupt dinner unless there was a good reason. Now Benton's phone is buzzing.

I catch a glimpse of a 202 area code before he says, "I've got to take this," and he answers, "Wesley here."

"Hold on," I tell Marino without saying hello, and Benton and I are both getting up from our chairs. "You know where I am so it must be important. I assume I need to get somewhere I can talk."

"Do it now." Marino's voice is hard.

"I'm walking out. Hold on," I say to him as Benton and I collect our briefcases.

We drop our napkins next to our barely touched salads and glasses of wine. We leave as if we're not coming back.

CHAPTER 9

WE'RE CALM AND RESERVED as we walk with purpose through the dining room, avoiding the curious glances of other couples being seated.

Benton and I are together but separate, each of us on the phone. To look at us, you'd never know anything out of the ordinary was going on. We could be talking to our Realtors, our bankers, our brokers, our pet sitters.

We could be a well-heeled couple getting calls from our adoring children, and Benton would be the rich handsome breadwinner. While in comparison I'd be the hardworking rather peculiar and difficult wife who always looks shopworn and halfway blown together. Our eyes are slightly downcast as we weave between tables, and I recognize the fixed stare, the flexing of his jaw, the tenseness of his hands.

I know the way he gets when something is serious. He's probably listening to his employer, the U.S. Department of Justice. Not his divisional office but Washington, D.C., possibly someone high up in the FBI or the director himself, and it could be the White House. It's not Quantico, where Benton got his start and used to work. That's not the area code I just saw on his phone when it vibrated.

My husband's special power is his ability to get into the mind of the offender, to discover the why and the what for, and unearth whatever traumas and bad wiring unleashed the latest monster into our midst. Benton's quarry could be one individual. It could be several or a group of them, and when he goes after them, he must become an empathic Method actor. He has to think, anticipate and even feel what evildoers feel if he's to catch them. But it's not without a price.

"Yes, speaking," Benton says, and he listens. Then, "I understand. No, I'm not aware of it." He glances at me. "It's the first I've heard." He looks down at the red carpet. "Please explain. I'm listening."

"I'm walking out," I quietly tell Marino.

Something has happened, and my imagination is getting the better of me. I sense a presence that's suffocating, heavy and dark. It's palpable like ozone in the air, like the eerie vacuum right before a massive storm breaks. I feel it at a visceral level.

"What is it exactly that you'd like me to do?" Benton turns his head away from people looking at us.

"Should be there . . . in three." Marino's voice is fractured in my earpiece, another bad connection, and everything that's weirdly unfolded in the past few hours suddenly is crashing around me. "No one saw anything . . . that we know of. But two girls, these two twins found her . . ." he says, and I do my best to decipher.

But it's as if I've walked into a tornado. There's so much flying around I can't tell what's up, down, inside out or backward.

"Hold on," I again say to him because I won't discuss a case until no one can overhear me.

"Turning off Kennedy . . . On Harvard Street now," his voice is choppy.

"Give me two more seconds. I'm finding someplace quiet," I reply, and I can hear the sound of his engine as sirens wail in the background.

Past Mrs. P's empty station, Benton takes a right at the entryway's round table with its sumptuous fragrant arrangement of cut lilies and roses. I keep going back to what he said just moments ago about an anticipated terrorist attack on the East Coast, possibly in the Boston area again. Now something has happened here in Cambridge, and he's on the phone with Washington, D.C., as the terror alert is off the charts. I don't like what I'm feeling.

I don't like the way Benton glanced at me as he said over the phone that he wasn't aware of something, that he hadn't been informed of whatever it is. As if there's something happening in the here and now that he should know about, that both of us should. Whatever's going on isn't simply a local problem, and as I think this I also know I'm ahead of myself. The two of us getting important if not urgent calls simultaneously doesn't mean they're related. It could be a coincidence.

But I can't shake the ominous signals I'm picking up. I have a feeling I'm going to discover soon enough that Benton and I are about to have the same problem but won't be able to discuss it much if at all. In our different positions we won't handle it the same way, and we could even end up at odds with each other. It wouldn't be the first time and certainly won't be the last.

"Doc . . . ? Did you get the part about . . . ? Interpol calling . . . ?" Marino says, and I must have misheard him.

"I can hardly understand you," I reply in a loud whisper. "And I can't talk. One second please."

Benton heads into the drawing room, and I wish the drapes had been pulled across the tall expansive windows. It's completely dark out with only vague smudges of distant lamps pushing back the inkiness, and I'm conscious of the night and what might be in it, possibly close by, possibly watching. Maybe right under our very noses. I detect something sinister has been tampering with us all day and probably for longer than that.

I RETURN TO THE entrance, where I avoid the old corroded mirror on the wall, and I stand with my head bent, facing the front door but not really seeing anything as I listen to Marino over the phone.

It's difficult to hear everything he's saying. We have at best a spotty connection, and I'm beginning to get jumpy. I don't know who's doing what or spying on whom, and in light of everything else it's hard not to feel hunted and disoriented.

"Okay, stop. You need to say that again only much more slowly." I huddle near an ornate cast-iron umbrella stand, and I don't want to believe this is happening. "What do you mean she's already stiff?"

"The first guy there checked her vitals said she's already stiff," Marino replies, and the connection is almost perfect suddenly.

"And have you seen this yourself or is it what you've been told?" I reply because what he's saying sounds completely wrong.

"I was told."

"Were there any attempts at resuscitation?"

"She was obviously dead," Marino says clear as a bell.

"That's what you were told."

"Yeah."

"What was obvious about it?" I ask.

"For one thing she was stiff. The squad didn't touch her."

"Then how did they determine she's stiff?"

"I don't know but apparently she is." Marino again reminds me he hasn't been to the scene.

"As far as we know, the first responding officer is the only one who's touched her?" I want to know.

"That's what I've been told."

"And what about her temp? Warm? Cool?"

"Warm supposedly. But what do you expect when it's still ninety degrees out? She could be out there all day and not cool off."

"I'll have to see when I get there. But the rigor doesn't make sense,"

I tell Marino. "Unless she's been out there much longer than one might initially assume. And that wouldn't make sense either. Even in this weather there are still some people out and about, especially near the water. She would have been found long before now, I would think."

For rigor mortis to be obvious, the victim would have had to be dead for several hours at least, depending on what muscles are noticeably affected and how advanced the postmortem process has gotten. The high temperatures we've been having would escalate decomposition, meaning rigor would set in sooner. But it's extremely unlikely that what Marino's been told is correct. That's also not surprising. Patrol officers are often the first responders, and they can't always know what they're looking at.

". . . Got him waiting with the twins . . . uh, who found the body . . ." Marino is saying, and then I lose the rest.

"Okay. You must be in a bad space again." I'm getting exasperated, but at least it sounds like he has the scene secured.

But I can't imagine what he meant when he said that Interpol was trying to call him.

"Looks like someone was hiding in the trees, waiting," he then says, and the connection is much better again. "That's what I'm guessing. No eyes or ears."

"Not if it were the middle of the day," I point out as I continue glancing around me, making sure no one can hear. "And if she's been dead for hours as her alleged rigor would suggest? There would have been eyes and ears because it would have been broad daylight, possibly early or midafternoon."

"I agree with you. That part can't be right."

"It doesn't sound it. But I'll see when I get there," I repeat. "What else can you tell me?"

Marino begins to describe what he knows about a violent death that may have happened within the past hour not even a mile from here. The woman's body is on the fitness path along the river. Some of her clothing has been ripped off, her helmet more than twenty feet away, and there's visible blood. It appears she died from a blow to the head, or that's what the first responding officer told Marino.

"He says you can see where she was struggling, moving around as her head was banged against the path," Marino adds, but what I alert on is his mention of a helmet. "Like someone was waiting until she was passing through a thick clump of trees where nobody could see, then grabbed her and she fought like hell."

"What helmet?" I ask. "The victim was on a bicycle?"

"It appears she was attacked while she was riding," Marino answers, and I can hear his excitement in his tense tone while I feel a chill along my spine.

I can't help but think of my encounter earlier today, first at the repertory theater and then on the sidewalk along Quincy Street. Suddenly the young woman with the British accent is in my mind, and I wish she weren't.

"She was on the path that cuts through the middle of the park," Marino is explaining, "and it happened in the spot where there's a small clearing in a stand of trees. I'm thinking it was planned like that to ambush her."

"And her helmet was off and some twenty feet from the body?" It's another detail that like her rigor defies logic, and I wonder what color the helmet is.

I hope it's not a robin's-egg blue.

"That's the story," Marino says, and I know exactly what he sounds like when something big goes down.

Not just big. But explosively bad. The blitz attack he's describing will create a public panic if it's not handled properly. I feel slightly sick inside. I remember the young woman on her bicycle looking at me quizzically as Benton handed her the bottle of water she dropped. She put her helmet back on before she rode off, and she didn't bother fastening the chin strap. I remember seeing it dangling as she rode off across the street, through the Yard, heading in the direction of the Square and the river.

This would have been close to seven P.M., barely an hour ago as the sun was setting. I tell myself if it turns out the victim is the woman I saw, it would be a bizarre twist of fate, an almost unbelievable one. I almost hope the detail about rigor turns out to be accurate. If it is, the victim couldn't be the young cyclist in Converse sneakers.

But even as I reassure myself, I also know that what Marino said about the rigor can't be true. Or the reporting officer is confused. Because I don't think it's possible—even in this weather—for a dead body on the fitness path inside John F. Kennedy Park not to be discovered for hours. I suspect the death happened recently, and then I envision the young woman's flushed face and smile again.

What doesn't kill you makes you stronger. I hear her voice in my head.

"I've already talked to your office," Marino says in my earpiece. "Rusty and Harold are bringing a truck."

"I need a big one."

"The MCC," he says, and the tri-axle thirty-five-foot mobile command center is a fine idea if there's a place to park it.

"We're going to need a barricade," I remind Marino, and I can't get the woman's face, her sporty sunglasses and self-assured smile, out of my thoughts.

"That's what I ordered. Remember who you're talking to."

When he headed investigations at the CFC, he was in charge of our fleet. In some ways he knows more about the nuts and bolts of our operations than I do.

"I want a place to duck out of the heat and away from the curious," I reply. "And we'll need plenty of water."

"Yeah, there's not exactly a 7-Eleven handy, and the park is dark as shit. We're setting up lights."

"Please don't turn them on yet. The scene will blaze like Fenway."

"Don't worry. We're keeping everything dark until we're ready. Doing what we can to keep the gawkers away, especially any assholes trying to film with their phones. There's student housing everywhere. Eliot House is right there on the other side of Memorial Drive and it's as big as the Pentagon, plus you got the Kennedy School, and traffic on Memorial Drive. Not to mention the bridge is right there, and across the water is Boston. So we got no plans of lighting up the scene right this minute."

"Do we have a name?" I ask.

"An ID was found on the path near her bike. Elisa Vandersteel, twenty-three years old from the UK. Of course that's if it's the dead lady's. I'm guessing it probably is," Marino says, and my mood sinks lower. "I'm told the picture looks sort of like her, for what it's worth. And I just pulled up in front of the Faculty Club. You coming out?"

"Where in the UK?" I almost don't want to ask.

"London, I think."

"Do you know what kind of shoes she had on?" I envision the cyclist's off-white Converse sneakers, and I'm pretty sure I caught a peek of bike socks, the kind that are below the ankle.

"Her shoes?" Marino asks as if he didn't hear me right.

"Yes."

"Got no idea," he says. "Why?"

"I'll see you in a minute," I reply.

CHAPTER 10

I STEP AWAY FROM THE front door, pausing by the antique entry-way table with its big flower arrangement.

Inside the drawing room Benton is discreetly tucked to one side of a window near the baby grand piano. He's on the phone, his face hard and somber. There's nobody else inside with him, and I wish I could tell him about the woman on the bicycle. He saw her too, and now the worst may have happened.

But I don't get any closer. I know when not to disturb him, and I notice that Mrs. P is back at her station, her round old-fashioned glasses staring at me. As I glance at her she quickly looks down and begins to open menus, checking the printed pages inside. I can tell she senses something is wrong.

I can't hear what Benton is saying to whoever he's on the phone with, but I get the impression based on his tone that he's not talking to the same person he was a moment earlier. I catch his eye and indicate I have to go, and he nods. Then he turns away. He doesn't place his hand over his phone to ask what's happening or offer what might be going on with him. And that makes me wonder if we really are being contacted about the same case.

But I don't see how that would be feasible. At this stage there's no reason I can think of for the FBI to be interested in a local death, possibly of a young woman from London named Elisa Vandersteel. But it's disturbing that Marino mentioned the International Criminal Police Organization, Interpol. I don't know why he did or if I might have misheard. But I can't stop thinking of the cyclist with the blue helmet and Converse sneakers who called me the *peanut-butter-pie lady*.

I realize the ID found near her body might not be hers, but when I met her she sounded British, possibly from London, and my stomach clenches harder. I feel a sense of urgency that's personal. As if I knew the woman who's been killed. As if I might be one of the last people she ever spoke to or saw. And I will myself to control my thoughts.

I can't say for a fact whose dead body is in the park or how the death occurred or why, I remind myself. I open the door and step out into the dark oven of the patio, where no one is sitting in the stifling night air. I follow the walkway, looking all around me with every step I take. I listen for the quiet nocturnal sounds of insects, of birds lifting off branches in a startled burst, their wings whistling.

I listen for the creaking of old trees, the rustle of leafy canopies or chirp of a katydid. But it's dead quiet except for traffic that gusts like the wind, rushing, then lagging before it picks up again. I'm aware of the solid roughness of the bricks beneath my softly tapping shoes, mindful of the thick static air and the bright bug eyes of vehicles on Quincy Street.

I pass the same foliage and rockery I did earlier when I was with Benton, but it seems I'm on another planet now, surrounded by unfamiliar voids of lawn, and hulking dark shapes and shadows. Nothing moves except traffic beyond the split-rail paling silhouetted ahead. I can see the libraries sleepily lit up across the street in the Yard, where I was walking not even an hour and a half ago. I reach the sidewalk, and Marino's SUV is parked at the curb behind Benton's Audi.

It seems like déjà vu as I climb in and stare at the rear of my husband's blacked-out Batmobile illuminated in the glare of headlights. Only he's not in it now, and I feel a pang of loneliness as I see the empty dark space where he was sitting behind the wheel, watching us in the rearview mirror but a very short time ago.

Benton is still inside the Faculty Club, and I continue watching for him to emerge from the red front door, to see him illuminated in the entrance light as he steps outside and follows the walkway. But there's no sign of him. He must still be on the phone, and it enters my mind that in the midst of all this chaos he has to take care of banal matters such as paying for a dinner we didn't get to eat. I didn't think of asking for the check. I simply walked out.

As I pull my door shut and set my briefcase by my feet, I ask Marino what else he instructed my two autopsy technicians Rusty and Harold to bring to the scene.

"And have they already left?" I pull my shoulder harness across me and the steel tongue snaps into the buckle that as usual I had to dig out of the crack in the seat. "Because I need protective clothing and a scene case. I don't have anything with me, not even a pair of gloves. And there's no time for me to stop by my office."

"You need to relax," Marino says. "I've got it covered."

He looks the way he did when I saw him last, except he's taken off his tie. I see it on the backseat, sloppily coiled like a polyester snake.

"Please assure me we're keeping the lights off." It's not possible I'm going to relax. "We turn on portable floodlights and we may as well send out invitations and a press release."

"Remember where I used to work? Remember who used to take care of all that and still knows how?" He checks his mirrors. "I know the drill." His eyes are darting and he's sweating. "I guess Benton's staying?" Marino stares at the Faculty Club, boxy and dignified in the distant dark.

A pale gold light fills the tall twelve-paned windows, and I can see inside the drawing room, the masculine leather furniture, the sparkling chandelier, the gleaming baby grand, and I look for Benton. But there's no way he's lingering in front of windows for all the world to see.

"I'm not sure what he's doing," I reply. "He was on the phone with Washington when I was leaving."

"Let me guess," Marino says, and right off he's assuming Benton's call is related to what's just happened in John F. Kennedy Park.

"I don't have any idea," I reply as we pull away from the curb. "I don't know what's going on but he did mention earlier that the terror alert is elevated."

Marino turns on his emergency lights but not his siren. "Something's going on, Doc. I'm just telling you. And he's not passing along the info because that's what the FBI does, doesn't matter that you're married to them."

"I'm not married to the FBI. I'm married to Benton." I've said it before and I'll say it again.

"If the reason he's on the phone with Washington is the Vandersteel case, there's no way he's going to tell you," Marino says as if he knows my husband better than I do. "He could be talking to Interpol, which might explain the call I got—that's assuming news of the case here has shot up the chain already, and if so I'd like to know how the hell that's possible. But Benton won't tell you shit unless it suits his purposes because right now he's the Feds. And yeah, you're married to them. Or maybe worse? He is."

"This is several times now that you've mentioned Interpol." I'm not interested in hearing his disparagements of Benton, the FBI or anything else at the moment. "Why?" I ask.

"They didn't call you too, did they?" Marino glances at me, his brown eyes glaring and bloodshot.

"No." I'm mystified. "Why would they and about what?"

MARINO GUNS A RIGHT on Harvard Street, and the route he takes basically will retrace my steps from my earlier ill-fated walk.

Only now it's completely dark, and the stars and quarter moon are blotted by a hot haze that for days has been filmy over the horizon, intensifying the colors at twilight from pastel tints to wide brushstrokes of gaudy orange, magenta and deep rose.

"Let me start at the beginning and spell it out," Marino says. "I was actually on my way to the CFC."

"What for?" I look at his wide-eyed flushed face as he streaks past apartment buildings, a bookshop, a bank, a café and other businesses that form blurred chains of light on either side of the two-lane road.

"Because Lucy and I were trying to see if there's anything else we could figure out about the bogus nine-one-one call made by someone using voice-changing software," he says, and that addresses at least some of what I've been wondering.

Unsurprisingly, Lucy picked up on the subtle but odd uniformity of what we suspect is an altered voice on the audio clip. She must have said something to Marino and also to Benton.

"She's in her lab," Marino says. "Or she was right before I called you."

"Then what?" I ask him as we speed through the middle of the Harvard campus. "You're with her at the CFC, and what happened next?"

There are more people out now, on the sidewalks, walking through the Yard. But certainly it's nothing close to the usual crowds, the typical hustle and bustle of Cambridge, which I've always said is a concentrated version of any huge metropolis in the world and all the problems and advantages that go with it.

"Then I get the call from Clay," Marino says.

"Do I know him?"

"Tom Barclay."

"The investigator?"

"Yeah."

"I see," I reply, and this changes things.

I look out the windows, and the park and the river are just minutes ahead. I can see the brick Widener Library with its teal cupola, and the stone slate-roofed department of linguistics. I'm surprised and unsettled by what Marino just told me. If Tom Barclay was the source of the information, that's unfortunate.

"I see," I again say. "So it wasn't a patrol officer who was the first responder."

"Nope. It was Clay," Marino answers, and Clay, or Investigator Barclay as I know him, recently was transferred from property crimes to the major case unit.

I haven't really worked with him directly but one of my medical examiners had a case with him earlier in the week and complained about him. Barclay is much too sure of himself and doesn't know when to shut up. He may have attended the crime-scene academy but that doesn't give him the expertise to identify and interpret artifacts such as rigor and livor mortis, and other changes that occur after death. A little knowledge can be a dangerous thing when you're cocky.

"The detail about rigor is perplexing and troublesome," I tell Marino over the thunder of his driving like a rocket. "He's been around dead bodies before."

"Not many."

"But some. And he should recognize certain obvious postmortem changes," I add, "and hopefully not confuse or misrepresent them. But it would seem like a strange mistake to make if he's stated for the record that she's already going into rigor when in fact she's not. And he shouldn't be stating anything to you that you in turn pass on to me. All of it constitutes a paper trail, a record that we might wish we didn't have."

I emphasize *for the record* because Marino's relaying to me what Investigator Barclay reported could become problematic if it's documented or circulated. The dead woman and any associated biological evidence are my legal jurisdiction, meaning I'm present in an official capacity.

I'm not here as Marino's mother, wife, friend, partner, mentor or pal, and very little is private anymore. Unfortunately, any information we exchange doesn't constitute some sort of legally protected small talk. We can get asked anything when we're under oath.

"Clay's new. He's never worked a homicide, and he thinks he's a genius. Beyond that what can I tell you?" Marino replies. "I guess we'll see for ourselves, but he said she was stiff. He touched her and she felt as stiff as a mannequin. That's what he told me."

"If he wasn't sure or didn't know, I wish he hadn't said it." This is disappointing and may come back to bite us. "It's worse because it's a detective saying it."

"I know," Marino says. "That's why I'm always telling him and everyone else to think before you open your damn pie hole and be careful what you write, e-mail and post on freakin' Facebook."

At Harvard Square, the SUV's strobing red and blue lights bounce off street signs and are reflected in the windows of buildings and cars we pass. I remind him of Interpol, steering him there.

"Why were you called?" I want to know.

"The million-dollar question."

"And when was this?"

"Let me roll back the tape so you can appreciate the timing," Marino says. "First I get the call from Clay. I tell Lucy I gotta go and am heading downstairs—"

"You were actually with her in her lab when Investigator Barclay called you?" I ask, and Marino nods, explaining he'd just gotten there and they were getting started going over the 911 recording.

"Then my phone rings and it's Barclay. He says he's at a homicide scene in JFK Park on the riverbank."

"Did he actually use the word *homicide*?" I ask. "Because I wish he hadn't said that either."

"He said it looked like an attempted sexual assault, and that she was beaten to death."

"I don't know why you bothered to pick me up." Cops like Barclay can create dangerous problems. "It appears he's happy to do my job." I'm going to have to have a word with him before the night is over. "Why did I bother interrupting my dinner?"

"Yeah he pisses me off too," Marino says. "You got no idea. Talk about someone who doesn't look before he leaps. It never occurs to him that maybe he's not a damn expert at whatever it is."

"I hope he's not freely offering these same opinions to everyone he talks to," I add, "because this is how misinformation ends up all over the place. Let's get back to Interpol. Tell me about the phone call."

"Like I was saying, Clay asked me to meet him at the scene. Then he wanted to know if he should contact your office, and I said I would take care of it. By the time I'd walked out of Lucy's lab, taken the elevator down to the lower level and was getting in my car in the parking lot, my phone was ringing again," Marino tells the story loudly, over the noise of the engine.

"This time the call's from an unknown number. You know, when a call comes up with a row of zeros? Like when caller ID is blocked and it's not somebody in your contacts list?" he says. "So I answered, and it was Washington, D.C."

CHAPTER 11

"IT WAS INTERPOL," MARINO states as if there can be no doubt about it.

I ask him how he could be so sure. "You said the number was blocked. So I'm not clear on how you knew who was calling," I add, and other drivers are moving out of our way.

"The person identified himself as an investigator from their Washington bureau, the NCB, and said he was trying to reach Investigator Peter Rocco Marino of the Cambridge Police Department."

Interpol's United States headquarters, the National Central Bureau (NCB), reports directly to the attorney general. And neither the NCB nor Interpol's global headquarters in France would be interested in any U.S. case unless there's reason to suspect criminal activity that extends beyond our national borders. That thought brings me back to the cyclist with the British accent, and I hope she's not dead.

I envision her blue helmet with the unbuckled chin strap, and I should have said something. I should have told her to fasten it.

"I asked the NCB guy what he was calling in reference to, and he said he was aware of the developing situation in the park on the waterfront," Marino explains.

"Those were his exact words? *The developing situation*?" Now I'm really baffled.

"I swear to God. And I'm thinking, What the hell? What situation could he know about? How could he know there's a body in the park by the water here in Cambridge?"

"I don't understand . . ." I start to say.

"I asked how he could be aware of any situation period around here," Marino talks over me. "What was his source? And he said that was classified."

"I don't understand," I repeat myself. "How is it possible that Interpol's call to you was in reference to Elisa Vandersteel, assuming that's who's dead?" It's completely illogical. "Was her name mentioned?"

"No, but he was talking about a sudden death. That was how he phrased it, *a sudden death that had international consequences*, which is why Interpol is involved," Marino says.

"Elisa Vandersteel would have international consequences," I reply, "since she's not American. Once again, that's assuming the driver's license is the dead woman's."

"It felt like that was the situation he was referencing. That he somehow knew about it."

"Tell me how it's possible? I've never heard of something like this happening," I reply. "The local media hasn't even caught wind of it yet. Is there something on the Internet I've not been told about? How could Interpol know about a death before you've been to the scene or called the medical examiner?"

"I asked Lucy if anything had been tweeted or whatever," he says. "I called her right after I hung up from talking to the Interpol investigator. Nothing's out there about the Vandersteel case that we know of. Assuming that's who she is. But you're right. It seems Interpol knew before either of us did, and I don't understand that either."

Marino's portable radio is charging upright in the console, and it hasn't escaped my notice that there's very little chatter. In fact it's so quiet I forget the radio is in the car until I notice it. I've heard nothing go over the air that might alert anyone about the dead body awaiting us at the park.

"But how would Interpol investigators or analysts know about a body found in a Cambridge park near the water in the past thirty-some-odd minutes?" I ask. "I'm sorry, something's off about this, Marino. And it's not the way the process works. Local law enforcement requests assistance because there might be an international interest—"

He interrupts, "I know how it's supposed to work. You think this is my first friggin' rodeo?"

"I don't believe I've ever heard of Interpol initiating contact about a homicide scarcely anyone knows about yet," I emphasize. "We don't know she's a homicide for that matter. We also haven't verified the victim's identity. We don't know a damn thing."

"All I can tell you is the investigator who called said he was from their counterterrorism division. He said he understood we have a situation," Marino uses that word again. "A death with international consequences, and I got the feeling he was thinking about terrorism, based on the words he used. I sure as hell wish I had a recording of what he said."

"And where did the information come from?" I'm going to keep pounding that drum. "Just because a British driver's license was found on a bike path? And how would he even know about that unless Barclay told him? This is absurd."

"When I asked him how the hell he could know about anything going on in Cambridge, and why he was calling me directly, he said they'd received e-mailed information that listed my name and number as the contact." Marino stares straight ahead, and he must be thinking the same thing I am, but he won't want to admit it.

"Interpol doesn't work that way." I'm not going to back down because this is something I know about, and Marino has been duped. "And they don't hire psychics with crystal balls who can predict cases before the rest of us know about them, last I heard." I instantly regret saying this because he'll take it as a slight directed at him, when it's not. "It's implausible if not impossible that they could know about a scene and a dead body we've not so much as looked at yet."

"Well I'm not the one who's pals with the secretary-general," Marino replies with a sarcastic snap. "Maybe you should call him up and ask him how the hell they found out so damn fast."

I've been to Interpol's headquarters in Lyon, France, numerous times, and am on friendly terms with the secretary-general Tom Perry, who's actually American, a Rhodes scholar, a former head of the National Institute of Justice, and a bona fide Renaissance man.

"If need be I will," I reply reasonably, ignoring Marino's sting, careful of my tone because I don't want to argue with him. "How was it left?" I ask.

"The investigator said the Washington headquarters, the NCB, was contacted but didn't say by who. He said it was protected information, the same shit I use as an excuse all the time. So I didn't think much about it," Marino explains, but I can tell he's thinking about it now.

"This is sounding too much like the nine-one-one complaint," I reply, in hopes he'll make the same connections I am.

I'd rather he draw his own conclusion so he doesn't kill the messenger.

"Yeah, and the guy coughed."

"Who did?"

"The Interpol guy coughed several times and I remember wondering if he had a cold. And now that I'm thinking about it, the person who left the bogus nine-one-one coughed too."

Marino has a hard edge to his glumness, and his face is deep red.

"I'm beginning to think that whoever murdered Elisa Vandersteel has anonymously reported his own damn case to Interpol because he wants the entire damn planet to know about it," he then says above the noise of his car, and I can see his pulse pounding in his neck. "And God only knows who else has been contacted."

That may be Marino's biggest worry. But it's not mine.

THE ANGRIER HE IS the calmer I get.

"There had to be a source," I persist anyway, because I deal with international cases far more often than Marino does, and I know the routines and the protocols. "Did a police officer contact Interpol? In other words did another cop contact the NCB in Washington about the Cambridge case? Because that shouldn't be classified."

"Got no idea who the source was but somebody sure as hell told somebody something," he almost yells over the roar of his engine. "Hell no, Barclay didn't, though. He wouldn't without clearing it with me. He wouldn't even think of it."

"Interpol's very careful who it talks to. You have to be authenticated and verified." I gently lead him closer to what will most assuredly be an unpalatable truth.

"I don't think it was a phone call. It sounds like they got an e-mail," Marino says, and the ugliness he's about to face is going to enrage him.

I look at his profile inside the dark SUV, at the big dome of his bald head, his strong nose, and the hard set of his heavy mandible.

"I do know that e-mail is the quickest and simplest way to report something to them," he's saying. "The forms and everything are right there on the Internet. They've got it all on a website. It's easy but it's also going to be monitored and traceable."

"So we certainly would expect that the Washington office of Interpol, the NCB, would know if an e-mailed tip was bogus," I say pointedly. "In other words, the NCB should know if it weren't from a real member of the law enforcement community or someone else in an authorized position to report an incident or a threat." I know what I'm suspicious of, and Marino doesn't like the tack I'm taking.

"You sure as hell would think so," he says with a hint of defensiveness, which is what I expect because he should know what's coming.

He should have figured it out before I did, but it's an unpleasant truth. And those take longer. They're harder to swallow.

"And it also could be that Interpol hasn't been contacted by anyone legitimately," I suggest. "And that you weren't either," I add, and he acts as if he didn't hear me.

"You would think the investigator who called me could have helped out a little by saying they weren't sure the tip was credible, that maybe some whack-a-do is jerking everybody around." Now Marino sounds personally offended, and he continues to ignore what I just said. "But I took what I was told at face value."

"Are you absolutely certain it was an Interpol investigator who called you?" I begin to confront Marino with what I suspect, and he's silent.

To borrow his colorful and bewildering vernacular, this is the real piece of cake, the poison in the ink, the snake under the tent, and the elephant in the woodpile. I'm asking him who he was really talking to, because all the signs point at his having been played for a fool. Or at least that's exactly how it's going to feel to him.

"I'm wondering what made you believe it was Interpol on the phone besides what the person claimed?" I try that approach next, and I can feel Marino getting stubborn like concrete setting.

Then he says, "I guess the only way I'm going to know is if I try to call the asshole back."

He picks up his cell phone from his lap. He unlocks it and reluctantly hands it to me as if he's turning over evidence that will get him into a world of trouble.

"Open it to my notepad," Marino says with his unblinking eyes fixed on the road, "and you'll see the number. Just click on the app and you can see where I typed what he gave me."

"Why? So you could call him back and report what we're about to find?"

"Hell if I know. He just gave me a number and said to update him, that we'd touch base tomorrow," Marino says, and this is sounding only more like a taunt, a hoax, with every second that passes.

Throughout my career I've worked closely with Interpol. We've always enjoyed a close relationship because when it comes to death and violence the world is a small place. It gets smaller all the time, and it's increasingly common for me to deal with color-coded international notices about fugitives and people who have vanished or turn up dead and nameless in the United States.

I also deal with Americans who die abroad, and now and then a decedent turns out to be undercover law enforcement or a spy. I know how to dance the dance with the Department of Justice, the Pentagon, the CIA, the United Nations Security Council and various international police agencies and criminal tribunals. I can honestly say that what Marino is describing to me isn't at all the way the process works.

"Then you want me to call this?" I look at what he typed in an electronic note, a phone number with a Washington, D.C., area code.

"Why not?" he says, and he's like a pressure cooker about to blow.

"I don't want to talk to whoever it is since it's your phone and not mine." I look at the phone in my hand, at the number displayed on an electronic message pad.

"Quit thinking like a damn lawyer. Just call it. May as well go ahead, and both of us can listen to it on speakerphone. Let's see if the investigator answers."

"You never did tell me his name. Who will you ask for?"

"John Dow. Dow as in Dow Jones." Marino's jaw muscles clench.

"Or as in John Doe?"

"I'm pretty sure he pronounced it Dow." The redness in his face is spreading down his neck.

I click on the number and am given the option to CALL, which I select, and I wait for it to connect. And it does, ringing loudly, wirelessly through intercom speakers in the SUV.

"Thank you for calling the Hay-Adams. This is Crystal, how may I assist you?" a female voice answers.

"Hello?" Marino says with a blank expression that turns into a murderous scowl. "This is the Hay-Adams? The hotel?" He turns his baffled furious face to me and silently mouths, *What the fuck?*

"This is the Hay-Adams in Washington, D.C. How may I assist you, sir?"

"Would you mind reading back your number to make sure it's what I was given?" Marino says, his glaring eyes on the road.

"Were you trying to contact the Hay-Adams Hotel, sir?"

"It would be helpful if you'd tell me your number. I think I might have dialed the wrong place," Marino says, and after a pause the woman recites the same number that's in the electronic note I looked at.

"Thanks. My mistake." Marino ends the call. "Goddamn son of a bitch!" He slams his meaty fist on the steering wheel.

What he wrote down is the general number for the hotel. It's what was given to him by someone who identified himself as a counterterrorism investigator for Interpol. This is worse than a typo or even a deliberate and mocking misdirect. It's personal, and not just directed at Marino. It may not be directed at him, period, but now's not the moment to tell him that. The Hay-Adams means nothing to him and I doubt he's ever stayed there.

But the hotel is close to the Capitol, the White House, and convenient to FBI headquarters, and also its academy and behavioral analysis unit in northern Virginia. The Hay-Adams is our first choice when Benton and I are in Washington, D.C., together, and we were there several weeks ago for business and pleasure. We visited museums, and Benton had meetings in Quantico while I conferred with General Briggs about our space shuttle presentation at the Kennedy School.

I think back to anything else that stands out about the trip. But nothing extraordinary occurred. I had work and so did Benton. We were in and out of offices and around a number of different people. Then the last night we were there we had dinner with Briggs and his wife at the Palm with its cartoon-covered walls.

We sat in a booth near a host of iconic characters. Nixon, Spider-Man, Kissinger, and Dennis the Menace, I recall.

CHAPTER 12

SIRENS SCREAM AS A Cambridge patrol car squeals a tight left off Winthrop and falls in behind us. We're a light show flashing along John F. Kennedy Street, and other drivers are slowing down and moving out of the way.

"Shit, shit, shit. Damn son of a bitch," Marino continues cussing a blue storm, to borrow another of his uniquely crafted clichés.

He's glancing in his mirrors as I sit back in my seat, hoping we don't crash. We're not going as fast as it seems but it's nerve-racking, and Marino's in a treacherous mood because of the phone call to the Hay-Adams Hotel. He rarely treats a death scene as an emergency. Usually lights and sirens aren't needed. Usually it's too late for us to prevent or save much, but he's impatient, aggressive, in a blind fury.

"Jesus Christ! Who the hell was that? Who the hell was I just on the phone with?"

He's been going on and on since he ended the call. There's nothing I can say, and I know when it's best to mostly listen. Marino needs to vent, then he'll be okay. But he won't forgive and forget. He never does. Whoever makes a fool of Pete Marino will have hell to pay. It may take years. In some instances it's taken decades.

"I can't believe it. I freakin' can't believe it! And what the crap does

...erts think he's doing?" Marino glares into the rearview mirror at the marked unit flashing and wailing behind us. "Did you hear me ask for his assistance? Did you hear me request a backup or yell *Mayday*?"

He glances angrily at me, and he's almost shouting. I'm silent as I sit snugly strapped in my seat, watching the lights pulsing in my side mirror, waiting for him to calm down.

"No, I didn't think so," he loudly answers his own questions. "This is what's called playing cops and robbers. The idiot Roberts is all dressed up with no place to go because I don't need his damn help."

Marino glares in the mirror every other second, his jaw muscle doing its rapid-fire flexing again. He snatches his portable radio out of the charger.

"Unit thirty-three," he holds the radio close to his lips, practically spitting he's so pissed.

"Thirty-three."

"Ask one-sixty-four to call me." He's instantly polite with a touch of sweetness as he talks to the dispatcher he refers to as Rosie.

"Roger, thirty-three," she says, and her tone is different with him too, and it needles me a little.

Marino loves women but he's never known what to do with them besides the obvious courting, badgering, acting out, being led by the nose and in general being controlled by his *lesser member*, as Lucy not so delicately puts it. No relationship he's had has ever lasted, not with his former wife Doris, who in my opinion he's never gotten over. He's also fallen out with me more than once, badly, almost irreparably.

I think of him flirting with my sister in Miami. Benton swore the two of them started something when we were there earlier in the summer, and I wonder how I could have missed the cues. I watch him return the radio to the charger as Rosie calls unit 164 and passes on the message.

I check my phone for any further updates about when my sister is set to land at Logan. I'm about to send Lucy a message about my inability to show up at the airport in light of what's just happened, but I'm distracted again when Marino's cell phone rings through the SUV's intercom.

"What can I do you for? What's up?" A male voice fills the car, and Officer Roberts sounds hyper and too cheerful.

"What's up is you." Marino isn't nice about it. "I see you bird-dogging me and need you to peel off and get the hell away." He sounds vicious.

"You're one to talk, all lit up like the Fourth of July. You know what they say. Monkey see, monkey do—" Unit 164 fires back as if he's having a grand time, and Marino interrupts because now he's really angry.

"Turn your fucking lights and fucking siren off, Roberts. If I need a meat puppet you'll be my first damn call," Marino snaps.

If he had a handset and could hang up with a slam, I'm sure he would. But he can't. He presses a button on the steering wheel to end his tirade.

"I'm not sure what he was responding to," I puzzle. "I've not heard anything on the radio that might hint we have a possible homicide in the park."

"He knows something big is going on there. He may not know what but everybody out here knows something's up. The radio silence is deliberate, and then he sees us go by, and that's his excuse to fall in behind me," Marino growls.

I remind him that it might not have been the best idea to turn on his own lights and siren. Certainly it's attracting attention.

"Well that doesn't mean you follow me like a damn parade. It's not a damn party or a spectator sport," Marino talks at the top of his voice. "Everybody wants to be a damn detective until they have to do paperwork, deal with lawyers, get sued, get called out at all hours and all the other bullshit we put up with."

I can see the patrol car in the side mirror, dropping back, receding into the distance. The red and blue strobes have gone dark, the siren ended in a whimper. Unit 164 slows and turns left on South Street as we flash, pulse, yelp and wail through a well-lighted stretch of restaurants, coffee shops, taverns and breweries.

"Maybe it really was Interpol," Marino says, and it's a good thing I'm accustomed to his non sequiturs. "Maybe I wrote down the number wrong." He picks up where he left off about the bogus phone call from a bogus investigator. "Maybe that's all it is."

"I seriously doubt it. I'm sorry to say but I think the call you got is exactly what it appears to be, Marino, and I'm sure it's upsetting." I don't add that it might be somewhat the way I felt when Benton played the 911 recording for me that Marino refused to share.

I know all too well what it's like to be falsely accused, excluded, belittled, treated suspiciously or simply tormented and harassed. But when Marino is upset, he doesn't necessarily compare notes with others, including me. There are no other notes. Only his.

"Wait till I get my hands on whoever it is," and he's enraged all over again. "How the hell did this person come up with my name and get my cell number? Where did he get the information? How did he know to call me about anything?"

"I don't know." I'm saying that a lot.

"Well it's the biggest and most important thing we need to find out. Who gave the info to this asswipe joker?"

"It's probably not the biggest or most important thing we need to find out at the moment." I stare at him, and I hate that someone has targeted him like this.

I know how Marino gets. He can't endure being boondoggled. He can't tolerate being made to feel as unimportant and powerless as he did while he was growing up on the wrong side of the tracks in New Jersey.

"I recommend you put this on a shelf for now," I tell him. "We'll worry about Interpol later. At your earliest convenience I suggest you have Lucy take a look at your phone to see if she can trace the unknown call that supposedly was from the NCB's counterterrorism division."

"Right," he says tersely, and he's furious with himself.

MARINO WAS TRICKED, AND it will be unfortunate if other cops find out about it.

I think of Roberts, for example, who Marino just emasculated. The way he goes after his comrades will come back to him a hundredfold if they discover he fell prey to a hoax of the worst order. They'll be merciless, but it's not a joke. It's no laughing matter. Marino might have been talking to the same anonymous person who, it would seem, used voice-altering software to complain about me in a 911 call today.

Marino could have been talking to Tailend Charlie, for all we know. Or if Elisa Vandersteel is the dead woman and she's a homicide, then Marino might have been talking to her killer. There's no telling who Marino was on the phone with but I'm convinced it wasn't Interpol. I'm no-nonsense as I tell him he really must let it go. With what we have ahead of us there's no room to spare for personal outrage or embarrassment.

"Let's just do this." I raise my voice above the noise of our roaring through Cambridge in a juggernaut of brilliant strobes and urgent tones. "It's been a hell of a day but we've been through much worse. How many years has it been? And here we are. We're still here, and we'll figure it out. We always do."

"That's the damn truth," he says, and I feel him glumly settle down a little, getting steadier. "I just can't believe it happened."

"I know. But it could happen to anyone."

"Even you?" He glances at me, and I nod. "Bullshit," he says.

"Anyone at all," I reassure him, but it's not entirely honest.

I seriously doubt I would have fallen for the same ruse the same way Marino did or at all. I would have asked more questions. I would have been suspicious instantly if I'd gotten such a call on my personal cell phone from a so-called NCB investigator. I would have recognized the corruption of a process I know better than Marino does.

"Well I feel stupid as shit," he confesses, and suddenly I feel stupid too but for a very different reason.

I suddenly remember Dorothy again. I'm startled and dismayed as I envision the disapproval, the *I told you so* look in her eyes and the gleam of satisfaction. She loves it when I screw up, and by the time I'd gotten into Marino's SUV at the Faculty Club my attention had been diverted from my sister and her last-minute plan of an unscheduled visit.

She's on her way here even as Marino and I are headed to a death scene, and I think of his flirting with the dispatcher Rosie. His annoying womanizing enters my mind. I resist looking at him as I'm unhappily reminded of what Benton accused, and it's more disturbing when I think of Marino's repeated offers to pick up Dorothy at Logan tonight.

Last I heard she's supposed to arrive from Fort Lauderdale around nine thirty but she's going to be late, according to Lucy. It's already almost eight thirty, and I have no doubt my sister is expecting Benton and me to be waiting for her with bells on no matter when she lands.

That's not going to happen, and Marino can't be there either, not that I'd encourage it. Next it occurs to me as an additional blow that I left my shopping bag in the cloakroom at the Faculty Club. I won't have gifts for the chronically dissatisfied Dorothy. Dammit. That figures, and the fact is I can't possibly do anything for her right now. I can't pay attention to her or make the slightest gesture of welcome. I've failed, and that's exactly how she'll look at it.

She'll view it negatively and as an unfairness directed at her personally. It won't occur to her that she wasn't quite as inconvenienced as the person who's dead. Dorothy's not even as inconvenienced as I am, but that won't enter her head. Once again I'm the busy and inaccessible Big Sis, and if she reaches out and makes herself vulnerable, this is what happens. I can hear her now. I could script it.

I send a text to Lucy and Janet: *Unable to make it to airport. Possibly you could get Dorothy? Or she could Uber? Very sorry.*

Almost instantly Janet answers: *No problem. We'll take care of Lucy's mom. Maybe stop by later? We'd love to see you.*

It always jolts me when Dorothy is referred to as Lucy's "mom." It never sounds right, and it's at moments like this when I'm reminded of how bonded I am to a niece I've raised like a daughter. I admit I might be a little possessive, just the tiniest bit territorial and jealous.

CHAPTER 13

THE BULKY SHAPES OF centuries-old trees and tall dense hedges are etched against the night as we enter the John F. Kennedy Park.

Marino has slowed the SUV to a crawl. He's turned the emergency lights and siren off. I count four patrol cars and one unmarked SUV parked bumper-to-bumper barely off the pavement. Deeper in it's too dark to make out much, little more than impressions of something there. Maybe a distant mountain range. Maybe thick woods in murky shades of dark muddy colors.

If I didn't already know what was around me, I couldn't tell from what I can see. The darkness transforms benches, paths, trash cans, the bend in the river into a scene that could be almost anywhere. But I would know Boston across the water. Instantly I would recognize the Hancock skyscraper topped by its lance-like antenna, and the Prudential Tower. I couldn't miss the lit-up Citgo sign, also known as the *C-it-Go* sign because so many Red Sox home runs have sailed over it.

We can drive but only so far, as there are no roads through the park, which is wide where we are but in other parts very narrow. Motorized traffic is prohibited inside the acres of well-kept grass, shrubs and hardwood trees that stretch between the Charles River and Memorial Drive. I've been here many times. It's a favorite hike from our house near the northeastern edge of the Harvard campus.

If Benton and I keep up a good pace we can make the round trip on foot in roughly an hour. That's if we take the most direct route, and we don't always. Now and then we wander from one newsstand and outdoor café or market to another, making our leisurely way to the water, especially when the weather is as sublime as it can be in the spring and fall. On Sundays when it's warm and not raining we love to drink Peet's coffee and read armloads of newspapers on a bench by the Charles.

In the winter we might hike or snowshoe here and sit bundled up and close to each other, sharing a thermos of steaming-hot cider. All of this is going on in my mind as an emotional subroutine that I don't focus on but can't block. I feel the distant echo of nostalgia, of loss, as I'm reminded of how rare it is that Benton and I have had much time to ourselves for leisure—for doing nothing, whatever that means.

We treasure conversations and activities that are unencumbered by broken laws and tragedies. We treat it as a special occasion if no one is committing violent acts or has died during the hours or a weekend when Benton and I are paying attention to each other. This is why our regular outings at the Faculty Club are important and cherished. It's why having favorite secret places like hotels, the ocean, the river, and scenic areas where we hike is necessary to good relationships and our good health.

The park is a popular place to get away, to have a picnic, to sunbathe, read, study or play a pickup Frisbee game. Only cyclists and people on foot are allowed but that doesn't stop Marino from sacrilegiously bumping his big police vehicle over grass and a narrow unpaved path. He halts between a big maple tree and a tall iron lamp that glows wanly in the near pitch-blackness, the SUV nose-in toward the Charles River. The headlights illuminate the red-roofed brick boathouse, and to the left of it the bridge I drove past during my fateful ride with Bryce what now seems days ago.

I watch a lighted necklace of cars moving to and fro overhead, their lights diamond white and blood red. And below, the water is sluggish, greenish black and rippled. I don't see any boaters out. Most of them will have gone in at sunset. On the opposite shore, Boston's Back Bay is softly illuminated by the glowing windows of old brownstones and row houses. In the distance, the downtown skyline sparkles, and the night sky is a lighter shade of black, a deep charcoal over the harbor and the ocean, which I can't see from here.

Marino turns off the engine, and we open our doors. No interior lights blink on because he's always kept those switches off for as long as I've known him. It makes no difference what he's driving. He doesn't want to be an easy target, a deer in the headlights as he puts it, and we never have been in all of the miles I've ridden with him. Most vehicle-related mishaps when we're together occur because I can't see where I'm stepping, what I'm sitting on or exposed to when I'm in and out of anything he pilots.

But to give him credit, he's much more meticulous about his cars, trucks and motorcycles than he ever was when we first started working together. I'll never forget his tricked-out Crown Vics with their monster engines, and their long looping antennas bobbing like fishing poles. The ashtrays overflowed, the windows and mirrors at times were opaque from smoke. There were fast-food bags and chicken boxes everywhere, and usually I was sitting on salt that looked like sand everywhere. If you didn't know what it was you might think Marino lived near a beach.

Overall he's become more highly evolved. He still smokes but nowhere near as much, and when he does the great outdoors is his ashtray. He wouldn't think of dirtying or stinking up his car, not that this is anything to brag about. When he eats while on the road he doesn't rip into the packets of salt and ketchup the way he used to, and he's much better about cleaning up. Nonetheless I prefer to see what I'm climbing into when he rides me around after dark.

I've earned my share of purple hearts from grease and various condiment stains on pants and skirts. I've banged my lower extremities against riot guns stored between or under seats, and slipped on running boards that are slick with Armor All. I've snagged my hose on a deer antler and hooked my thumb on a fishing lure in the glove box, which also is never lighted. Once we bumped over a bad pothole, and a *Playboy* centerfold fell out of the visor and into my lap. It was several editions old. Marino had forgotten it was there, I guess.

I lower my pumps to the dirt path, standing up, and the heat slams into me like a wall. It's not as bad as it was when I walked out of the Faculty Club but that doesn't mean it's much better than tolerable. It doesn't mean it's safe for long exposures without risking hyperthermia, and I'm assuming we'll be working the scene for hours.

When the truck is here it can serve as a staging area where we can duck into the air-conditioning at intervals. We'll have plenty of water, snacks, and urine-collection devices, UCDs—more popularly known as *piddle packs*.

"We've got to figure out exactly how we're going to do this," Marino says, and we shut our doors.

The quiet heat is broken by the rumble of traffic on the street behind us and on the bridge. I hear little else. Maybe a plane passing overhead. Nothing is stirring, the heated air inescapable.

"A high recon," I reply simply as I shoulder my messenger bag. "Then a low one where we move in and collect evidence."

"You going to leave the body out here even longer than it's already been?"

"Longer than what? We don't know how long it's been. We know when the police got the call, which I'd estimate was what? Thirty or forty minutes ago? I'll factor all of this in, and the numbers and data will be as exact as anything can be. It's business as usual in other words, and will be fine."

"So we just leave her as is." He pushes a button on his key fob and pops the tailgate.

"Why are you worrying so much?"

"Because I wish we could get the body out of here. That would solve most of our problems, Doc."

"And at the same time create bigger ones. I don't want to wait any longer than necessary but I don't have much choice if I want to see what I'm doing."

"It's just too bad this had to happen with Dorothy flying in," he says, and that may be the very last thing I want to talk about right now.

"Plus I have nothing with me, no protective clothing, nothing," I pick up on what I was saying before he rudely brought up my sister. "I came straight from a dinner where I didn't have my car or anything else. Under normal circumstances, I wouldn't have left for the scene yet."

We've walked around to the back of the SUV, and I don't rub it in that Marino continues to enjoy a special status and special treatment. Had he taken the required steps that other detectives don't typically deviate from, he would have called the CFC investigative unit he used to head.

He would have discussed the case with whoever answered. After routine questions were asked and an electronic report was created, one of my medical examiners on call would have been contacted. Most likely that doctor would have responded but only after a truck and all needed supplies and personnel were deployed first.

If I ended up at the scene at all, it wouldn't be now. It might not be for another hour at least. I probably could have finished my dinner with Benton first, and if I'd had enough wine I wouldn't have shown up at all. I wasn't supposed to be working tonight. I was to be with my husband and go pick up my sister. But Marino bypassed all of the usual protocols and checks and balances just as he always does.

I won't tell him that I don't really mind. When he calls I know it's serious. We have a routine that's familiar and comfortably rutted like an old wagon trail. I watch him lift open the tailgate, and of course no light goes on. I may as well be staring into a cave.

"I'VE GOT GLOVES, COVERALLS," he says halfheartedly because he knows I can't wear anything that might fit him. "And the usual stuff, except no thermometer. I should just toss one in so you have it if you need it. I keep meaning to get around to it."

"We're going to have to wait," I say it again, and I have no doubt he won't be the only one who's about to get impatient.

Everyone will be champing at the bit to collect whatever forensic treasures might be out here. Every cop—and Marino most of all—will want to know what happened to the victim. I can't begin to answer that until I examine her, and I can't do that until I deem it safe. Right now it's not.

Turning on the lights at this exposed location would be the same as doing it inside a glass house. Anyone around us will have a ringside seat, and as I spell this out, Marino agrees reluctantly.

"We'll start with photographs. We'll get the lay of the land," I say as we continue to discuss what makes the most sense. "I'm sure the truck will be here any minute."

"But it will be another good twenty or thirty minutes after that with all the setting up to be done." Marino is halfway inside the back of his SUV, using his phone flashlight to illuminate the precisely arranged and packed crime-scene accoutrements and equipment. "And it's going to be hard as hell to see in the meantime." His voice is muffled inside as he roots around. "And my damn night vision's not what it used to be either. It's like everything turns to shit the minute you hit forty."

I stare through the velvety darkness at the river flowing sluggishly like liquid dark glass. Marino hasn't seen forty in a while, and when he gets like this there's not much I can say. But I don't blame him. I would be licking my wounds too if I'd just been duped the way he was.

"Getting old sucks," he gripes, and I know when he's feeling belittled and obsessive. "I hate it. I freakin' hate it," he adds, and the Interpol impostor has done a number on him.

"You're not old, Marino." I've heard enough, and we have a lot to take care of. "You're in great shape and weren't born yesterday. You're experienced. So am I, and we know exactly what to do out here. We've worked far more difficult scenes than this. Forget about the phone call for now. Put it out of your mind. I promise we'll get to the bottom of it. But that's not what should be preoccupying you at the moment."

He continues digging around inside his truck, and I begin my scan as if I'm a lighthouse sweeping everything around me, looking for what needs to be protected or ignored. Since we don't know what happened and exactly where, we'll start well outside the perimeter the police will have secured.

I can't see any yellow tape from where we're parked, but I have a pretty good idea it begins at the clearing where a dead body and a bicycle await us. But if this is a case of violence involving the perpetrator and victim physically encountering each other, then the clearing isn't where the scene begins. It can't be. And Marino is thinking the same thing.

"Whoever did it had to get in and out of here somehow," he says. "Unless it's a damn elf that lives in a tree."

"Assuming Investigator Barclay's description of the body has even a semblance of truth?" I reply. "If she really were assaulted and beaten? Then yes, her assailant or someone involved had to access the park. Whether she was killed here or dumped, the person was in and out, and we can't assume he didn't take the same route we're about to. I'm not saying it's a *he*."

"Yeah I know." Marino hands me a box of extra-large nitrile gloves that he'll use and I won't. "But if it was a sexual assault or an attempt, we're probably talking about a male. I'm already looking for tire tracks, especially gouges and flattened areas of grass. So far I'm not seeing it, but he could have entered the park a number of different ways."

"A lot of streets dead-end here and along the river," I point out. "And there's no wall obviously, so he could have been parked in a variety of nearby locations. But from there how did he get the body in here?"

"Carried it." Marino is shoving heavy cases of equipment around in the back.

"I doubt it."

"I didn't say that's what I think. I'm just saying it's possible."

"How would that explain her bicycle being near her body?" I ask.

"Exactly, because I think we already know she wasn't dumped." He tears open a cardboard box. "She was murdered right where she was found." He hands me one folded pair of disposable coveralls, still in the cellophane package, size double-XL.

"Let's be reminded that we don't know that she was murdered." I watch him and I constantly look around. "We have no idea why she's dead."

Lights reflected in the water's slow current flicker like a vast school of silvery fish, and on the other side, Boston is a glittering empire of centuries-old stone and brick, and modern high-rises. But almost no ambient light dispels the darkness immediately around us, and I dig into my messenger bag for the small tactical flashlight I always carry. I force the box of gloves, the coveralls to fit inside so my hands are free.

"We have to establish the perimeter," Marino says. "We've got to start somewhere but as dark as it is? We're pretty much guessing."

"That's why we start here. We'll look where we're going and get an overview," I reply, and I deeply regret what I'm wearing.

I might have to burn this suit when I finally scrape it off me. I don't enjoy disposable clothing that swathes me in bright white Tyvek rather much like a building under construction. But right about now I find myself coveting, almost lusting for, a loose-fitting pair of coveralls and lightweight ankle boots.

"We can mark anything we see with cones or flags and then come back a second time once we have the luxury of time, privacy, and appropriate visibility," I continue the discussion with Marino. "I'm assuming you talked about barriers with Rusty or Harold? I know we have the basics in our big trucks, but there's nothing basic about this situation. The scene is wide open from virtually every angle and perspective once we turn on the lights."

"I told Harold we're going to need more than the usual walls that we prop up with a few sandbags to make sure people can't see shit from street level." Marino slides a big scene case to the lip of the open tailgate. "But for something like this, you got that right. We're going to need a tent because you got all kinds of people looking down at us from buildings and the bridge."

I glance up at the long string of headlights moving above us, crossing the river in both directions. I watch aircraft lit up like small planets, clustered around Logan Airport, and I think of Dorothy again. Marino digs in a box of evidence-marking cones in bright primary colors, each of them numbered. He stacks a dozen of them, and it always reminds me of the Cap the Hat board game that my father found at a yard sale in our Miami neighborhood when I was a little kid.

"I said we want a roof," Marino tells me what he told Harold. "I said we're going to need the full monty out here."

CHAPTER 14

WE FOLLOW THE SAME dirt footpath we just drove over, gradually veering off it and into the grass. Dry and several inches deep, it whispers against my shoes and tickles my bare ankles as we watch where we step, moving deeper into the wooded park, toward the hard-packed sandy fitness path that winds through the middle of it.

The tall iron lamps are few and far between. They would offer little more than vague yellowish smudges as you sit on a bench or take a stroll at night. It's very dark in here, and I have my small tactical light while Marino has his phone flashlight pointed out and slightly down.

In his other hand he tugs the heavy-duty black plastic scene case that's big enough for a small body. Its wheels make a quiet gritty crunch as he rolls it along, leading the way, both of us careful not to trample evidence or stumble. So far we haven't seen anything that might make us stop and plant a small colorful cone.

The parched grass is a carpet of brownish-green sharp little blades in the glare of our lights, and my scuffed tan leather shoes are vivid. I can hear fragments of conversation up ahead, what sounds like children talking in excited quiet voices. It's not a happy excitement but a different brand of cortisol-fueled enthusiasm that I associate with fear, with shock. But there's something else I'm picking up. The childish sounds don't strike me as normal.

They bring to mind haunted places with otherworldly conversations that drift on the air in creepy tales. Here, then gone, the laughter of dead children frolicking in the woods, of dead children picking berries and playing hide-and-seek or tag.

The peculiar disembodied voices in the distance ahead remind me of horror movies, and I feel a chill touch the back of my neck as the park spreads out darkly, peacefully, on either side of the fitness path where someone has died. Someone I may have met twice earlier today, and I continue to hope I'm mistaken.

We approach a clump of trees with full canopies that offers a perfect place for a predator to lie in wait. Marino points this out to me as we walk deeper inside shadows where the dead and the living are gathered, waiting for us. It feels uncanny and weird as if we're headed to a surprise party where everyone crouches in the dark until the guest of honor appears and the lights switch on.

I remember the early years when we really didn't have to worry about cameras everywhere and huge indiscretions trending on the Internet before I can finish an autopsy or get lab results. In the old days every Tom, Dick and Harry weren't filming with cell phones. By the time photo journalists showed up with telescopic lenses, the body was either gone, safely zipped up in a pouch, or detectives would be gathered around holding up sheets or their coats to protect a victim's privacy. Life and death are much more complicated now.

"I don't think this was random," Marino is saying. "Someone knew her patterns."

"Do we know if she had patterns?" It's my way of cautioning him again about jumping to conclusions, but it's a waste of breath.

"Everybody has patterns," he says, and I listen as I wait for Rusty and Harold to rumble up in our diesel mobile command center.

I'm wondering where they're going to park it and what commotion it's going to generate in the very lap of Eliot House. Looming over the park is one of the biggest housing complexes on the campus with its seven brick buildings and numerous courtyards that remind me of Oxford and Cambridge or the palace of Versailles. I imagine students peering out their windows and venturing outside.

The truck will be spotted immediately, and if people zoom in or get closer they'll see OFFICE OF THE CHIEF MEDICAL EXAMINER and the CFC crest and Massachusetts state seal on the doors. I expect that any minute the Harvard campus will begin waking up to the stunningly sad realization that someone has been killed virtually under its proverbial nose. The second we turn on the lights we're going to need more uniforms for crowd control.

"Because there's nothing to stop people from ducking under the tape," I say to Marino as we inch our way through the woods. "There's nothing to stop traffic on the bridge from detouring so people can drive through the park to rubberneck. This could become a major fiasco pretty fast."

"I'll bring in more units when we're ready," he says, and I begin to make out the scene materializing several hundred feet ahead. "If I make the request now? A squadron of cars roll in and only draw more attention. The minute the tent's up, I'll request backups, as many as it takes."

I count the silhouettes of the six battery-powered LED spotlights that have been set up on tripods. They're perched about like tall praying mantises, quiet and dark as if sleeping.

I see the shapes of uniformed cops milling around, talking in the hushed way people do when it's dark. The sound of childish voices is an indistinct and perplexing staccato in the impenetrable background. I can't determine the source but it's eerie, as if the dark wooded area is haunted by agitated sprites.

Marino and I duck under the yellow perimeter tape, which is where I thought it would be. We enter a clearing in the trees where the body is half on the path, and half on the grass. I can make out the paleness of her bare arms and legs, and the whiteness of her sports bra and light color of her shorts. She's on her back with her legs straight but splayed, her arms up and spread as if she's been positioned in an X.

What I see sends a mixed message of mockery, of sexual degradation—and also nothing like that. At first glance it seems she's been displayed to shock whoever discovers her, but it's unusual that her shorts and bra are still on. Typically when a body is lewdly, hatefully displayed it's nude. Often other contemptuous touches are inserted and added to further disgrace and disfigure, and I'm not seeing anything like that yet.

But I've also learned the hard way to be overly conservative about making assumptions based on previous cases I've worked. A detail in one death may mean something else entirely in another. As we get closer I make out that the bicycle is on its side in the middle of the unpaved gritty path. I recognize the tall broad-shouldered Cambridge investigator Tom Barclay off to one side, near the trees, about fifty feet from the body. The spritelike voices I've been hearing belong to the two girls he's with, and they look too young to be out alone at this hour. But it's hard to tell.

They could be ten or twelve or maybe slightly older, and they're identical twins, one in pink, the other in yellow. Restless like two plump little birds, they turn their heads in synchrony, their eyes darting about, and it's obvious there's something not quite right about them. As we approach I can see that Barclay is shining a light on whatever he's holding. He's asking a question I can't quite hear.

"I might have," the girl dressed in pink drawls loudly in the voice of one who doesn't hear very well as she peers at what Barclay is showing the two of them on his phone, and Marino and I get closer.

"I don't know. Usually there's lots of people and I stay out of the way of bikes," the girl in yellow says slowly in the same blunted tone, and no matter what I was told, I can't quite believe what I'm seeing in the uneven illumination, the chiaroscuro created by our flashlights.

During one of our badly connected phone conversations as Marino was on his way to pick me up, he mentioned twins. I didn't give it much thought but to stand before them especially under the circumstances is extremely disconcerting. I find myself literally doing a double take as I look from one to the other, both of them dark-haired with identical unflattering helmetlike cuts.

The matching unstylish glasses they have on remind me of yearbook pranks, of inking nerdy black frames on the face of a rival's photograph. The girls are built the same, under five feet tall and heavy. They wear striped T-shirts, shorts and sandals that fortunately for me don't match. If the twins weren't wearing different colored clothing I'm not sure I could tell them apart.

"Wait here, okay? You know what to do, don't you? You stay right here and don't go anywhere. Stay. And I'll be back." Barclay talks to the girls as if they're a lower order of a pet such as a rabbit or a lizard.

He strides toward us, and I check my phone to see if there's any word from Rusty and Harold.

I HEAR THE TRUCK as I'm about to call, and I press END.

The rumble of the diesel engine is unmistakable, and I look back in the direction of John F. Kennedy Street. I can see headlights cutting through the park as a white CFC truck that's bigger than an ambulance bumps off the pavement and creeps under trees. The low-hanging branches scrape the boxy metal roof, making a terrible screeching sound that has the effect of nails on a chalkboard.

"Good. Maybe we can get going here so we can figure out who we need to be notifying and talking to," Barclay says too authoritatively as he reaches Marino and me. "The sooner we can process the scene and get the body to the morgue, the better," he adds as Marino ignores him.

My eyes have adjusted to the contrasting shades of light and shadow, and I can better make out the twins some distance from us where Barclay was a moment ago. A female uniformed officer is with them now, asking if they need water or food. She wants to know if they'd like to wait in an air-conditioned patrol car. She says it as if they've been asked this before, and they shake their heads no. I have a pretty good idea what will happen next.

In a while she's going to transport them to the department and place them in a daisy room, as police call a comfortable nonthreatening setting they use for interviews with children. A counselor will be in to talk to and evaluate the girls, but the female officer isn't going to mention that out here in the middle of the park.

She's not going to explain that the twins will be treated the same way abused children are, and I can't help but feel judgmental. It's not appropriate for me to have personal opinions about cases I work, but it's inevitable some things are going to hit me harder than others. I'm not good with bad parents, bad caretakers and bad pet owners.

The twin sisters are young and impaired, and what sort of person would allow them to be out and about unchaperoned, especially after dark? Is anybody wondering why they aren't home and where they are?

"We can turn on the lights whenever you're ready," Barclay tells us rather than asks.

"The problem, Clay, is the minute we do it's like we've lit up a baseball field," Marino answers in an artificial avuncular tone, as if the young investigator is dim-witted and useless but a nice enough boy. "And if you build it, they'll sure as hell come. So nope, Clay."

Marino says the name every chance he gets. "Not yet, right Doc?" He looks at me.

"Flashlights only for now," I agree, and the diesel sound gets louder, then stops as the engine is cut. "It's going to be difficult enough when people start noticing our mobile command center parked out here in addition to all the police cars." I look at the twins watching us with owl eyes. "It's pretty obvious there's something going on, and I don't want to draw attention until we can set up a barrier."

I explain that right now the body is exposed to anyone who happens by or trains a telescopic lens on it. I can't turn the lights on, and I can't work without them, and it's a familiar catch-22. I wouldn't think of examining the body in situ without lighting if I'm given the choice, and I can't cover her with a sheet before I examine her or I run the risk of disturbing or displacing evidence. So for the moment we're stuck in the dark with only flashlights, and my attention wanders back to the twins again. I can't stop looking at them.

I'm keenly aware of their disproportionately small heads, their thin upper lips and flat midfaces. They probably won't get much taller, will have an ongoing struggle with their weight, and their small eyes are spaced far apart like a nonpredatory animal, a horse or a giraffe. The thick glasses, hearing aids, the silver braces on their teeth and everything else indicate a catastrophic failure that likely happened in utero.

Possibly it was due to what the unborn twins were exposed to, and if what I suspect is correct, it's unspeakably tragic. It's careless and cruel. Fetal alcohol syndrome is preventable. Just don't drink during pregnancy, and I wonder if the two girls are in special classes in school. I worry how functional they are, and what obstacles we face in using them as witnesses in this case.

I wonder how much I can rely on what they tell me now about how they happened upon the body and what they might have tampered with. Are they cogent? Are they truthful? And what kind of parents or guardians would allow them to wander about at night or at all?

I feel anger stir like an ember glowing hotly when it's fanned. Then Barclay is next to Marino and me, showing us the photograph on his phone of Elisa Vandersteel's driver's license.

"That's what I found on the path," Barclay says proudly, as if he discovered the smoking gun. "Obviously, I didn't pick it up. I thought I'd wait until you got here." He directs this to Marino as I look at the photograph on the phone display.

Elisa Ann Vandersteel. DOB: 12–04–1998. London, and the post code is the exclusive area of Mayfair, on South Audley Street near the Dorchester Hotel and the American embassy. The photograph could be the woman I encountered twice earlier today, but I'm not certain.

I'm not going to say anything to Marino or anybody else until I have more information. Any sightings of the victim are important in determining when she died, and I'm mindful of being cautious about what I pass along without verification. Not that driver's-license portraits are very good in general, but in this one Elisa Vandersteel is heavier than the cyclist I met. The face in the picture is broader, and the brown hair is short, whereas the young woman in Converse sneakers was lean and had a ponytail. But we don't know how old the photograph is. She might look very different now.

"Anything else?" I ask. "Any other personal effects. A lot of cyclists have bike packs or saddlebags for their wallets, keys and other belongings."

. I don't add that I don't remember seeing something like that when I encountered the cyclist on Quincy Street. But Barclay says he didn't see a bag of any sort attached to the bicycle or nearby.

"That doesn't mean there wasn't one," he adds. "It might have been stolen by whoever did this."

"And we don't know if this is a homicide." I'm just going to keep saying it. "We don't know anything yet." I return his phone to him.

"How many people have you had to chase off since you got here?" Marino asks him what's gone on since the call was broadcast over radio.

"A handful have wandered in or tried to."

"How close did they get?" Marino has yet to really look at him while they talk.

"They didn't get anywhere near."

"At least not the ones we know about." Marino abruptly walks off in the direction of the twins.

"A couple of students, three to be exact," Barclay tells his retreating back. "I turned them away before they could see anything. They couldn't see there's a dead body," he directs this at me, and I wonder what he was doing before he showed up here.

CHAPTER 15

HE'S SLEEK AND QUITE an eyeful in parachute pants, a polo shirt, and leather high-tops, everything black.

His pistol is holstered on his right hip, his detective's badge displayed on his belt, and Investigator Barclay looks like the star of his own TV show with his lean muscular build, Ken-doll face and buzz-cut blond hair. I can smell his cologne from several feet away, and I know his type, what we used to call a hotshot.

Marino has cruder terms for vain young bucks like Clay, as he hails him. I can't imagine the two of them are friendly with each other or would be under any circumstances imaginable. As this is going through my mind I have second thoughts about Barclay's nickname. Or better put, something comes to me as a warning.

"Does everybody call you Clay?" I ask, but what I'm really wondering is if anybody does besides Marino.

"I don't know why he suddenly started doing that unless it's to tick me off as usual." He watches Marino talking to the twins. "My first name's Tom, my middle name's David. People call me Tom. It's just another one of his stupid jokes that he thinks are so brilliant. I guess his point is to encourage other corny bullshit. First it's *Clay*. Then it's *Dirt*. Or *Play-Doh*. Or if I do something wrong my name will be

Mud. But it goes with the turf when you get promoted to working major cases." He shrugs. "You get picked on."

Barclay continues to nail Marino with a stare, and Marino continues talking to the twins as if he's oblivious. But he's not. The sophomoric jokes, the juvenile behavior are a special skill set of his, and he has the acumen of a hawk. He doesn't miss Barclay's slightest twitch, and it's a good thing I didn't call him Clay. Marino would have thought that was hilarious, and it may very well be that he's the only one who's ever called him that.

But chances are good that Marino won't be the last. Unfortunately when he comes up with a nickname or new "handle" for someone, there's no undoing it. I wouldn't be surprised if soon enough everyone in the Cambridge Police Department was talking to and about Clay Barclay, as if the lame redundancy really is his name.

"How you doing, Doctor Scarpetta?" He's boisterous and too friendly as if we've just run into each other at a reception or in a crowded bar.

"Thanks for doing a good job keeping things quiet out here . . ." I start to say.

"If this was in daylight can you imagine a more exposed spot?" He watches me dig in my bag for a notepad and a pen. "Not to mention working a scene when it's over a hundred degrees. At least it's a cool eighty-eight now."

I'm methodical and not in a hurry as I pull out Marino's package of coveralls and the box of gloves. I set them on top of his nearby scene case. Then I walk back to Barclay, my tactical light pointed down at the grass with each step.

"I'll take the ambient temperature as soon as the truck is here," I let him know, and the real point I'm making is he needs to be careful about throwing around information the way he's been doing.

I'm mindful that he's already gone out on a limb by deciding the victim is Elisa Vandersteel when identity hasn't been confirmed by DNA, dental records or any other legitimate means. And an ID found on the fitness path in a public park isn't a confirmation. Not even close.

He's also said she's an assault, a murder, and I can't know any such thing when I've not so much as looked at her yet. Possibly most dangerous is what he's also passed along to at least one person—Marino—that the body is as stiff as a mannequin. In other words, it's in an advanced stage of rigor mortis. That directly impacts the estimated time of death, and I wish Barclay had kept his opinion to himself.

These are the sorts of seemingly benign mistakes that can haunt you in court, and time of death is especially tricky. It's not an exact science but is crucial to any alibi. It's a favorite bone for defense attorneys to chew on, and how quickly strangers can lose faith in what an expert witness like me testifies. I have no intention of causing jurors to doubt my credibility because an inexperienced detective thought he could do my job for me at a death scene.

While it was appropriate for Barclay to check that the victim was actually deceased, he shouldn't have begun playing the role of a medical examiner by making determinations about rigor mortis and how advanced it is or isn't. He needs to be careful about information he finds on the Internet. He shouldn't accept as gospel what the temperature in Cambridge is based on a weather app.

What part of Cambridge? There could be quite a difference between a shady spot near the water and the hot bricks of Harvard Square, for example.

"I'm assuming you got the temperature from some sort of app on your phone," I say to Barclay after a silence I can tell he's eager to fill. "So the detail about it being eighty-eight degrees Fahrenheit or thirty-one degrees Celsius? We'll keep that out of any reports since we don't know what the temperature is in the exact location where the body was found."

"If you got a thermometer I can put it over there next to her," he says, and I realize how aggressive he is.

"No thanks. That's not what I was suggesting. I don't have my scene case yet, but when I do I'll handle any temperatures that need to be taken of the body, the ambient air, and all the rest." I speak slowly and in a measured tone, resorting to what I think of as my neutral voice. "It might be cooler here because of the river," I suggest as if it's no big deal.

But he knows it is. He feels disrespected and criticized, and I'm witness to his mood's rapid shift. It's something I suddenly remember observing about him on the few occasions I've been in his presence. He's volatile. He goes from hot to cold with not much in between.

"If only there was a breeze." He looks away from me, toward the river, and it's obvious when his narcissism is winged. "It's hard to breathe. Damn suffocating."

He's practically turned his back to me.

"WHAT TIME WAS THE body found?" I ask him that next, and he can keep his back to me the rest of the night if it makes him happy.

After a sulky silence Barclay says, "We got the call about forty-five minutes ago. But oh! Wait a minute!"

He turns around and feigns a eureka moment, flashing his white teeth in the dark.

"The time came from my phone." He throws a snarky dart, and it won't find its mark with me.

"Is that okay? Or should I trust my watch instead?" he asks, and I won't engage.

"The time I have written down for when I got the call is nineteen-oh-six-hundred hours." He says it as if I won't know what that is.

I jot it down. "Twenty-three-twenty Zulu time. Twenty minutes past seven EDST." Then I ask, "How was the call classified when it was broadcast? What was said exactly? Because it would seem the media isn't aware of anything yet."

"It came in as a ten-seventeen." He waits for me to ask him what that is, but I know the police ten-codes probably as well as he does.

I've been hearing them my entire career, and a 10-17 is common. It literally means "meet complainant."

"I'm assuming it was about the twin sisters," I interpolate, and Barclay stares at me as I think, *What a dick.*

He says nothing went out over the air that might alert reporters monitoring Boston-area law enforcement radio frequencies. This continues to argue against Marino's suspicious phone call being from anyone legitimately involved in the case. It would seem Barclay absolutely didn't contact Interpol's National Central Bureau in Washington, D.C. I have a feeling that Marino's right. The inexperienced investigator probably wouldn't think of it and might not even know what the NCB is. Not every cop does.

Marino certainly didn't initiate the contact, and of course I didn't. It couldn't have been anyone at my office. We didn't know about the death at the time the alleged NCB investigator called Marino's cell phone. What's becoming more apparent is that the person responsible is someone up to no good, to understate the problem.

"I happened to be on Memorial Drive and got here in maybe three minutes max," Barclay then answers what I didn't ask about why he was the first responder or paid attention to a low-priority call.

Meeting a complainant suggests someone wants to talk to a police officer, usually to report a concern or upset of one sort or another. A general request like that could be about anything. Much of the time it's about nothing, and it surprises me that a detective would pay much attention to such a call unless it was specifically directed at him. But Barclay is new to the Major Case Squad. Maybe he's overly eager. Maybe he was bored.

"And the two girls who found her?" I ask, and I'm watching Marino talk to them out of earshot. "Are they students? Because they look too young for college."

From where I'm standing they're barely pubescent, and I'd hazard a guess neither is old enough to have a driver's permit.

"No, ma'am, they're not in college," Barclay says, and he flips through pages in his notebook. "They go to the school near Donnelly Field, in the eighth grade. Or that's what they told me and I got no reason to think they're making something up or hiding anything. Or that they knew the victim. They said they didn't."

These strike me as callous remarks to make about two girls who have been traumatized by a discovery that will stay with them the rest of their days. I wonder if he's implying that he briefly considered them suspects—if it crossed his thoughts that the twins might think it was a fun idea to ambush someone on a bicycle. I suppose anything is possible, and I notice his small flashlight is turned off. It's as if he's forgotten he has it, and he checks through his notes. He finds the page he wants as if he can see in the dark like a cat.

The girls live near the Highland Laundromat off Mount Auburn Street, he tells me as he loudly flips through pages. It makes sense that their route would have taken them from Harvard Square, along John F. Kennedy Street toward the river. The plan was to walk along the water through the park, then cut up Ash Street, which would take them home. All told the outing was just under a mile round trip.

"Usually they would cut over to Mount Auburn, which is more direct," Barclay explains what he gleaned from questioning the sisters. "But it's so hot they've been detouring through the shaded park and sticking near the water as much as possible."

"Why were they out at all?" I'm making notes.

"They said they were heading home from the Square, from Uno's, and I'm thinking who can eat pizza in this weather? I heard on the news this morning that in another day the heat will break. Then it's rain and we'll go straight to winter. You grew up in Miami, right? So I guess this weather's a piece of cake for you. Not me. This is way too hot for my thick blood."

I don't ask where he's from but it's probably not here, not originally. He has a trace of a midwestern accent.

"I've only been to Miami a couple times," he says, and I don't follow up on that either.

CHAPTER 16

HE WAITS TO SEE if I'll engage in small talk and banter, but I'm not interested. My attention keeps going back to Marino talking to the twins some distance away, angling his phone flashlight in a way that won't illuminate much to anyone who might be watching with binoculars or a telescopic lens.

But I recognize what he's doing. He wants to see the expression on the sisters' faces as he questions them, and I can tell that the girls find him reassuring. I intuit it by the way they gaze up at him. I sense it by how they cluster close to him beneath the dark canopy of a spreading oak tree as if they're passing through an evil forest and Marino is their guide.

"Anyway," Barclay says, pointing toward rhododendron bushes about twenty feet ahead of where we are, and to the left of the body. "You might want to be careful where you're walking around here and I don't mean because of any evidence we've not collected yet. But one of the girls got sick over there."

"When was that?"

"When I first got here, right as I was walking up. She was coming out of the bushes, wiping her mouth on the back of her hand and kind of glassy-eyed. I don't know which one or if she threw up or what. Trust me, that's one thing I decided not to investigate too closely."

"Do you know if either of them touched the body?" I get to the most important question. "What exactly did they tell you they did?" I glance at the time on my phone, and the glow from its display is bright like a TV screen in the dark.

It's 8:22 P.M., and I make a note of it.

"When I got here there was no one else around, and they weren't close, were at least twenty feet from her," Barclay says. "They were real shook up, and they said they didn't touch it. I must have asked them half a dozen times, and they said no. The closest they got to it was maybe a yard," he adds, holding his hands about three feet apart as if I can't envision what he's describing.

"It?" I ask.

"The dead lady."

He continues to regard the victim as an object while he treats me like a lesser mortal who has no right to be here. I'll take it a little longer. Then I'm going to share a few of my thoughts with him. I'm going to give him some free advice.

"They wandered close to check it out, and then retreated, were probably scared shitless," Barclay says. "They stayed back and called the police."

The girls have matching backpacks, and I have no idea what might be inside them. But at a glance I don't see that either of them has a phone.

"How did they call for help?" I ask.

"I don't know. Nine-one-one." It's his way of flipping me off.

"I'm aware that nine-one-one was called. My point is at least one of them must have a phone."

"I don't know. I didn't search them," he says. "But tell you what. When I get them in the daisy room and can distract them, I'll go through their backpacks. I guarantee their phones and who knows what else is in there."

I return him to the subject of the body being found, and he tosses out the same details I've already heard. The girls were walking home and noticed something ahead on the path.

"They got closer," Barclay says, "and at first they thought it was someone who'd been in a bad bike accident. Like it was getting dark and she ran into a lamppost or something, hitting her head so hard it knocked her helmet off. They could see blood and that she wasn't moving."

"What do you mean *at first*?" Before I talk to the twins I want an idea of how much he may have tainted them. "At first they thought she'd had a bike accident? That's what they said?"

"Well I doubt they think that now. They think somebody did something bad to her."

"How did they get a good enough look to notice blood and decide she was dead?" I ask, and if the girls suspect foul play it's probably because Barclay has his mind made up about what type of case this is.

He hasn't hesitated saying it's a homicide—a sexual one at that.

"It's extremely dark, and the shadows are especially thick where she is," I point out. "Do they have a flashlight? Because I don't know how they could have seen very much otherwise."

"Maybe in one of the backpacks. I don't know. They told me they were pretty sure she was dead. They said she smelled dead."

"That's interesting. Meaning what?"

"And they also said she smelled like a hair dryer." He smirks.

"I'm wondering what they meant by that," I reply, and he laughs.

"Who the hell knows? They're retarded, right?"

"It's not my job to test their IQs and I doubt it's yours either, and that's not a good word to use." I look on as Marino takes photographs and sets down a numbered cone, and it's all I can do not to blast Barclay but good. "The girls meant something by what they said," I add in my most reasonable tone. "It would be smart to figure out what it was instead of assuming they're talking nonsense."

"Probably what they were noticing was the blood. Blood plus heat equals an odor. Kind of a metallic smell? Like a hair dryer maybe? And her blood's going to be decomposing for sure in no time at all because of how hot it is."

"Unless you want to swap jobs with me, Investigator Barclay, that's another detail you really shouldn't be discussing." I glance back at the sound of footsteps and wheels rolling slowly along the gritty path.

"Another detail? As in more than one?" He might be flirting now. "But hell yeah. I'll swap jobs anytime. I've always thought I'd be a good doctor."

I DETECT LOW VOICES, and Rusty and Harold with all their gear and equipment are two floating lights and a shadowy caravan. I can just make them out as they enter the woods that lead to the clearing.

They wear hands-free headlamps like miners to light their way as they steer two trolleys. I don't have to see them to know they're loaded with a mountain of scene cases, boxes, sandbags, and the privacy barrier, which is disassembled and packed inside what looks like a stack of long black body bags. Tied down with bungee cords, the bulky dark shapes of the advancing cargo bring to mind a morbid Santa's sleigh as it lumbers closer. I send Harold a text:

Once inside the tape, begin to unload. Will check with you in a few.

"It should take no more than twenty minutes to get all this set up," I say to Barclay. "While this is going on Marino and I will do a walk-through, taking photos, getting an idea what we need to identify, protect and preserve before we assemble the barrier in place over the body. Once that's done we'll turn on the lights and I'll examine her inside an enclosure that affords us privacy."

"How big an area can it cover?" Barclay stares back at my transport team.

"Big enough to enclose the bike and the body," I explain. "What we're putting together is basically a tent. And if you've never been through this before, we have to take steps in a well-thought-out logical order so one procedure doesn't mess up another."

I watch the twins talking to Marino, and I look at the bicycle some twenty feet ahead of where I'm standing, and then the body a good ten feet beyond that. Usually when I conduct a high recon or preliminary walk-through I get the lay of the land and a good idea of what I'm dealing with. But what I'm seeing out here is a contradiction. It's haphazard, almost quirky, as if someone staged the scene but didn't have a clue what it should look like.

Had the victim fallen from her bicycle, her body wouldn't be ten feet from it. A bicycle can't throw you like a horse, and even if it could, what I'm seeing doesn't add up. Why is her helmet so far from where the bicycle went down? Even if her chin strap wasn't fastened, that still wouldn't explain it. How did she hit her head so hard as to be killed almost instantly, it seems. I also can't imagine that she died in the position she's in with her arms up, her legs wide, her knees and elbows barely bent as if she's in the middle of a jumping jack.

"You ready to take a look at her?" Barclay asks, and what I'd really like is for the overbearing new investigator to leave me alone with my thoughts for a moment.

"And it goes without saying that you didn't disturb the body. You didn't move it." I click my pen closed and ask in the way of a coda.

"I said I didn't. I checked her vitals, and it sure seems like she's been dead for a while."

"Her vitals? Where?"

"Her wrist. I'm pretty sure it was her right one. I picked it up to check for a pulse, and her arm was stiff. That was it. That was all I did. Like I keep telling everybody I didn't move her," he says, and I wonder who *everybody* is.

I suppose Marino could constitute a crowd all by himself when he's after someone.

"When the squad got here did you tell them you were sure she'd been dead for a while?"

"I gave them my opinion. I said she was already stiff, and yeah she was warm because you could fry a freakin' egg out here."

"One thing you really should keep in mind, Investigator Barclay, is it's important not to be the origin of unsubstantiated opinions." As a parting gesture I offer him a piece of my mind, a free moment of mentoring that he's certain not to appreciate.

"No matter how well intended your opinions may be," I add in a quiet voice that means business, "be very careful before you speak. I don't care what you're told or what you see. I don't care what you're absolutely certain you believe. Think twice. Think three or four times."

"I have a right to my opinion—" he starts in, and I cut him off.

"Not if it has to do with science, medicine or some other area that's not your expertise. I advise that you report your observations but don't interpret or make decisions based on them." I don't take my eyes off him. "Because loose talk and misinformation are fodder for lawyers."

"I'm just telling you she's stiff and therefore been dead awhile . . ."

"Paralysis can make someone stiff. That doesn't mean the person's dead. Again, please don't interpret or offer your opinions—especially not medical or forensic ones."

"Since I'm the one who witnessed it, that makes what I'm saying a fact, not an opinion," he fires like a loaded bowstring. "And maybe there's an odor. I might have smelled rotting blood." After a hostile pause he takes the next shot. "And now I'm getting what all the chatter was about. All the shit that was on the radio earlier."

I don't ask him what he means. I have a feeling I know as I'm unpleasantly reminded of the 911 complaint about my supposedly fighting with Bryce and disturbing the peace. Maybe Barclay knows all about it. Maybe everyone in his department does. I conclude my business with him by asking that he wait over there, and by that I mean a healthy distance from me.

He stalks off toward Marino and the twins, and the dashing investigator whose name isn't Clay doesn't like me. It couldn't be more apparent. Not that I particularly care. Marino walks in my direction. He crouches by the big black plastic Pelican case he rolled from his SUV.

"You need to keep your eye on him." I say it under my breath. "Because he's brand-new and already he doesn't think he answers to anyone. An attitude like that will get only worse."

"I got his number more than you know." Marino moves around the case unsnapping clasps. "He's got a weird thing with older women, some fucked-up mother complex. I'm just giving you fair warning."

"I remind him of his mother?"

"An aunt, a mother. Because you're older than him."

"That doesn't mean I remind him of his mother or aunt or anyone else for that matter."

"I'm just telling you he thinks he's a gift to women but unlike yours truly here he doesn't like them. Not really." He opens the lid of the case.

Inside is a supply closet of forensic necessities perfectly organized and neatly packed. He finds a camera and a large flashlight with a detachable shoulder strap. Then he pulls disposable booties over his shoes, and he works a pair of gloves over his huge hands.

"I know these will swallow you, Doc." He hands me a pair of booties and gloves.

I ask him for two rubber bands to adjust the booties, making them half the size so I don't walk out of them or step on my own feet. I pull on the extra-large gloves and have inches of room to spare in the floppy purple nitrile fingers.

"Let's go," he says, and we move on to the second stage, the inner perimeter, not bothering with other protective clothing, not yet.

There's no risk of contamination if we're careful not to step on or disturb anything. With rare exceptions we won't collect evidence until the inner scene is protected and the lights are on. We start in the clearing, using our flashlights to sweep the gritty swath in front of us, and the trees and grass on either side.

With each step Marino stops as if he sees something. He leans closer, grunts softly, indicating it's nothing, and he takes photographs. I hear the constant whir of the shutter. The blinding bursts of the flashgun are disorienting as we continue our well-practiced synchronized approach. It's a deeply ingrained procedure, like the proper way to hit a tennis stroke, and we rarely need to coach each other anymore.

"Stop," I say to him as the silhouette of an unlit lamppost materializes in the dark up ahead, close to the overturned bicycle at the outer rim of the clearing, just before the woods begin again.

The lantern on top of the black iron pole is out, and we shine our lights at it, discovering a glass pane is wide open, the bulbs inside shattered. Bits of broken glass flash and flare as we probe the grass, and splinters sparkle all around the bike.

"From this perspective, it almost seems it might have crashed into the lamppost," I comment. "Maybe what Barclay suggested is right."

"He's never right," Marino snipes.

Perhaps the person riding couldn't see and had an accident. But that wouldn't explain the destroyed lightbulbs inside a lantern some ten feet off the ground. It wouldn't explain why the body isn't nearby.

"Got no idea." Marino stares up at the dark metal frame of the lantern at the top of the lamppost. "Maybe somebody opened the access pane and smashed the bulbs."

"It's weird that the glass is blown all over the place. How would that happen if you opened the pane and smashed the bulbs? And unless you're a giant I don't think you could reach the lantern to unlatch it."

"I'm thinking the same thing. How come the glass is blown everywhere? The bulbs couldn't have been shot out or the outer glass panes would be broken, and I don't see how a rock could do it unless you were up on a ladder and used it to smash the bulbs." He shines his light around, looking for one anyway. "But to be honest, we don't know for sure when the damage happened."

"I wouldn't expect the park to leave a broken light out here for very long," I reply.

"Well it sure as hell makes it darker in this immediate area where she went down on her bike when she got attacked," he says as we probe nonstop with our lights. "So maybe some psycho smashed out the lamp. Maybe he shimmied up the lamppost, who the hell knows, and then waited for her or some other victim. That's exactly what it's looking like, meaning this was premeditated."

"Or maybe the light was already out and she had an accident." Not that I think this at all, but I'm reminding him to be cautious about locking one idea or another into his mind. "We don't know for a fact that she was assaulted," and I've said this multiple times but nobody seems to be listening.

Another step, and another, then one more until we're about four feet from the bicycle on its side. The body is some ten feet from it, and already I can see the drag marks.

"Dammit!" I mutter, and regardless of what Barclay claimed, I had a feeling this was what I'd find. "She's been moved."

CHAPTER 17

THEY'RE EASY TO DISCERN when you're accustomed to looking for disturbances in soil or foliage. It's second nature for me to scan for anything that might suggest an area was trampled on and disturbed either accidentally or deliberately.

The drag marks indicate the body was moved but not much, and that's another oddity to add to a list of them. Her upper body is in the grass. Her hips and legs are on the path, and I can see the displacement of the gritty surface that begins inches from the backs of her low-cut socks. What immediately comes to mind is at least one person began pulling her and either was interrupted or stopped for some other reason. And I wonder what happened to her shoes.

Her shoes like her shirt seem to be missing, assuming she was wearing them prior to her death. Maybe they're out here somewhere, I decide. There may be quite a lot of things we find once we have proper lighting, and I envision the cyclist in the blue helmet again.

I remember her sneakers. I've been hoping the dead woman isn't wearing Converse. I can't be sure since something has happened to her shoes. She's not wearing a blue paisley bandanna or gold necklace like the cyclist was. But something could have happened to those too, and it's an act of will not to take a close look right now, to stride right up and satisfy an unbearable curiosity mixed with dread.

I could get inches from her. I could shine my flashlight on her face to see if it's the woman with the British accent. And if both of them are Elisa Vandersteel. But I know better. I need to work my way to the body one little piece at a time, patiently, carefully. Pretending I don't know what might be up ahead in the dark. Pretending not to care. I'm not supposed to have feelings or reactions about anyone I take care of or investigate but of course I do.

I glance back at the distant racket of Harold and Rusty unloading the trolleys and unzipping the big black vinyl bags. I hear the low murmur of the two of them talking.

"Do you mind?" I trade my small tactical light for Marino's big one.

I crouch down in the middle of the path, looking all around, making sure I don't compromise or interfere with whatever might be out here. The turbo six-thousand-lumen light is made of metal and weighs several pounds. It has a wide lens with six LEDs, and the brilliant beam paints over the path, igniting hard-packed sandy minerals like quartz and silica.

They sparkle like something alive wherever the light touches, and bits and slivers of broken glass flicker and flare when I illuminate the area around and under the bicycle. I do this slowly, thoughtfully, and I pay attention. Once a scene has been entered and intruded upon, there's no going back. There's no undoing it, and when possible I take all the time I need no matter how much it might irritate everyone else. I point the light past the bike, another ten feet to the body.

I can see more clearly where her heels dragged through the loose surface as she was pulled a short distance; at most eight inches, it looks like from here. I can only suppose this must be what Investigator Barclay misinterpreted as evidence of a struggle. She has on grayish-looking footie-type socks similar to what the cyclist had on but I won't be able to tell until I get closer.

"I'm not sure what's happened out here but I'm not liking it," I say to Marino. "Something's very off about this. It's as if her bike went down right here where the lamp's access pane is open, the bulbs shattered and glass everywhere. Yet her body's over there? And I doubt she rode a bike in her socks. I need to get closer. If you don't mind hanging back for a minute, and keep taking pictures." I get up from my crouched position.

I make scraping sounds as I move about in my ill-fitting jerry-rigged shoe covers. I direct the beam along the path, following it to the body, and from several feet away I see the long brown hair is in disarray. I see her attractive young face with its turned-up nose and delicate chin, her pale skin, the dirt on her parted lips, and her eyes staring dully through barely open lids. The sunglasses she had on earlier are missing, assuming the dead woman and the cyclist I met are one and the same.

I'm increasingly convinced they could be, and that's thinking of it conservatively. That's not including what my gut is telling me. In the intense light I can see that the shorts are light blue, and there are pinstripes in the socks. Soaked into the grass under her neck is blood. From where I am I don't see a lot of it, and I don't notice bruises, lacerations or other injuries to her face. Only dirt and vegetable debris, as if she took a tumble.

But the position of her arms is telling. They're over her head, widespread and palm up, and that corroborates my growing conviction that she was pulled by her wrists. It never ceases to amaze me what people don't think about in the uproar of the moment. It would have been simple to brush away the drag marks and position the body, making it not quite so obvious what was done after the fact. I glance at the twins again, and their faces are riveted to me. I have a bad feeling they're lying.

They claim they didn't get near the body, no closer than three feet, according to Barclay. But somebody did. It may have been more than one person. There may have been two people of similar strength and each one of them pulled the dead woman by an arm, then stopped. I wonder again about the helmet some twenty feet away, upside down in the grass like a beached turtle. Did someone toss it there? What happened to her shoes and shirt? What about sunglasses, a necklace, a bandanna? If she had them, where are they?

I paint the light over the bicycle as I slowly make my way around it. I look for damage to the tires, the white frame with blue accents and a racing stripe, and the gel seat. I don't notice dents or scrapes. But the black plastic phone holder clamped to the flat handlebars is empty. The clamp that would have held a phone in place has been released. There's no phone in sight, and I get that feeling again, only more strongly. It comes back as a pang in my stomach accompanied by a sinking sensation, and I take a deep, slow breath.

I try to control my thoughts about the woman I encountered twice today as I brace myself for an inevitability that's crashing over me like a tidal wave. The bike's definitely familiar. I didn't have a reason to study in detail what she was riding but I'm certain there were blue markings on a light-colored or white frame. I remember noticing the blue was the same shade of robin's-egg blue as the helmet she had on, and my light picks it up again in the grass near a Japanese maple tree.

"That's just weird," I say to Marino, and I envision the face of Elisa Vandersteel in the ID I just looked at. "The helmet's some twenty feet from the body. Why?" I ask.

"It could have happened when she resisted, maybe tried to run from whoever grabbed her," he proposes, but so far I'm not seeing evidence that she fought anyone or ran anywhere.

"Or did the sisters toss it there, and if so why?" I reply. "And it would seem unlikely that they would remove the victim's shirt, but where is it? Where are her shoes?"

I don't mention the phone, bandanna, the necklace or the sunglasses, because I wouldn't know about them if I'd never seen the woman before. I'm not ready to introduce the subject to Marino. If it's even remotely possible I'm mistaken about having met the victim earlier, it could launch him in the wrong direction. It could hurt the case in court. I shine the light and comment that the area around the bicycle and the body aren't very disturbed except for the drag marks.

"I see nothing so far including blood that might indicate there was a pursuit or a struggle," I'm explaining. "But what I do see isn't making sense as I continue to point out. It's chaotic."

Then my light flicks past what looks like two shiny threads curled on the path inches from each other.

THE SEGMENTS ARE SIX or seven inches long, and I realize what we've found is a delicate gold chain that's been forcibly broken into pieces.

"Possibly part of a necklace," I say to Marino as I look back at the overturned bicycle.

It's close by, several yards behind us, and I scan the path around the broken chain, looking for any sign of a confrontation, a struggle. But the tan unpaved surface is smooth and undisturbed as if nothing dramatic happened here.

"A necklace someone ripped off, and it doesn't look like it's been out here long." Marino sets down another tiny evidence marker, a blue cone with the number 7. "I wonder if something was on it, a locket, a cross or whatever that might have looked valuable. Or maybe it was taken as a souvenir."

"Possibly," I reply, and I sweep the area around the pieces of the chain, looking for a pendant, ring, lucky charm, anything at all that might have been part of a necklace.

A skull, for example, like the cyclist had on. It was hard to miss when we met at the box office and then again on the sidewalk. I noticed a necklace with a gold skull, a cartoonish whimsical one. I remember she flipped it around to her back as she pedaled off, making sure the dangling chunk of metal was out of her way and didn't hit her in the teeth as she rode, I can only suppose.

As I walk through the grass I don't see her shirt, and I remember it was a beige tank top, a Sara Bareilles tour souvenir from several years earlier, I'm pretty sure. I see nothing like that. But I finally find her sneakers scattered, one here, the other way over there, off-white Converse, the laces still tied in bows as if she literally were scared out of her shoes.

I may not be sure of her name but I have little doubt that she's the cyclist I saw earlier at the theater and then in front of the Faculty Club, and I keep myself in check. I can't react to it. I can't give any indication I have a personal reaction to anything I'm doing out here. And I make a decision as we set down cones, making notes and taking photographs. It's time to give Marino a heads-up.

"I can't prove this," I say to him, "and I'm not sure it matters. But I may have seen her earlier tonight."

"You're shitting me." He stops walking and stares at me as if I have five heads.

I briefly explain it to him, starting with my encounter at the American Repertory Theater, and then later in front of the Faculty Club.

"Benton and I both met her on the sidewalk," I add. "And this would have been about six forty-five as the sun was setting. But it wasn't dark yet."

"If that's who it is then she couldn't have been dead very long when the girls found her," he says. "We got the nine-one-one call at about seven thirty."

"Which is why what Barclay said is illogical," I answer. "If she'd been dead less than an hour when he checked for a pulse, she shouldn't have been in full rigor or even an easily discernible stage of it."

I glance back at the twin sisters, and their attention is all over the place as Barclay talks to them. I'm reminded that they aren't as comfortable with him as they were with Marino, and it's obvious. Since he was with them they've turned into a matching pair of frightened bookends, weary and wild-eyed.

I catch Barclay saying something to them about their mother. He's asking about her in a way that makes me suspect he was asking earlier. They shake their heads, and if there's a father in the family mix, I've yet to hear a mention.

"She usually asleep this early . . . at eight thirty?" Barclay says.

"It depends."

"Sometimes."

"When she doesn't feel good."

"Maybe that's why she's not answering the phone . . . ?" he asks, and I can't tell which girl is responding to him.

"No," one of them says. "Don't wake her up if she's asleep. She won't like that."

"When she doesn't feel good she doesn't like it," the other echoes, and I sense they're accustomed to taking care of their mother.

I can catch only snippets of the conversation but it's enough to indicate trouble. I wouldn't be surprised to learn that Mom is divorced, and the reason she's not answering the phone is because she's drunk. She probably hasn't a clue that her daughters haven't returned home, and I hope I'm wrong. I unlock my phone and I send a text to Harold:

Heading your way.

I say to Marino, "I think we've seen enough for now. Let me make sure Rusty and Harold are on the same page with us about how to set up. I'll be right back. Then we can suit up and hopefully get the lights turned on in a few minutes."

Marino stares in the direction of crime-scene tape in the woods, about the length of a football field from where Rusty and Harold are waiting. Then he looks at the twins some fifty feet ahead to the left, at the outer edge of the grassy clearing, close to trees. Their eyes dart around restlessly as Barclay continues saying things I can't hear.

"I'm going to wander over and talk to them," Marino lets me know.

"I'll meet you there." I look at the twins looking at us. "It would be very helpful if they told me in their own words what they might have done out here. That's what I'd like to find out before anything else if you have no objections."

"Yeah," Marino says. "I think we already know there's something they're hiding. Like why the dead lady was dragged, and why her shit's everywhere or missing."

CHAPTER 18

Rusty AND HAROLD ARE the CFC's *Odd Couple*. My two top autopsy technicians are so different from each other they shouldn't get along.

Rusty in his surf pants and hoodies looks like a hippy leftover from the golden era of tie-dye and Woodstock while Harold is a former Army man who eventually became a funeral-home director. He has thinning gray hair, a neat mustache, and lives in suits, single-button conservative ones in solid subdued shades of black and gray.

"How long are we talking about?" I look at what they have to assemble with nothing to guide them but flashlights. "Can we be up and running in twenty minutes max?"

"I think so." Harold crouches, and then Rusty does, their head-lamps flicking over the roller storage bags unzipped and spread open all around us.

Inside are folded aluminum frames, polyurethane-coated black sidewalls and an awning fabricated of heavy-duty black polyester. Still tied down on the trolleys are the requisite sandbags, ground stakes, the scene cases, the boxes of gloves, and the plastic-wrapped packages of disposable protective clothing.

Any additional supplies we might need including water and nonperishable food such as protein bars will be inside the big truck. And I plan to head that way soon. I need something to drink and to get out of the heat for even a few minutes. More importantly, I want to call Lucy, and I don't intend for anyone to hear our conversation. I'm going to ask her about a twenty-three-year-old woman named Elisa Vandersteel whose driver's license lists a London address. I want to see what Lucy can find out about her, and we need to start now.

It doesn't matter that the identity isn't certain. At the moment and after what I've seen so far, a confirmation will be little more than a formality. The rest of the story is a baffling mystery, as are other disturbing events that continue to unfold, and we should get started on any line of inquiry that might be helpful.

Who was Elisa Vandersteel? Why was she in the United States? What was she doing in Cambridge, and was riding her bicycle along the river at sunset a habit? If she did it routinely, then a stalker or some other dangerous person could know.

"I'm sorry to make this so inconvenient," I explain. "But the thing we really have to worry about is up there, and I don't mean God." I point up, indicating the bridge, the surrounding buildings, and also news helicopters that will show up the minute the word is out. "We have exposure from every direction including overhead."

"That's what we get paid the big bucks for," Rusty says, and he says it a lot.

"Do you know what killed her?" Harold asks.

"I've not examined her because I don't want to get that close until we have privacy and adequate light. But from a distance I can see signs of trauma. It appears her body was repositioned and moved."

"Well that's bad," Harold says. "You're sure she's been tampered with?"

"There are drag marks."

"Crap," Rusty replies. "A couple kids found her?"

"And who knows what all they did before the police got here," Harold adds somberly.

"Some of her belongings also appear to be unaccounted for. Others are scattered, and possibly a necklace was broken and whatever might have been on it is missing at the moment." I don't mention the gold skull.

I don't want to tell anybody what to look for. I continue to remind myself to be careful about influencing the investigation because of a personal theory I might have based on an experience that may be nothing more than a fluke. So what if I met Elisa Vandersteel—if that's what turns out to be the undisputed truth? What does that have to do with her death or anything we may or may not find here?

Even as I try to dismiss the encounter as irrelevant I know it's not. If nothing else, it won't be helpful if it comes out in court that I met her not long before she was murdered. It won't make the case stronger. Quite the opposite. The defense will use it against me. I'll be accused of not being objective, of being influenced and distracted by crossing the path of the victim not once but twice just hours before her death.

"Forcibly removed," Harold assumes about the broken chain I mentioned.

"Assuming the jewelry is hers, that's what it looks like," I reply.

"Sounds like there was a violent struggle and the perpetrator tried to stage something after the fact," he suggests, and their headlamps are blinding when they turn toward me.

"There was violence," I reply. "But I can't say if there was a struggle because I don't know enough yet. As soon as we have the enclosure up, I'll know a lot more."

"We had a discussion about what would be best. We thought you'd want the canopied tent, and we recommended that to

Marino." Harold always sounds a little unctuous, as if he's greeting people at the chapel door or giving a tour of a casket showroom or a slumber parlor. "We know the area of course. But we also pulled up a map."

I glance up at Eliot House's upper-story student apartments, and I can see several people looking out the lighted windows. I look at the bridge, and there's a steady stream of cars on it in both directions. Aluminum clinks and clacks, and I hear the sound of bags shoved around on the ground.

"Will you post her tonight?" Rusty asks.

"Usually I would wait until the morning. But this isn't usual," I reply.

"Because I'm wondering if Anne should come in." He lifts out another folded frame that's cumbersome but lightweight, and his headlamp is a blazing Cyclops eye. "If so, she should be heading back to the CFC now, in other words."

The scaffolding of tent sections going up around us brings to mind a crazed Stonehenge fashioned of silver tubes.

"I'll get a van for transporting her when it's time." Rusty is talking about the body now.

"How do you plan on handling that?" I ask. "Without driving right through the middle of the scene."

"I think we pull in as close as we can without messing up anything," Rusty says. "Then by the time you're ready for us to carry her out, she'll be pouched with an evidence seal. And that's all anybody's going to catch on camera, just the usual pouched body on a stretcher. I'm thinking we'll have her in the receiving area by nine P.M. if all goes well." The two of them look at each other, and nod.

"I can notify Anne," Harold says.

She's the CFC's chief forensic radiologist, and I'm going to want the victim in the CT scanner as soon as possible. I reply that yes, Anne needs to come back in if she can. It would be wise to mobilize now, I couldn't agree more.

"You're thinking she was murdered," Rusty says.

"I don't know what I think yet."

"To play devil's advocate," he adds, "I'm wondering if she could be a heat-exposure death. Like she's riding her bike, faints, wrecks and hits her head. We sure have had our share of heat-related fatalities of late, a lot of them weird-ass stuff."

"A bike accident wouldn't explain her belongings strewn everywhere," Harold says thoughtfully.

"It depends on who touched her stuff and when it happened," Rusty disagrees. "You know, like if somebody was looting? Like in small-plane crashes? If you don't get there fast, people steal everything."

"But not out here. That's not going to happen here," Harold says somberly.

"Stealing happens everywhere." Rusty unrolls another section of black polyurethane siding.

I tell them more about the twins who found the body, and that we can't be certain who did what. Kids don't always understand consequences, Rusty drawls in his slow amicable way, the headlamp cushioned by the do-rag over his long shaggy hair.

"They move something, take something. They don't know any better at first." He interlocks the frame of a large panel. "Then maybe they freak out and lie because they're afraid of getting in trouble."

"We'll build the components here out of the way," Harold says to me as I survey the trolleys and what I want from them now. "Then we'll finish the final assembly in the target area when you're ready and feel it's safe for us to work over there."

"We'll mark off a perimeter, and you can set up the tent right over the bicycle and the body." I add that Marino will use spray paint to clearly designate the footprint for the tent, a safe zone for laying something down.

I take off the ill-fitting gloves he gave to me, and the huge shoe covers fitted with rubber bands. I drop them into a bright red biohazard trash bag.

I COLLECT MY GEAR, grabbing a scene case, what's essentially a large tough plastic tool chest. I pick a box of purple nitrile gloves size small, several pairs of shoe covers with traction soles, and packaged hooded coveralls. I leave Rusty and Harold to their construction project, and follow the path, reentering the clearing.

I direct the flashlight downward and slightly ahead of me, careful I don't step on any possible evidence even though Marino and I already have been over this area. I never stop looking down and around because it's quite possible to walk past something several times without noticing it. So far I've seen nothing except the victim's scattered personal effects that we've already marked with cones. The park is clean. Any scrap of litter I notice appears to have been out here for a while.

I'm aware of my breathing, of the sound of my feet on the gritty path, then the swishing as I walk through grass. I hear the steady rush of traffic on the bridge, the rumble of trucks and cars, and the whine of a motorcycle on John F. Kennedy Street. The air is hot and heavy. It doesn't move. I slow down as a figure materializes in the darkness up ahead, striding toward me. The female officer I saw earlier approaches me with purpose.

"Doctor Scarpetta?" She's keyed up, almost breathless, stopping several feet from me, directing her flashlight at the ground. "You ever notice how you find something when you're not looking for it?" The shiny steel nameplate on her short-sleeved dark blue uniform shirt reads N. E. FLANDERS.

"It happens all the time," I reply. "What did you find?"

"I was walking over to check on your guys, see if they needed anything." She stares off in the direction of Rusty and Harold. "And I noticed something. It's probably nothing but it's a little strange. I think someone was sick in the bushes over there. I'm pretty sure it's recent." She turns and points behind her. "In the woods just off the path and not very far from the bike and the body."

"Investigator Barclay mentioned that one of the girls might have been sick," I reply, and I get the feeling Officer Flanders knows nothing about this because he didn't bother sharing information. "He told me that when he first got here he saw one of them coming out of the bushes, and that it appeared she might have thrown up."

"Someone did for sure."

"I'm happy to look if that's what you're asking. I was headed that way."

"What time frame are we talking about for getting some lights on out here?"

I tell her it shouldn't be long for the tent. After that, I'll get the body to my office as quickly as I can.

"If you don't mind me saying so, it doesn't seem right to just leave her lying there out in the middle of everything."

"I'd do her a far greater disservice if I compromised evidence in any way," I reply.

"We can't put anything over her? A sheet or something?"

"I'm afraid not. I can't risk dislodging or losing evidence, especially trace evidence. If I cover her before going over her carefully with a lens, I won't have any idea what I might be messing up."

"Well if she's been out here for a while anyway, I guess waiting an extra half hour isn't going to change anything," Officer Flanders decides.

"What makes you think she's been out here for a while?"

"Well that's what Barclay thinks."

"It would be best if we don't circulate rumors," I reply, and she shines her flashlight on what I'm carrying.

"Can I help with something? It's too hot to be hauling anything heavy."

"I'm fine. And if any of you need water or to step out of the heat, we have our truck."

"As long as there's nothing dead in there," she jokes.

"You'll be happy to know that we don't transport bodies in the same truck where we rest, drink, eat, and work. We'll have a van here for the body," I explain, and Officer Flanders has a broad face that's neither pretty nor unattractive.

She's what my mother used to call "plain," by which she meant an unremarkable-looking girl who was worse off than "the ugly ones." That's how she would say it, and her explanation for such a vile state-ment couldn't have been more logical. At least in her limited way of thinking, and also in Dorothy's because she shares the same point of view. Pretty girls don't try at all because they don't have to. Ugly girls try harder for obvious reasons.

That leaves plain girls, which usually is synonymous with smart girls, and they need to try but don't know any better or can't be both-ered. So plain girls have the distinction of finishing first and last in the categories of accomplishment and attractiveness respectively. It's my mother's own weird version of "The Tortoise and the Hare," I sup-pose, only there's no moral and no one really wins.

N. E. Flanders is the brand of plain that Dorothy wouldn't have a single kind word to say about. I estimate the officer's age is mid- to late forties, her chunky short-waisted figure not helped by her creaking black leather duty belt and low-riding trousers. Her dark hair is tucked behind her ears in a pageboy, and a white T-shirt peeks out of the open neck of her uniform shirt.

"I'll show you." She motions me to follow her. "It's a rag, a cloth, a towel, I don't know. But someone threw up on it as best I can tell. I mean I didn't get more than a few feet from it, and I didn't touch it of course."

We light our way as we walk, looping around the bicycle, and stopping at the edge of the woods between the path and the river. I recognize the clump of rhododendron bushes Barclay pointed out earlier, and as Officer Flanders probes the dark dense shadows with her light, I smell the evidence before I see it.

"There." She points the beam of light at what looks like a wadded-up cloth caught in branches near the ground as if shoved there.

I set down the scene case, and as I bend closer and shine my light I decide what the officer has discovered isn't a rag or a towel. It's a shirt, off-white, possibly beige, and I can make out a portion of a date, a partial image of a silkscreened face. I remember the woman on the bicycle was wearing a beige Sara Bareilles concert tank top.

"I assume this hasn't been photographed." I unfasten the clasps of my scene case.

"No. All I did is notice it with my light. And then I saw you coming."

"We need to get Marino here." I balance on one leg at a time, pulling the shoe covers with traction soles over pumps that are still damp and sticky against the bare skin of my feet.

I work my hands into a pair of gloves, small ones that fit this time. I open a transparent plastic evidence bag, and next retrieve a pair of sterile disposable forceps. I explain that typically I wouldn't store anything in plastic unless the item is completely dry. Blood and other body fluids including vomit will degrade and rot as bacteria and fungus proliferate, and any evidence such as DNA will be lost.

I'm explaining this to Officer Flanders when I hear Marino before I see him. His big bootie-covered feet are getting closer on the path.

"What's up?" his voice booms in the dark, and I show him what we've found. "What makes you think it's hers?" He directs this at me, and I'm relieved he makes no allusion to what I told him a little while ago.

He doesn't ask me if the shirt looks familiar. He doesn't come right out and confront me with what I remember about how the cyclist looked or was dressed when I encountered her twice earlier.

"It's a T-shirt, and it's wet, apparently covered with vomit," is what I say. "It would appear to be recent since nothing would stay wet out here for very long."

As he takes photographs I explain that the shirt is too messy for a paper bag. I'm going to package it in plastic but only temporarily. I'll have the CFC truck deliver the evidence directly to my headquarters. I'll make sure everything is properly preserved. We'll recover any evidence from the shirt and hang it in a drying cabinet—I spell out exactly what we'll do. Then I cover my nose and mouth with a surgical mask.

"How 'bout you go over and hang out with the two girls," Marino says to Officer Flanders. "Keep everybody away from them, and don't ask them nothing. Just stay with them, and the Doc and me will be right there."

She walks off, and I hand Marino a mask. He puts it on and starts taking photographs.

"Shit," he complains, and underbrush crackles and snaps beneath his feet as he moves around. "Some things you never get used to. Goddamn it!"

"Are you all right?"

"It's like when some kid throws up on the bus. Then everybody does."

"Well don't unless you're going to do it in a bag. Would you like one?"

"Hell no. I've been around worse shit than this."

I hand him the pair of disposable forceps and he grips the shirt with them, extracting it from the rhododendron bush. He guides it over the transparent plastic bag I hold open, and I can see at a glance that the T-shirt is from a Sara Bareilles concert and it's damaged. There are tears in the cotton fabric but I don't notice blood. If the victim was wearing the shirt when she was attacked or injured, there should be blood on it.

Marino and I discuss this briefly because it doesn't make sense.

"I'm not getting how her shirt came off." He continues to poke around in the bushes. "And there's no blood on it?"

"I need to examine it carefully, which I'm not going to do out here."

"Unless the girls did it. Maybe they took it off the body because they wanted it."

"Then why does it have tears in it? Why is it damaged?" I pinch the bag's seal closed with my fingertips.

"How do we know it wasn't already torn?" Marino says.

I don't recall that the cyclist's T-shirt was torn. But I wasn't looking carefully. At the time I had no reason to make a mental note of her every detail as if I were filling out an investigative report in advance.

"We'll figure that out when we get it to the labs," I reply. "But what I can tell you with certainty right now is there are multiple tears in the shirt and it's covered with vomit."

"Then what? How did it end up in the bushes? The answer is: It didn't walk here by itself. And there's a lot of disturbed dead leaves and soil back here."

He looks in the direction of the twin sisters. I can see Officer Flanders's back, and the moving beam of her flashlight as she's about to reach them.

"Come on." Marino steps out of the bushes, onto the grass. "Let's go find out what the hell they did."

CHAPTER 19

I INTRODUCE MYSELF AS KAY Scarpetta, which means nothing to them.

I don't say I'm a doctor, a Ms. or a Mrs. Maybe I'm a cop. Maybe I work with social services. I suppose I could pass for Marino's girl-friend. I can't tell what the twins think of me or what assumptions they might make about my reason for showing up to chat with them about a dead body they stumbled upon.

"How are you both holding up?" I set down my scene case and smile.

"Fine."

They look flushed and tired but from what I understand they've re-fused every opportunity to sit in an air-conditioned car. They're con-tent to stand outside in the hot dark night, and it occurs to me they might crave attention. I have a feeling they spend much of their time picked on or ignored, and I wouldn't be surprised if they put up with more than their share of being ostracized and bullied.

"She'd like to ask you a few things," Marino says to them about me. "Then we'll get you someplace where you can get cool, have a nice drink, a snack. How would you like to see what a real police department looks like?"

"Okay," one of them says.

"Where are the TV cameras?" the other asks. "How come this isn't on the news? It should be on the news!"

"We don't want any TV cameras or reporters here right now," Marino replies.

"But why aren't they?"

"Because I'm in charge," Marino says flatly. "That nice lady officer you were with a few minutes ago? Officer Flanders is going to give you a ride to my headquarters in her police car."

"Are we in trouble?"

"Why would you be in trouble?" Marino asks.

"Because somebody's dead."

"Because somebody did something bad."

As Marino and I were walking here, he informed me that the girls are fourteen years old. Their names are Anya and Enya Rummage—as in the ROOMage and not the RUMmage sisters, God help them, I can't help but think. What unfortunate names for identical twins. As if they don't get ridiculed enough, I'm guessing. I give them another reassuring, sympathetic look as if all of us are out in the miserable heat and in this mess together, which of course couldn't be further from the truth.

"I'm wondering exactly where you were when you noticed the body," I say to them as if I'm perplexed and need their help.

"There." Anya in pink points toward the distant trees behind us where Rusty and Harold are assembling the tent scaffolding.

"So you were walking through the woods, following the path toward the clearing," I reply.

"Yes, and we saw the bike on the ground."

"Then we saw her."

"When you were entering the park from John F. Kennedy Street, did you see anyone? Hear anything at all? I'm wondering how long she might have been here when you found her."

They say they didn't hear or see anything unusual as they cut through the park. They didn't hear anyone talking and certainly they didn't hear shrieks or someone yelling for help. As both of them continue to recount what happened, I get a picture of them walking along the fitness path the same way Marino and I did a while ago.

When they reached the clearing they saw what they at first assumed was a bicycle accident. It was almost completely dark by then, and there was no one else around. The park was empty as far as they could tell except for "animals," they continue to say. A squirrel, possibly a deer, they tell me. I ask what time it was when they discovered the bicycle and the woman's body, and the girls shake their heads. They don't know.

"Then what did you do? Do you think you can describe for me exactly what happened next?" I ask, and both of them look at Marino for approval, and he nods. "How close did you get to her?" I inquire.

"Tell her. It's okay," he reassures them. "She's a doctor and is trying to help."

But it's not quite the right thing to say. The twins stare in the direction of the body as if it's not too late for a doctor's intervention.

"I'm a doctor who works with the police," I explain to them without using any of the buzzwords like *medical examiner, coroner* or *forensic pathologist*. "We need to find out what might have happened to the person you discovered. It's my job to figure out now she got hurt and died."

"She must've wrecked," Enya in yellow says. "Or someone jumped out at her maybe because she couldn't see very well. You ride slow because you can't see? And then a bad person is waiting to get you."

"It was too dark," the other sister says.

"Too dark to be riding a bicycle through the park?" I go with their train of thought, and they nod.

"So what made you decide to walk through here?" Marino asks. "Did you worry about how dark it is?"

"No because we do it all the time."

"Not all the time," Anya in pink disagrees. "Not usually after dark but our pizza was slow."

"Because you added sausage. Even though I didn't want it."

"So what if I did?"

"You got here and it was dark. And you weren't scared walking through here alone?" Marino asks, and they shake their heads.

"We watch out for cars. And there's no cars through the park. Mom doesn't like us walking around cars."

"We don't come here in the rain, though."

"We only walk through here sometimes. Not in the winter or when it's too cold near the water."

"Mostly when it's hot."

"Mom gives us money for food when she doesn't feel good."

"She doesn't feel good today."

"She's very tired."

"She's asleep and doesn't want to get up."

I look from one face to the other, from Anya to Enya. Or maybe it's Enya to Anya. Both of them have on stretch shorts with drawstrings, and tees with tulip hems. As I continue to ask questions, they tell me the same story I heard from Barclay. They got close to the body but didn't touch it, and their eyes jump around as they describe this. When I ask them how long they waited before they called the Cambridge police, neither of them replies, and they won't look at me.

I ask Enya, the sister in yellow, if she made the call, and she shakes her head, no.

"What about you?" I ask Anya in pink.

"No." She shakes her head vigorously, and now both of them stare at me.

"Maybe you'll let me see your phone," Marino says. "I'm betting one or both of you have a phone, right?" And the girls indicate they don't. "So neither of you called the police?" Marino asks. "Now come on. Somebody had to, right? How'd we know about it if you didn't call us?"

"I didn't call the police," Enya says slowly in her blunted tone.

As both of them continue to assert what seems a blatant lie, I get a sneaking suspicion it isn't. I have an idea what might have happened.

WE KNOW THE CAMBRIDGE police received a 911 call about a person down in the park, and that would indicate the girls had access to a phone. But if they literally don't own the phone in question, then that might suggest they used one that belongs to someone else.

To this equation I add my earlier observation when I briefly looked at the bicycle on the path. The phone holder on the handlebars is empty. If the woman I met earlier was Elisa Vandersteel, as I suspect, then I saw her clamp her iPhone into the holder before she rode off across Quincy Street and into the Yard. So what happened to her phone after that? I might know, and if I'm right it could explain why Anya and Enya are swearing they don't have a phone.

Maybe they don't—not one of their own. They claim they didn't call the police, and very possibly they couldn't have. Not literally if the phone didn't belong to them—not if it was locked and they didn't have the password. They absolutely couldn't dial the Cambridge Police Department. They couldn't even call 911 without getting past the locked screen, and I doubt they'd know how to do that in emergencies unless someone had shown them.

I propose this to Enya in yellow. I ask her if she knows what an iPhone is, and she does. It would seem her mother has one, and yes she understands about swiping the locked screen to the right, to the password keypad. At the bottom on the left side is the word *emergency*. All you have to do is touch it and you're given a dial pad that allows you to enter your country's emergency three-digit number, which is 911 in this case.

So neither Enya nor Anya dialed the Cambridge Police Department's general number. One of the sisters pressed EMERGENCY, and then entered 911, afterward pressing SEND. Literally, that's what Anya in pink—not Enya in yellow—admits to having done.

"How'd you know to do something like that?" Marino acts impressed.

"Mom showed us," they say in unison.

"She showed you how to use her phone in case there's ever an emergency?" I suggest, and they nod.

"If we need to call an ambulance," Anya adds.

"Is that what you thought you were calling? You thought you were asking for an ambulance?" I ask, and they verify that was their intention.

"Then you didn't think about the police," Marino picks up where I leave off. "You didn't know the police would come if you called for help. That's not who you were asking for."

They confirm that they didn't want the police and never intended for them to come. They tell us they wanted to help her, and the police don't help anybody. The police are who you call when you want to get someone into trouble.

"When someone's mean," Anya says, "and you have to lock them up in jail."

Marino and I realize without having to say it that the girls weren't deliberately misleading us about the phone and who they did or didn't call. It's clear there are limitations in what they comprehend, and an emergency isn't the same thing as a crime. One requires medics. The other the police. What this might suggest is that at first the sisters weren't sure the victim was dead, and they weren't assuming she'd been attacked. Their immediate thought was she'd had an accident, and their response was to get medical help, which is exactly as their mother has taught them, it seems.

"You weren't asking for the police to come." Marino makes sure. "You wanted an ambulance."

"Yes."

"Did you think she was alive?" He's going to keep asking until he gets a satisfactory answer.

"She didn't move."

"And the bad smell." Anya in pink wrinkles her nose.

"Can you describe it?" I ask.

"It smelled like mom's blow dryer when it won't work."

"You noticed an odor that reminded you of your mother's blow dryer?" I try to decipher what she means, pretending it's the first I've heard of a strange smell.

I'm not going to let on that Barclay told me something similar.

"It gets too hot," Enya says.

"An electrical smell?" I suggest as I think of the broken lamp.

"If you thought somebody had done something bad to her would you have called the police?" Marino then asks, and after a pause the girls shake their heads in unison.

They shrug and say they don't know. Then he points toward the clearing, asking them to remember their initial impression when they saw the bike and the woman on the ground. They continue to assert that they thought she was in an accident at first.

"You wanted to help her," he says, and they nod. "You saw she was hurt," and they nod again.

"We didn't want her getting more hurt."

"Like if another bike might run over her," Anya in pink says, and her handoff couldn't be smoother.

"That's the danger when someone's down in the middle of the path, right?" Marino doesn't miss a beat. "Maybe you moved her out of the way a little? So no one would run over her?" he asks, and they nod.

It's as simple as that.

"What happened to make you sick?" Marino asks either one of them since we don't know who did what.

"My stomach," Enya says.

"And the shirt you cleaned up with?" Marino boldly powers forward. "Did she have it on when you first saw her?" He assumes the girls removed the shirt from the body, but they shake their heads, no, and they don't look unnerved.

They don't look the least bit frightened or unhappy anymore.

"It was in the bushes where the thing was. It scared me and made me sick." Anya points.

"Hmm," Marino frowns. "I'm wondering if it's the same bushes where we just found it."

"All I did was see what it was. And then something was in there." Her eyes suddenly widen behind her glasses. "It tried to kick me and I screamed."

"Who do you think it was?" Marino asks as if her comment was normal.

"It might have been a deer."

"And maybe she heard it too as she was riding past, and it scared her. So she wrecked."

"Did you actually see a deer?" I ask.

"I heard it," Anya says excitedly. "I heard it running away."

"What about you?" Marino asks Enya.

"I heard it too!" she exclaims the way kids do when they realize everyone is eager to hear a story they're telling. "I heard it run away in the dark, and then the policeman got here."

"So let me make sure I get this straight," Marino says. "You heard something run out of the bushes, and then Investigator Barclay showed up. You got any idea how many minutes passed between when you heard the commotion in the bushes and when Barclay got here?"

"One minute," Enya says.

"I don't know," Anya chimes in.

"One minute and I don't know?" Marino looks at both of them. "Which is it?"

"Maybe more than one minute. I don't know."

"I was scared and then he was walking toward us. Are we in trouble?" Enya looks uncertain again.

"Now why would you be in trouble?" Marino asks.

"I don't know."

"Hmm." He pauses, puts on the big act of entertaining an unhappy thought. "Wait a minute. Hold the phone. Have you done something I don't know about? Something that you're worried might get you in trouble?"

Technically, the answer is yes. It appears they've tampered with a crime scene and perhaps tried to abscond with an expensive phone taken from a dead person. Even if they borrowed it initially, it would appear they intend to keep it unless there's a better explanation for what happened to it. But I think it's safe to say they won't be held accountable—nor should they be. I'm not sure they know better.

Then as if Enya can read my mind she picks up her knapsack, which is in the grass by her feet. It's pink with small hearts, and her sister's is just like it. Enya digs into a front pocket and slides out an iPhone in an ice-blue case—like the one I saw the cyclist clamp into the holder on her handlebars.

Marino doesn't touch the phone. He doesn't act surprised and certainly not suspicious or judgmental. He opens a brown paper evidence bag and holds it in front of Enya. He instructs her to drop the phone inside it.

"Well now that's really helpful," he says to both girls, and I can imagine Barclay's smoldering resentment when he finds out what Marino's just done. "You know what I can't figure out?" He looks at both of them.

"What?"

"How you got hold of this. How did you manage that?"

Anya in pink admits with a hint of pride that she saw the phone "on the handlebars" and "borrowed" it.

"That was a pretty smart idea to borrow the phone to call for help," Marino says, and they look pleased.

He wants to know if they'd mind him taking a peek at what's inside their knapsacks. Maybe there's something else they have that might be helpful.

"Okay," Enya says, and she takes his hand.

She presses it to her face as if she might love him.

CHAPTER 20

TWICE NOW IN THE past forty minutes I've trekked alone through the clearing, following the path to the edge of the park where an auxiliary diesel generator hums in the dark.

I'm getting more frustrated with each minute that passes. I was hoping to be back at my headquarters before now, and yet I've scarcely started. The body should be in the CT scanner. I should be setting up my autopsy station.

Already I should have a good idea what happened to her, and I don't. Not to mention hypervigilance is fatiguing. When you have to think about everything you do and say, and watch every place you touch or step, it wears you down. Especially in this weather.

It's already 9:30 P.M. and the tent isn't close to ready. I could put on the big show of hanging around outside instead of retreating to the quiet comfort of an air-conditioned monster truck. But there's not much I can help with at the moment, and one thing I've learned over the years is to pace myself. If I don't keep hydrated, if I'm not careful about overheating, if I don't plan and strategize I won't be much good to anyone.

The CFC's mobile command center is the size of a small yacht hitched to a super-duty crew cab, white with the CFC crest and the state seal on the doors. There are no windows in the trailer. But inside it's lit up and cool, a combination lounge and war room where first responders and other essential personnel can rest, work, teleconference, use computers, and safely store evidence destined for the labs. When I stopped in here the first time it was to drink water, change my clothes, and safeguard the packaged soiled T-shirt by locking it inside an evidence mini-refrigerator.

Now I'm back again, fortifying myself with more water and a protein bar while trying not to fantasize about the dinner I missed at the Faculty Club. I'm hungry and restless as I wait to hear from Lucy. She was pushy about having a discussion with me a while ago when I couldn't talk. Now that I'm alone with a few minutes to spare, of course I can't get hold of her. I'll have to see what I can find out on my own about Elisa Vandersteel, and I sit down at a workstation.

Logging onto the computer, I spend a few minutes searching the name, and it gives me an uneasy feeling when nothing comes up, not a single file returned. I try the surname Vandersteel and Mayfair, London, and have no better luck, which is odd. It's pretty difficult to avoid any mention on the Internet these days but if my searches can be trusted, it would seem that Elisa Vandersteel doesn't exist.

She also isn't on social media, it seems. I can't find her on Instagram, Facebook or Twitter, and that's extremely unusual for someone young. The woman I noticed taping up recipes at the ART certainly didn't seem shy or introverted. I also realize that doesn't mean much. One can be confident and friendly but private, and maybe she's had issues in the past that cause her to stay below the radar. But the more key words I enter without success, the more wary I get.

I think of the photograph of the UK driver's license that Investigator Barclay showed me. I remember that the street listed in the Mayfair address was South Audley, not far from the American embassy. But I didn't pay close attention to the house number. I search what I recall and nothing comes up, and I'm grateful that my routine searches aren't the final word on Elisa Vandersteel.

I'm not Lucy. I can't begin to approach her level of technical sophistication, and as soon as we have a private moment I'll get her to search. I check my phone again, and can tell by the digits displayed in the icons of certain proprietary apps whether anything new has landed. Nothing has that I consider a priority at the moment, and I hope Lucy's all right. When I think about what's happened so far today I can easily imagine her state of mind. I have a very good idea what she's thinking.

Or better put, who's shadowing her thoughts, gaining on her in leaps and bounds right about now, and it's depressing. It's a falling off the wagon of sorts because an enemy, a nemesis will become an addiction if one's not careful. Lucy isn't and never has been. She can't be. It's too personal for her. She's going to get worked up and paranoid in a way that Marino, Benton and I never have and won't when it comes to a certain human virus who infected her decades ago.

I decide I may as well head back out into the elements to see how we're coming along with the canopied barrier, which has been trickier than we anticipated. Spray-painting the footprint has been a frustration and a headache because we can't turn on the auxiliary lights without exposing the entire scene to anyone who might be watching and ready with cameras. It's very dark despite the multiple flashlights poking and prodding. The terrain is uneven, and there are tall hedges, benches and lampposts in the way.

The first attempt wasn't working so we had to stop, and trying again has proven a worse mess than imagined. First Marino's bright orange outline had to be painted over in black, then the area was measured again and reconfigured as we made sure we weren't going to be setting the tent on top of evidence. The second attempt wasn't much better, and as I'm thinking this I'm well aware that Marino, Rusty and Harold are still at it and will be for a while longer.

It's become quite the engineering challenge to enclose the bicycle, the body, and as many personal effects as possible while avoiding bushes and trees, and causing any potential damage to the scene. But if they don't manage to get the tent pitched fairly soon, I'm going to have to improvise. This has gone on too long already. It's not according to plan, and someone's going to say something. Probably Tom Barclay.

Marino wouldn't allow him to accompany the twins to the police station, and the cocky and annoying investigator is still here, trying to watch everything I do while pretending he's not. Maybe he's hoping to learn something that might make him better at his job. Maybe he's waiting for me to screw up.

But most likely he's simply behaving in character—a magpie carrying every glittery bit of gossip back to his nest. Information is his currency, and while he may not mean any harm, people like him are dangerous.

I GET UP FROM a chair bolted to the stainless-steel diamond-plate floor, and the mirror-polished metal is cold beneath my bare feet.

I was able to ditch my silk blouse, my skirt and suit jacket for a pair of teal-green scrubs but sadly I'm stuck with my scuffed clammy pumps. Storage bins in here include scene gear for all conditions except the Sahara Desert, which is what it feels like in Cambridge of late. But in general the CFC isn't prepared for unrelenting extreme heat because it almost never happens in New England.

I can't exactly trade my uncomfortable shoes for what's available, which are rubber hip waders and waterproof fire boots, one size fits all. Opening a cabinet, I find a fresh pair of shoe covers with grip soles. I step back into my damp pumps, and the thin leather linings have become unglued and feel slimy against the bare soles of my feet.

I pull on the booties but I won't bother with coveralls or gloves yet. I check my phone again, and still nothing.

I've let Lucy know that I need her help, but I haven't said why. I'm not about to immortalize my suspicions in writing or voice mails no matter how safe I'm told my communications are. Especially when my phone has been acting up the way it has, and Lucy is even more careful about leaving an electronic trail than I am. I wonder what she's doing. I wonder if she's working in her lab or the Personal Immersion Theater, the PIT.

Or maybe she's with Janet and Desi, and as I envision the three of them I think what an extraordinary family they've become. Janet is an environmental attorney. She's former FBI, and her history with Lucy includes college and Quantico. They practically grew up together, and I couldn't ask for a better partner for my niece. I would choose Janet time and time again were it up to me. She's humane, smart and gentle—as was her sister Natalie, who died a year ago this past summer.

Janet and Lucy have created an ideal home for Desi, all of us an extended family, a supportive and protective matrix. He would be an orphan otherwise, and what a loss that would be. Such an irresistible lovely boy, the incarnate Christopher Robin, my sister says, his blue eyes mesmerizing, his mop of light brown hair streaked blond by the sun.

Nine now, Desi is growing up fast, all legs and arms, and his face has become more angular. He's nimble, fearless and scary smart, and I've begun to tease Lucy that at last she's met her match. Who wouldn't want to be part of a family unit like that? And I'm unpleasantly reminded of what Benton said before our dinner was interrupted.

He suggested that Dorothy and Marino might have more than a playful flirtation going on. Now she's on her way here when she's never bothered once the entire time I've lived and worked in the northeast. Marino has bonded with Desi, taking him fishing, teaching him how to play baseball, giving him his first taste of beer, and the track my thoughts are running along is too unpleasant to dwell on.

It's distasteful if not enraging to imagine Dorothy with Desi. My selfish sister who couldn't be bothered with Lucy. My male-addicted only sibling who always forgot about her daughter the instant the newest suitor was at the door. And now all I hear from Dorothy is Desi this and Desi that, as if there's nothing she adores more than to nurture and attend to a child, especially a male child. It's obscene. It's the height of hypocrisy, and then I can't bear to think about it anymore. I blank it out.

Dorothy should be landing at Logan fairly soon, assuming her plane hasn't been further delayed. Lucy, Janet and Desi are probably picking her up, and that's why Lucy isn't getting back to me, I tell myself. She's busy driving one of her demanding supercars or tricked-out armor-clad SUVs. But who knows what anybody is doing, including my husband. I have no idea what Benton's phone call from Washington, D.C., was about. I haven't a clue where he is.

It's surreal that our dinner date has come to this, and then I click on the phone app for the security cameras we use to monitor the dogs. Sock and Tesla were in the living room a while ago. Now they're sleeping in their memory-foam bed in the kitchen, and I back up the recording to when Page the dog sitter is walking in. Obviously Benton has let her know something has come up and we're not certain when we'll be home.

Clearly she's staying over, in pajama bottoms and a T-shirt, bare-foot, no bra, and I don't like it when she's in the downstairs guest room. I don't want to say such a thing out loud but it's true and probably means I'm a selfish person. I sincerely dislike having anyone in our house but there's no choice now that Tesla is in the mix. She needs training, socializing, and she shouldn't be left without human companionship for long periods of time.

I watch Page filling the dog bowls with filtered water she pours from a pitcher. A friend of Lucy and Janet's, she's imposing, her upper-body strength from competitive swimming impressive, almost unbelievable for a female. It's entered my mind that she might take steroids because I can't quite believe her bulk is solely from long hours in the gym or some earlier stint in the Navy when she was accepted into the Basic Underwater Demolition or BUD training program for SEALs.

Tall with curly dark hair, all brawn, Page is the gentle giant with dogs, kind but in control. She couldn't be more thoughtful or attentive toward an aging greyhound rescued from the racetrack or an English-bulldog puppy once abused by children and abandoned.

"Who's gonna potty and then get a beddy-bye treat?" Page asks Tesla and Sock.

I hear their nails click furiously as they run to the back door.

WALKING THROUGH AN AIR-CONDITIONED cloud of LED light, I pause in the galley with its coffeemaker, small refrigerator, microwave and laminated white countertops.

Tossing empty water bottles into the recyclable trash, I look around at the workstations, equipment cases, forensic instruments, and multidrawer cabinets of tools and other supplies. I make sure there's nothing else I need for what I'm about to do. I don't think there is. And Harold and Rusty know the drill. On my way here I gave them my scene case and other necessities. They will have everything set up under the tent by the time I get there, and everything will be as it should.

But I'm restless and my mood is tense, my thoughts burdened. When I think of the second time I encountered the woman who I now believe is dead and about to become my patient, she literally rode off into the sunset. I don't know where she went after that or when she finally entered the park, but it was completely dark by seven thirty.

Supposing she was killed around that time, it means that for the better part of two hours her body has been left out in the middle of a public park surrounded by Harvard student housing and other populated buildings. In an ideal situation I would have gotten her out of here a good hour ago.

This is taking too long but it's not surprising. Things rarely go as quickly as we'd like, and in a difficult death investigation it's the rule rather than the exception that very little goes as planned. But the world is less forgiving than it used to be, and already I'm preparing for criticism.

Someone will decide I didn't show proper respect, that I carelessly left a dead body exposed for all to see. I'm callous and uncaring. Or I'm negligent. I'll read about it in a blog or hear about it on YouTube. I always do.

CHAPTER 21

I SCROLL THROUGH THE LATEST news feeds, and so far so good.

There's no mention of the police or personnel from my office work-ing a bicycle accident, an assault or anything else at the edge of the Harvard campus. I see nothing about a dead body in a Cambridge park or even the most vague allusion to the *developing situation* on the waterfront that the alleged Interpol investigator mentioned to Marino.

I come across nothing I consider a cause for concern except what Benton told me earlier about the elevated terror advisory. I skim an online article in the *Washington Post* about the bulletin published earlier today:

> . . . The Secretary of Homeland Security has issued a Na-tional Terrorism Threat Advisory alert due to an imminent threat against transportation hubs, tourist hot spots, and the sites of major public events such as sporting competitions and concerts. Of specific concern are possible planned attacks in Washington, D.C., Boston and their neighboring communi-ties. This is based on detailed chatter U.S. intelligence has intercepted on the Internet suggesting these potential targets, and that self-radicalized homegrown actor(s) could strike with little or no notice . . .

When the status has gone from *elevated* to *imminent* the threat is considered credible and impending, and that makes me wonder about airport security. It will have been beefed up—especially in Boston. That may be why my sister's plane was delayed. It could explain why the TSA was overwhelmed in Fort Lauderdale, the line of passengers out the terminal and on the sidewalk "unless you're first class like me," as my sister informed Lucy, who then passed it along to the rest of us.

I don't have any updates directly from Dorothy. She can't be bothered to tell me she's running late or that she's on the plane. I had to get the information secondhand, and even so I don't know what to expect. I guess it really doesn't matter since I'm not the one picking her up anyway, and I feel a twinge I recognize as disappointment with a sprinkle of hurt for good measure.

A part of me expects more of my only sister. I always have, and for me to feel that way after all I've been through with her is not only baseless it's irrational. It's time to get over it. Dorothy has always been exactly who she is, and for me to hope for anything better reminds me of a quote attributed to Einstein: *Insanity is doing the same thing over and over again and expecting a different result.*

Dorothy is predictable. She does the same thing repeatedly and expects not a different result but the same one she got the last time she did whatever she wants with little regard for anyone else. So maybe she's the sane one, I think ruefully, and as I go through my messages and alerts I'm surprised that General John Briggs just tried to get hold of me. For some reason I missed a call from his home phone minutes ago.

I have a special ring tone for all of his numbers, and I make sure my ringer is turned on. It is. But it was silent, and I don't know why because our electronic communications are excellent in here. They have to be. Lucy makes sure of it in all of our vehicles, utilizing range extenders, boosters, repeaters or whatever it takes. And I'm seriously beginning to wonder if there's something wrong with my smartphone. It isn't one you can buy in a store or online, is virtually *hack-proof* according to Lucy. But maybe she's wrong. It depends on who's doing the hacking.

She's constantly developing special apps and encryption software that aren't available on the open market, doing everything possible to make sure our computers, radios, phones and other devices are as secure as anything can be in this day and age. But nothing is infallible. I touch the PLAY arrow, expecting to hear the voice of the chief of the Armed Forces Medical Examiners, the head of U.S. medical intelligence, my friend and former mentor Briggs.

But it's his wife who tried to reach me, and I know instantly that her news won't be good. A classic military spouse from an earlier more traditional era, Ruthie has devoted her life to her formidable husband, moving with him whenever his newest orders have come in, running interference and enabling him while she prays he doesn't get hurt, kidnapped or killed in the destabilized war-ravaged hellholes he frequents.

Iraq, Afghanistan, Syria, Turkey, Cameroon, Yemen, and she's never really sure. Often she's not told but lives the anguish of knowing that whenever he boards a military transport jet or lands on an aircraft carrier she may never see him again. Her life has been Briggs and nothing but Briggs, and if she doesn't want someone to access him, that person won't, including me. Depending on what's at stake, if he doesn't want to deal with me directly, it's Ruthie I hear from.

So I'm accustomed to her mediation, her triangulation, and now and then it tests my patience. But she sounds unusually raw and emotional in the message she's just left, and I can't tell if she's been crying, drinking, is sick or maybe all of the above. I play the voice mail again. Then again, pausing at intervals, listening carefully, trying to determine if something is wrong with her or if she's simply feeling bad about the reason she's calling. I'm pretty sure I know what it is. I've been expecting it.

"Kay? It's Ruthie Briggs," she begins in her slow Virginia drawl, and she sounds tired and congested. "I'm hoping you'll pick up. Are you there?" she says stuffily. "Hello, Kay?" She clears her throat. "Are you there? I know how busy you are but *please* pick up. Well when you get this please call me. I want to make sure you've been told . . ."

But her voice is muffled, and then it's as if she's swallowed her words and I can scarcely hear her. It occurs to me that she might be holding something, perhaps tissues in front of her face, and that she's turning away from the phone as she speaks.

"For the next little while I'm at this number, then . . . Well as you can imagine there's a lot to do, and I just can't believe . . ." Her voice quavers. ". . . Well please call me as soon as you can." In her befuddlement she leaves her phone number as if I don't have it.

And the voice mail abruptly ends.

IF WHAT I SUSPECT has come to pass, there's no reason for Ruthie to be upset. It couldn't be helped, and at least the cancellation isn't as last minute as it could have been.

All along I've been primed for getting a call literally right before Briggs and I are supposed to be onstage at the Kennedy School. At least I've been given almost twenty-four hours' notice, and it's not like I haven't been warned repeatedly. He's told me from day one that he might not be able to appear with me tomorrow night. It all depends on the mood at the Pentagon and NASA, he's said, and he's apologized in advance for what's probably just happened.

Most likely Ruthie tried to reach me to tell me I'm on my own tomorrow night. Briggs won't be on the panel with me. So it's not really a panel anymore because that leaves me alone onstage. But I'll manage, and it occurs to me that were I to step outside the mobile command center I could see the imposing red-brick complex from here, tucked behind trees.

The Kennedy School backs up to the park, and I can't help but think about how everything seems weirdly linked and familiar. It's as if I'm traversing a landscape that's turned out to be an intricate maze, and I don't know how big it is, what it connects or how to get out.

I'm not going to learn anything further about why Briggs has had to cancel until I talk to him, assuming I can reach him. He also could have been deployed somewhere, and I know how much he hates to let anyone down, especially me. Big Army man that he is, he'll duck a confrontation if it includes being the bearer of bad news. I redial his and Ruthie's home number. No one answers, and I hear a peculiar clicking on the line.

"Ruthie, it's Kay. I'm sorry I missed you," I leave her a voice mail, and now I'm hearing an echo as if two of me are talking on top of each other. "For some reason my phone didn't ring. I'm working an outdoor scene and may be in spots where the signal is bad or I can't answer. But please keep trying me."

Then I send a text to Harold and Rusty, making sure that one of our transport vans is on the way. It may have to wait awhile but let's go ahead and get it here, I tell them.

10-4, Boss. Moving slow. Unavoidable. Stay cool ALAP, which is Rusty speak for *as long as possible,* and he includes a frowning, red-faced emoji.

On the right side of the trailer, beyond the galley, is a deep stairwell that leads outside. My Tyvek-covered shoes thud down the metal steps, and at the bottom I open the door. I emerge outside in the hot night and am blinded by blazing HID headlights. I hear the guttural rumble of a powerful engine. I smell high-octane gasoline exhaust that can't be coming from the mobile command center's auxiliary diesel generator. Then everything goes silent and black.

"Hello?" A thrill of fear touches the roots of my hair as I hear the swish of grass, of someone walking fast. "Who is it? Who's there?"

A lean figure materializes in the night like a ghost rushing toward me.

"AUNT KAY, IT'S ME. Don't be startled," Lucy says, but it's too late.

My adrenaline is out the gate. Flustered, I click on my tactical light then point it down so I don't blind her. Just as quickly I turn off the bloody thing, feeling foolish, then angry.

"Dammit, Lucy!" My heart is flying, my thoughts scattered like a flock of crazed birds. "Don't sneak up on me like that." My pulse pounds. "Jesus. It's a good thing I don't have a gun."

"I don't know if it's a good thing. Especially now."

"I could have shot you. I'm not joking."

"There's nothing to joke about, and I wasn't sneaking." She's scanning all around us as if we're not alone. "I just this second pulled up and saw you walking out. I was coming to find you."

"Why?" I take a deep slow breath, and the hot air seems to barely fill my lungs.

"I'm glad you're okay." She looks at me, then back at the street, and up and around as if we're about to be attacked.

"What do you mean *especially now*? What's going on?" Something is, and she's in high gear. "Why wouldn't I be okay?"

"You've been leaving me messages," she says, and I detect the brittleness in her voice, the flinty aggression. "So here I am. Let's go inside."

I recognize her mood and probably know what it means. "I didn't demand we talk in person. I have a simple question, and a phone call would have been fine. I was going to ask you to search a name for me—"

"It's too hot out here," she cuts me off, not seeming to listen.

"What's the matter?"

"I don't like what's going on." Her staring eyes are deep-set shadows, her mouth grim.

"Someone's dead, and there's nothing to like about that or a lot of things at the moment." But I know that's not what she means.

"I don't like it," she repeats, and her attention is everywhere again. "I've been trying to tell you. There are things you don't know, and it's fucked up." Her low voice is fierce in the dark, and I get a feeling deep down, a mixture of emotions that I can't easily describe.

Disappointment. Frustration. The numbness of homicidal rage turned stony and cold like something ancient that's petrified. I've become increasingly desensitized, especially in recent years, and it's true about crying wolf. Lucy may not do it audibly but I know when a certain subject is constantly on her mind.

She rarely comes across as excitable. She's not the sort to go off the rails, to be impetuous, to act nervous or scared or raise her voice. But she can't fool me. I can always sense when she's about to fly apart the way she is right now. It won't be pretty. It never is. When she gets like this I usually know why. Or better stated, I have a good idea who it's about.

"What is it that's fucked up, Lucy?" I brace myself for what's next as my eyes adjust to the dark again.

I'm pretty sure I know what she's going to say. I could have predicted her reaction after the 911 complaint that we now think was made with voice-altering software. If she knew about another bogus call a little while ago, this one supposedly from Interpol, she'd be only more convinced of her curdled worldview. Lucy accepts as unimpeachable her own version of original sin, which is that all horrors and humiliations come from the same malignant source.

As if there's only one devil. Only one mortal enemy. Only one cancer. And if only that were true.

"Let's go inside and get something to drink." Her face is so close to mine I can smell cinnamon on her breath and the subtle spiciness of her Escada men's cologne.

She's acting as if we're being watched. Maybe she worries she was followed here, and I stare past her at what's parked behind the CFC truck. She jokingly considers her Ferrari FF a family car because it has a backseat and a boot for luggage.

I can't make out the color in the dark. I know it's a vivid shade of blue called Tour de France, and the interior is quilted *cuoio* or a racing-yellow Italian leather. But she could have thundered up in anything, an Aston Martin, a Maserati, a McLaren, a different Ferrari.

Lucy is a genius. I don't use the word lightly or as a term of endearment. It's not an adoring aunt's hyperbole but an accurate description of someone who by the age of ten was programming software, building computers and acquiring patents for all sorts of inventions. Before Lucy was old enough to buy liquor or vote she'd earned an incomprehensible fortune from creating search engines and other technologies.

While still in her teens she landed on the *young and filthy-rich list,* she likes to quip, and began to indulge her passion for helicopters, motorcycles, speedboats, jets and other fast machines. She can pilot pretty much anything, and I focus my attention on her all-wheel-drive FF with its long sloping nose parked silently, darkly on the grass. She drove it to work this morning, and the reason I'm certain of this is because the Ferrari was picked up by the CFC security cameras while I was upstairs in my office, sitting at my desk with its multiple computer displays.

On one of them I watched Lucy drive her four-hundred-thousand-dollar so-called family car inside the bay where ambulances and other transport vehicles pick up and deliver bodies. Not even the cops can park in there, and I was unhappily reminded that often she tucks her expensive modes of transportation out of the dirt and grime, out of the weather. It's rather selfish, and now and then some members of the staff make comments. But that's not what has me thinking about this now. It's the flight suit she has on.

When the cameras picked up Lucy this morning as she climbed out of her electric-blue 650 horsepower V-12 coupe, she was wearing ripped-up jeans, a baggy T-shirt and sneakers. I remember she was holding a large coffee, and slung over a shoulder was her tactical black backpack, roomy with lots of compartments, basically a portable office and armory.

Now that I'm thinking about it, the backpack is what she typically carries when she's flying somewhere. Then at some point today she changed into one of her flame-resistant flight suits in lightweight khaki Nomex, the CFC crest embroidered in red and blue on the left chest pocket. It's not uncommon for her to fly her twin-engine bird whenever and wherever she pleases.

But it's late. It's pitch dark. We're in the middle of an extreme weather alert and a difficult death scene. Her mother is on a plane headed to Boston. I don't understand.

"I'm wondering why you changed your clothes." I bring it up tactfully, and she looks down at her flight suit as if she's forgotten what she has on. "Are you flying somewhere? Or maybe you were earlier?"

But it wouldn't make sense. At its most miserable today the temperature crept past a hundred degrees with more than 70 percent humidity. The hotter and more humid it is, the less efficient the helicopter, and Lucy is meticulous about weather conditions. She has to factor in payload, torque, engine temperatures, and I think back to how many times I was around her today.

At a staff meeting, on the elevator, and I ran into her in the break room when I was looking for Bryce. The last time I saw her probably was around four P.M. after I left the autopsy room with my assistant chief, Dr. Zenner, and we walked past the PIT.

Lucy was inside replacing several projectors, and we chatted with her for a while. She wasn't in a flight suit then.

CHAPTER 22

SHE'S BLASÉ ABOUT IT, claiming she spilled coffee and had to change her clothes.

I know when my niece is evasive. It's as obvious as her rose-gold hair and as plain as the narrow nose on her intensely pretty face. I check my phone, mindful of the minutes creeping by, and still nothing from Harold or Rusty about how the tent is coming along.

Usually Lucy would volunteer right about now, asking if she could go check on them. Technical engineer that she is, maybe there's something she could do to help. But she doesn't offer and isn't going anywhere. It's obvious she has an agenda, has shown up unannounced for a reason, and I may as well see what it is as I wait, tamping down my impatience, glancing at my phone every other second.

I don't want to hound Rusty and Harold. It's not helpful if I continue interrupting them while *they struggle with their erection,* as Marino put it rather horribly the last time I checked. But probably I shouldn't stand out here in the dark talking to my niece either. A better idea is to head back to the clearing and find out for myself how things are going. I want to make sure no one is overheating or needs anything, and I'm mindful of rumors.

I don't want an ugly one starting about my sitting in the air-conditioning, relaxing with my feet propped up while everybody else toils in what feels like Death Valley after dark. I don't want it said that I was taking my sweet time fraternizing with my niece, who thundered up to the scene in a Ferrari that costs more than a lot of houses. My mother still preaches that appearance is everything. These days she has no idea how right she is.

It doesn't take much for people—especially cops—to question your competence and credibility. It takes less for them to wonder about your honesty, and even less than that to doubt your human decency. Any suggestion that I'm entitled or lazy could influence a jury in a negative way. The truth is almost anything can.

"Lucy, I need to head out and check on things . . ." I start to say, and she moves closer to me, touching my arm in a way that's arresting.

"Let's cool off and get something to drink," she replies, and it's not a suggestion.

I glance around at flashlights probing the distant night. I look back at the jeweled vehicle lights flowing along John F. Kennedy Street, and up at the steady traffic on the bridge. I survey the growing number of police cars parked everywhere. No one is inside them. I don't notice a single person near enough to eavesdrop.

But I don't doubt that Lucy feels the breath of the enemy on the back of her neck, and nothing I say is going to change that appreciably. It's like people who suffer from post-traumatic stress disorder. You'll never convince them there's nothing to feel anxious about. You won't talk them out of their nightmares and phobias. It won't help to wish them happy thoughts and sweet dreams.

Lucy's early passions, triumphs, disasters and flirtations are part of her programming. Most indelibly etched are her Quantico experiences, what truly were the very best and worst times of her young adult life. With my blessing and under my direction she took a road less traveled and slammed head-on into a monster. Their collision was cataclysmic and I never saw it coming. Lucy's not the same, and neither am I. No one would be.

Psychic injuries can become faults that like disk errors and other glitches aren't always fixable. It's disturbing to contemplate how often my niece's hair-trigger responses aren't warranted by what she's convinced she perceives. Most of the time I don't say much. I wait for her to have clarity, and she doesn't seem to have that as often anymore. It's gotten increasingly difficult to be sure what to trust. What's real? What isn't? Even Lucy doesn't always seem to know, and if I could wipe the monstrous psychopath Carrie Grethen off the face of the earth it would be for that alone.

She's managed to rob my de facto daughter of any peace of mind she might have had in this life, and I can't seem to do much about it. God knows I've tried. God knows how much I regret the damage that's been done. Were I really Lucy's mother, I'd be a failed one. She's the most important thing I should have gotten right.

I won't forgive Carrie Grethen for that either, and it's moments like this when I recognize how much I want her eradicated. Completely and forever. Like a plague. Like a scourge.

"All right." I go along with Lucy's request in a noncommittal way, revealing nothing important on the off chance we're not alone. "We'll duck out of the heat and grab a drink but we need to make it quick. As you've probably gathered, setting up is taking longer than I'd hoped."

"Murphy's Law."

"Once we're ready to go, I can't stall."

"He who waits." Lucy chats away in slangy clichés, and it's obvious she's doing it for the benefit of whoever she thinks is watching us.

Lately it seems all I hear about is spying, tailing, peeping, trolling, spoofing, stalking, hacking, sniping, snooping. And maybe Carrie really is out here in the dark somewhere having a grand time monitoring our every word, our every move.

The more I think about her, the more I seethe, and I say nothing else to Lucy. I'm silent as I enter my personal access code in the digital keypad on the trailer's side door.

"BE CAREFUL." MY NIECE'S cinnamon breath is in my ear, and I'm aware there are telescopic lenses that could capture the numbers and symbols I entered.

I know there are all kinds of skimmers that can grab data from a considerable distance. I couldn't be more mindful that Carrie is adept in such things and so much more, and I'm worn out from the warnings. In addition to Lucy's deadly projections I have to contend with Marino's endless fear-biting hypotheticals about all the different ways I might be followed or stalked and for all sorts of far-flung reasons.

"I'm always careful." I open the aluminum door. "Not infallible but certainly not cavalier," I add as I step inside, and the cold air is biting.

Lucy follows me in, shutting the door after her. "I still think we should switch our vehicles to fingerprint locks."

"I know you do, and maybe someday it won't be so impractical." The air-conditioning is a relief but I'm going to freeze.

"I just wish these suckers were armored. They should be."

"That would be even more impractical. Are Janet and Desi okay?" I bring them up now that we're inside the trailer's metal stairwell, which isn't bulletproof but at least no one can overhear our conversation.

"They're at Logan driving around in circles because there's no place to wait longer than a nanosecond." She tugs on the door handle again, double-checking that it's secure. "I told Janet not to head out so early but she did anyway, don't ask me why. Mom isn't close to landing yet."

"Do we have an idea why?" I start climbing the steps.

Lucy is right behind me. "First there was a delay in Fort Lauderdale because of an unattended bag at the same gate Mom was using. So her flight took off more than an hour late because of that, and then she was sitting on the tarmac for a while."

"And you know this how? I wouldn't think a left bag at my sister's gate would be trending on the Internet."

"Mom's been e-mailing updates to Janet," Lucy says, reminding me that my sister can't extend the same courtesy to me.

"And I guess it's one of those situations where there's not time to go home." The hurt I feel is as old as time, but I won't let it show. "She'd much rather have to turn around and go back," I add.

"Also traffic is backed up in New York airspace like it has been all week because of the heat wave. Sea fog, thermals are a problem because the air is so much hotter than the water right now, and a lot of flights are on ground holds or are being rerouted. Depending on fuel, Mom won't be landing until at least ten thirty."

I check the time and it's almost ten.

"And she's got luggage," Lucy says. "A lot of it."

"Sounds like she's planning to stay with you awhile."

"I just hope her damn phone battery doesn't die, and I'm worried about Janet connecting with her. Apparently Logan's a real shit show, and you know Mom," Lucy says as our feet thud dully to the top step. "Usually the last one on the plane. Good luck with her bags being there, and Janet can't possibly go inside to help."

"It's going to be a very late night for Desi."

"He's been texting me that the traffic is terrible. State troopers are herding everyone, barely letting you stop your car when you drop off or pick up."

"Well I'm sure he must be excited about Dorothy's visit," I comment halfheartedly as we enter the bright white Formica and stainless-steel galley.

"Yes, since she spoils him rotten. Have you talked to Benton?"

"Not since the Faculty Club," I answer, and Lucy's green eyes have that distant look I know so well and have come to dread.

She may be here in the flesh but in spirit she's somewhere else, some remote emotional space she doesn't share. Beautiful, brilliant, in her midthirties but much younger than that in many ways, and compared to most of the population, Lucy has every advantage. How sad that an obsession would become the path of least resistance for an over-achieving highflier like her. Not that there's anybody like Lucy, and her uniqueness is part of the tragedy.

What a waste that she naturally gravitates to Carrie's isolated hate-ful place like water seeking its own level. Lucy believes she's the cap-tain of her own ship, the master of her own fate. That she has free will. But I'm not so sure anymore.

"Why? Have you talked to him?" I ask.

"Yes," she says, and I would remove this curse from her if I could.

I would take it upon myself if it meant freeing Lucy. I would do almost anything. And strangely I think of the woman on the bicycle and what she said to me before she rode across the blistering hot street:

What doesn't kill you makes you stronger.

But what if it *does* kill you? That's what we should be asking be-cause Carrie isn't making us stronger. It's too late. We crossed that divide two years ago when she let us know in the worst way imagin-able that she's still alive. Since then we're on the side of diminishing returns as she's chipped away, bled and maimed us while we flail in a state of perpetual sensory deprivation.

We don't see or hear Carrie. We don't experience her unless it's on her terms, and her greatest gift is her implied nonexistence. Saying she did something heinous has become rather much like saying the Devil did. Except I have provable scars from her, and a lot of people have died.

"I've been curious about what Benton's doing." I sound calm, which isn't at all how I feel. "He got a call from Washington about the same time Marino called me about this case. How did he seem to you?"

"Hard to tell. I'm pretty sure he was in a car when I reached him," Lucy says.

"A car? Or his car?" I lean against the countertop across from her. "I'm wondering if he's with other FBI agents, if something's happened. He mentioned the terror alert's been elevated and includes Washington, D.C. And also here, the Boston area."

"He didn't offer what he was doing or who he was with," she says, and in the bright light I can make out the subtle bulge of the pistol beneath the cuff of her right pant leg.

CHAPTER 23

THE HOLSTER IS STRAPPED above her boot.

I can't tell what she's carrying but it's probably her Korth PRS 9mm. There's no telling what she has in her car, a high-capacity pistol for sure and possibly a lot more firepower than that.

"I don't know if he was driving or being driven somewhere but his tone made me think he wasn't alone." Lucy plants the palms of her hands behind her on the edge of the counter.

Hoisting herself up, she sits, resting her back against a cabinet, her booted feet dangling, the pistol's black holster peeking out. She folds her strong graceful hands in her lap, and I'm aware of the plain platinum Tiffany wedding band on her left ring finger.

None of us were invited when she and Janet were married in a civil ceremony on the Cape last year after Natalie died. But as Lucy and Janet both explained, they didn't do it to prove their love and commitment. They didn't need to prove it to each other or anyone else, they said. They did it because they intend to adopt Desi.

"You called Benton for what reason?" I ask. "And when was this?"

"A little while ago. After I listened to the latest from Tailend Charlie," she says to my dismay.

"Why on earth would you bother him about that with everything else going on?" I can't believe it.

"There are new developments you're unaware of. Some old developments have resurfaced too. It's important or I wouldn't bother you." Yet as she says this I have my doubts.

There's something Lucy isn't telling me. I can see it in her face. I can feel it. Benton is involved, and I ask her again if he's okay. She says he's really busy, and I reply that all of us are. Then she proceeds to explain that Tailend Charlie's latest audio clip was sent at the usual time, twelve minutes past six P.M. More than three hours ago, and my frustration boils over. I don't see why this merits our undivided attention in the middle of a death investigation.

"I don't mean to be rude," I say to her. "But that's not new information, Lucy. Every one of his crank communications is sent at six-twelve P.M. As you continue to point out, it's intentional, and let me guess? The new recording is cookie-cutter identical to the others except for the content of the message. In other words the recording is canned and precisely twenty-two-point-four seconds long."

"And two-twenty-four was the street address of your house when you and Mom were growing up in Miami." Lucy isn't going to back down from what she's decided without the benefit of real evidence.

"Two-twenty-four and twenty-two-point-four aren't the same thing at all."

"Symbolically they are."

"I'm not sure we should be so quick to assume intentional symbolism." I pick my words carefully so she doesn't get defensive. "The time stamp of six-twelve, the length of two minutes and twenty-four seconds, could be nothing more than meaningless remnants of programming code."

"And six-twelve also is the exact time the bullshit nine-one-one call was made to the Cambridge police," Lucy reminds me as if she didn't hear what I just said.

"That's true. But all of it could be coincidental . . ." I don't finish because I know it probably isn't.

I check my phone again. Nothing from Rusty and Harold, and I send Marino a text:

How are we doing?

"Listen, Aunt Kay," Lucy says to me as I look down at my phone, waiting for an answer from Marino. "I don't like to admit that I was at a disadvantage because of multiple things happening at once."

She pats down the pockets of her flight suit, sliding out a small tin of her favorite cinnamon mints. They rattle softly as she opens the lid, offering them to me, and I think about her choice of words. *Multiple*, as in many. There's something she's not going to tell me, and I take a mint. The fiery-sweet flavor rushes up my nostrils, making my eyes water.

"When we talked a couple hours ago I was preoccupied with the nine-one-one call." Lucy tucks the tin back in a cargo pocket, buttoning the flap. "I was tied up with trying to figure out what the hell happened, who was behind it and why. I can't do everything at once."

"Not even you can." I move the mint to the other side of my mouth and take a sip of water.

She goes on making her case, claiming that early this evening we were attacked simultaneously on multiple fronts—and she uses that word again.

Multiple.

"The timing is deliberate. I believe we're talking about connected attacks that involve the same person or persons. And that suggests to me there are more on the way," she adds.

But the real problem isn't what's been done or might be next. Or how. Or why. It's the *who* in the equation, and all along I've maintained it's obsessive and dangerous to assume that behind every aberrant act is the same diabolical puppeteer.

I'm not naïve about Carrie Grethen. I'm intimately familiar with her nefarious proclivities and treacherous capabilities. I know what it is to be physically mauled by her, almost die at her hands, and work her crime scenes and autopsy her victims.

So it's not as if she's an abstraction to me. But unfortunately she's not the only horror show, and I open the text that just landed. Marino writes:

A clusterf**k. Stay put for now. Nothing U can do.

I wish he hadn't called the scene out here a clusterfuck. I hope that doesn't come home to roost at some point.

"Suffice it to say that what little I could decipher in the audio file was worse than usual." Lucy continues telling me about the latest harassment from Tailend Charlie. "It's too close for comfort, and no telling about the rest of it."

"What does Benton say?" I ask.

"I wasn't going to get into it with him on the phone, not with other people around, especially a bunch of suits," she answers, and I puzzle over how she can know who he's with if he didn't say. "And I sure as hell wasn't going to bring up the stuff about Natalie," she adds to my astonishment.

"You mean Janet, not Natalie." I assume Lucy has misspoken.

"I mean Natalie," Lucy says. "You'll get it when you start thinking about her last few months, when Janet and I were frequently in and out of Virginia. Then you and Benton were with Natalie a number of times late in the game when she was in hospice in particular, and if you think back to some of the things she was saying? They take on a very different meaning now, a disgusting one."

"I can't fathom why you and Benton would be talking about her in the context of everything else." I feel a flutter of uneasiness as I wait for the rest of the story.

"Remember the fights you and Mom used to have when you were kids?" Lucy adds to my confusion. "Remember what you nicknamed her after you got really pissed off?"

"*SISTER TWISTER*. BECAUSE OF her wicked pinching in addition to her other ambushes. Twisting and yanking your hair or cutting it off in your sleep or who the hell knows. Although to hear her tell the story it was you who was the nasty fighter." Lucy reminds me of what I've not thought about in years.

"Dorothy's always been quite the fiction writer." That's as much as I'm going to say.

I've spent most of my adult life being extraordinarily circumspect about what I tell Lucy about her mother.

"We've got to figure out who might know what went on in your house when the two of you were growing up in Miami." Lucy plugs her phone into the charger on the countertop she's perched on.

"Who besides my mother and Dorothy? And me obviously? No one comes to mind but I'll give it some thought." I open a closet and find a dark blue CFC windbreaker to put over my scrubs because I'm getting chilled.

"I suspect that certain things are connected and have been for a lot longer than we've realized," Lucy says. "Going back to summer before last when Natalie was dying, and longer ago than that."

"Such as?" I zip up the windbreaker, and it's so big it hangs midthigh. "What things?" I open the stainless-steel refrigerator reserved for beverages and edibles, no evidence allowed. "Water or Gatorade?"

"Starting with I no longer believe her death was the private family matter we thought it was. Gatorade would be good. In a bottle, not a can."

"Cool blue or lemon-lime?"

"There should be orange."

"Natalie's death wasn't private?" I question as I root around for orange Gatorade. "As in someone was spying on her? I've not heard you mention this before as if it's a certainty. I know only that Natalie was very paranoid. She worried she was being monitored."

"She should have been worried. That's what I'm getting at. I think someone was attempting to spy during her most intimate final weeks, days, hours, moments with all of us." Lucy's green eyes blaze. "I can't say for sure how far it went because none of us were expecting surveillance or looking for it. So things could have been missed."

"Because we didn't take Natalie's fears seriously enough," I say.

"No we didn't. And what I can't swear to now is whether there were any other devices in her house or later in hospice. I wasn't looking for them."

"Any others?"

"Besides Natalie's computers, specifically her laptop." Lucy opens the bottle I handed to her. "But we can't be sure what else might have gone on. I wasn't conducting counterspy sweeps every time I went to Virginia. Janet wasn't either. We didn't think we had a reason."

"And now you're sure there was spying going on?" I ask, and Lucy nods. "As Natalie was dying?"

"During some of it, I'm guessing. We may never know how much."

"It would take a very special type of degenerate to do something like that."

"And we know exactly who fits the bill. I have a very strong feeling she's up to something really special this time."

She means that Carrie is, and I'm back to the same suspicion, only more strongly. Something else has happened. But she's not sharing that information with me for some reason, and I keep thinking about Benton. She was talking to him earlier. I don't really know about what. Lucy isn't going to say a word if he's told her not to, and I herd her back to what started this conversation.

I ask her if Natalie might have been aware of the nickname I coined for Dorothy when we were kids. Might she ever have heard someone mention Sister Twister?

"If so, I don't know about it." Lucy tilts back her head and takes a swallow of Gatorade.

"I'm wondering if the subject may have come up in Carrie's presence years ago when she, Janet, Natalie and you were still friendly with each other."

"I don't think so."

"I can't see any other explanation for how some anonymous cyber-menace would know unpublished personal details about my family. Unless it came directly from the source," I add.

"You mean unless it came from Sister Twister herself. My mother the mad pincher," Lucy says, and I don't correct her.

It's not true that pinching and pulling hair were Dorothy's real crimes but I'm not going to tell Lucy that. I've never elaborated on just how sneaky, untruthful and violent my sister could be, grabbing an arm, an ankle, and twisting the skin quick and hard in opposite directions. What was called a snakebite or Indian sunburn back then was her specialty.

When executed with sufficient skill and force, it's quite painful and leaves little evidence beyond a redness that early on I learned not to complain about. If I did, Dorothy simply would say that I had a sunburn. Or I was suffering from an allergic reaction. As usual I was wrongly accusing her. I was trying to get her into trouble, and when questioned, she would concoct the most elaborately imaginative false-hoods to explain my inflamed sore flesh.

If I was sitting near the windowsill reading, and my arm or ankle got burned, she'd tell our mother. Or the sun hit me at a certain angle while I was sleeping. Or I must be coming down with a fever, a rash. Possibly I got a spider bite or was developing an allergy to gardenias, to mangoes. Or I was "coming down" with cancer like our father.

Dorothy got exponentially bolder and out of bounds as he got sicker. She decided he wasn't able to stick up for *Daddy's pet* anymore, rendering me defenseless, she assumed. I wasn't. But I didn't tattle or retaliate with corporal punishment.

There are better ways to deal with bullies, and in some respects I'm actually grateful to my sister. Thanks to her I learned the art of silence, the power of listening and the added potency that comes with waiting. As our father used to say:

A volte la vendetta é meglio mangiata fredda.

Sometimes revenge really is better served cold.

"What I'm wondering is if my sister might have mentioned the silly nickname to Natalie, to Janet." I suggest this to Lucy because I'm se-riously beginning to wonder who Dorothy has been talking to—not just recently but over the years.

"I don't know," Lucy says, "but there's no way Mom ever passed on that story or anything else to Carrie."

"Not unless we're mistaken in what we've always assumed about the two of them not knowing each other. Are we absolutely certain of that?"

"They've never met and Mom knows nothing about her." Lucy's adamant, and I'm going to push harder.

CHAPTER 24

WHAT ABOUT IN THE very beginning?" I ask Lucy. "Are you sure you didn't mention Carrie when you started your internship at Quantico? It would make sense when you went home to Miami or talked on the phone if you might have said something to Dorothy about your FBI supervisor, your mentor—especially one who gave you so much special attention."

Carrie couldn't have been more generous or charming, and Lucy was flattered out of her mind. She didn't have a chance.

"I know you don't like to think about it," and I don't want to be provocative, "but you were bowled over by her in the beginning. You couldn't talk enough about her. At least to me."

"I think you know why I didn't mention her to Mom." Lucy's stare has turned hard and edgy. "I didn't talk about Carrie or anybody else I so much as had a beer with."

Dorothy is bitterly disappointed by her only child's "lifestyle," as my sister continues to refer to being gay. It doesn't matter how many times I tell her that who any of us falls in love and partners with isn't a lifestyle like belonging to the country club or living in the suburbs. My sister doesn't get it. In my opinion she doesn't want to get it because it's easier for her to define Lucy as a bohemian or a tomboy, which is Dorothy's euphemism for being gay. It's easier if Lucy and I both suffer from penis envy, and that's my sister's euphemism for not being male-dependent the way she is.

Penis envy really is a thing, she loves to declare, preferably in front of our mother. Or more recently, in front of Marino when we were in Miami this past June and he was giving Dorothy motorcycle rides and who knows what else.

"There's quite a lot Benton and I don't discuss with Dorothy," I reassure Lucy. "She wouldn't have any idea who Carrie Grethen is unless you've shared that part of your life. Or someone else has." Marino enters my thoughts, and I hope Benton is mistaken.

It gives me a sick feeling to think of Marino being sweet on Dorothy, of him talking to her about us or anything else that's none of her business and is possibly dangerous. The idea is too galling, and I dismiss it.

"You're saying that Tailend Charlie mentioned Sister Twister." I get back to that because I want to make sure I'm clear on where it came from. "As you know, Lucy, I've not listened to the audio clip yet. So I'm assuming it's not been transcribed or translated unless you got someone else to do it."

"I haven't and won't," she answers. "It's important you do it since you're the intended target. The recording was made for your benefit."

"It hasn't been translated and yet you know what it says?"

"Bits and pieces. Easy ones." Lucy takes another swig of Gatorade. "My Italian may be clunky but I know *sorella* means sister, and I recognized *Sorella Twisted* or *Sister Twister* when I played the clip. I've heard the nickname from Mom when she's regaled me with stories of how terrible you were to her."

I feel another rush of resentment that's as fresh as it's old.

"I recognized your name, your initials, and the word *chaos,*" Lucy continues to describe what she could make out in the most recent audible harassment. "Apparently *chaos* in Italian is pretty much the same thing in English."

"In Italian there's no *h*. It's spelled *c-a-o-s*." I pronounce it for her.

"Yes." Lucy nods. "That's exactly what I heard. *Chaos is coming,* or something like that."

She goes on to explain that the audio file is consistent with the others I've received since the first day of fall.

"Cheesy rhymes, insulting, and promising your death," Lucy says.

In each of them the Italian-speaking voice has been synthesized. The lyrical baritone sounds like my father, who died when I was twelve.

SHE FINDS THE AUDIO file on her phone and turns up the volume as high as it will go, touching PLAY. The familiar computer-manufactured voice begins loudly:

Torna di nuovo, K.S. A grande richiesta!

The rhyming cyber-threats greet me with the same opening line every time. Translated: *Back again, K.S. By popular request, no less!* And as I listen, I feel blood vessels dilate in my face. My pulse picks up.

I don't want to hear a voice that sounds like his because then he's in my mind again. As if my father's still here. As if he's still alive. But he's not. What I'm hearing isn't him, and he would never talk to me unkindly. He would never wish me dead, and pain flares. I go hollow inside.

"I don't have time to deal with this now." I tell Lucy to stop the recording, and she does. "You think Tailend Charlie is Carrie Grethen. That's what you've come to tell me," I address the elephant in the room.

"I think she's behind it, that it's part of something else she's up to. Yes. That's where I am in this." Lucy's face is defiant.

"You've decided it."

"Because I know."

"And I needed to be told immediately because if Carrie is Tailend Charlie?" I fill in the blanks. "Then maybe she's also the one who disguised her voice and called nine-one-one about me. Maybe she's doing everything that's going on right now including magically interfering with the damn tent so I can't work the damn scene."

"Try not to get so irate. Especially not in this heat. It's not good for you."

"You're right, it's not."

"I believe she's in league with whoever Tailend Charlie is." Lucy's green eyes are unblinking. "Carrie's found someone to help her. It's her MO. It's what she does when she's mounting her next major offensive. She builds her army of two."

"Her latest Temple Gault, Newton Joyce, Troy Rosado." My mouth is as dry as paper, and I take another swallow of water, careful to keep my sips small so I'm not constantly looking for a piddle pack.

"She's taken about a year to regroup after her last bloodbath when she killed Troy's father. Then when she'd used up Troy she almost killed him. Carrie's easily bored." Lucy says these things as if there can be no debate. "You don't really think she's been sitting around doing nothing since then, do you?"

I keep my eyes on her and don't say a word. There's not much to say. She's either right or she isn't, and I have nothing to add.

"Hell no," she answers her own question. "We know Carrie better than that by now. She's been industrious while she's been away." Lucy's tone lacerates. "And her newest minion is some techy-geek anonymous worm who calls himself Tailend Charlie," she adds, and for an instant I'm stunned by her jealousy.

Lucy is threatened by my latest cyber-stalker because so far she's failed at tracking him, and Lucy doesn't fail. Yet she's rather much failed at everything she's attempted since Tailend Charlie's mocking communications began. Failure is Lucy's Kryptonite. She can't endure it.

"I don't know who he is but Carrie isn't working alone," Lucy says as I'm distracted by my phone on the countertop.

The display suddenly has illuminated for no apparent reason.

I pick it up, unlocking it, taking a look. The ringer is turned on, the ring tone on vibrate, exactly as I set them. Apparently I haven't missed any more calls due to some sort of glitch, and nothing looks out of the ordinary.

I place the phone back on the counter I'm leaning against, and it unsettles me that Ruthie Briggs hasn't tried me again. Nor has she texted or e-mailed.

"After a while certain things can suddenly make more sense." Lucy is talking about Natalie's death a year ago almost to the week, on September 18, and I'm becoming obsessed with the damn tent.

It's now past ten and nothing from Rusty and Harold. Not a peep from anyone. What the hell could be taking so long? I start to send Marino another message but I hold my horses. I don't need to drive everyone crazy. When they're ready for me, they'll let me know.

"Janet had been careful about getting the necessary passwords," Lucy is talking about Natalie's electronic devices now. "I just figured she was so overwhelmed she forgot or wrote down something wrong."

After Natalie died it turned out Janet and Lucy couldn't access the most important device of all: the personal laptop that had been in Natalie's bedroom and later in the hospice facility. The password she'd given Janet didn't work.

"And getting into it wasn't a piece of cake." Lucy avoids the word *hack*. "Natalie worked in digital accounts management. She was computer savvy."

I look at Lucy as she talks, and her eyes are windows to the carnage inside her. It wouldn't show up on a CT scan. It wouldn't be visible in an autopsy. But evidence of the massacre is beneath the surface like the footprint of a fort rotted away centuries ago and buried by layers of sediment and soil. Lucy has rebuilt her big powerful life on top of what Carrie ruined, and were the two of them face-to-face in mortal combat, I no longer wonder who would emerge liberated and whole.

I'm confident that neither of them would.

"I honestly thought Natalie was going overboard in her worries about spying," Lucy continues to explain, and I can tell she feels guilty. "I worried she was getting demented, that the cancer had spread to her brain."

"Understandably," I reply, but what I'm thinking is there are some things that can't be restored anymore.

There are some battles that can't be won. And if I imagine Lucy and Carrie in a duel, who would kill whom anyway? I hope I'm wrong. I hope it won't prove to be the case that they can't go on without each other. What would motivate either of them in their endless bloody tennis match if the other wasn't across the net? I don't know the answer but as Benton likes to say about dysfunction, *It's hard to give up your iron lung.*

"I remember you telling me that Natalie had covered her computer cameras with tape," I bring that up. "A lot of people do it but apparently she didn't until she knew she was dying."

"She put black tape over the webcams on her desktop, a tablet and also the laptop," Lucy replies. "It's an easy low-tech way to prevent someone from using your own computer to spy on you. Natalie routinely disabled built-in cameras on any personal electronic device she owned because she knew they can be activated remotely. And if the hacker is really skilled he can remotely alter the camera chip, disabling the indicator light so it no longer turns on when you're being secretly recorded."

"So taping over the camera lens was added for good measure," I reply.

"At the time it just seemed wacky."

"But what if it wasn't?"

"That's why we're talking about this," Lucy says. "I should have taken her seriously. If she hadn't been so sick and saying such weird shit, I would have."

"Did she ever mention concerns about Carrie?"

"No reason. All of us thought she was out of the picture for good."

"Because she was locked up in a forensic facility for the criminally insane," I presume. "And then after she escaped she got killed. Or that's what we believed."

"Like the rest of us, Natalie was convinced Carrie went up in flames with Newton Joyce when his helicopter crashed off the coast of North Carolina," Lucy says.

"Who did she think was spying on her?"

"The Feds. Or maybe a foreign government, other lawyers, lobbyists, reporters. You name it. The law firm she was with dealt with a lot of heavy-hitting politicos."

"And when she was moved to the hospice facility, this personal laptop went with her." I envision it on the bedside table where Lucy had set it up.

CHAPTER 25

I DON'T RECALL SEEING BLACK tape over the camera lens on the silver frame of Natalie's personal computer. But I'm remembering other things that were going on at the time.

Almost concurrently, Lucy was finding oddities in the CFC computer system. Then as more weeks passed she confirmed that someone had hacked into our e-mail and possibly the database. Months later after Natalie died, Lucy began to find other reasons for concern, she says.

"I was going through her computer logs, checking all processes that were running and at what times of day and night," she explains, and it's the first I've heard her go into detail about what she did back then. "And I found possible indicators of Trojan horses, of malware parading as legitimate programs, of a number of things."

"I assume you discussed this with Janet?" I ask because Lucy's never discussed it with me.

"I told her I wasn't sure. For example, there can be lots of explanations for a corrupt registry file. There can be more than one reason for a number of things. And if there's no cause for suspicion because you're far more worried about losing somebody you love and dealing with her seven-year-old kid? Then maybe you're not really looking either."

"But now you're suspicious."

"It's gone way beyond that."

"You've decided it was Carrie who was hacking. It was Carrie who was spying on Natalie, and basically on all of us." I don't ask because it's not a question.

"She was probably using a RAT, a Remote Administrator Tool to control Natalie's computer or computers." Lucy moves around the small galley as she talks, opening cabinets and cupboards like a fidgety kid. "And who knows how long it had gone on."

"How old was Natalie's laptop?"

"She'd refurbish and upgrade her personal computers, keeping them for a while. The one in question was six years old at the time, and some of the questionable files went back that far. So it's possible she was being hacked even earlier but those computers or devices are long gone. I can't check."

"If Carrie had been monitoring Natalie for at least six years," I reply, "then it wasn't triggered by her diagnosis or even by you and Janet getting back together. None of that had happened yet."

It's not adding up that the spying went on for an extended period of time. If it continued even after Janet and Lucy broke up well over a decade ago, why would Carrie still be watching Natalie? As I remember it, Carrie found her boring and referred to her as *The Old Shoe*. But clearly there's a lot I don't know, and I don't want to interrogate my niece.

I've never been given a satisfactory explanation for why she and Janet reconnected several years ago after more than a decade of being apart. I don't know if they were in contact all along or whose idea it was to get back together. But one day Janet reappeared, and next I knew Natalie was in hospice care and Desi was living here.

"Carrie's an addict, you know," Lucy then says as she walks into the main area of the trailer, her booted feet loud on the shiny steel floor. "She's addicted to us. In a sick way we're all she's got."

"She doesn't have us. She's never had us." I feel myself harden with anger.

Lucy sits down at a workstation and wakes up the computer mounted on the built-in desk.

"Somewhere mixed in with her mutated alchemy is this raging insatiable need to be important to someone." Lucy types a password. "And when she's in control of her victim—because everyone she partners with is a victim—she couldn't be more important to that person. For a while she's God. But then it always ends the same way. And she's alone again. The irony is, she needs us."

"She's not God and I don't give a damn what she needs." I return to the same bolted-down chair I was sitting in earlier.

"Benton says if you can't see her as a human, you'll never figure her out." Lucy's eyes meet mine. "And if you never figure her out, you'll never stop her."

I take a look at my phone again. Nothing. What the hell is going on? And I halfway expect that we're going to open the trailer door and find the entire park has vanished. As if we're in some hideous twilight zone and are being controlled remotely the same way Natalie's laptop may have been.

"Even if Carrie's behind all this, please explain how she would know the first thing about my father." I'm thinking of the canned recordings that sound like him, and I type a text to Marino as I talk. "If she's partnered with some other deranged person, how would he or she know?" I say to Lucy. "My father wasn't recorded, as far as I know, and Carrie never met him. She hadn't even been born by the time he died."

"I have to think there must be something of him out there somewhere," Lucy says, and it's not the first time she's said it.

"I'm not aware of it."

"You've never heard a recording of him but you can still hear him in your head."

"Like it was yesterday."

"What about Mom?"

"I don't know what Dorothy remembers."

"And there's no way she has a recording or knows about one?"

"She wasn't helpful. I asked her that a few days ago when we were discussing her trip." I didn't tell her why I was curious.

"There must be some kind of recording somewhere," Lucy says. "There has to be, and if there is? All someone had to do was get hold of it and pull out phonetic blocks and fabricate sentences. You could do the same thing to synthesize a voice speaking in Italian."

"Why can't we find this person?" I ask her point-blank. "What's so different this time that you haven't been able to trace a single communication from Tailend Charlie?"

"I think we're dealing with someone who's setting up virtual machines. If it were me, that's what I'd do."

"Please explain what you mean."

"It means we're sort of screwed," she says.

"WHAT YOU DO IS hack into some open machine or network. University campuses are prime targets for this, and we've got more than our share around here," Lucy explains what she believes Tailend Charlie is doing.

"Once you create your own virtual machine, you use it to create a virtual mail server," she adds. "After every e-mail you eradicate the server and create a new one, and this goes on and on into perpetuity."

"And there's no trail, no IP or anything?" I assume.

"Maybe there will be an IP in the packet logs of routers along the way. But it's the worst kind of wild-goose chase. Every time you track down an e-mail it's gone and a new one pops up from a totally different location."

"It sounds like something Carrie would do," I admit. "It's technology I can imagine her knowing about."

"You can pretty much take it to the bank that she knows the same things I do," Lucy says reluctantly, and it's hard for her to give Carrie that much credit.

It's even harder for me to hear it. Then Lucy brings up Bryce and I've been waiting for her to get around to him. She says he has no concept of who he leaks intel to in the course of what he considers normal conversations.

"Including the detail about a fake tattoo, which couldn't have been visible to anyone who might have been watching." Lucy picks up her phone. "He would have had to pull down his sock, and even so, the tattoo is small and faded after he scrubbed the hell out of it."

She explains that when she heard about the 911 call she asked Bryce to take a photograph of the tattoo and e-mail it to her right away. She hands me the phone, and the marijuana leaf above Bryce's right ankle is Crayola green but dull. It's about the size of a quail egg.

Now that I'm looking at the image I'm not surprised that none of us at work today were aware of the inconspicuous temporary tattoo. I don't see how anyone could notice it without being in close proximity to Bryce as he has his sock pulled down or off. Or maybe the wrong person somehow heard about Bryce's botched party trick, and from there the detail somehow found its way into the false 911 complaint made to the Cambridge Police Department earlier this evening.

"The pool of suspects should be small," Lucy concludes. "It had to be someone who knew what Bryce was doing last night."

"What did he tell you?" I ask.

"That he got a fake tattoo at dinner with friends. Nothing was posted on social media, and he hasn't a clue how anybody would have known beyond the buddies he was with. That's the extent of his note to me. I've not actually talked to him."

205

"Maybe we should." I take another sip of water and try not to think about how empty my stomach is or how late it's getting.

I block out the *grand cru* Chablis Benton and I didn't drink, and the clammy shoes that feel glued to my bare feet. I keep checking my phone. According to Marino's latest update a few minutes ago, the tent's not completely set up yet because there was a problem arranging the panels around several large trees. A section of scaffolding collapsed. Then the canopied roof didn't fit quite right. Or something like that.

"Have you ever told Bryce that when you were growing up in Miami, some of the kids in school called you a Florida cracker?" Lucy asks that next, and I'm feeling pelted by rotten eggs from my past.

"You've got to be kidding," I reply.

"Tailend Charlie again, and he had to get it from somewhere. That's why I'm asking."

"Sister Twister and Florida cracker are mentioned in the latest rhyming tripe?"

"Yes," Lucy says, and indignation stirs in its secret place.

I feel shame that was dormant but the anger is very much alive as my privacy, my past, continues to be invaded, distorted and vandalized by some anonymous bastard bard.

"Let's get to the bottom of this," I say from my metal chair as I dig my hands into the pockets of my windbreaker. "Bryce knows something even if he doesn't think he does. Let's ask him."

Several clicks of the mouse, and Lucy opens a file. Then in no time she has my chief of staff Bryce Clark on live video, the app her own enhanced rendition of Skype or FaceTime. She goes straight to the point, asking him if he knows much about my childhood in South Florida. Might he have been discussing it with anyone? Especially recently?

"Well we all know they were as poor as church mice," he replies.

"But I can't say exactly what she might have mentioned when we've just been sitting around shooting the breeze. Is she with you?"

"Yes," I speak for myself.

"Not that it's very often we have nothing better to do than sit around the office shooting the breeze, right, Doctor Scarpetta?" He waves, his attractive boyish face staring blearily from the computer display. "Full disclosure?" He holds up a brown bottle of Angry Orchard hard cider with its whimsical scowling-apple-tree label. "My second one but I'm not drinking on the job since I'm home? Even if I'm talking to you?" He's saying this to me, I think, and I'm not sure if it's a question or a comment, if he's being funny or not, and that's not unusual with him.

"The friends you were telling me about earlier." Lucy rests her chin on her hand, addressing him on the computer display as if he's sitting across the desk from her. "Do you talk to them about work?"

"Never inappropriately," he says, and I can tell from the background that he's sitting in his living room and has paused the TV.

"What about her?" Lucy says to him as she looks at me.

"Are you suggesting I'm disloyal?" Bryce protests. "Are you saying I'm talking about Doctor Scarpetta behind her back?"

"I'm not saying anything. I'm asking questions. Are you sure there's no possibility one of these friends you had dinner with last night might have posted something about your tattoo online? Not that I've seen anything anywhere yet . . ."

"You won't because there's nothing," he retorts. "Why would it be on the Internet?"

"That's exactly what we're trying to figure out. How someone might have known about it," Lucy says.

"Perhaps someone who had no idea it could cause a problem?" I offer him a chance to save face.

"Hell no. Anyone who matters knows that stuff like that can get me into trouble because of who I work for," he says as if suddenly I'm not present anymore. "That anything can be used against anyone in court."

He rambles on for a long moment, suggesting in his convoluted way that it's routine for him to be called to testify in trials and have his credibility attacked. It's not. He's never summoned for anything except jury duty, and he's always excluded.

"Where did you go last night?" Lucy asks him.

"We had two other couples over for Mexican home cooking, our specialty, as you know." Bryce smiles on the monitor, warmed by the memory. "Firecrackers with fresh jalapeños, a seven-layer dip with my famous guacamole, plus tacos, and the most amazing margaritas made with a really nice *añejo* tequila that we've been saving since Christmas? The one from your mom?"

My mind blanks out for a moment. Then I realize he's referring to Dorothy. It dawns on me what he's talking about.

CHAPTER 26

IN MIAMI OVER THE holidays last year, I got my fill of hearing about my sister's wonderful generosity and what *a simply scrumptious doll she is,* to quote Bryce.

It seemed that every time he and I had business to discuss over the phone, the topic of conversation managed to bounce back to Dorothy. If he thought she was in earshot, he'd tell me to pass along how much they were enjoying the tequila. Or he'd yell hello as if she could hear him. Or he'd ask me to convey a comment or a question. It was rather awful.

"Oh, what's the name?" Bryce snaps his fingers several times on the computer display. "This really fancy Patrón and it came in a leather box? And she has this fantastic recipe with agave nectar and fresh lime juice, straight up like a cosmo in a chilled glass, no salt. I told her I would practice so we can have her over while she's in town. And as you can imagine, the six of us had *way* too much fun." He rolls his eyes. "Just ask our cranky neighbor."

"Which friends are you talking about? Who were you drinking tequila with?" Lucy wants to know. "And when did you tell my mother this?"

Bryce recites four names I've heard him mention often over the years as Lucy begins typing information into search fields. My slightly tipsy chief of staff continues to defend what he perceives as the tarnished honor of his best pals, who he's known "since forever?" He says it like a question.

"And you know what? I can promise you they have nothing to do with the lying piece of shit who made the nine-one-one call about Doctor Scarpetta abusing me in public," he adds with feeling.

"I didn't abuse you." I remind him to pay attention to his choice of words. "Please be careful what you say, Bryce."

"I'm just repeating what was reported to the police by some jerk-off concerned citizen." His face is sincere with his fixed blue stare and spiky blond hair.

"When did you tell my mother you would make her margaritas?" Lucy steers him back to that.

"Well today's Wednesday. So I guess it was Monday night when we were going over her flight info and other things."

"And the fake tattoo? Where were you when you were messing around with that last night?" Lucy asks. "And who saw?"

"Wow! Get out the rubber hoses! Or these days, the waterboard? In our living room. There was nobody else there. We were safe and sound in our own home. It's too hot to go out and I'm not one for making scenes. Not that a fake tattoo and margaritas are a felony, last I heard."

"What time was it?" Lucy asks.

"Let's see. It was after dark obviously, and we'd eaten. I'm thinking around the same time it is now. Nine forty-five, ten o'clock. Maybe as late as ten thirty, which is about when I realized to my shock that the tattoo wasn't *temporary* as advertised? It wasn't going to come off easily, and I'm thinking of contacting the company about it and complaining."

"So let's talk about nicknames for a minute," Lucy says.

"Well I'm sure I have a lot of them. And maybe I don't want to hear what some of them are?"

"I'm actually talking about your chief," Lucy says to him as she looks at me.

When she quizzes him about nicknames from my childhood that he might have overheard, he asks, "Like what?"

"You tell me." Lucy isn't going to give him certain unseemly details if he doesn't already have them.

"She might have been called a know-it-all." Bryce frowns the way he does when he's thinking hard. "But that's to be expected, I guess. No insult intended," he adds for my benefit, I assume.

"Let me know if you think of anything else," Lucy says to him. "Any comment, no matter how innocent. Any person you know who might have passed along something without realizing it."

He promises he will, and with a click of the mouse he vanishes from the monitor.

"That narrows it down but doesn't make me feel any better." Lucy swivels her chair around, facing me as I recheck my phone for updates. "If this business with the fake tattoo had gone on in a bar, a restaurant or somewhere else in public?" she says as I read a text from Harold:

Tent up and ready for you.

"It might make more sense that someone could have been watching. But in the living room of his own home?" Lucy is saying.

The scene is waiting. I tell her I've got to go, and then I ask her to see what she can find out about Elisa Vandersteel. I tell her briefly about running into the woman who I fear is now dead, and if Lucy is surprised, she doesn't show it. But I catch a flare in her green eyes like light touching an emerald.

"How did you get the name?" She goes into interrogation mode, and I tell her about the British driver's license.

"Where was it and why are we thinking that's who she really is?" she then asks.

"On the fitness path between the body and the bicycle. Marino can e-mail you a picture of it."

"Most cases aren't complicated, Aunt Kay. Most end up being pretty much what they appear to be. But this one isn't going to be simple." She sounds reasonable but beneath her calm words is a threatening undercurrent, and I get up from my chair.

"There's something you're not telling me." It sounds so trite.

I sound naïve, almost laughable, because there's always something Lucy isn't telling me. There's plenty I don't tell her either, especially about Dorothy.

"I have a hunch about something. That's as much as I'll say right now." Lucy stares at me the way she does when she doesn't want me asking her anything more about a particular subject. "I'll be back with you when I have info I can confirm."

I remember what she said earlier. She referenced *multiple things happening at once,* and I inform her about the phone call Marino got allegedly from Interpol. All Lucy has to say about it is *more of the same.*

"Lucy, don't be so quick to decide everything is Carrie." I come right out and say it.

"I haven't decided anything," she replies, and I feel her stubbornness like a slab of concrete beneath thin carpet.

"Well you know where I'll be. And I'm sure it comes as no surprise that it's not looking like I'll see my sister tonight." I stubbornly avoid referring to her as Lucy's mom or mother whenever I possibly can. "Please tell her I'm sorry Benton and I couldn't pick her up—that both of us apologize."

I almost say that we're looking forward to spending time with Dorothy, that we can't wait to have her over to the house, to cook for her and take her to the theater. But it wouldn't be true, and Lucy knows it's not. I can't tolerate the idea of lying, especially to someone who's been hoodwinked and mistreated by a parent who isn't a nice person unless it suits. Maybe I'm not a nice person either because there are some things I simply can't forgive. And I can't forgive my sister. I won't.

"Tell her I hope she isn't too exhausted after what's sounding like a not-so-pleasant flight," is the best I can muster as I open the door at the bottom of a metal stairwell that brings back memories of riding the school bus.

I remember missing it because Dorothy thought it was amusing to change every clock in the house. She thought it great fun to hide my homework, and I would miss the bus because of that too.

"I'm going to work in here for a while." Lucy's voice follows me out into the hot darkness where the greedy night crouches, waiting for me like some insatiable entity cloaked in suffocating black.

THE HUMMING VIBRATION OF the truck's generator, the sounds of traffic begin to recede into the inky distance behind me.

As I head back to a clearing I can't see it anymore, just a dark void because of the black tent up ahead, acres away, I'm haunted by what I just heard. It's been a while since I've thought about what happened ten months ago when Dorothy gave Bryce and Ethan a very expensive bottle of tequila.

I remember thinking it odd that she was suddenly extravagant with people she'd never shown any interest in, although typically my sister is quite the hit with gay men. She adores South Beach, and it adores her back. She finds it gratifying and entertaining to *dress to kill*, as she puts it, to hold court in gay bars, to march in gay pride parades or better yet ride on a float, preferably in a formfitting low-cut dress, showing off her eye-popping curves, waving to all her fans as if she's Sofía Vergara, whom Dorothy idolizes.

Whatever Italian my sister learned as a child, she's managed to forget so completely she can barely say *ciao* or order pasta, although she doesn't bother with either. I'm not sure when it happened, but somewhere along the way Dorothy decided she's South American.

She's fluent in Spanish and all things Latino. The Miami Sound Machine. The hip-hop scene. She loves Cuban and Mexican cuisine, and suddenly Bryce does too. I didn't give her handmade aged tequila much importance until a few minutes ago.

I didn't realize what it might signify and why would I? It's not out of the ordinary for my sister to make grand gestures when the mood strikes. It's not unusual for her generous acts to be at my expense. Not so coincidentally I was in Miami with Dorothy and my mother when Bryce and Ethan received the Gran Patrón, specifically the Burdeos, which of course is Spanish for "Bordeaux," and that's the type of barrels it's aged in.

In other words, I heard all about it ad nauseam, and as I think back I recall assuming Dorothy's motive was to outdo or annoy me, and so what? I wasn't going to give her the satisfaction. But I find myself facing the ugly possibility that her Christmas splurge wasn't random or whimsical.

It wasn't simply her showing off and rubbing my nose in it. Not during the holidays or later at Easter, on Bryce's birthday or Ethan's and most recently and significantly Desi's. She's sent a deli basket, scented candles, potpourri, and treats for their pets. Desi got a Miami Heat jacket and a check, and I remember that Dorothy also called him.

All this when she didn't used to give any of us the time of day, really. Certainly she never paid attention to my chief of staff on the rare occasion she would call me at work. Until not so long ago she was condescending and dismissive to Bryce on the phone. She had no interest in Desi until his mother died. Dorothy never wanted to come north for a visit until now, and I wonder how often she and Bryce talk.

I will myself not to think about this now. Each gritty step I take along the unpaved path draws me closer to a young woman who shouldn't be dead no matter the cause. Still nameless and a mystery, she patiently awaits me inside a tent beyond the woods on the far side of the clearing.

Now that I'm seeing what Rusty and Harold have been struggling with for the better part of two hours, I understand what a job it was— or to quote Rusty's favorite shopworn pun, what an *undertaking*. Several acres away, the rectangular enclosure could accommodate a small wedding or a funeral.

The pitch-dark boxy shape blocks out tall old trees and shrubs, and the vague stars and quarter moon. I no longer can see the smudged lamps, the lights reflected in the river or the spreading empire of Boston neighborhoods and skyscrapers on the other side.

As I walk closer it's as if I'm reaching the end of the earth or diving in a shallow reef that abruptly drops off thousands of feet to the lightless bottom of the sea. I have the eerie sensation of floating in outer space, of being jettisoned to some awful remembered place where I don't want to be. And what continues to enter my mind is something Benton began to say at the beginning of our time together what now seems a different life ago.

I remember his exact words long before we had any concept of how trite and understated they one day would prove to be:

Carrie Grethen hasn't finished ruining people.

That was the simple prediction Benton Wesley, the FBI's legendary profiler, made long before we knew who she was, long before she was apprehended. He continued to predict her malevolence after she was indicted and convicted, and he didn't stop voicing his warnings when she was locked up on the women's ward of Kirby Forensic Psychiatric Center in New York City.

CHAPTER 27

CRIMINALLY INSANE, DEEMED MENTALLY unfit to stand trial, Carrie was warehoused on Wards Island in the middle of the East River, and it was a catastrophic mistake.

I don't know why it surprised anyone when she escaped. Benton had predicted as much, and he said that the miscreant who airlifted her to freedom, Newton Joyce, wasn't the first or last Clyde to her Bonnie. As a child, Joyce was horrifically disfigured in a fire. After his death, police searched his house and found a freezer full of his victims' faces. Carrie had encouraged him to keep the souvenirs. They probably were her idea.

I'm sure there were other partners after him, who knows how many before she exploited and had her fill of Troy Rosado. Carrie has a pattern of partnering with people she's convinced she can control, usually fatally flawed males like Troy, like Joyce, and before them Temple Gault, who Carrie worshipped and couldn't dominate.

A rare breed of glorious monster, Gault was a self-indulgent flamboyant Caligula, only he also was disciplined and supremely competent. Slight and limber, he was lithe and as lethal as a razor-tipped whip. He could strike as fast as a cobra, slicing open a throat or kickboxing the person to death, and he had a fetish for biting. As I walk through the heavy hot air I see his light blond hair, his blue eyes wide and staring like Andy Warhol's.

I've hardly thought about Temple Gault in years, and it's as if he's suddenly all around me. For an uncanny instant I feel his evil presence in the stagnant night, and I'm grateful he and Newton Joyce are gone for good. Dead. Unfortunately Carrie isn't, and I envision her dyed black hair and baseball cap, her unnaturally pale skin that she obsessively protects from ultraviolet light and toxins. This was what she looked like about a year ago, at any rate, and we have no idea about her appearance now. It could be anything.

But I would know those eyes, eerily blue like cobalt radiation, as if the decay of her very core emits a sapphire glow that darkens with her worsening moods, deepening to an angry purple like a damselfish when it turns aggressive. Carrie once was physically exquisite, born with exceptionally beautiful attributes and a stellar intellect. Her splendor was part of her curse.

The rest of it was her deranged religious freak of a mother who was pathologically jealous with a plethora of personality disorders and delusional ideations. Carrie had no siblings that would survive. After her birth, her mother miscarried twice. The brother born on the third try died soon after the father went to prison, and I remember looking up the autopsy records and lab reports when I was the chief in Virginia.

I remember thinking that a lot of mysterious deaths like eleven-month-old Tailor Grethen's were signed out as sudden infant death syndrome or SIDS when maybe they shouldn't be. I remember wondering how he really died as I imagined little angelic-looking Carrie doing something undetectable to her precious baby brother. Wedging his head between the mattress and the side of the crib. Positioning him in a way that ensured he couldn't breathe. Smothering him. To quote Benton quoting Gilbert O'Sullivan:

Alone again, naturally.

Carrie would remain an only child in a blighted universe all by herself. Homeschooled, she had no classmates, friends or ordinary activities. She didn't go to the movies, take music lessons, play sports or read for pleasure. The only television programs she was allowed to watch were fundamentalist religious ones about Jesus and judgment, about who's saved and who isn't. *The Jim and Tammy Show. The 700 Club.* Jerry Falwell. She listened to TV preachers threaten eternal damnation and other hellfire scares, and by the time she was six, Carrie knew all about sin.

Her mother made sure of it. Benton believes she not only didn't stop her daughter from being sexually abused, it was the mother's idea. She egged it on, enticing a host of men with her pretty child as a party favor. Carrie was lagniappe, a little something extra that her mother freely offered and would severely punish her for afterward. Carrie was forced to beg for forgiveness, to forsake her evil ways and perform degrading acts of penance after every battery and rape.

Her superior mental discipline and ability to dissociate have made her a supremely successful psychopath, possibly the most successful one he's ever encountered, says Benton, who has studied and pursued her much of his career. She can transport herself mentally, detaching herself so completely that she doesn't feel stress or pain, and she knows how to wait. Carrie will delay gratification for decades if the reward is worth it, and lying and truth are different sides of the same reality to her. She could say the world is flat, the moon made of cheese, and she'd pass a polygraph.

Emotions such as fear, remorse and sorrow are colors missing from her palette, and it was Lucy's bad luck that this perfect storm of a malicious human being would be her supervisor at the FBI's Engineering Research Facility. My innocent and immature niece literally was assigned to Carrie during the college internship I personally arranged, using my influence and connections. Lucy wasn't much more than a child at the time.

She never really had a chance to fall in love with the right person, and maybe she would have if I'd not had the bright idea of sending her to the FBI Academy. If only she'd never stepped foot in Quantico, Virginia. Maybe her first significant relationship wouldn't have been with someone who seduced her, stole her heart and in some ways her very identity and soul. Maybe Lucy would have felt differently about Janet long ago and also now. I wouldn't want to be Janet.

I wouldn't want to be the one who comforted Lucy after Carrie came close to destroying all of us. It's not a level playing field. It never has been, and Janet's smart enough to realize there are but a few degrees of separation between murderous hate and erotic love. They are different extremes of the same raging passion, and she evokes neither in Lucy.

Janet is somewhere between the best and the worst of everything when it comes to life with my niece, and I constantly feel bad about it even as I say nothing. It's not my business. But I worry I'm to blame. Maybe Lucy would have been better off had I not tried to do so much for her, had I not insisted on rescuing her from powerlessness, from loss and every other perceived bogeyman that plagued my childhood.

Maybe Dorothy is right when she says that I'm the one who's done the real damage to a niece I couldn't love more were she my own daughter. The irony is that Dorothy doesn't know about the worst mistake I made. She doesn't know about Carrie Grethen. My sister could be sitting next to her on the plane and not know who she is or why it matters.

Heading toward the big boxy tent silhouetted against the night, I realized how unsettled I am by Lucy showing up and giving shape and form to her worst fears. I resent walking around in the dark with Carrie on my mind, and I feel myself begin to resist her as I've done countless times.

"How are we holding up?" I say to one of the uniformed cops as my sweat-soaked Tyvek-covered feet quietly crunch past on the unpaved path that stretches ahead of me.

"Hanging in."

"Stay cool," I say to another officer.

"You too, Chief."

"If anybody needs any water, let us know," I offer the next one I encounter.

"Hey, Doc? We got any idea yet what happened to her?"

"That's where I'm headed," I reply, and I have a similar exchange with all of them.

There are at least twice as many uniformed officers stationed about, and I have no doubt that Marino's made sure the park is surrounded and buttoned up. No one uninvited can come in and out, and I find myself constantly listening for news helicopters, grateful I'm not hearing them yet. I don't need them hovering low and churning up the scene with their rotor wash.

I reach the tent and for the second time tonight am startled by a figure stepping out of the shadows.

"Marino's inside waiting for you," Investigator Barclay says officiously as if I've just shown up late for an appointment.

VELCRO RIPS AS I push my way through the side flap of the canopied enclosure. For an instant I'm dazzled by auxiliary lights, the scene as bright as an operating room. I stop just inside, setting down my shoulder bag, placing my phone on top of it.

I survey some forty-by-thirty feet of the John F. Kennedy Park that includes the iron lamp with its shattered bulbs, the bicycle and the body, all of it lit up like high noon. Marino and I are alone, no one else allowed inside until we say so. He moves about in white protective clothing that starkly contrasts with the black-paneled walls and twelve-foot-high black roof supported by a scaffolding of gunpowder-gray aluminum poles.

As I watch him make notes and take photographs I feel as if we're immersed in a black-and-white postmodern photograph. The only noticeable colors are the margins of green grass, the tawny fitness path, red biohazard warnings, and the dead woman's light blue shorts. From where I'm standing I can't see the blood but it will be coagulated, tacky and a dark reddish brown on the way to dry black.

That's based on what I noticed earlier when I got close, and also on the weather conditions, which remain extreme. Already I can feel the trapped humidity from the river. The hot air is sticky and low pressure like a tennis bubble. There's a plastic smell, and it won't be long until the stuffy environment bristles with a foul stench as bacteria teem and dead flesh and fluids putrefy.

"I went through the knapsacks," Marino calls out to me, and I assume he's talking about Enya and Anya.

"Are the girls safe and cool in a daisy room, I hope?" I find an equipment case to sit on so I can suit up.

"Eating snacks, drinking sodas. Flanders is babysitting, and I've got a couple uniforms making a wellness check on the mom." Marino's booming voice is amplified by the enclosure.

"She's still not answering the phone?"

"Or the door. Poor kids. I feel bad for them."

"And they're still saying she's supposed to be home?"

"Asleep in bed when they left the house, and I have a feeling I know what that means. Dead drunk, how much you want to bet?" Marino says. "I'm going to have to get DCF involved because it's obvious there's a problem."

The Department of Children and Families is the agency in Massachusetts responsible for neglected and abused kids. I tell Marino that no matter what happens in this case, he should make certain the twins are safe. It would seem they don't have adequate adult supervision. The way they're headed they're going to end up hurt or worse, and I don't think they understand the different kinds of trouble they can get into.

"Like stealing. Like tampering with evidence and obstruction of justice," Marino agrees. "Call it what you want? That's what it is when you pick up something that's not yours at a scene and decide to keep it. And guess what?" He hunches his shoulder to wipe sweat off his chin. "It turns out they were in possession of the dead lady's sunglasses. Which is too freakin' bad because I would have liked to see where they found them. How close to the bike or the helmet, that sort of thing?"

He lowers the camera and heads toward me as I begin pulling off the shoe covers I wore walking here.

"Do I dare ask what else was in their knapsacks?" When children stumble upon a violent scene it's bad for every reason imaginable.

"Leftovers from dinner," Marino says as he reaches me. "Bread wrapped in napkins, little packets of stuff like Parmesan cheese, red pepper flakes, salt, salad dressing." His big face is framed in white Tyvek like a nun in a habit, his cheeks bulging and a sweaty deep red.

"Sounds like they're not being properly fed." I look up at him from where I sit. "But you're not really going to know until you get inside their house. Are you okay, Marino? I'm worried you're very hot."

"Well they don't exactly look like they're starving. Yeah I'm hot. This sucks."

"One can be overweight and malnourished," I remind him. "In fact that's often the case, especially if the diet is mostly sugar and fast food. And left to their own devices, that's what kids will eat morning, noon and night."

"It appears they were telling the truth about having pizza for dinner and why they were out wandering around," he says. "I get the feeling they do this sort of thing a lot in all kinds of weather, probably because you're exactly right. Their mother's not taking care of them."

"It may be that she's never taken care of them, including when she was pregnant." I suggest that the twins may be suffering from fetal alcohol syndrome.

"That would explain why between the two of them they couldn't light up a ten-watt bulb," Marino says. "They're street-smart but that's about it. And it's shitty. Little kids shouldn't have to be street-smart."

"The sunglasses they picked up," I go back to that. "What do they look like?"

"Maui Jims, sporty ones."

"Rimless with amber lenses?" I inquire as I get a sinking feeling again.

"Yeah," he says. "They were near the body, according to Enya. The lenses are dusty and scratched real bad, and I'm thinking the victim may have been wearing them when she was attacked. Assuming they weren't already damaged."

"We need to be careful about saying she was attacked." I don't like it when he makes me feel like a scold.

"When you saw the lady riding her bike earlier did you notice if her sunglasses were damaged?"

"I didn't notice, assuming that's for sure who this is."

"I think we know." He pulls off his gloves and tosses them into the nearby biohazard trash bag hanging on a metal stand. "It's hard to imagine we're talking about two different women who look similar, are about the same age, and both had on Converse sneakers and a Sara Bareilles concert T-shirt. And maybe the same type of sunglasses. And they appeared in the same part of Cambridge at the same time."

"Even if they're the same person that doesn't mean we know who she is." I'll continue reminding him to be conservative even if he doesn't listen.

"And the other thing the girls had squirreled away?" He picks up a roll of paper towels, tearing off several squares to wipe his face. "A pendant. A gold skull about the size of a quarter, like from a necklace. I'm thinking it came from the broken gold chain."

"Where was it found?"

"They said on the path near the bike. Based on where they showed me, I'm thinking it was in the general area where the pieces of chain were." He tosses the wadded paper towels into the bright red trash bag next, and I follow them with my used shoe covers.

"The woman I encountered earlier was wearing an unusual necklace shaped like a skull. It was gold and looked fairly substantial, not flat like a medallion but rounded with contours," I inform him. "I noticed her flip it around to her back, tucking it into the back of her shirt when she rode across Quincy Street, heading into the Yard."

"It's gotta be her, and I'm not liking that you saw her twice right before she got whacked. I keep worrying that she's got some connection to you, Doc."

"I can't imagine what it would be," I reply. "I don't believe I'd ever seen her before today."

Then I tell him about my Internet searches for Elisa Vandersteel. I couldn't find her in London or anywhere.

CHAPTER 28

THE DRIVER'S LICENSE COULD be fake," he says. "These days technology makes it a piece of cake to counterfeit IDs that look like the genuine article."

"It's odd that whoever Elisa Vandersteel is she doesn't seem to be on social media either," I inform him. "What young person isn't these days? And I came across nothing in the news about anyone with that name that might be her. But I only looked for a few minutes."

"I agree it's strange. Unless she had reason to stay below the radar." Marino pulls down his white hood, patting dry his shiny head with paper towels. "Jesus, I'm sweating like a whore in church. Or she had a fake ID card, and there's no such thing as an Elisa Vandersteel with that DOB and address. And maybe that's why there's no one with that name on social media."

"Lucy's working on it. Let's see what she comes up with." I tear open a packet of coveralls.

"More than she's been coming up with, I sure as hell hope." It's an unfortunate dig at her failed efforts with Tailend Charlie, and I won't get into it with him.

I scan the lighted area of the park inside the flat-topped block-shaped enclosure, my attention wandering over the grass, the hard-packed path, the laid-down bike and the body. The scene looks eerily undisturbed as if it's not possible someone died violently here.

"How are we doing?" I ask Marino to fill me in on what might have developed since we last communicated. "Have you found anything interesting that we missed the first time? We're going to want to wrap this up as quickly as we safely can. It's awful in here, and I don't want either of us or anyone else getting overheated."

"Mostly I've been collecting what we already know about. The pieces of gold chain, the driver's license. And her helmet, which didn't look damaged to me."

"Do you think Enya and Anya might have picked up other evidence?"

"Where would they hide it? I searched their knapsacks, and we've got the glasses, the skull pendant, the phone. Plus we found the shirt one of them threw up on in the bushes."

"Unless they hid something somewhere," I propose. "Money, for example. Credit cards, cash? The victim was riding her bike out here alone with no money and no keys?"

"All I can tell you is they swear they didn't *borrow* anything else." Marino takes off his gloves and unzips a small black Harley-Davidson cooler bag that belongs to him personally. "They turned their pockets inside out for me. Nothing."

"I suppose it depends on whether they trust you enough to be truthful," I reply as he lifts out a dripping bottle of water and offers it to me. "No thanks. I'm all set at the moment. It depends on whether you trust them in return," I add about the twins. "Do you?"

"Hell, by now I've got them thinking they're going to be sworn in as junior detectives any minute. So I'm pretty sure if they had anything else they would have handed it over."

"I'm also curious about why they didn't bother picking up the driver's license." I begin working the synthetic white pant legs over my horrible shoes. "It was still on the path when Investigator Barclay arrived. I'm wondering how it got where it was and why the girls took other things but left that for some reason."

"Probably because, the way they figure," Marino says, "a dead person's ID would get them caught red-handed. It's not like they thought it was fine and dandy to take the belongings of someone who's been injured or in this case killed. Point being, at some level they know right from wrong. They were thinking finders, keepers. And they assumed the dead lady wasn't going to need sunglasses, a phone or a gold skull pendant anymore."

"They said that?"

"Pretty much."

"Well she wouldn't be needing money anymore either."

"I know. But unless they've got it hidden in their underwear?" He gulps the water, and the bottle is almost empty when he returns it to the cooler bag. "But I'll have Flanders check into that because there was no way in hell I was going to and be accused of manhandling them."

"Let's hope there's nothing else they've squirreled away that the victim wasn't going to need anymore." I replay my encounters with the cyclist when we were in front of the Faculty Club.

I didn't notice much in the way of jewelry.

"I didn't see a watch, for example," I pass on to Marino. "But the phone, the sunglasses and any other items Anya and Enya picked up and tucked inside their knapsacks will be a problem if this goes to court."

"I hope they didn't mess up anything that matters." He splays his fingers, working his hands into new gloves. "Not that there's anything much to mess up. So far I'm not seeing discernible footprints, no fresh cigarette butts. No blood drips or anything that might make you think there was a struggle. It's like she was already dead when she hit the ground."

"It certainly appears that she didn't move." I stand up and work my arms into the slippery white sleeves. "Based on what I'm seeing, I suspect once she was on the ground she was unconscious and dying," I add as my phone rings.

It's Lucy, and I put on my earpiece. I tell her I hope she's found something.

"South Audley Street, Mayfair. Off Grosvenor Square," she says.

"Elisa Vandersteel's address?" I sit back down on top of the equipment box, and I look up at Marino.

"A six-thousand-square-foot house valued at around thirty million pounds," Lucy tells me. "That's the address on the driver's license, and one of the reasons her name's not coming up in ordinary searches is it's not her or her family who lives there."

"The address is fake then."

"It's not. The owner is the CEO of a tech company, William Portison. British, went to MIT, wife's name is Diana." Lucy's voice sounds in my earpiece. "Does that mean anything to you?"

"I don't think so."

"That's who owns the house where Elisa Vandersteel was living as an au pair for the past two years," Lucy says with no lack of confidence. "It could explain why the Portisons' ritzy Mayfair address is on her British driver's license. And being an au pair might be why she's not on social media. Not every employer wants that if they're private and careful with their kids."

"You might be right but it's odd," I reply.

"A lot of au pairs work in exchange for room and board," Lucy says next. "They basically become part of the family."

"Yes but usually not literally," I reply. "I wouldn't think living with a family entitles you to hijack their address and use it as your own. If the South Audley Street house isn't Elisa Vandersteel's legal residence, then it really shouldn't be on her driver's license or other forms of identification. If nothing else it presents a liability to the Portisons."

"Well it seems they didn't stop her from using it when she moved to London two years ago and got the license," Lucy says. "She lists it on a number of things and got mail there. So I assume they knew what she was doing."

"Moved from where?" I ask.

"CANADA," LUCY SAYS IN my earpiece. "She exchanged her driver's license for a British one. And the obvious reason to do that would be if she planned to drive in the UK for more than twelve months."

She goes on about it with a certainty that perplexes me, and I'm not going to ask how she's managed to find out all this. When I searched the Internet for Elisa Vandersteel I came up empty. But I don't know where Lucy looked. Possibly the Deep Web, the Undernet, and I don't venture into the Bermuda Triangle of cyberspace, where terrorists and deviants prowl, and unsuspecting people and their property are wrecked and forever lost.

Lucy reminds me rather constantly that nothing is private anymore. Maybe what I'm seeing with the Tailend Charlies of the world is simply the price of doing business these days. But I admit I hate it. At times I feel like Rip Van Winkle waking up to discover decades have passed. Only it feels more like a century. Life used to be more civilized than it's become, that's for sure.

"And it's likely her work visa was up or a problem of one sort or another," Lucy adds as if she's had access to a dossier, "which explains why she's no longer in London."

"The woman I met earlier today definitely sounded British, not

Canadian," I reply. "In fact, my first thought was that she might be from London."

"Elisa Vandersteel was in London for the past two years but not from there."

"And before that?"

"A student at Leicester University, and before that it was Toronto, where she was born."

"And do we have any idea why she was in Cambridge?" I ask. "It would seem she has something to do with the repertory theater or the musical *Waitress* since that's where I ran into her the first time."

"She's not a student here," Lucy says as if it's common knowledge. "Her name also doesn't come up with the ART, the Loeb Center, *Waitress,* or anything related or even similar. Maybe she was a volunteer or something. It will be easy enough to find out."

"I'm wondering if she might have been living with someone here the same way she was in London." I tell her about the young man she kissed in front of the Faculty Club.

"That's my guess. She's staying with someone, explaining why I'm not finding anything to indicate she has an address in the greater Boston area. There's nothing listed in her name. No rentals. Nothing owned. Not even a hotel room or sublet that I'm seeing so far," Lucy says, and I feel Marino's curious stare.

"We got an ID?" he asks, and I indicate it's looking that way.

The UK driver's license found on the fitness path is genuine. The dead woman is twenty-three-year-old Elisa Vandersteel, a college graduate, a former au pair. But we won't release her name publicly until we've gotten a confirmation with DNA or dental charts and have notified her next of kin. For now Marino and I will assume this is who we're dealing with, and I feel stunned all over again.

I feel horrible. Actually I'm not even sure how I feel, how I should feel, how anybody should feel. It's as if I had a chance to change Elisa Vandersteel's destiny, and I didn't. She was in front of me twice today mere hours before her death. But it made no difference. If only I could have stopped her. If only I'd suggested she fasten the chin strap of her helmet or that she get out of the heat. Maybe I could have gotten her to think twice.

Maybe she would have changed the ultimate route she took or changed something, anything at all. If only I could have delayed or diverted her, maybe told her not to ride alone after dark through a deserted park. Of course I didn't know she was going to do that. I didn't know enough to tell Elisa Vandersteel a damn thing that might have prevented her from dying. And I need to stop this or I'll drive myself crazy.

"Her father was Alexander Vandersteel, and he committed suicide in 2009 at the age of forty-one," Lucy tells me what she's finding so far, and I hear keys click in the background as she continues her searches. "I got his obituary right here, and it looks like he ran a charity that got decimated by some Madoff-like investment scam. He hanged himself from a rafter in the garage," she says, and I can't imagine a detail like that was in his obituary.

"What about Elisa's mother?" I stand up and zip the coveralls to my chin but save the dreaded hood for later.

"Not sure yet," Lucy says. "But her parents were divorced."

"So let me see if I have this straight. The father's dead, who knows about the mother, and they were divorced," I repeat. "I guess we go to plan B because it would seem that Elisa Vandersteel's familial relationships may not help us with her identity."

I sit back down and start pulling on a new pair of shoe covers.

"We're probably not going to be able to confirm who she is," I add, "until we recover certain personal items such as her toothbrush, her hairbrush."

"I'm guessing she was staying with someone around here," Lucy says. "And I can promise that somebody at the theater is going to have at least some of the answers we need. I thought I'd wander over there before everyone's gone for the night, just do a little snooping, maybe find out where the boyfriend lives and where she's been staying. I'll find something."

I glance at the time on my phone. The evening performance at the repertory theater will have ended more than an hour ago.

"How will you explain your interest?" I inquire. "We want to be careful about word getting out."

"Oh I forgot. I'm new at this," says my former FBI, ATF agent niece who spent years undercover and doesn't need my coaching.

I tell her to be careful, and she says she'll see me later.

"Probably back at the office at some point," she adds, and I don't ask if Dorothy and her mountain of luggage are in the car with Janet and Desi yet.

I end the call, not inclined to bring up my sister in front of Marino, who watched me the entire time I was on the phone. I have a feeling he's thinking about her but I'm not going to give him an entrée to talk about it. If what Benton said is true and Marino and Dorothy have started something unbeknownst to me, I don't want to hear it now. I have enough to deal with.

"Ready?" I say to him.

CHAPTER 29

THE AMBIENT TEMP'S EIGHTY-SEVEN degrees," Marino says, and I spot the thermometer he placed on top of my scene case near the body.

I pull on purple nitrile gloves, and already I'm sweating through my scrubs.

"Thanks." I find my notepad.

"What are you going to do about taking her temp?" he asks. "I'm worried we should have just gone ahead and done it when we first got here."

"With flashlights in the dark when we don't know what evidence we might be disturbing or contaminating?"

"I know. And I'm with you, Doc. But just saying I've heard some comments, you know, cops talking about you sitting in the cool truck and not bothering."

"And we've heard such comments before, and we'll hear them again."

"Should we turn her over or something? Because I don't see how you're going to put a thermometer in her armpit when both arms are straight up." He lifts his arms above his head, and when he's swathed in white protective clothing I'm reminded why Bryce sometimes calls him The Yeti.

"We're fine at the moment. I won't need to turn her to take her temp."

"Okay. But it seems like the longer she's out here . . . ?"

"I know how it seems," I reply. "But as you've pointed out, her arms are straight up over her head. Even if I reposition her, it wouldn't be ideal for getting a core temperature."

That leaves the option of using the rectum. But there's no way I'm inserting a thermometer and possibly introducing injury or have some pugilistic defense attorney accuse me of it. I'll opt for the less convenient technique of making a small incision in the right upper abdomen to get the temperature of the liver.

I'll do this before anything else, and I return to the body. Kneeling close with a sterile disposable scalpel, I get a whiff of decomposition and another odor that's most noticeable near her head. The stench from blood breaking down is mixed with something else, and I try to isolate what it is.

"I'm smelling something acrid," I say to Marino as dark red blood oozes from the tiny buttonhole incision I make.

"I don't smell anything." He looks away as I push in the long thermometer.

Marino's not squeamish until he is. Then some things really bother him. I reposition myself closer to Elisa Vandersteel's head to find the source, getting down on my knees, leaning close to look carefully.

"Not me," Marino says. "All I smell is rotting blood."

"This." I show him singed hair near her neck and right jaw.

"Shit. I swear you're part bloodhound."

I also notice tiny fragments of glass. They shine like grains of sand in her disarranged ponytail, but I see nothing like that on her clothing, skin or adhering to the dried reddish-brown blood in her right ear.

"So maybe she has a head injury," Marino says as he follows where

I'm touching and looking. "That can make you bleed out of your ears."

"It depends on what type of head injury."

"How about one caused by a gun?" he proposes, and he's not being funny. "We don't know that she wasn't shot." His eyes are hidden by his camera again as he takes more photographs. "We've sure as hell seen our share of cases where you don't know they've been shot until you get them to the morgue."

"At the moment we don't know much," I agree, and I have little doubt that at this early stage of things Marino wishes the victim had been blasted with a shotgun, had a knife in her back or an ax buried in her head.

Then he'd know exactly what he's dealing with, and most of all he wants to work the case because he's already working it. It's natural to want to fit facts with a gut feeling, and that's the problem I routinely face because it's hard for cops to back off. There's no conquest, commendation or adrenaline rush if Elisa Vandersteel died from natural causes or an accident.

"She could have been shot." Marino doesn't stop but he will eventually. "And if you were shot in the ear at close range you could get burned hair from the muzzle flash."

"I'm fairly certain that's not what we're seeing." I study wisps and stubble that remind me of melted nylon as I think about what Anya and Enya said they noticed when they were close to the body.

They mentioned an odor that reminded them of their mother's overheated blow dryer, and possibly what they were detecting was burned hair. If so they were telling the truth about that, and the more I observe at close range, the more reality shifts right in front of me.

What began as the scene of an attempted mugging, robbery or sexual assault turned deadly is quickly becoming something else entirely. Marino won't want to hear it. Not at first. But after spending most of my professional life with him, I'm used to talking him down from the ledge, and he returns the favor. Now and then I'm guilty of bias too. I don't know anybody who isn't.

Marino probably is the most relentless cop I've ever worked with, and his kneejerk reaction will be to resist the track my thoughts are taking. When a detective worth his salt sinks his teeth into a theory, he doesn't want to let go. If one isn't careful, an investigation becomes a competition, a contest when it shouldn't be about winning. It should be about truth.

"Maybe she burned her hair when she was drying it after the shower this morning," he suggests. "It's important to remember we don't know when it happened. Maybe it's got nothing to do with what killed her."

"She dried her hair after the shower this morning?" I call attention to what he just said. "Do we know that's what she did?"

"Negatory since we barely know who the hell she is. But what I'm trying to say is we have no idea when it happened. I've seen people burn their hair from grills, the stove, cigarette lighters," he reminds me.

But what he's really referring to is that he's experienced each of the above more than once. Marino hasn't changed much. He still makes me crazy when he starts squirting lighter fluid during backyard barbecues. I can't count the times I've said to him: *What is it you don't understand about more not always being better?*

"Back in the days when I had hair to worry about, I scorched it when I was lighting a flare one time," he says, and I remember that too. "Took a long damn time to live that down." This was in Richmond, and he didn't live it down. "Point being, we don't know when she singed her hair and it might have nothing to do with anything."

HER EYES STARE DULLY at me from slitted lids.

If only you could speak, I always think. She will in her own way and in her own time. The language of the dead is silent and difficult, and the message I keep getting is Elisa Vandersteel looks remarkably clean and uninjured. I haven't turned her over yet, and I'll know more when I can examine her internally. But already I feel confident that her singed hair is directly related to her death.

That doesn't mean she's a homicide. I believe she was killed by a predator but that doesn't mean it was human. She may be an electrocution, and I'm scanning for any possible source of current. I'm looking around for something damaged, a shorted circuit that she could have come in contact with.

My attention continues going back to the obvious suspect, the iron lamp with its broken bulbs. I keep looking up at the sky only to be reminded that I can't see it because of the canopy. I'm thinking about power lines and lightning, and I tell Marino that whatever singed her hair likely occurred at or around the time of her death. If she'd burned her hair at an earlier time I don't believe we'd smell it now.

"Except I don't smell it." He bends close to the body, shrugging his broad shoulders.

"And I do," I insist. "And if it's this noticeable it probably was even stronger when Enya and Anya showed up a couple hours ago and found her."

Marino looks at the body, and he looks all around the lighted area of the park boxed in by the tent.

"The one thing that sticks out like a sore thumb is the blown-out lamp." He comes around to the idea begrudgingly, and now we're getting somewhere.

"That's exactly what I'm wondering. The damage to the lamp is telling us something important," I reply, and we start talking about power lines.

Most of them aren't underground in Cambridge, and Marino is quick to assert that if one were down we would have found it by now.

"Probably the hard way. Or the twins would have lit themselves up," he adds. "So tell me how it could be an electrocution, Doc? She would have had to come in contact with something electrically charged, and I'm not getting the mechanics of how it could have happened."

He points out there are no accessible electrical panels that might have live circuits, and no cords or tools to malfunction.

"And I'm not seeing transmission wires, cables, nothing like that exposed on the ground anywhere," he continues going down the list, and he should know.

Marino has his own machine shop. He has a monster garage, and thinks nothing of building an addition to his house or overhauling the engine of his truck. On more than one occasion in the past he's been the jack-of-all-trades I called in a pinch when I had a problem or electrical emergency. Especially in the earliest years when I lived alone, he was always over at my house for one reason or another, installing motion-sensor lights, repairing the garage door, changing the oil in my car, swapping out the garbage disposal.

"And it's a damn good thing, right?" he says. "Or maybe all of us would have been fried the minute we started walking around out here."

"That's an unpleasant thought." I step back on the path, looking at the lamp, at the pattern of broken glass.

The lightbulbs didn't merely crack or shatter. They were exploded with enough force to send pieces and shards many yards away. The lamppost is about ten feet tall, and I can't see the damage to the lantern. But clearly Marino has.

"The screws are still in the sockets, the three bulbs are totally destroyed." His face is red and sweaty as he circles the lamppost, looking up, his hands on his hips. "For the most part the filaments are gone."

"How can you see from here?" The lantern is too far above my head for me to look inside it.

"While they finished setting up, I used a stepladder and took photographs, which I can show you later," Marino says. "The metal latch is missing, maybe explaining why the glass door is open, and the question once again is when. Did the exploding bulbs cause the little latch, the hook, to break off? Or was it even there to begin with? We'll keep looking but it's not showed up so far."

I walk over to the bicycle on its side, and the rear tire is closest to the park entrance where Marino and I came in when we first got here. Apparently Elisa Vandersteel did the same thing, and I remember her pedaling through the Harvard Yard. I imagine her turning right off John F. Kennedy Street, entering the park from the east.

From there she would have followed the fitness path to the clearing, riding west as the sun slipped behind the trees and the shadows got darker and longer. Based on the position of the bike, something happened right here where I'm standing on the path, the iron lamp but several yards to my left. Her body ended up some ten feet away with glass in her hair, and her helmet is farther away than that.

As I think of lightning deaths I've worked I'm reminded that at first blush it almost always seems we're dealing with a violent assault. Clothing can be ripped, tattered or torn completely off, and I think of the T-shirt in the shrubbery. Shoes or boots will split wide open or come off like the Converse sneakers. Jewelry melts or breaks, and I envision the segments of gold chain we found. The broken ends looked shredded, and that's consistent with an electrical discharge. The current hits a metal object, dramatically heating it up, and it disintegrates.

Often victims are critically injured when the explosive force of an electrocution or a lightning strike hurls them to the ground. It's not unusual to die from blunt-force trauma, and it could be that's what killed Elisa Vandersteel. But I have my doubts.

CHAPTER 30

My COVERALLS CRINKLE. THE thin white material is slippery and whispery as I sit back on my heels to take a closer look at the unpaved path and the nearby grass.

It's past eleven, and the stench of decomposition has made the air deader and thicker. It's close to unbearable in here. But at least we're not dive-bombed by flies. The tent helps keep them out, and as a rule they're not active at night, not hunting for putrefying wounds and orifices in which to lay their eggs.

I study glass fragments as small as grains of salt that rained over the bicycle, sparkling like diamonds on the frame, the tires, and blades of grass.

"Not that I'm an expert in exploding lightbulbs," I say to Marino as I return to the bike's rear tire. "But right here where she went down there's a fair amount of glass that's been pulverized into dust."

"I've seen that before in electrical fires and arcing. Lightbulb glass is really fragile, and you give it enough juice it will blow to smithereens." He squats close to me, and I feel his heat and smell his sweat. "But some of what we're noticing probably is from the powder that coated the inside of the bulbs."

We look up at the empty lantern with its open access door, and below it a whitish residue is visible on the black iron frame. When the glass fragments blew out, they created a trail of what looks like fairy dust sparkling and twinkling across the fitness path, through the lawn, to the trees.

In my head I play it out like animation, envisioning the lamp violently exploding and the bicycle going down. The two events happen simultaneously as Elisa Vandersteel is jettisoned from the saddle. If that's what occurred, it could explain the tiny particles of glass on top of the downed bicycle. It might be the only explanation for the sandlike fragments caught in her hair.

"Well I think you're right about her burned hair being related to this." Marino cranes his neck looking up at the black iron lantern again. "But if the lamp malfunctioned as she was riding by? Wouldn't you also expect her to have cuts from flying glass?"

"That's a good point, and I can only say I've not yet seen any injuries like that." I think about how low Elisa Vandersteel might have been as she was riding by.

The lightweight hybrid has a small aluminum frame, low-rise handlebars, and a gel seat that I estimate would be approximately four feet off the ground were the bicycle upright. When she rode through the Yard she was bent over but not tucked into a racing position. I estimate the lantern would have been at least seven feet above her head when the lightbulbs exploded out the open door.

"The greater the mass, the greater the velocity," I'm explaining this to Marino. "And the bigger pieces, the shrapnel, would have flown over her head. But powder wouldn't travel far. It would drift down. That's assuming she was on her bicycle at the time, and I'm not seeing anything to make me think she wasn't," I add. "All of this is hypothetical. But it's significant that there's glass in her hair. It couldn't have landed on her where she is now."

"Nope. There's nothing over there because all the glass blew that way." He points in the general direction of the Kennedy School. "So we really don't think she was grabbed off her bike." He looks at me, and it's a good sign that he's started using the word *we*. "We're thinking there was no assailant—that she was just riding through the park and got zapped by a faulty lamp or heat lightning or something crazy like that."

"It's a possible scenario," I reply. "I don't see any sign of a physical confrontation."

"Then we're not calling this a homicide. Are we calling it anything when people ask?"

"It's undetermined for now. The less said the better."

"That's for damn sure. But to throw her ten feet like she was shot out of a cannon? All I can say is there must have been a hell of a lot of force. And I guess her helmet ended up even farther away than that because it's lightweight."

"And because possibly the chin strap wasn't fastened." I tell him when I saw Elisa Vandersteel ride across Quincy Street toward the Harvard Yard, the strap was dangling.

"Shit," he says. "Well that answers that."

"We'll know a lot more when it's determined exactly what happened to the lamp," I reply. "It won't be fun if you have to dig up the entire thing and haul it to the labs."

"Done it before. Will do it again."

I busy myself with my scene case, finding clear plastic and brown paper bags. I gather rolls of masking tape, Sharpies, and a gunshot-primer-residue collection kit I use when traces of debris are destined for the CFC's powerful electron microscopes. Changing my gloves, I return to the body. I kneel by her head, and in the intense illumination of the auxiliary lights, my flashspun polyethylene-covered knees are bright white against the green grass.

I remove the cap from a carbon-covered metal stub. I press the adhesive side against Elisa Vandersteel's scorched hair, collecting bits of glass, fibers, particles, anything I find. Sealing each stub inside a sterile vial, I label and initial it, prepping in the field, preparing specimens for the trace evidence lab.

This will make it easier for my chief microscopist Ernie Koppel to do the analysis when he gets to work first thing in the morning. The evidence will be waiting. It will save us time if all he has to do is sputter-coat the samples with gold. Then he'll mount them in a chamber and vacuum it down.

PALPATING THE SCALP, I dig my fingers through Elisa Vandersteel's tied-back long chestnut hair. Gently, carefully I work my way around the curvature of her skull, and my gloves are smeared dark red.

"She's got a wound to the back of her head," I tell Marino, and I'm aware of the side of her face resting against my leg.

She's as warm as life, and I feel a flutter around my heart again. It's as if I've been touched by the breath of God, reminded of what I'm dealing with, and I steady myself. I can't have a personal reaction right now, and I move blood-crusted hair out of the way to measure the laceration with a small plastic ruler.

The injury is not quite two inches in length over the occipital bone. I tell Marino that the laceration was caused by skin splitting as a result of blunt-force trauma, and this likely is the source of most of the blood we're seeing.

"Possibly from striking her head on the hard-packed path," I add.

"And the reason there's blood under her back is because she was dragged and that's where it ended up." Marino is looking down at Elisa Vandersteel's feet with their light gray-and-white-striped bicycle socks. "And we can account for how that happened. We know who did that much at least."

He takes more photographs of marks in the dirt that are no more than six inches long, terminating at the back of the heels. The girls didn't pull her very far in their effort to get her out of harm's way. They didn't succeed if their goal was to make sure she didn't get run over, as they put it.

Her body isn't even close to being completely off the path, but I'm bothered that their impulse was to move it at all. I wonder if this is what they habitually handle at home, perhaps when their mother is in a drunken stupor or passed out cold on the floor.

I gently touch the wound to the back of the head, spreading the irregular ragged edges so I can see the slender threads of tissue bridging. They're a clear indication this isn't an incised wound caused by a weapon with a sharp edge. I tell Marino that the scalp and subcutaneous tissue were split by a crushing force over a bony prominence of her posterior skull.

"So she must have been alive when she got that or she wouldn't have bled out," he says.

"But she didn't bleed out very much, which suggests she didn't survive very long. The scalp is incredibly vascular," I explain. "There would be a lot of blood everywhere had she survived long enough to move, to walk around or try to run from someone."

I continue working my fingers through her hair, checking for boggy tissue or fractures. There are no other injuries to her scalp or skull, not that I can feel or see, and I ask Marino to bring a hand lens from my scene case. I hear him step away. Then he's opening drawers, and next he's back with the magnifying lens. I use it and a flashlight to get a better look at Elisa Vandersteel's right ear.

"No abrasion, charring, stippling or any other sign of injury," I inform him. "I'm seeing only dirt and dried blood, and I'm not likely to know what caused the bleeding until we get her into the CT scanner."

Placing my hands under the back of her head, I lift it a little. I turn it to the right, and there's dried blood in her left ear too.

"If she's an electrocution, why would she have blood in her ears?" Marino asks.

"Ruptured eardrums are the most common cause." I open her eyes wider.

I check them for burns, for hemorrhages, and the blue irises are becoming cloudy. Sliding the long thermometer out of the incision in the abdomen, I wipe off blood so I can read the calibrations. Elisa Vandersteel's core body temperature is thirty-four degrees Celsius or ninety-four degrees Fahrenheit, and that would be about right if she's been out here for several hours.

"And her rigor's beginning, which is also consistent with that. I can feel a little resistance as I move her neck." I show Marino. "But her right hand and wrist are completely stiff, as Investigator Barclay noted earlier, and it's beginning to make sense."

As I lift her arm I notice that on top of her wrist is a peculiar whitish linear burn about three inches long and so fine it's as if she were scorched by a fiery spiderweb. It wasn't noticeable when her arm was raised over her head, so I'm just now seeing it, and I wonder if her right hand was near her hair when it got singed. If so, what did she come in contact with? Marino takes photographs, and I show him that the right wrist and hand are as rigid as iron.

"Yet rigor's only moderately advanced in her right elbow and shoulder." I lift her arm again to demonstrate. "It's barely noticeable in other small muscles and not apparent anywhere else including her left arm." I move that too. "I assume when Investigator Barclay checked for a pulse, the wrist he touched was her right one."

"I'm going to ask him," Marino says. "But that's the only thing that adds up. And from that he decided she was in full rigor all over."

"She's not, and it would have been even less advanced a few hours ago. She would have been limber except for this." I indicate her right hand and wrist. "And I'm reminded of what we see in an electrocution when the victim touched something like a hot wire—and that's what the white mark looks like on her anterior wrist. It looks like a burn from touching something extremely hot, the kind of burn you get when you scorch yourself on the red-hot burner of a stove."

"But a burn wouldn't give you instant rigor," Marino says. "And that's what this is even though I'm not sure I've ever seen it in person before."

A cadaveric spasm or "instant rigor" supposedly can occur when the death is preceded by a violent expenditure of energy that depletes muscles of oxygen and adenosine triphosphate (ATP). And the result is rigidity. The phenomenon is rare and believed by many experts to be apocryphal. But for sure something odd has happened here.

"So if her right hand was in contact with an electrical current," I tell Marino, "theoretically this could cause the muscles to continuously contract or clench, to go into what's known as tetany."

I pull the body partially on its side, just enough to check the back for livor mortis, or the settling of uncirculating blood due to gravity. I see only a slight pink blush. When I press down my thumb, the skin still blanches. Livor is in the early stages, and this also is consistent with her not having been dead very long.

There's also no question that when she landed on the ground she was either shirtless or her shirt was bunched up. Her back has the scratches and abrasions I'd expect in a bicycle accident, and there's dirt on her white sports bra.

When I turn the body a little more I'm surprised by what at first looks like a necrotic tattoo.

"What the hell?" Marino says.

"Her pendant," it dawns on me.

CHAPTER 31

THE BURN IS SHAPED like a skull.

"You can see the face. Well almost," I show Marino as we change our gloves, and we have a red biohazard trash bag full of soiled ones by now. "You can make out an eye and part of the grin, at any rate."

"Was she wearing the necklace backward when you ran into her?" He blots sweat on his chin with a paper towel, careful not to drip anywhere important, including the body.

"I wouldn't think so because I noticed the gold pendant was a skull with a whimsical face."

"Then it had to be turned over when it burned her, and it had to be inside her shirt so it was directly against her skin." He states what he wants to be true.

Marino doesn't want to think anything that might feed into his phobia of things that creak, groan and go clank in the night. He's getting spooked. I would expect as much after today, and it seems far from over.

"If you saw an injury like this and had no idea?" He goes on and on about it. "In the Salem days this would get you hung as a witch. They'd say it had to be a witch who zapped this person, and you'd better hope you never gave whoever it was the evil eye."

"Well fortunately we don't live in those days. But you're right. I probably would have been hanged as a witch." I pick up my hand lens, and he takes close-up photographs of the burn.

Dry and dark reddish brown, the partial impression of the skull's grinning face was caused by sparing when the metal pendant got extremely hot. The debossed or depressed mouth and an eye weren't in contact with skin, and those areas aren't burned. They've remained pale, explaining what looks somewhat like a grotesque emoji in the middle of Elisa Vandersteel's upper back. Even I would be the first to say that it's bizarre.

"It looks like a dead head." Marino's eyes race around. "Like something supernatural, like a stigma."

He means a death's-head and a stigmata, and the burn only looks like that if one knows what caused it.

"Can you help me hold her please?" Sweat runs down my chest, my belly, between my thighs, and the scrubs under my coveralls are soaking wet.

Squatting across from me, Marino steadies the body as I turn it completely on one side to give me a better look from head to toe, front and back.

"That's weird too," he says about the delicate whitish linear burns I find on the right shoulder and posterior base of the neck. "More of the same thing she's got on her stiff right wrist, and they're on the same side of her body. But if they're burns, they don't look anything like the one here." He indicates the angry red wound caused by the pendant.

I explain that when burns look leathery and white it usually indicates full thickness or third degree. I suspect that these whitish linear marks are from direct contact with whatever may have electrocuted her.

"Such as wires." I give him a hypothetical. "Except they would have to be very fine, almost hairlike."

"What wires?" Marino looks around nervously as if they might be close enough to get him.

"I have no idea—assuming that's what we're dealing with," as I notice she has something in the interior pocket of her blue running shorts. "The other burn is from the gold pendant making contact with this same electrical source. That's my guess."

Digging my fingers under the waistband, I find the small interior pocket and the hard flat shape inside it. I pull out a black plastic fob that appears to have a serial number on it.

"Bingo. Maybe it's the key to where she lives," Marino says as I drop the fob in an evidence bag I hand to him.

I get up and look around at the trees, the lamp, the trail of exploded glass. I try to come up with what could have been long and linear like fine wires that she might have come in contact with as she rode her bicycle out here. I think of her pedaling through the shadows, through the stifling heat, perhaps getting anxious and weary as it got later and darker.

Then suddenly something sears her bare right shoulder, the back of her neck, scorching her between her shoulder blades. It must have been excruciatingly painful and terrifying as she frantically grabbed at whatever it was, burning and shocking her right hand. It must have felt as if she were being attacked by an invisible swam of hornets, and that might be the last thing she was conscious of as her bike went down and she was thrown clear.

Such a scenario could explain the linear burns, and it could account for her asymmetrical rigor. A powerful electrical current striking a gold pendant and passing through her body would have heated up moisture, turning it to steam, and that could have blown off and damaged her shoes and clothing. Heat could have broken the gold chain we recovered, and I check her neck again, looking for any sign the chain burned her before it broke free.

Using a magnifying lens and moving her hair, I find what look like several red hash marks, tiny red burns no bigger than dashes on the right and left sides of her neck. There's nothing in front, and then I envision Elisa Vandersteel again, hot and sweaty but alive and friendly on the sidewalk in front of the Faculty Club. She was wearing a neckerchief.

A blue paisley print, I'm fairly sure, and I recall having the impression it was somewhat faded, possible a little frayed as if it might be something old. I ask Marino if a neckerchief has shown up, and I describe it. Did the twins possibly have it in a knapsack, and he didn't realize where it came from?

"Nope," he says. "I didn't see anything like that but I'll have Flanders double-check while she still has them in the daisy room."

"If not, then it should be around here somewhere," I reply, "unless she took it off after I saw her on Quincy Street. The important point is if she were wearing something like that it might have protected the front of her neck if the fabric was under or partially under the chain when it got heated up. If we find the neckerchief there may be burns that would verify this."

Then I tell him we also need to check on whether there might have been thunderstorm activity reported in the area early this evening. And I add that flipping the necklace around to her back may have been the worst thing she could have done.

"Even though she would have been sweaty and electricity loves sweat. But even so, skin isn't the best conductor," I explain. "But finding a chunk of gold is another story, and that may be why she's dead."

"Because the current would have hit her heart." Marino watches me work a small brown paper bag over one of the hands. "And there's a lot of resistance to pass through, which is why some victims have nothing more than burns after the fact. I know a guy who lost a finger but that was it."

"If the electrical charge didn't pass through her body, it's possible she would have survived," I agree. "And I'm betting we're going to discover her head injury isn't what killed her."

"That's why I'm careful about wearing jewelry when I'm around anything that can shock me. It used to piss off Doris because first I wouldn't wear the big clunky silver ID bracelet she gave me. Then I wouldn't wear my wedding ring, and she'd say it was so I could screw around on her." Marino confides this as if it's a new story, and at this stage of things very few of them are.

He hasn't stopped talking about his ex-wife in all the years they've been apart, which is at least twenty. Doris was his high school sweetheart, an uncomplicated woman, long-suffering until she wasn't anymore and ran off with another man. I know Marino hasn't gotten over her. I just hope he doesn't finally do it now because of my sister, and I try to block out what Benton said at the Faculty Club.

I secure the bags at the wrists and ankles with masking tape, making sure no evidence is added or lost during the trip to my headquarters.

"Now what?" Marino says at the sound of male voices outside the entrance of the tent.

I turn around as Velcro rips, and it's Investigator Barclay again, poking his head inside.

"You need anything?" he calls out.

"Yeah as a matter of fact, *Clay*?" Marino yells back. "I need you to stop coming in here and asking us that!" He rolls his eyes, and slowly shakes his head.

He waits until Barclay is gone to ask about the "freaky pattern" we sometimes see in lightning strikes, usually on a victim's chest or back. It reminds him of flying over the Low Country in Lucy's helicopter, he says. All those tidal creeks branching out everywhere through the salt marshes and mud flats, and what Marino refers to is arborization.

Also called *Lichtenberg figures,* it's the peculiar reddish pattern a lightning strike often leaves on the surface of the skin. If you don't know what you're looking at it's a freakish sight, and what causes it isn't completely understood. A good possibility is capillaries rupturing along the path the electric discharge takes through the body. And Elisa Vandersteel doesn't have a hint of this.

What bothers me more is if she were struck in her back and a thousand volts passed through the gold pendant, stopping her heart, then where's the exit? Lightning is predictable and it's not. It's as if it has a mind of its own, as if it's alive. It wants to race to the ground like some wild beast burrowing, and it's not uncommon to find an exit burn on the bottom of a victim's foot.

She doesn't have that either, nothing but dirt on her socks. There's not an exit anywhere I can find, and I tell Marino I'd like to see the pendant Anya and Enya picked up. He walks back to his big scene case.

PAPER RATTLES AS I open what looks like a plain brown grocery bag, and I work it over the hair, the entire head, all the way to the base of the neck, using more masking tape. I tear it with my gloved hands instead of using a blade.

I like something I can remove easily once the body is on the table in the autopsy room. A hair, a fleck of paint, a fiber, DNA—it could be anything. I'll move heaven and earth not to lose or contaminate it. But if one doesn't understand my reasoning, what I've just done looks like an appalling way to treat a dead body. It's what Marino calls a *whack and sack.* That's your reward for getting hit by a train, killed in a plane crash, for being murdered. *Dr. Death comes along and bags your pieces and parts like trash collected along the highway,* according to him.

At least I repositioned her arms from straight up over her head to down by her sides so we can fit her into a final bag, the biggest one, a body pouch, and I'm reminded that death and dignity don't belong in the same sentence. Opening drawers in my scene case, I find a sterile needle, and then Marino is back. I recognize the thickly contoured gold skull with its deep-set blackened eyes and gap-toothed grin.

I feel the weight of it inside its labeled bag, noting that the pendant doesn't look damaged, just dusty. I touch the needle to it through clear plastic and feel the faint magnetic tug.

"It must be gold-plated steel or there's some other alloy present. Gold is an excellent conductor of electricity but it wouldn't get magnetized unless it's not pure." I return the bag to Marino, and my fatigue is on its way to crushing.

I don't feel very good. I should take a break but there's not time.

"If it was lightning," Marino counters, "how come I didn't hear any thunder around here late this afternoon or early evening? You can't have lightning without thunder."

What he says is true because lightning causes thunder. One can't exist without the other. I propose that we might not detect so much as a rumble if the storm is twenty or thirty miles from here. We might not have a clue there's anything to worry about as we step outdoors for a walk, a swim, a game of golf. But a flash of lightning can travel a great distance from the storm generating it.

"That's where we get the expression *a bolt out of the blue*." My tongue is making sticky sounds as I talk. "And when you look at a chaotic scene like this you can understand people coming up with such ridiculous things as an *act of God* or *spontaneous human combustion*. When what they probably were dealing with was a damn lightning strike." I'm beginning to get irritable, to have sharp corners. "It would have been especially confusing if the nearest storm was many miles away, having already moved through."

"Except no storm has moved through," Marino says as Tailend Charlie violates my thoughts again, and I remember looking into the etymology after receiving the first mocking audio clip from him.

I say *him* but I don't know if the person is male. For the sake of convenience I refer to him as such, and Benton believes it to be true. My profiler husband says my cyber-stalker-poet is a man, an older intelligent and highly educated one, and the question from the start is why he gave himself a handle that's archaic British slang.

A *tail-end Charlie,* as it's more typically spelled with a hyphen, can mean the last batsman in cricket. But it also can also refer to a gunner in the rear of a fighter plane or the last thunderstorm in a squall line. As I pass this along to Chicken Little Marino, I realize all I'm probably doing is reinforcing his fear that the sky really might fall on our heads.

"In other words, just when you think something's over, the freakin' worst is yet to come," he complains as a whiff of rubbing alcohol fills my nostrils.

I watch him open packets of antimicrobial wipes, cleaning the six-inch plastic rulers we use as a scale when photographing evidence.

"One more curious coincidence in a day full of them." I'm aware that my stomach is somewhat unsettled.

"Yeah but is it really a coincidence?" Marino places each disinfected ruler into a sterile bag, returning all of them to a labeled drawer in his photography case. "You're saying it is, right? Because you only started getting those recordings a week ago. And now here we are." His eyes dart around as sweat trickles down his shiny red face framed in Tyvek.

I'm not saying anything one way or another, and I don't answer him as my patience rubs thinner. Everything is catching up with me. It's as if I feel the earth shift beneath my feet, a sinkhole about to open up.

"And if you think about it, Doc, a bolt out of the blue *is* a tail-end Charlie because it's the last part of a storm that's moved on, right? Kind of like a last flash for good measure."

I watch him drop wadded sanitizing wipes into the trash.

"What I'm saying is a rogue thunderbolt, in other words literally a tail-end Charlie, might be what killed this lady. Sure it could just be coincidental in a day full of shit like this—to quote you. It may have nothing to do with your rhyming troll." His bloodshot eyes look at me. "But what if it does?"

I don't reply because that's what I'm afraid of. I don't want to give my fear a name or form. I don't want to think or say it.

"What if it's all connected somehow?" Marino continues poking a stick at it. "What if it's all coming from the same source somehow? I mean we sure as hell have to consider it on top of everything else that's been going on."

It's overwhelming to contemplate a link between Tailend Charlie and Elisa Vandersteel since both are linked to me. It might imply that Carrie Grethen is behind all of it. Behind everything, and I'm too worn down to read tea leaves, to speculate anymore. Instead I suggest to Marino that we rely on science. Since nothing else seems very trustworthy, I advise that he check with the National Oceanic and Atmospheric Administration.

"NOAA should be able to tell us everything that's gone on weather-wise." I unlock my phone and my vision is bleary. "We'll find out if there was any thunderstorm activity within fifty miles of here." I feel whoozy and peckish as I text Rusty and Harold that we're ready to transport the body.

It's getting close to midnight and time to clear out. I've done as much as I can at the moment. The tent was a Rubik's Cube to set up, and we stopped taking breaks as the work dragged on stress-fully, miserably. We're behind and overheated. I feel dehydrated, my mood deteriorating precipitously, and I have a headache that's getting worse.

When I hear familiar voices and Velcro ripping again, I'm dizzy and jumpy as I turn around. I almost lose my balance.

". . . They're just finishing up . . ." Investigator Barclay pushes through the tent's opening.

I can't see Benton but I hear him mention something about blocking in several police cars. He'll be out of their way in a few minutes, he says in a commanding serious voice, and I feel a nudge of dread.

CHAPTER 32

"Like I said? Be ready because it stinks like holy hell in there . . ." Barclay announces in a stage whisper.

He's annoyingly present and officious as he holds open the tent flap for my important FBI husband, practically saluting him, showing him into our glaringly bright, baking-hot, airless, foul-smelling theater, where I'm about to pass out.

"Whatever you need, you know where I'll be."

"I've got it from here." Benton has had his fill.

"I almost went with the FBI, you know. I got no problem working with you guys," as if everybody else does. "Well you got my number if there are any other questions?"

"That's it for now." Benton's politeness hardens like epoxy as he tells the overbearing obtuse investigator he can leave—that nobody minds.

As I listen I'm finding it difficult to kneel in the grass, to concentrate. I'm packing up my scene case, feeling a little drunk, and I wonder what questions Benton was asking Barclay. What were they discussing as the presumptuous investigator escorted him here? I slam down the lid of what's nothing more than a big black toolbox.

"Bet you don't know many agents who started out as police investigators? Because I would think that would be a big draw . . ."

"You need to go," Benton snaps at Barclay.

And heavy plastic clasps snap. And my heart lurches. I feel strangely shaky and emotional.

Keep breathing. Keep moving.

SINCE I SAW BENTON last he's taken off his suit jacket and his tie. The sleeves of his white shirt are folded up to his elbows, and the pistol holstered on his hip is exposed.

He didn't drop by to say there's a lovely bottle of French Chablis waiting at home. He's here on official Bureau business, and I think of Lucy as my pulse hammers. I ask if she's okay and feel a stab of nausea.

"She's fine." Benton watches me from just inside the tent, near the equipment cases.

I'm getting increasingly agitated. Hostility smolders and sparks like an aggravated dragon while I act like everything is normal.

"We need to talk, Kay."

But I'm wondering how the hell he knows Lucy is fine unless he's been in communication with her recently. And if so, why? Don't gild the lily. Don't sugarcoat. Just tell me what I don't want to hear, tell the damn truth for once.

"Is she still working in the truck?" I hear myself ask even as I know the answer.

"No." Benton stares at me, and Lucy wouldn't still be here.

That was hours ago when we talked inside the air-conditioning, and the stench is putrid and pervasive now. I'm insulated in it like a foul rotting gauze that I taste in the back of my throat as the dragon salivates, swallowing hard.

For God's sake, don't throw up.

I'd never live it down, and I watch Investigator Barclay vanish through the tent flap, what's become the wormhole to a parallel universe. He won't go far. No doubt he'll hover within earshot as he's done most of the time Marino and I have been working in isolation, conversing in private, speculating secretly, gossiping just between the two of us, not realizing some asshole wannabe was out there listening.

No telling what Barclay relayed to my husband, in other words to the FBI. After what Marino and I have been through with this scene, and the biggest damn threat is one of our own. The thought penetrates furiously as my heart pounds harder, and my eyes are watering. I take deep slow breaths, blinking several times, well aware that a common symptom of heat exhaustion is irritability. But knowing that doesn't do any good once you're caught in a vortex of uncontrolled fury.

"Hey Benton? Did Dorothy get in okay?" Of course Marino would ask sweetly, warmly about a woman who devours men like tartare.

Innamorato pazzo! as my father used to say.

Marino is crazy in love. Now that I'm looking for it, I can see it plain as day, and I pay attention while Benton tells him in a leaden voice that Dorothy is fine.

Other than one of her absurdly ostentatious oversize designer bags being lost, that is. I don't say it out loud.

She's landed safely with almost all her luggage, Benton informs us about my vain self-important inconvenient sister who's always treated her own flesh and blood like shit.

"But she's finally in the car at least?" Marino has to make sure about his intended paramour. "Because I've not gotten a text from her in the last couple hours. She stopped answering."

Sotto l'incantesimo! my father would declare. Marino is under the spell. He and Dorothy have been in contact even as I've been by his damn side working this motherfucking scene, and he never let on. Then I'm horrified that I just said something so hideous as that out loud. Maybe I didn't. Maybe I thought it but didn't say it.

Marino's not behaving as if I did. I look closely and suddenly there are two of him all in white like Pillsbury Doughboys. Neither seems offended. But I can't tell and I close my eyes. Then I open them and Marino is by himself again and acting normal for him. I hope I didn't say *motherfucking*. Not that I'm a prude. But I rarely talk like that. I'm not thinking straight. I'm about to erupt like a volcano. My electrolytes are in the toilet, and it's bewildering.

"As long as she's okay," Marino is saying to Benton. "But the airport's a nightmare because of the elevated terror alert and who knows why else." He tries to be nonchalant about it and fails.

"She's with Janet and Desi." Benton's eyes don't leave me.

"Then she's in the car on the way to their house?" Marino probes but Benton isn't paying attention.

"We need to talk, Kay. I need you to come with me," and I detect sadness beneath my husband's iron will.

I push back my hood, my hair plastered to my scalp. I pick up my scene case, and it seems incredibly heavy as I make my way to him.

"What's the matter, Benton?" Marino yells. "You getting bored hanging out with pencil necks? Couldn't stand missing out on all the excitement? Wanted to drop by and see what real investigators do?"

He's behind me, loud enough to break the sound barrier and not picking up on cues. Marino's too busy making cracks about the *FIBs,* as he calls the FBI when he's not calling them something worse. Then he falls silent mid-snark because Benton's grim expression is as rigid as a mask. He's oblivious to everything except me.

"Shit." Marino realizes something is seriously off. "Hey? What's going on?"

"You don't look good, Kay." Benton couldn't be more gentle or somber. "I need you to sit down."

He starts to touch me but I move away. I have blood on the cuffs of my sleeves. I need to decontaminate. I have to get out of this synthetic clothing before I suffocate. I feel claustrophobic wrapped up from stem to stern like a house under construction, and I'm breathing faster and shallower.

I will myself not to show that I'm on the brink of collapse. I'm keenly aware of the danger signs. One of them is not sweating enough. I'm not anymore.

"How about sitting down and drinking something?" Benton says because he's thoughtful.

He always has been, from the first time we found ourselves in the same room together, and I couldn't take my eyes off him. Benton was considerate and kind when he didn't have to be, when most people weren't. He didn't follow the lead of his male compatriots and think of me as tits and ass in a lab coat. He never called me *ma'am* or *Mrs*. He'd say my name the way he still does. As if he meant it.

"Do we have Gatorade? Anything like that out here . . . ?" He's asking because he would do anything for me.

"Not that I'm seeing so far but I'll keep digging." Marino is crouching by his Harley-Davidson cooler bag, and I blearily watch his thick fingers find the small metal tongue.

I hear the sound of a zipper as I sit down on top of my scene case. I begin taking off my coveralls, and everything's a struggle.

"We need to talk about Briggs," Benton says.

"Is this about him canceling?" It sounds pathetically lame when I ask, like wishful thinking on my part.

I know that's not why my husband, why Special Agent Benton Wesley has come for me. He didn't show up to pass along information about my event with Briggs but to haul me away because the U.S. government wants what only I can give. Or give up, and that's the more likely story. Whatever the FBI demands won't be in my best interest. It never is one hundred percent of the time.

"I'm sorry," Benton says as I reach down to pull off my dirty grass-stained shoe covers. "I didn't want you hearing this from somebody else."

"Ruthie tried to get hold of me and sounded upset." Blood pounds in my head. "That's what I thought she was calling about." But it wasn't, and I should have put more effort into finding out what she really wanted.

"He's gone," Benton says. "I'm sorry, Kay."

"FUCK!" MARINO VIOLENTLY TWISTS the cap off a bottle of water, handing it to me as his face turns a deeper shade of red. "What the hell are you talking about?" He glares at Benton. "He's *gone*? General Briggs is dead?"

"I'm really sorry," Benton says to me, and how ironic that he would resort to a euphemism.

Gone. As in *passed away. No longer with us. Not here anymore.*

That can't be right. That's not what he means. But it is, and dread nudges harder. It throws an elbow into my solar plexus, knocking denial right out of me.

Dead.

Briggs went swimming at six P.M., and forty-five minutes later was found facedown in the pool, and I try to comprehend it.

Dead.

The stagnant foul air seems smoky as if I'm looking through a veil. I take another sip of water warm enough to bathe in. I pour it into my hands. I splash it on my face. I dribble it over my bare arms. I dig my fingertips into my temples as my head aches miserably, looking up and down, blinking several times.

I get back on my feet as Marino machine-guns questions, demanding to know if the FBI is thinking that what happened to Briggs *is connected to the dead lady here in the park*. It's unwise for Marino to ask that. He just made it easier for the rug to be pulled out from under him, and he does that a lot.

"Kay? You should sit." Benton's face is blurry. "Please take it easy. I want to make sure you can walk back. We probably should have you transported. What about a wheelchair?"

"Good God no. Just give me a few minutes." I'm a little queasy.

"Sit and drink water please."

"I'm fine." But I'm wobbly on the way to worse if I'm not careful.

I don't want to be sick, and I look away from him, from Marino. Don't stare. Fixating is a recipe for disaster, and I look here. I look there. Up and down. Moving around. I don't allow anything to hold my attention for more than a second or two, barely stopping my eyes from moving. Don't fixate because that's when it will happen.

That's when you lose it, and I can't count the people I've collected off the epoxy paint–sealed floor or presented with the ubiquitous plastic bucket. Mostly cops who gather around the stainless-steel autopsy table as if it's no big deal, and I always see it coming.

That fifty-yard stare as my scalpel slices through the chest, making the Y incision, running down the torso, detouring around the navel, reflecting back tissue with quick deft flicks of the blade.

Exposing gastric contents, the intestines, and it's not aromatherapy, to quote Marino. Only he pronounces, even writes it *Romatheraphy* with a capital *R*. As in the Eternal City. As in Romulus and Remus.

Two
Four
Six
Eight
Remember
Not
To
Fix-ate!

My little morgue ditty. Rhymes are an easy way to remember. Keep moving. Look here. Look there. Don't stare. I recite my little ditty in my mind because I'm the one who needs it this time. And I keep my eyes moving. And my attention wanders . . .

Over the grass.

Across the tawny dirt path.

Back to the dead woman forlorn on her back.

In her white sports bra.

Her blue shorts.

And gray-striped socks.

Her head, each hand, each foot wrapped in brown paper like an uprooted tree in a burlap diaper.

Dead.

Packaged as evidence, disgraced and depersonalized, and that can't be the bold, proud, spirited woman I met earlier today. Not once. But twice. Attractive, quick-witted, fit, overflowing with confidence and life. Reminding me of Lucy. How could she be reduced to this? To detritus hauled away and carved up?

What doesn't kill you makes you stronger.

But it did kill her, and what a strange thing to say, as if a part of her knew and was trying to laugh it off. I should have stopped it somehow. She was in my presence twice and I didn't stop anything.

I look around the black cubical tent with its exposed gray aluminum frame. Then back at the body, and I remember her strong tan shoulders and bright smile as she taped recipes to the walls inside the Loeb Center. I remember her dropping her water bottle on the sidewalk in front of the Faculty Club.

You're the peanut-butter-pie lady.

She was hot, her tan skin covered in a sheen of sweat. The sun was going down. There were smudges of peach and pink along the horizon, and I watched her ride across Quincy Street.

Dead.

I look up at the trees. Their heavy green branches are motionless in stifling air that would be a clamorous symphony if odors were musical instruments in an orchestra of stench. I'd be hearing minor keys, sharps and flats, a crescendoing chaos swelling with percussion. Heavy with bass strings. Building to a suffocating coda.

Then the house would go dark after the encore of death, and the bloated teeming crowd would be too turgid and foul for me to force my way through anymore. Looking for an exit. Not finding one. There isn't one. Briggs would be the first to say it. I can't show up at the morgue in Baltimore for him.

It would only give the bad guys something to dig up that doesn't need to see the light of day, Kay.

I can hear him as if he's standing in front of me with his deep dimples and big smile. There's really only one rule in life, he preached. To do what's right. But he didn't always, and I wipe my eyes on the backs of my hands.

CHAPTER 33

I REST QUIETLY ON TOP of my hard black boxy perch. I keep my back straight, breathing slowly, deeply, trying not to slouch.

I bought the heavy-duty plastic scene case on sale at Home Depot years ago, and it's an appropriate throne for the *Queen of Crime,* for *Her Travesty* and *Royal Hardship*. Bryce is quite the pun meister. He calls me a lot of things when he thinks I can't hear him.

I wait for my molecules to gather, for the dizziness to pass. My brain seems to slide around heavily, slowly, inside my skull like an egg yolk as I turn my throbbing head this way and that. I listen to Marino and Benton. Sipping water, I look closely at who's talking. Back and forth like a Ping-Pong match. Point and counterpoint like a Gregorian chant. The Pugilistic Crank versus the Unflappable Stoic.

I have a ringside seat as Marino questions, and Benton deflects and evades, not answering anything important about what's happened to our mutual friend John Briggs. But it's not lost on me that my husband doesn't hesitate to probe about the dead woman in our midst, a twenty-three-year-old Canadian who shouldn't be on the FBI's radar, certainly not yet.

I also don't trust Benton's imperviousness to the helicopter that's begun flying up and down the river. Or maybe it's more than one.

But he acts as if he doesn't notice what at this hour isn't a sightseeing tour, and it sounds too big to be a local TV news crew. I have a feeling the Feds have started showing up or are about to, and I don't think Marino suspects what's going on. Probably because oblivion is better, and as I rest and hydrate I give him another second or two before he faces reality in a most unhappy way. I know a not-so-friendly takeover when I see one.

". . . The question's also going to be why she really left their employment," Benton is talking to Marino about the Portisons in London and their former au pair Elisa Vandersteel. "Because if the family was happy with her they would move heaven and earth to hang on to her. Why did she leave?"

"Maybe her visa."

"There are ways around that if the family wanted to keep her and she wanted to stay. The two boys are older though. Thirteen and fourteen, and it may be as simple as they don't need someone looking after them anymore."

"What two boys? How the hell do you know that? Did Lucy tell you?"

But Benton doesn't feel obligated to answer questions unless it suits him. He's asking and commenting about the case as if he's in charge, and Marino is beginning to fidget and get flustered. After carefully packing his Pelican case, he's suddenly kneeling back on the grass to reopen it as if he doesn't know what to do with himself.

"Yeah, I know what the questions are," he retorts, unsnapping clasps, and he's getting defensive and louder. "You must have talked to Lucy and I don't know why because last I checked this wasn't your damn case."

"Maybe she found out something from the people at the theater?" Benton doesn't answer that question either as he looks toward the body some fifty feet away. "For example, what or who brought her to Cambridge?"

Marino opens the big lid on his scene case.

"The question is whether Elisa Vandersteel was an intended target or simply random—in the wrong place at the wrong time."

"Whose question?" Marino begins rechecking the evidence he packaged, and I see his paranoia and anger grow by leaps and bounds. "I thought you were here to talk about Briggs." His hot flushed face stares warily at Benton as the truth sinks in.

Something has happened to the jurisdiction in the Vandersteel case. That would explain why Benton is here. If the FBI has taken over the investigation it would make sense that he's been prowling around the scene inside the tent, watching where he steps, scanning trees, the grass, the path, and the damaged lamp and exploded glass. When he's not looking at me, he's looking at everything else, and it's beyond his usual curiosity.

I can tell when he's making assessments. I know when he's in his profiler mode. I also know that the FBI shouldn't have been invited to assist in the Vandersteel case—not at this early stage. But Benton's demeanor, his heavy energy and quiet gravitas, are telling me he doesn't need an invitation.

What that suggests is a fait accompli, and it's a thought I find disturbing and unsettling. We don't know if she's a homicide, and since when is the FBI interested in electrocutions or lightning strikes?

I have no doubt Barclay divulged all sorts of things as he escorted Benton through the park. But by that point most of the damage had been done. A decision had been made or my husband wouldn't have shown up here to begin with, and Benton can't just walk in uninvited and help himself to a case. There's a process, and I wonder when Marino's going to catch on that Benton isn't treating him like an investigative colleague anymore.

I watch him pack up his coffin-size scene case, obsessively fussing with it the way he does with one of his monster tackle boxes or tool chests.

". . . A heart attack is my vote." He's like a moth batting against a window screen, determined he's going to extract more from Benton about Briggs, about anything.

But what I'm really witnessing is the agonal stages of Marino's lead role—or any role—in the Vandersteel investigation. He won't be involved with what's happening in Maryland either. But then, technically he never was.

". . . That's why I'm wondering if Ruthie said anything about him not feeling good," Marino says as Benton ignores him.

Marino hasn't been informed outright that his case has been co-opted by the Feds, and since they aren't collaborative that's the same as being fired. Something like that wouldn't come from Benton. That's not how it's done when a local investigator is removed from a case—or more accurately stated, when a case is removed from a local investigator. Benton won't be the one to say it and he doesn't have to for the ugly truth to be all around us like the stench and the heat.

"Like maybe he hadn't been feeling right, was having chest pains. Or maybe it had to do with the pacemaker he got eight or nine months ago?" Marino has begun to bluster, and Benton isn't answering. "But I can see you aren't going to tell me shit. In other words you're being a typical FBI dickwad."

Benton isn't really, and were Marino not so distracted by his discomfort and fatigue, by his usual power struggles and insecurities, he might realize what's glaring. Briggs had a top-level security clearance and regularly advised military leaders, the secretary of state and various directorates including the Departments of Defense and Justice.

He attended social events at the White House and was accustomed to briefing the president. For obvious reasons he's of keen interest to the U.S. intelligence community, which isn't going to insert itself directly into the domestic investigation of his death. The CIA is sneakier than that.

Typically it uses the FBI as a liaison or a front because global spy-masters aren't supposed to deal directly with domestic medical examiners, cops and the likes. That's a sanitized way of saying that in the real world the CIA is the invisible witch rubbing the FBI's crystal ball, diverting and deploying its agents and experts like a squadron of flying monkeys.

What happens next suddenly and without warning is they descend upon your scenes, your witnesses, your offices, paper records, database, labs, morgues, your very homes and families. There's no regard for what damage might be done, and cops like Marino may never know what hit them or the reason. Having a major case overtaken by the Feds is every investigator's nightmare—especially if the agents involved are secretly doing the bidding of some cloak-and-dagger organization like the CIA.

I watch Marino watching Benton look around, assessing, contemplating, carrying himself as if he has the right to be here while I scarcely know the smallest thing about my mentor, my friend found dead in a pool. What pool? Was this at Dover Air Force Base in Delaware? I know he swam there religiously when he was overseeing the Charles C. Carson Center for Mortuary Affairs.

Or was Briggs traveling? He would use the hotel pool if there were one. But I have a feeling I know, and it would be tragically ironic. It would seem like an Old Testament judgment as I envision the quaint stone house in its charming Bethesda neighborhood off Old Georgetown Road. Briggs bought the property decades ago. One of the draws for him was its close proximity to Walter Reed National Military Medical Center, where we once worked together.

"Here." Marino looms over me, and I realize he and Benton have stopped talking.

Marino has dug up a sports drink that's as hot as the humid foul air. The bottle was hiding inside a rucksack for God knows how long but I don't care. I wipe lint and grime off it, twist the cap, releasing the seal with a pop. The fruity flavor is salty and cloying, and I feel it instantly like the hit of a cigarette or a shot of Scotch.

"I don't know if something like that can go bad after a while," Marino watches me sip, and his clothing is several shades darker from sweat. "Sorry it's not cold."

ON THE DECK BEHIND the house is the Endless Pool Briggs was constantly repairing.

I can see it in my mind as vividly as a photograph, and it pains me unbearably. Too frugal and stubborn to replace it, he held it together with spit and rubber bands, he liked to quip. To him it was a functional exercise machine no different from a treadmill or a stationary bike, and swimming in place was part of his daily routine when he was at his and Ruthie's Maryland home.

I was witness to it when I would stay with them, and the appointed time was six P.M., the witching hour between work and Johnnie Walker, as he liked to say. He'd step down into water heated to eighty degrees Fahrenheit, and turn on the current, selecting whatever resistance suited his mood and conditioning. Then he'd swim in place for thirty minutes. No more or less, and after all we've been through? After all my complaints about his jerry-rigged engineering? This is how it ends?

I ask Benton that. I need to know it for a fact. Where was Briggs? Was he at the house in Maryland? I want to know for sure and don't care if Benton doesn't want to talk in front of Marino or perhaps at all. I don't care whose case it is. I need to know a few things. I need to know them now.

"Yes, in Bethesda," Benton answers me while communicating with a look not to push him too far, that we can't be talking about this here.

"Where was Ruthie?" I push a little more. "Was she home?" He can tell me that much.

"She was making dinner."

The kitchen sink overlooks the redwood deck and fenced-in yard in back. But one can't see the pool because it's off to one side near the bird feeder and the toolshed. I told Briggs more than once it wasn't safe. If he had a heart attack, if something happened, very likely no one would see him in time.

I badgered him about getting a defibrillator, about installing security cameras. When he got the pacemaker, I gave him a CCTV starter kit so Ruthie could monitor his exercise from different areas of the house.

Thanks but no thanks, he let me know. *I don't need to be spied on more than I already am.*

Approximately six hours ago, I'm told, he headed out the back door with his towel, his goggles, barefoot, and in swim trunks. I've been to the residence countless times. I can see the Endless Pool about the size of a home spa. I recall Briggs installing it on the deck maybe fifteen years ago when old football injuries started acting up and he began referring to himself as the *joints* chief of staff.

He gave up running for swimming, and at their Maryland home he'd wage war against the Endless Pool's artificial current. If he wanted to build endurance he didn't go longer but harder. He'd wear water mitts or scuba fins to increase resistance, and I ask if he had on either. Benton doesn't seem to know, and I watch Marino pick up a handle of his big Pelican case, rolling it closer to the tent entrance as I hear voices and the clatter of a stretcher.

Then Marino's cell phone startles the stifling quiet, the ring tone a World War II air-raid siren, an urgent alert I've heard before but not often. He steps away from his scene case and us as he answers someone high up in the Cambridge Police Department food chain.

"Yeah, I'm still here and about to wrap it up. What? You're kidding." His voice is exasperated but restrained. "Yeah, I'm hearing you. Not that I'm surprised." He glares at Benton. "When the hell was this?"

The tent flap opens again, and Harold walks in, weary but tranquil, smiling sympathetically at me. He asks if I need anything, and I would see it on his face if he'd heard the news about Briggs. The CFC exists because of General John Anderson Briggs. He helped shape the place and has spent considerable time with us over the years. Harold, Rusty and the rest of my staff will be crushed. But not as crushed as I'll always be.

". . . That figures. It's nice of him to tell me himself seeing as how I've been standing here talking to him for the past fifteen friggin' minutes." Marino gestures on the phone, stealing resentful sidelong glances at Benton.

"It's still hot as Hades out there." Harold solemnly nods, looking at me as if I'm a prospective project for an undertaker.

I can imagine him contemplating different glues and shades of makeup and whether I'm going to need putty.

"If you don't mind my saying so, Doctor Scarpetta . . . ?"

"I do mind, Harold. I don't need to hear that I look worse than some of my patients right about now."

"Goddamn son of a bitch." Marino has ended his call.

"You just look like you could use a break someplace cool, Chief." Harold takes my empty sports-drink bottle from me, studies it with a frown before tossing it in the trash. "You did notice this was expired?"

"Well that makes two of us, Harold. Thanks and you know where I'll be." I look down at my damp dirty scrubs, at my loathsome pumps. "I'll see you back at the ranch."

"Well I don't know about you walking anywhere. You still look pretty hot to me . . . Oh dear." As he's pulling on a pair of gloves. "I didn't mean that kind of *hot*. Anyway I'm not sure you should exert yourself in the least." His concerned face appraises me too carefully.

"Don't even think about it." I wag a finger at him.

"We do happen to have a stretcher handy and it's as clean as brand-new—"

"No. Thank. You." I emphasize each word like a gunshot.

"Fine. But we'll be bringing up the rear if you start feeling faint. It's a bit of a hike, and there seem to be a lot of people. Law enforcement of one sort or another," he adds, signaling that there are cops or agents in the park who weren't here earlier.

"What about the media?" I ask.

"Oh no. They can't get in. The park is completely sealed. They have the entrances blocked and have even closed off Bennett and Eliot Streets and University Road. Cruisers are all over the place, most of them with their emergency lights off, and there are a lot of unmarked cars lurking about. And I've been hearing a helicopter. Actually, it could be more than one."

Then he goes on to give me an update in the same earnest soothing tone. He says my troops are being mobilized, and that confirms what I suspect. He realizes it's not happenstance that Benton is here. Harold recognizes the signs of a coup on the way, and he's taken it upon himself to mount a defensive front while the new day is still young.

My radiologist Anne has agreed to come in to work right away, he confirms. So has Luke Zenner, and Bryce is already there. Rusty has driven the mobile command center back to the CFC and returned with a van to transport Elisa Vandersteel's body. Harold has saved me hours and possibly a lot more than that. This is one of many reasons why I couldn't possibly replace him, and I tell him thanks.

"I can use all the help I can get," I add. "I think the long night might have just gotten longer."

"I'm afraid you're right, Chief." His smile is somewhere between unctuous and pious.

Benton loops the strap of my briefcase over his shoulder, pretending he didn't hear anything we just said. He follows me as I duck through the black fabric flap, passing from glaring brightness to the pitch dark. For an instant I can't see. But the great hot outdoors is a pleasant relief, and I fill my lungs with air that's not as stifling and doesn't stink.

"How are you feeling? Are you okay to head out? Tell me the truth," Benton says, and maybe it's my muddled condition but I feel a vibration.

"As long as I don't jog." I detect the unmistakable *thud-thud*.

"Slow and easy please," he looks at me as my attention is pulled toward the river.

The *whomp-whomp-whomp* reverberates in my bones, percussing in my organs. I scan around us as mechanical turbulence bounces off buildings and bridges, making it difficult to pinpoint the location of what sounds big and scary.

I'm fairly certain it's the same helicopter we've been hearing or another one like it, and I notice a bright white light in the distant dark to the northeast, a searchlight probing, headed toward us. We stop walking to watch the blazing finger pick its way along the MIT and Harvard campuses.

It paints over the ruffled water, slashing through thick treetops and over the fitness path on this side of the river.

CHAPTER 34

THE BELL 429 THUNDERS in low and slow, whirling and churning, lit up and strobing at an altitude of maybe four hundred feet and a speed of sixty knots. Rotor wash agitates the canopies of trees, shaking them violently, and it's a good thing we've collected the evidence. I wouldn't be happy if this thing had roared in before the tent was up.

"I hope it doesn't decide to hover here," I raise my voice to Benton as if he has something to do with the deafening spectacle, and maybe he does.

The twin-engine bird roars past in a fierce wind, and I recognize the gun platforms on the skids, the fifty-million-candlepower NightSun on the belly, the rescue hoist, the Forward-Looking Infrared (FLIR) camera.

The silhouette of the twin-engine warship brings to mind a monster tadpole, a carnivorous one, and I notice the doors haven't been removed or opened. Typically they would be if this were a tactical operation or a search-and-rescue mission, and that hints the objective is surveillance. But as far as I'm concerned, mostly what I'm seeing is for show.

"One of yours?" I ask Benton, our necks craned, looking up. "Because it's not Boston, the state police or Med Flight. It's not the Army,

Marines, Navy or Coast Guard. And it's certainly not Lucy even though she changed into a flight suit a few hours ago. That's definitely not her helicopter," I add.

The searchlight is long and linear like a stick of neon-bright white chalk as the unmarked blacked-out bird banks sharply downriver, doing a one-eighty at the Harvard Bridge, near my headquarters.

"It wasn't my idea," Benton says as we stand outside the tent, looking up.

"And what idea are we talking about? Thundering up and down the river for what purpose?"

"Suffice it to say Carrie Grethen feeds off the attention but so do certain other people."

By *certain other people* he means his own, his fellow agents, and we watch the helicopter scream past again.

"I was against it, saying she'll only get off on it if she's goaded into overdrive. She'll just kick it up even higher, but I was outvoted," and that's all he's going to say about it.

The rest I can probably guess with a high degree of accuracy. The FBI is searching this area of Cambridge, and I'm betting they have choppers up in Maryland and possibly other places. If this is for Carrie Grethen's benefit it's truly stupid, and Benton is right about that. In fact the idea of intimidating her in such a fashion would be laughable if anything were funny at the moment.

The Bureau's big machines don't impress her, and more likely they've been deployed for appearance sake, to make sure the taxpayers know that Federal agents have stormed in to save the day. That's what Benton meant when he referenced that Carrie's isn't the only ego in the mix. There's nothing like being splashy. There's nothing like giving a false but dramatic impression, and this is why cops like Marino snipe about the Famous But Incompetent, another moniker tossed around about the FBI. It's why they're the FIBs.

It's why Marino resents and distrusts them, and as I think of Elisa Vandersteel's body being loaded on a stretcher right about now, I feel a rush of indignation. The FBI with its expensive equipment and slick agents hasn't mobilized for her sake. She's nothing more than a means to an end, and I ask myself the same thing I always do. What are the Feds really after?

The answer is almost always going to be mundane if not predictable. Add politics to power and season liberally with publicity. Then stir in the elevated terror alert for the Boston-Washington area that Benton mentioned earlier, and that's probably what I'm dealing with. In summary, it's why Marino has been marginalized and I'm about to be if I'm not clever.

"Remember this isn't a race," Benton says, and he's setting a very slow pace as we trek back to where he's parked near the entrance at John F. Kennedy Street. "If you start breathing hard or feeling unsteady, we're pausing and taking a break."

Overhead on the bridge, the traffic is much lighter between Cambridge and Boston's Back Bay. There aren't many cars or motorcycles, mostly trucks at this hour as the Charles River flows sluggishly like molten glass in the uneven glow of lamps along the shore. The helicopter is gone, at least for now, and our footsteps are quiet.

"What's really going on?" I ask. "I know what I think but would rather hear your side of things."

"Uh-oh. We're already talking about *sides*."

"Because you can't be on mine and I won't be on yours. Despite Marino's claims to the contrary, I'm not married to the FBI."

"I wanted to check on you for a lot of reasons, and it was important I tell you myself about Briggs. But that's not the only reason I'm here."

"Obviously not. You've been walking around and asking questions about a case that shouldn't be any of your business. You don't simply show up and insert yourself into a local investigation, and that tells me other things have gone on. Clearly they've gone on stunningly fast, in the blink of an eye."

"Yes, they have because so much has happened at once," and he tells me that before he got here he was on the phone with Gerry Everman, the commissioner of the Cambridge Police Department.

Benton doesn't say who initiated this conversation, but I can guess. The FBI did, and when they take over an investigation this is what it's like. It feels exactly the way it does right now as I walk with their senior profiler through the park toward densely shadowed trees beyond the clearing.

I listen to our shoes on the hard-packed path with its loose sandy surface that's a poor medium for footwear or tire tracks. Distant traffic sounds like a gusting wind. I catch fragments of conversation in the impenetrable dark, and am vaguely aware of people I can't quite make out talking in hushed voices.

I feel eyes on us as I catch the silhouettes in uniforms and field clothes of cargo pants and polo shirts. Cops, possibly the Feds, and I think about Harold implying it was getting a little crowded out here.

"ELECTRICAL? I GET THE impression that's what you're deciding." Benton is almost too quiet to hear, and I walk very close to him. "It seems she was riding past a lamp and was electrocuted."

"And then logic begins to fail us because what I'm seeing is confusing if not contradictory." I take his hand and don't care who sees it. "Was the problem the lamp? Or was the lamp blown up by the same electrical current that killed her? And where did this current come from? If it came from the lamp then how does that explain her injuries? She has a linear pattern of burns that don't make sense. And

I don't understand the FBI's interest this early on when there are more questions than answers."

"It's almost like she encountered exposed wires, from what I've gathered."

"Yes, I'm sure you've gathered quite a lot," I reply. "But there aren't any wires that we could see, and they would have to be some distance off the ground if they were going to make contact with her neck and shoulders. It's as if she was riding along and passed under something that's no longer present or visible."

"Or something passed over her," Benton suggests.

"Obviously you're assuming homicide when I don't know that for a fact yet."

"But why she would be targeted is a mystery," he says. "Elisa Vandersteel has no connection to us that I can fathom, and no connection to Briggs. I also don't see why she might be of interest to Carrie Grethen. The victimology perplexes me. Something's not right."

"Does it bother your colleagues? And yes, something's not right. That's quite an understatement."

"Elisa Vandersteel was a soft target. Random, in the wrong place at the wrong time. Briggs was a hard target. That's the theory."

"Is it your theory?"

"I'm not sure I have a theory but I know Carrie Grethen kills for a reason," Benton says. "She's not into random slaughter but rather prides herself on what she perceives as her own moral code and decency. It's not her MO to destroy people who don't deserve it, in other words. So why would she target a twenty-three-year-old Canadian au pair whose dream was to be an actress?"

"It sounds as if you might have learned more about her."

"Apparently the reason she was in Cambridge is she'd gotten an internship at the repertory theater, was helping in stage management in hopes of getting a chance to act. She'd started there about two months ago, at the beginning of August. Was bright, a hard worker, funny, but very private. This is according to several theater people Lucy's already talked to."

I think of the young man who handed Elisa Vandersteel a FedEx envelope in front of us, and I ask if anyone has tracked him down yet.

"There's a lot to dig into but she was seeing someone who works in the events-planning office at the Faculty Club. Apparently he's a vocalist who she met when he auditioned for *Waitress* but didn't get the part."

"Do they know his name?"

"They couldn't remember it."

"Do they have any idea why Lucy was asking about her?"

"I don't think so. She wandered backstage as if she was looking for her and started chatting. I definitely have the impression that Elisa Vandersteel was living with this guy we saw on the sidewalk."

"But we don't know where." I think of the key fob I found in her pocket.

"Not yet but it's close enough for her to get around on a bicycle, it would seem."

"Have you told Marino all this?" As I ask I remember that he has custody of Elisa Vandersteel's phone, and Benton saw her talking on it the same way I did.

But he doesn't bring it up.

"No, I've not told him," he says, and it occurs to me that he's not bringing up her phone for a reason.

Benton saw her talking on it the same as I did when we were on the sidewalk in front of the Faculty Club. He hasn't asked about it. If I don't mention it, he probably won't. Maybe someone else will but Benton will feign ignorance. Why would he know that Elisa Vandersteel had a phone? And I feel sure he hasn't told his compatriots that he encountered her not long before she died.

Already Benton is letting me know in his own subtle way that he's not going to interfere with me even as he does.

"Do you intend to tell Marino what you're telling me?" I ask. "And if not, when will he be informed that he's been fired from his case?"

"No one's been fired, Kay," Benton says slowly, gently, in rhythm with his steps.

"Technically, maybe not."

"I think we understand each other."

"Yes, and what I ask is you remember the most important thing."

"It doesn't need to be said."

"But I will say it anyway. She deserves the best we can give her." I mean that Elisa Vandersteel does.

"And I have no doubt you'll make sure she gets it, Kay. I can count on you to do what it takes."

He's letting me know that he personally won't get in my way. But the Bureau is another story. Then he asks my opinion about the cause of death, and this is when we step up the tempo and the subtle moves in our dance.

I'm required to pass along information even as the parties involved interfere with me. I won't withhold appropriate details from my FBI husband. I give him far more than I would most. But I don't tell him everything.

CHAPTER 35

I EXPLAIN WHAT I CAN say with reasonable certainty, handing off to Benton what I would to other officials who have a right to know. But I'm nicer about it and we're holding hands as we walk through trees, rooftops peeking over them to our left, the glinting dark river to our right.

"An electrical charge passed through the pendant she had on, magnetizing it," I'm saying. "She was thrown off her bicycle, lacerating her scalp. Some of her belongings were scattered, and based on glass in her hair," I conclude, "I believe this happened at the same time the lamp exploded. But I can't tell you much more than that when she's not been examined at the office yet."

"It's sounds like you're talking about lightning."

"Similar, yes. But not quite, which is baffling. Lightning could account for the burn caused by the pendant but not the peculiar thread-like linear burns she has. I honestly have never seen anything like this before."

"Which brings me to the question we wouldn't want anyone to know we're asking," Benton says. "Is it possible we're dealing with some sort of DEW, a directed-energy weapon?"

"As opposed to what? Heatstroke? A heart attack?" I'm aware that the leather insoles of my ruined shoes make quiet squishy sounds as I walk.

"As opposed to sabotage," Benton says. "Such as doing something to booby-trap the lamp or an Endless Pool so that they malfunction catastrophically."

He turns to look behind us as if he can see the shattered lamp with its swath of exploded glass. But all of that is under the tent. It's like looking back at a black hole at the far end of the dark park with its smudges of illumination, and I detect people moving about almost invisibly. They keep their distance from us, watching in the velvety blackness, their tactical lights probing and flaring.

"This is what the Bureau is thinking?" I ask. "That someone targeted two different people in two different places with what's basically weaponized electricity?"

"Like a particle beam, a laser, a rail gun that uses energy instead of projectiles. The technology's out there. It's been only a matter of time before something terrible happened."

"And the delivery system in these two cases?"

"Something like a long-range laser gun. A manned aircraft. Or much more problematic would be a UAV, an unmanned aerial vehicle converted into a weapon of assassination or mass destruction."

"As in a drone you can buy off the Internet?"

"This is what we've been anticipating, and you've been hearing me say it for a while, Kay. A drone is going to take out a major passenger jet, a government building, a world leader. Sufficiently weaponized, a drone could take out a lot more than that. We're waiting and watching because it's a certainty when the capability is there."

"And unfortunately drones are everywhere. Not a day goes by when I don't see them somewhere," I reply, and it gives me an uneasy feeling that I spotted one earlier today. "Even when I was walking to meet you, even in this heat, there was one flying around," I add.

"Did it seem to be following you?"

"I didn't think that at the time. But as we're talking about it I remember being aware of one at the Square when Bryce was holding forth through the open car window before I went inside The Coop. And then there was the drone as I was walking through the Yard afterward. But I can't say it's the same one, and it didn't come close."

"Depending on how technically sophisticated the device is, it might not need to get close if it's being used to spy or stalk," he says. "Did you notice how many props it had? Was there anything about it that caught your attention?"

"It looked like a big black spider against the sun. That's the only impression I recall having because I didn't pay attention to it. I imagined some kid hanging out in his dorm room and having fun flying the thing. I honestly gave it almost no thought."

"Kids are high on our list for this very problem, only we've been expecting homemade weaponized UAVs—drones armed with explosives, with firearms, pipe bombs, poisonous chemicals, even acid. But there are worse things to fear. Especially if the objective is to terrorize," and as he talks I remember what Marino said a little while ago:

. . . *If you think about it, Doc, a bolt out of the blue is a tail-end Charlie . . .*

"You're right," I tell Benton. "You wouldn't want the public to know you're asking questions like this. People would be afraid to leave their homes if they thought they might get attacked from the sky while they're swimming or riding a bicycle. What about burns? Do we know if Briggs has them?"

"There's a burn on the back of his neck. A round one about the size of a dime."

"Round?"

"Yes, and it's red and blistered," he says as I think of the skull pendant Elisa Vandersteel was wearing.

"Do we have any idea what caused this round burn?" I ask.

"No, but it must be something he came in contact with while he was in the pool."

"What about jewelry, anything metal he had on?"

"Nothing except the copper bracelet he always wore. The one that turned his wrist green."

"If it has alloys mixed in with the metal, it might have been magnetized."

"It was very weakly when the death investigator from the medical examiner's office thought to check. Apparently electrocution was top on the list because the pool clearly had malfunctioned for one reason or another," Benton continues telling me what the police have said.

When they checked they discovered the pump, the wiring to the lights, everything was fried, and I envision the gray 30-amp breaker subpanel on the back of the house, 50 amp, to the left of the door that led into the kitchen. I tell Benton I'm fairly certain the pool was the only thing on it, and he replies that the breaker was thrown.

Then I ask about the main breaker panel outside the house. Was anything thrown in there, and he says no. This suggests the possibility of a transient high-voltage electrical source that came in contact with Briggs or the pool while he was swimming. And this sounds much too similar to what we've been saying about the Vandersteel case.

"Something that was there but isn't now," I follow what Benton is considering. "Something like manufactured lightning—or a directed-energy weapon, a DEW in other words."

"Imagine if the water became electrified, and you have a pacemaker," Benton adds, and my thumb finds his wedding band, a simple platinum one, as I'm reminded of Marino's refusal to wear jewelry because it's dangerous.

I ask if Briggs had on anything else metal. Was there anything on his person or around him that could have completed the circuit if he'd come in contact with an electrical source?

"Just the bracelet," Benton says. "He wasn't wearing his wedding band or his dog tags."

"He wouldn't have been. He always took them off when he swam. The last time I stayed with them he'd place them in a dish on the kitchen table," I recall.

"That's where they are in photographs I've seen."

"Everything seems pretty normal." I stop again to shake another small rock out of my shoe. "He did what he usually does, and yet you instantly suspect foul play? I don't care that he's a three-star general with a top-level security clearance. Even spies can drown or have a heart attack. What did you say that got your employer sufficiently interested to mobilize this fast?"

"Literally all it took was one phone call," and Benton brings up the one he got from Washington, D.C., as we were leaving the Faculty Club.

IT WASN'T HIS DIRECTOR or the attorney general on the line.

My husband was being spoofed. He says he got the same type of call that Marino had gotten minutes earlier, and I don't know how Benton found out about that. Possibly Lucy told him. But as I replay what happened as we were leaving our untouched dinners, I realize that Marino was on the phone telling me about Interpol contacting him even as Benton answered his own bogus call.

"Someone supposedly from the National Crime Bureau, the NCB." Benton unlocks his phone, and the display is dimmed sufficiently so that it's hard to see from a distance. "And this person said he'd e-mailed me a photograph, and sure enough he did."

He holds his phone so I can see the picture, and I try to remember anyone acting oddly, perhaps loitering near us some ten days ago on Saturday night, August 27. I search my memory for someone who might have paid too much attention, staring or hovering, especially showing undue interest in General Briggs when we had dinner with his wife and him at the Palm in Washington, D.C., not even two weeks ago. The restaurant was packed with mostly a business crowd, and I remember it was loud.

"You weren't aware of anybody taking photographs, and haven't a clue who might have . . . ?" I start to say as Benton shakes his head, no.

On the phone's display, Briggs is all smiles but the picture has been Photoshopped to include a heavy black *X* over this face. His arm is around Ruthie as they sit across from Benton and me. We're raising our glasses in a toast at our booth surrounded by cartoons of Dennis the Menace, Spider-Man, Nixon.

It was a festive evening with plenty of shoptalk mixed with pleasure, and Briggs and I discussed our talk. We enjoyed several Scotches as we fine-tuned logistics about tomorrow night's event at the Kennedy School. As I look at the photograph I find it gut-wrenching and stunning that a happy moment captured in time would turn into something like this.

"Obviously someone was in the restaurant or near a window at some point while we were eating dinner," I say to Benton. "Do you think it was Carrie Grethen?"

"Frankly yes. I think she or someone directed by her were nearby or passing through, depending on what technology was used. But someone obviously and deliberately took the picture of us and I was none the wiser either."

"And the point?"

"Destablizing us is certainly a big part of it," Benton says. "Keeping herself constantly at the center of our focus is important. She wants to remind us of her presence and that she's smarter than we are, always one step ahead. Never forget this is a competition."

But I do forget. I can't possibly spend my waking moments thinking about something like that. I've never understood people, including my own sister, who devote most of their resources to besting someone, to winning a match that's one-sided and imagined.

"She wants our attention and our fear," Benton continues to tell me what Carrie craves, and I've been hearing it forever. "Most of all she has to overpower us, to get in the last word. Control and more control."

"Who do you think you were actually talking to when you saw the 202 area code for D.C. and took the call?" I ask. "Did you assume it really was an NCB investigator?"

"I wasn't sure what was going on at first. The person sounded male and reasonably credible until he launched in about the *developing Maryland investigation*. That was the language, and I had no idea what investigation he was talking about. So I listened, and I asked why he was calling me specifically and how he got my cell phone number. He said I was listed as the contact person on the case."

"What case specifically?" I look down at my shoes, and one of the heels is coming loose.

"In hindsight, obviously Briggs, who I wouldn't know about until a little bit later. But at the time this so-called NCB investigator was vague. When I pushed him on details he was in a hurry. He gave me a phone number that turns out to be the desk of the Hay-Adams Hotel."

"And since that's exactly what happened to Marino," I reply, "it can't be a coincidence."

"I agree. Two bogus phone calls within minutes of each other, both supposedly from NCB about two different cases that have barely happened yet, mysterious sudden electrical-type deaths occurring almost at the same time hundreds of miles apart," Benton says, and I remember him in the drawing room of the Faculty Club, on the phone near the grand piano.

"When this so-called investigator was talking to you, did you notice if he coughed?"

"It's interesting you would say that. Yes, he sounded like he might have asthma."

It's possible Carrie is utilizing voice-altering software, and I wonder if she's sick or maybe her accomplice is. Benton may have been talking to one of them and had no idea. It's even more bizarre to think Marino might have been. I touch the left arrow at the bottom of the phone's display to go back a screen to see who e-mailed the photograph.

Tailend Charlie sent it to Benton's FBI e-mail address some four hours ago, last night at eight P.M. This was an hour and fifteen minutes after Ruthie discovered her husband in the pool, and maybe forty-five minutes after the twins discovered Elisa Vandersteel's body here in the park and helped themselves to her phone, calling 911.

"We're supposed to know Briggs was a hit," Benton says. "That's why I got the photograph. It's a way of claiming responsibility. Calling Marino was a way of doing the same thing about the case here in Cambridge. It's what terrorists do, and never forget that's what Carrie Grethen is. She and whoever she's in league with are terrorists who won't stop until they're eliminated."

"I'm glad she's telling us what she thinks we need to know." I feel a prick of anger.

"If she took out Briggs herself, and I believe she did," he says, "then that could place her in Bethesda some six or seven hours ago."

"Depending on how she did it," I remind him. "If you're talking about something like a laser gun fired from an unmanned aircraft? I'm assuming that can be done from the desk of someone sitting thousands of miles away." Even as I say this I know where Benton is headed.

He and his colleagues will be going south to Maryland. But I won't be going with them. They'd be wise not to ask.

"I'm supposing she might be in the D.C. area because of the photograph taken of us in the Palm," Benton confirms what I suspect. "And if the ultimate goal of what we're seeing is some coordinated attack using UMVs on a massive scale, then I can see her spending time in the Washington-Baltimore area," and there can be no doubt where this is going.

Or more precisely, where it's already gone. Over the next few hours, Benton will be on his way to D.C. or Baltimore. I'm supposed to be with him as FBI agents begin arriving at my headquarters, which conveniently will be missing its director and chief. Elisa Vandersteel's autopsy and virtually everything else will be witnessed and micro-managed.

We're about to be invaded. At least I'll be prepared, thanks to Harold, and I'm hoping Anne is already at the office.

CHAPTER 36

SHE ANSWERS HER CELL phone on the first ring, and I can tell she's expecting my call.

"I'm pulling into the parking lot now," Anne's voice is in my earpiece, and she doesn't bother with hello.

"Any sign of visitors yet?" I ask.

"Not so far."

There may be a lot of people in and out, and it doesn't matter if we didn't invite some of them, I tell her. It's of no consequence if we don't like them or completely understand who they are. They must be taken care of properly. So we need beverages, especially coffee, and most of all we need food.

"Not much is going to be open at this hour if you're hoping for something decent to eat," Anne's easygoing voice says as I begin to make out John F. Kennedy Street through dense trees up ahead, and I don't see any traffic.

"That's why we have the locked freezer in the break room," I begin to explain confidentially as if I'm telling her how to access Fort Knox. "There should be pizza I keep for emergencies. Meat, vegetarian and vegan. Gluten-free and regular."

"Seriously?"

"What did you think was in there?"

"The last lawyer you didn't like. I don't know."

"I'm still at the scene but heading back. Benton is dropping me off." I keep my voice down.

I glance back at him, and the hulking shape of the tent looms in the dark distance behind us like a flattened thunderhead. He's politely walking some distance away because he doesn't want to overhear what I say. If he doesn't hear it he doesn't have to tell anyone, and it won't be Benton who pulls the evidence out from under me. But he won't stop it from happening either. That's assuming I don't beat his colleagues to the draw.

I'm suddenly alert and in overdrive as I explain to Anne that I need Ernie Koppel to come in right away. I'll also require someone from the histology lab to prepare specimens for him. We're about to be interfered with, overtaken, and if we don't begin testing evidence immediately there's a good chance it will all end up at Quantico, at the FBI crime labs.

We talk about this obliquely. Nothing is to be put in writing, and we're very careful what we say over the phone. Hopefully, by the time the government makes its official requests, I'll have done most of the analysis. I'll have done everything I possibly can to answer questions that I worry might languish otherwise or never be asked. Elisa Vandersteel needs me to finish what I've started.

She deserves the best I can give her, and the first order of business will be the CT scan. I suggest to Anne that whatever left the odd linear burns might have deposited microscopic evidence in the wounds.

"Lightning wouldn't do that."

"You're exactly right," I reply. "It wouldn't."

"But an electrocution might."

"And if so?" I ask her. "Electrocuted by what? What looks like lightning but isn't? We need to find out exactly what happened to her if for no other reason than to make sure that it doesn't happen to somebody else."

"And while we may care about that? No one else will," Anne says, and I know what she's really saying.

If the evidence ends up in Quantico, we have no control over who finds out what. The Feds have their own agenda, and it's not the same as mine.

"He'll be autopsied in Baltimore tomorrow. Well actually *today*." Benton has wandered back and slides his hand out of his pants pocket, glances at the luminescent dial glowing on his wrist. "Christ. It's already half-past midnight. How did that happen?"

"I assume you've talked to Doctor Ventor or someone has."

The chief medical examiner of Maryland, Henrik "Henry" Ventor is one of the finest forensic pathologists in the country, both of us affiliated with the Armed Forces Medical Examiner System, the AFMES. Briggs trained us, was our commander, our boss.

"Yes, and he's already been in touch with the police," Benton says.

"I assume that's where you're headed after you drop me off," I add.

"I took the liberty of getting Page to grab your bug-out bag from the hall closet at home, and we have it with us. Any other items hopefully you can pick up at the office. I realize you need to get out of your scrubs and clean up a bit. Then we'll head out."

"I'm not going with you, Benton."

"We'd like you there."

"Even if I didn't have responsibilities here, I wouldn't get involved. I don't need to tell you why that is."

"We could use your help, and the other doesn't matter anymore."

"It shouldn't matter but it could. Imagine what it would do to Ruthie if I got asked the wrong thing under oath."

"I promise you won't get asked."

"That's a promise you can't possibly keep, Benton. I can't be helpful in Maryland right now but I could do some harm. And I need to finish this case. I'm not about to walk off in the middle of it. So I'm staying put."

He goes on to remind me that the Army CID, the Pentagon, the FBI and various intelligence agencies want Briggs's autopsy witnessed by at least one other senior forensic pathologist, preferably a special reservist with the Air Force who's affiliated with the AFMES. In other words, ordinarily that senior person would be me, he says as if I didn't just tell him no several times.

"Page will take care of Sock and Tesla. I expect we'll be there for several days," he adds, and I can't possibly.

Benton wants to go after Carrie with guns blazing, and I have no doubt Lucy is more than happy to accommodate. Neither of them is comfortable with the idea of my staying here alone in the house with Page and the dogs, and I'm not about to move in with Janet and Desi, especially now that my sister is here.

"You'll work both cases with us, Kay. It will be like the old days."

"It wouldn't. The FBI doesn't work *with* anyone, and I won't work *for* you or them. I work for the victim. Specifically, the dead woman I just spent several hours with in the tent."

"I don't want you staying here."

"I know you don't but that's the way it has to be," as we close in on headlights burning through the trees.

"Then stay at Lucy's new place in Boston. You'll be safe with Janet."

"I can't."

"Then they can move into our place while I'm gone, and all of you will be together."

I hear an engine idling, and Benton wouldn't leave his expensive Audi running with no one in it—not even for two minutes. He didn't come here alone, not that I'm surprised, and I wonder which agents are with him.

"I'm heading to Norwood, and from there to Baltimore," he says, and Lucy keeps her helicopter in Norwood, just outside of Boston, where she has her own hangar.

"I see. That's why she's in a flight suit. She's taking you," and I think about the timing of her showing up as I emerged from the trailer.

Benton must have let her know about Briggs's death hours ago.

"When I'm done here I'll come meet you," I promise as we approach a black Tahoe with dark-tinted windows and government plates.

The back door on the passenger's side opens, and I watch an unfamiliar man climb out.

"It will be at least a day or two," I say to Benton, "but I'll help Ruthie, do anything I can."

Off to our left the Kennedy School of Government hulks against the night, and for an instant it's hard to breathe.

CHAPTER 37

Roger Mahant is the assistant special agent in charge, the ASAC of the FBI's Boston division.

He's driving the black Tahoe. Benton's riding shotgun, and I'm in the backseat sitting next to a man I've never met before. He could be FBI but acts more like the CIA, quiet, unreadable, self-contained. I don't trust him or anyone at the moment, not even my husband, not professionally. He has to take their side in here. He has to be one of them.

So Benton can't tell me everything that's going on—not in front of them. He can't act like my husband or much of a friend. It's nothing new but feels more lonely than usual as he sits in the front seat, his back to me, saying little or nothing, in his sponge mode. You forget he's there while he soaks in everything around him, and I can tell when he's doing it.

"Something else to drink?" Mahant's brooding dark eyes look at me in the rearview mirror.

"I'm fine for now." I have my messenger-bag briefcase in my lap, and my arms are wrapped around it as if someone might try to take it.

Mahant saw me polish off a Fiji water and just now set the empty bottle on the floor like a litterbug. He looks at me constantly when he should keep his eyes on the road. I don't like it when he and Benton talk to each other in low quiet tones. It reminds me that my husband is part of a collective, a group, a tribe. I'm careful and observant as I sit quietly in back, out of my element and not in charge. The ride is a favor I didn't want but couldn't refuse, and any second they're going to pick my brain. They'll get every drop out of me before they finish what I've started—or they think they will.

In the few short minutes I've been inside the Tahoe I haven't asked questions. But I've gathered that the man in the backseat with me is from Washington, D.C., or that area. He might be from Quantico or Langley. I don't know what he does but it seems it was fortuitous that he was in Boston this week. I also don't know his name. He may have told it to me when I first climbed in but I don't think he did. I'm almost certain he didn't say a word as I buckled up.

The inside of the SUV smells like french fries, and the radio is on just loud enough for me to recognize Howard Stern bantering with his cohost Robin Quivers. I can't tell which taped segment it is. But I didn't realize Mahant is a fan of the show, and wouldn't have expected it. I almost like him better. But I don't. Even if I could it wouldn't be smart.

Don't let your guard down.

In his fifties, bald with thick-framed glasses, he has one hand on the wheel, and in the other he holds a Dunkin' Donuts iced coffee he sips quietly, politely, through a straw. He's cordial enough whenever I've been around him, usually at professional receptions, holiday gatherings, that sort of thing. But we don't socialize. I try not to with the FBI.

Briggs warned me from day one not to trust the Feds. I always found that amusing since he is the Feds—or he was.

Work and play with them but never show your underbelly, he would say. *And for God's sake keep your knickers on, Kay, or you'll find out the hard way it's a man's world.*

It doesn't matter that it's unfair, he'd declare with a pointed finger. If life were fair, people like us would be unemployed, and in my head I hear his resonating voice. It demanded attention no matter what he was saying or to whom. But keeping my knickers on wasn't in the cards, and Briggs wasn't solely motivated by his strong moral sensibilities, no matter what he claimed.

He had feelings that went back to our very earliest days. We both did, and it took but one kiss, one protest that we should stop, and then we didn't. I remember the sounds of our breathing, the pattering rain. I'll never forget when he turned the headlights off as we sat in his ruby-red Karmann Ghia in front of the shabby stucco building where I lived with a toxicologist. Her name was Lola, which is Spanish for Dolores. It means sorrows, and that suited her to a T.

We were so young and inexperienced, recent hires at the Miami-Dade Medical Examiner's Office, where Briggs was my supervisor, and Lola was never happy, especially with me. I disappointed and annoyed her constantly and didn't understand it then. No doubt it was out of spite that she wouldn't always tell me when she was coming or going, as if she might make me jealous. But that rainy windy night I knew she wasn't home and probably wouldn't be for a while.

Ironically she'd made sure to rub it in as if to imply that she had quite the life and I didn't. Briggs asked me about her because he found her peculiar and abrasive. What was it like living together? Did I worry she might poison my cereal? When would she be coming home, and then the heavens opened. We laughed at the deafening drum roll overhead, at the flooded glass, and he turned the wipers off. Surrounded by a deluge, we fogged up the glass, wiping it off to steal glances up at the second floor, at the empty unlighted window of the cracker-box apartment I had to share because that was what I could afford.

It was obvious no one was home, obvious why Briggs wanted to walk me up with the umbrella and see me in safely. He wasn't being a gentleman, and I was no lady. It was a perfect storm of circumstances and had been from the start when my rattletrap car with its worn-out clutch happened to break down on Dixie Highway after dark.

Lola happened to be out with an ex, she made sure I knew. My sister Dorothy happened not to answer the phone, and neither did my mother. Briggs happened to be the only person I could reach after I'd hiked along the shoulder of the highway to a gas station pay phone. He happened to drive me home, and afterward he happened never to tell Ruthie the truth.

She'd already decided I was a home wrecker even before I was one. Why let her know she was a psychic or a prophet? Why tell her she was right?

Why give her one more reason to shun you, Kay? I can hear Briggs arguing with me.

Confessing to his wife would have been an apocalyptic ending to my relationship with him. We wouldn't have worked together again. My days with the AFMES would have ended before they began because she was overly sensitive, fragile and possessive, and at the time she had a powerful father at the Pentagon. This was according to Briggs, his rationale for why he needed to keep certain things from her. It was for her good and mine. It was for the best. Those are the sorts of things he'd say. I always knew he was kidding himself, and it might have been the only time I would have called him a coward.

"You doing all right?" Benton turns around and looks at me in the backseat, and truth be told, he's a bigger man than Briggs ever could be.

My husband doesn't run from what he wants or pick something because it's safe. He doesn't lie about what he loves. He may be deliberate and take his time. But he won't give up or settle for less, and we don't keep secrets from each other. Not the kind that would fray the bond between us.

I INTRODUCE MYSELF TO the man sitting next to me as the Tahoe turns onto Memorial Drive. Then I feel silly.

He must know who I am and why the FBI picked me up. In a few minutes they'll leave me at the CFC because I'm not as cooperative as they'd like me to be, and I begin watching for my titanium-skinned biotech building. I stare out at the dark early morning as we follow the river, and I realize how tired I am. I feel defeated and guilty. It's true what they say about your sins finding you out.

Only in my case it's more appropriate to say that my sins tend to find me, period. There are consequences to everything. But when Briggs and I had our moment it couldn't have occurred to me that this day would come. I couldn't have imagined I'd be called upon by the government to assist in his autopsy but would have to recuse myself for reasons I won't discuss. Even if I weren't up to my ears in the Vandersteel case, I wouldn't go to Baltimore tonight. It wouldn't be right.

". . . So I was just wondering what people call you."

I realize the man next to me is asking a question as he offers a packet of tissues, gently nudging it against my wrist. I take it from his strong smooth hand, opening the little cellophane tab.

"Thank you." I wipe my nose, my eyes. "You were saying?"

"I'm sorry about General Briggs. I've actually said it a couple of times. I understand he trained you."

"Yes. Thank you."

"Then I was asking how you're doing, since rumor has it you were in pretty bad shape out there, got heat exhaustion."

"I'm fine."

"And after that I was curious about what people call you. Kay or Doctor Scarpetta? And can we get you anything? Food? Something else to drink?"

"No thank you."

"To which question?" He's being flirty right in front of my husband.

Or literally behind his back.

"I don't need anything," I say to whoever the man is, and I don't want to look at him.

And I don't want him looking at me as I see myself the way he must. Wilted, my makeup gone and forgotten, my hair out of control. My deodorant stopped working hours ago, and the only scrubs I could find inside the trailer are too big. Not dressed but draped, I constantly find myself tugging at the V-neck of my salty sweat-stained shirt because if my bra strap doesn't show, cleavage does. And while I'm used to Marino staring, I'm not so forgiving to a perfect stranger.

"Tell me your name again." He hasn't told me at all, and when he answers I think he's kidding at first.

"Andrew Wyeth," he repeats, and then I wonder if he's making a nonsensical joke or a snide allusion to my husband's wealthy late father, an art investor.

There were Andrew Wyeth watercolors in the Wesley house when Benton was growing up. I stare at the back of his head as he looks down at his phone, and he has no reaction to what the man next to me is saying. Benton is ignoring him. He's ignoring all of us even as he follows our every word and intonation with the keenness of a hawk. I know it for a fact because that's what he does.

"Just think of the painter and it's not me," Special Agent Wyeth says as he shakes my hand a little too long, a little too tenderly, and his humor doesn't penetrate my smoldering mood.

I don't want to be in this car. I don't want to be with them, and it's not easy when Benton has to act this way. When we're forced to pretend we have something different with each other than we really do, it makes me feel cheated and dishonest. As if we're having an affair again. As if I'm a home wrecker again.

Sometimes our little games make me feel alone and unsupported, convinced nothing will be handled properly unless I do it myself. That's the way I feel now. I'm on my own.

"Were you named for the artist?" I'm blandly polite and barely listening as I think of all I've got to do quickly, stealthily, without showing my hand.

"No, ma'am. My father was," Wyeth reminds me how much I hate to be called "ma'am."

Thirty at most but more likely in his twenties, he must be a wunderkind to be keeping such important company. While I can't see him very well in the dark backseat I don't need to. He's very nice-looking and has a soothing voice that inspires trust I don't intend to offer. Muscles bulge from the short sleeves of his polo shirt and strain against the khaki fabric of his cargo pants.

Veins rope, and he has so little body fat it's as if he's been shrink-wrapped in his own skin. I can't imagine how much time he must spend in the gym or what he eats. Very little. Protein. Juices. Kale. Healthy things like that, I imagine, and he smells good. A subtle woodsy manly fragrance with a touch of citrus and musk.

Calvin Klein.

". . . You'll be in the very capable hands of Boston's finest, ASAC Roger Mahant, who you know." Andrew Wyeth is winding up his pitch about what I'm in for. "I believe you've seen him throw back a few at festive gatherings, so you know how entertaining he can be."

"Hey, I'm sitting right here. I can hear you," Mahant jokes in the mirror while Benton continues to ignore us as he does something with his phone.

"He'll be spending some time with you, Doctor Scarpetta, mostly for observational purposes so we can be up to speed on what's going on in the Vandersteel case," and Wyeth must be with the Bureau to go on like this as if he runs the place.

"We'll need accommodations for a few of us," and it's Mahant talking now. "A fairly large office with a couple of desks, a table and chairs," he says impertinently. "We also need private access to at least one restroom, and of course parking," he adds outrageously as I decide, *What a prick.*

CHAPTER 38

THE LAST THING I want is federal agents roaming around my headquarters, and Bryce will be even more out of control. He'll be a hot mess. Everyone will be.

But there's not much I can do, and it does no good to get incensed. I need to be clearheaded, and then Benton is reaching over the back of the seat, handing me his phone.

"Police photographs taken at the scene," he says, and I brace myself as I begin to go through them.

There's nothing of Briggs *in situ* as Ruthie discovered him because when the rescue squad arrived the first thing they did was pull him out of the water. That was about the extent of any heroic measures because it was quickly apparent that he was dead. In the pictures I'm looking at he's faceup on the deck near the wooden side of the Endless Pool.

I recognize the outdoor furniture, the back of his Bethesda house and the yard, and it pains me to be so familiar with what I'm looking at, to think of all the stories. He's wearing what he called his *dogaflage,* the baggy swim trunks his skilled-seamstress wife made for him a few years ago as a surprise. The green-and-brown camouflage pattern includes the cartoon dog from *Family Guy,* and Briggs had multiple pairs that traveled wherever he went.

It's awful to see his strong vibrant face slack and suffused a deep purplish red with barely open eyes, and I can make out the impression left in his skin by the goggles he was wearing when he died. There's foam protruding from his lips, and Mahant asks me about it.

"That's what you see in drownings, right?"

"Sometimes." I have to watch every word I say with bureaucrats like him.

I don't want to read my casual comments in a report or hear them on the news. Already I can tell he's not going to grasp much of what I talk about while he believes he knows more than I do about everything. Picturing him and his subordinates in certain areas of the CFC is worse than a bull in a china shop. They can do real damage that can't be fixed.

"But you don't just drown in a pool not much bigger than a hot tub," Mahant says. "It's what? Four feet deep? So obviously something happened."

"You can drown in a puddle or a bowl of soup. But yes, something happened," I agree with his banal assessment as his eyes glance at me in the mirror.

"And the sudsy stuff coming out of his mouth is from breathing, meaning he didn't die instantly."

"Almost nobody does," I reply. "Unless you're decapitated or blown to smithereens your brain takes a moment to shut everything down. That doesn't mean he was conscious as he took an agonal breath or two and aspirated water. If that's what happened, it could explain external foam in the mouth or nostrils."

"You're telling me if your heart stopped you could still breathe? Like for how long and how many breaths?"

"I don't know. It would be a little difficult to research something like that," I reply, and Wyeth smiles and stifles a laugh.

I click on other photographs, finding a close-up of the copper bracelet, then several others of his body turned on its side to show the odd round burn on the back of his neck. I hope Briggs was instantly incapacitated, that he never saw it coming, and for an instant I envision the drone I noticed earlier, silhouetted blackly against the sun. I think how simple it would be to do something hideous with one.

"I assume you won't be starting the autopsy right this minute," Mahant continues talking to me as my thoughts jump disturbingly to another recent case.

"There's a lot to do before that," I reply as I think about the Cambridge woman electrocuted this past Monday night.

Molly Hinders was watering her yard at sunset, and was found sometime later dead in the wet grass with a burn on her head.

"And I won't have much of a staff until everybody starts coming in to work." I'm not lying but I don't intend to be helpful—not the way he wants me to be.

"So I should get back here at what time, Kay?" Mahant asks.

"Whatever works for you. We'll be here."

"But what time do you plan to do her autopsy exactly? I'm assuming you have an electronic schedule I can access so I don't have to bother you? Anyway, set the time and I'll plan to meet you."

"We don't really schedule autopsies in the way you're describing. We're not like a hospital OR or a doctor's office." I sound perfectly reasonable and not the least bit condescending even as I marvel over how uninformed he is.

"Yep. What's the hurry when your patients are dead?" Wyeth quips.

"Why don't we just set a time." Mahant isn't asking, he's telling, and he's about to be a real thorn in my side if I let him.

"That's a little tricky because first she has to go into the CT scanner . . ." I start to say but it's too much to explain.

I'm not sure the Boston division's second in command has ever been inside my building. I know I've never worked with him, and that's no surprise. Officials like Mahant are *pencil necks* and *suits,* as Marino calls them. They're not out in the field investigating, and when they do show up at a scene or the autopsy room you can be assured it's political. There's an agenda that likely won't be shared, and no matter how friendly and collegial the relationship begins, it goes off the rails fast and rarely ends well.

I have no intention of honoring any sort of schedule ASAC Roger Mahant might decide. But the writing's on the wall. He's going to do everything he can to insert himself into the business of the CFC, and I'll do everything I can to make him wish he hadn't. For better or worse I can be pretty good at that, and I remind him that when he comes back later to be sure to bring shower supplies and a change of clothing.

"Why?" His dark eyes are in the mirror.

"You'll want to clean up thoroughly afterward and stuff what you've got on in trash bags. I remind you that the odor gets into your hair, your clothing, way up into your sinuses. In fact, I apologize because it's never a good idea to be inside a closed car after you've been working a scene for hours where the body is decomposing rapidly."

Benton lifts his arms and sniffs his folded-up shirtsleeves. "I think I'm all right but I wasn't there long or on top of everything like you were," he plays along with what I'm up to.

Mahant cracks his window an inch, turning the air-conditioning as far up as it will go.

"We have disposable gowns, hair covers, gloves and such that we'll supply," I say to him over the blasting air. "And we're also taking care of food. You're just not allowed to have anything to eat or drink in the autopsy rooms. But there's a break area upstairs."

"Eating in the autopsy rooms? Judas Priest. Do people really do that?"

"Not anymore. When's the last time you had a tetanus shot?"

"Hell if I know." Mahant's reflection in the rearview mirror looks impatient and unhappy.

"What about hepatitis A and B?" I ask that next.

AROUND A BEND IN the river, the Cambridge Forensic Center comes into view up ahead near the Harvard Bridge.

My seven-story metal-skinned cylindrical building has been compared to a lot of things. An unjacketed lead projectile, a dum-dum round, a snub-nosed missile, a pickle. It juts up like a tarnished metal silo across the road from a different section of the same fitness path where Elisa Vandersteel was riding her bicycle when she was killed. The scene I just worked is barely a mile from my office, although one would never know it because Mahant had to take a circuitous route as we left the park unless he wanted to bother flashing his creds and asking police to move barricades from streets closed off.

He turns left off Memorial Drive. Then another left, and we stop in front of the CFC's ten-foot-high black PVC-coated privacy fence. I open my window and reach out to enter a code on a keypad mounted to the left of the black metal gate topped by triple-pointed spikes. With a loud beep it lurches to life and begins to slide open on its tracks.

The Tahoe drives inside the back parking lot, and I recognize the personal cars belonging to certain members of my staff. Bryce is here. So is Anne, and the Tahoe creeps past parked vans, SUVs and trucks, all of them ghostly white and silent at the quiet hour. We stop behind the unmarked white Ford Explorer in the first space to the left of a pedestrian door at the back of the building.

It's what I drove to work yesterday. But I left it here thinking I would be off the next day spending time with my sister, Janet, Lucy, Desi and everyone. I got a ride with Bryce, and then I would have ridden home with Benton from dinner. But nothing's turned out that way, and the next day is here. There will be no time off or family gathering in my immediate future, and I get out of the Tahoe.

"I'll be right there," Benton says to me, and he stays inside the SUV with the doors shut.

I can imagine at least some of what they're talking about. Mahant doesn't want me around when he and his cronies help themselves to my headquarters and everybody in it alive and dead. But that's too bad. No one is chasing me off, and I wait by the pedestrian door. I wait several minutes, then Benton steps out of the SUV. I scan my right thumb to unlock the biometric lock and we walk into a vehicle bay the size of a small hangar.

I smell fresh-scented disinfectant. The epoxy-sealed floor, the walls lined with storage cabinets, everything is spotless. Gleaming steel gurneys are neatly parked in a washing area, and in a far corner is La Morte Café, where Rusty and Harold drink coffee and smoke cigars at a table and chairs that can be hosed off.

"Lucy was able to hack into Elisa Vandersteel's phone," Benton starts in telling me what he thinks he can and probably more than he should.

As usual he's smarter than everybody else. He knew Lucy would get into the phone far more quickly than the labs in Quantico would.

"So we know who the boyfriend is, the kid we saw at the Faculty Club," Benton says. "Chris Peabody."

"As in Mrs. P?" I remember she mentioned her grandson was working part-time at the Faculty Club.

"Probably but we'll confirm. He lives in a one-bedroom apartment on Ash Street, west of here."

"Which was the direction Elisa Vandersteel was headed as she rode through the park," and I can tell by the look on Benton's face that he's very worried.

"The last phone call she made was to him at seven-oh-six P.M. as she was putting a FedEx in the drop box on JFK Street right next to the school of government," he says. "We know this because of the content of the voice mail when the boyfriend tried her back about ten minutes later, and based on everything else, I'm thinking she was dead by then. I'm thinking she did exactly what we thought, Kay. She entered the park off JFK Street, and as she rode near the lamp something got her."

"Does her boyfriend know?" I recall seeing him and other staff going in and out of rooms while we were at the Faculty Club.

No doubt there will be plenty of witnesses to vouch for his where-abouts at the time of Elisa Vandersteel's death, and it's unlikely he has anything to do with it. But Mrs. P's grandson is in for a god-awful time in every way imaginable.

"There are a lot of people to talk to. This is going to be a shit storm, and you've been up for twenty-something hours with no end in sight," Benton is saying. "Let Luke handle the autopsy, Kay. You've already done the hardest part. Why don't you come with us?"

"Us? Who else besides Lucy?"

"Wyeth." Benton walks me to the far end of the bay where a ramp leads up to another door. "As you may have gathered he's one of us, with our NCTC."

The National Counterterrorism Center monitors both domestic and international threats. It works hand in glove with U.S. intelli-gence agencies such as the CIA.

"If he's been in the Boston area for the past few days I assume he wasn't here because of Briggs unless you had intel about his death in advance," I reply, and our voices echo inside the vast hollow concrete space where we talk, just the two of us near a huge drain in the floor and a thick coiled hose. "And I hope that's not true. Because if you had even a glimmer—"

"We didn't. There was no forewarning that I'm aware of, just the photograph e-mailed, as I've said, and he was already gone by then." Benton uses that euphemism again.

Gone.

"Wyeth has been in the area on another matter." Benton pauses, his eyes on mine, and then he says, "I'm very concerned about the possibility of some major attack planned for the Washington area, and that what we're seeing right now is the tip of the iceberg."

He says he can't get into the details but Briggs was an important target in more ways than I know.

"It's been rumored on the Hill for a while that he's in line for an appointment to a cabinet-level position, something the new adminis-tration has in mind," Benton says. "I think Carrie is reminding us she can slay any dragon she likes and rob us of what we care about most. She can destroy our dreams. She can rob us of our family, and Briggs was exactly that, especially to you."

"I don't know if she's reminding us of that or anything." I take a deep breath as I feel angry and sad at the same time. "And rumors don't always have anything to do with fact. We should be careful what we infer and believe when there's so little we know," I add as the windowless bay door begins to retract.

The illuminated parking lot fills the opening as the massive rolling door lifts with metallic clanks, and headlights burn as the white van glides inside. Then the door begins to shudder down again loudly as Harold and Rusty climb out the front seat, walking around to the back, opening the tailgate, all of it amplified in here.

"I'll call you on a fuel stop." Benton hugs me, and the hard shape of the pistol on his hip reminds me that we never really know when we'll see each other again.

We don't live normal lives or have a normal relationship, and I'm not sure what it is to feel safe anymore. For a moment he holds me close, his nose and mouth buried in my hair as more headlights glare in the parking lot beyond. I swallow hard. This feels terrible.

"I'd appreciate it if you'd have Janet, Desi and Dorothy move into our place until I'm back. I know I've mentioned it but I mean it, Kay. Everybody's safer together," Benton faces me, his eyes unyielding. "I've already talked to Janet about it in case you decided to stay home, and I was pretty sure you would. Page can help as needed with the dogs," he adds as I catch Luke Zenner out of the corner of my eye.

My blond Austrian assistant chief walks up to us, and I suspect he was sleeping when Anne summoned him. Possibly sleeping with her, it also occurs to me, as Luke is impossibly attractive and quite the ladies' man. I can see the wrinkles from his pillowcase imprinted on the right side of his face. He hasn't shaved, and it couldn't have taken long to throw on a Patriots T-shirt, baggy Bermuda shorts, and a pair of moccasins.

"I'll be upstairs for a while and will fill you in later," I say to him, and it's my way of signaling that we can't talk openly in front of Benton right now. "I'm thinking we should put her in the decomp room. She's getting into rough shape really fast."

"I can imagine and it sounds like a plan," Luke says with his German accent as his blue eyes meet mine. "We'll get going on that, then," and Harold and Rusty are wheeling the stretcher through the bay.

They push it up the ramp, and through the door leading inside as Benton and I say good-bye, although we don't really use that word. We try not to speak in terms of endings but to leave our separations light and airy with a *See you later* or *I'll call in a bit*. As if everything is fine when it's not.

I wait at the top of the ramp, my messenger bag slung over a shoulder of my sweat-stained scrubs. I watch my tall husband with his wide shoulders, his long stride and straight proud posture as he walks away. He reaches the huge square opening, and it frames him like a painting as he turns to smile at me.

CHAPTER 39

THE FIRST STOP WHEN I enter my building from the bay is the brightly lit receiving area with its walls of stainless-steel coolers and freezers monitored by green digital readouts that turn yellow and red when they aren't happy.

The air is cool and pleasantly deodorized, and I'm greeted by bickering just inside the door, where Harold and Rusty have parked the stretcher on the platform floor scale. They've put on shoe covers, aprons, gloves and surgical caps, and I catch them in medias res, softly pecking at each other and oblivious to anyone who might be listening.

"Well what is it then?" Harold clicks open a pen and he has his notebook open.

"It's really annoying when you do this."

"Do what? I'm just asking for verification of what weight you said we should deduct."

"I didn't say because I don't need to." Rusty holds the long wooden measuring rod in one hand like a shepherd's crook as he unzips the pouch.

"Then what is it?"

"Why would it be different this time, Harold?"

"It's always smart to ask."

"And you always do. It's eighty-six pounds just like last time we weighed it."

"But you didn't check first when it was empty, did you. So we don't know that for a fact."

"No, I don't every single time because it's stupid," as Rusty measures the body from the top of the bag over Elisa Vandersteel's head to the bottom of the bags on her feet.

"What happens if we get asked in court whether we weighed the stretcher?"

"I've never heard anybody ask that or even bring it up except you."

"But they could and depending on the circumstances maybe they should. You never know when the tiniest detail can make all the difference. Let's see . . . if we subtract eighty-six from two-sixteen?" Harold does the math in his pocket-size notebook because he can't do it in his head. "We get a weight of one-thirty." He writes it down as I walk across the recycled-glass floor that's a shade of tan called truffle. "And the length?"

"Sixty-five inches."

I stop at the glass-enclosed security desk, what people here call the Fish Tank. On the outer ledge of the closed window is the big black leather-bound log, our Book of the Dead. It's anchored by a thin steel chain, and all case entries must be made in black ink with the ballpoint pen tethered by a length of the same white cotton twine we use for sutures.

I open the acid-free ledger pages, lightly rapping a knuckle on the glass to get my favorite security officer's attention. Georgia has her back to me as she collects a yellow RFID wristband from the 3-D printer. She returns to her desk and slides open her window.

"You look like you've lost more weight." I notice her dark blue uniform with its yellow trouser stripes seems a bit baggy as she sits back down at her computer, placing her hands on the keyboard, the mouse.

"Oh, now you're just being nice." She peers at me over her reading glasses as her peach acrylic nails begin clicking over keys. "Seriously, though?" Her brown eyes are pleased. "You can tell?"

"I certainly can."

"Almost ten pounds."

"I thought so."

"You've made my day and the sun's not even up yet."

"The most important question is what Weight Watchers has to say about pizza this morning. Is it legal?" I review entries about bodies delivered and picked up, catching up on what's happened since I was here last.

"That depends on what kind and whose it is. Now if it's your pizza, Doctor Scarpetta? I don't care if it's a thousand points because I'm eating it."

I watch her go through paperwork on her desk, accessioning the Elisa Vandersteel case, giving it a unique number.

16-MA2037

"But you might want to tell me what sort of party we're suddenly having," Georgia says, "and who I should be watching for in the cameras and worrying about. Am I right that we're battening down the hatches? Because you just say the word."

"It looks like we're having company, and we'll be as hospitable as we can muster." I'm careful what I say so nothing comes back to haunt me, and I turn another page in the log. "But no one's getting in the way of the work. We won't allow that."

"Well I sure knew something was going on with Anne showing up at this hour. And then Bryce wandering in, and after him Paula from histology? And now you and Doctor Zenner, and rumor has it Ernie Koppel's on his way. Damn." She glances up at me. "So who's the company we didn't invite?"

I tell her, and she blows out a loud breath and rolls her eyes.

"I could use some overtime help if you're interested," I add, scanning names, ages, addresses, suspected causes of death, and whether our patients are still with us or have been dispatched to a funeral home or cemetery.

"Starting when?" she asks.

"Starting when your shift ends six hours from now."

"O'Riley will be in then. At eight."

"Yes, and I'd like you to stay and help him, if you're willing. As long as you're not too tired." I want Georgia around because she's fearless and she's loyal. "Let's get as many backups here as we can."

"I'll get on the phone. It's better if I do it." She means instead of Bryce. "You know how he can get on people's last nerve."

"As many of our officers who are available. I want at least one on every floor if possible."

"To protect us from them." She means from the FBI, and I don't nod or answer.

I look her in the eye, and that's enough.

"You just let me know what you want me to do," Georgia folds her thick arms across her formidable chest, and I don't know how effective she'd be in a fight but I wouldn't want to challenge her.

"That will be largely decided by our guests," as I turn back several pages in the log, wondering if there's been a mistake.

"Well I can already tell you what they'll do," Georgia is getting worked up by the thought of her turf being overrun. "They're going to snoop into every damn thing they can while they have the chance."

"We won't give it to them," I reply as I continue to peruse the log, and I didn't expect Molly Hinders's body to still be here.

But it must be. Had it been released there would be a handwritten record of it, and as I read the entry made Monday, September 5, I'm reminded of the address.

Granite Street.

Bryce and Ethan live on Granite Street here in Cambridge very close to Magazine Park on the river. They moved there last spring, and I'm startled and not quite sure why.

"It appears Molly Hinders wasn't released after I left yesterday." I return the log to its spot on the ledge. "I thought she was being picked up by the funeral home. Did Doctor Wier run into some sort of problem?"

Lee Wier is one of my forensic pathologists, and she knows what she's doing because I trained her.

"Well that's turned into quite the cluster F."

I have a bad feeling Georgia's right about that. Molly Hinders is Investigator Barclay's case, and Marino needs to intervene.

"That poor lady couldn't have worse luck. Now everybody's drunk and fighting while she's all by her lonesome in a damn cooler," Georgia is telling me as I keep thinking about what Dr. Wier said as she was going over the case during staff meeting several mornings ago.

When Molly Hinders's body was found it was near a plugged-in stereo speaker that had fallen from its mount and was on the wet grass. It was the only explanation for how she could have been electrocuted in her backyard as she watered her plants with a hose. But it's really never made sense to me that a speaker circuit could kill anyone.

HER SCALP AND HAIR were burned from coming into contact with the electrical source that killed her.

This was the early evening of the Labor Day holiday, and she'd returned home from kayaking on the Charles River. She removed her kayak from her car's rooftop rack, dragged it into the backyard, then entered the house and poured herself a glass of wine. Still in her bathing suit, she went out to water the backyard, where there's a stereo system, a wrought-iron table and chairs, and a barbecue under a partially covered pergola overgrown with vines.

When the police arrived the stereo system had no power because the ground-fault circuit interrupter—similar to a breaker—had been tripped. That alone should have prevented her from being shocked, much less killed. For some reason it didn't, and I've found this puzzling from the start. But the case didn't grab my attention then the way it does now. Molly Hinders is reminding me too much of Elisa Vandersteel and General Briggs.

"Please explain why Molly Hinders is still here," I ask again.

"From what I gather," Georgia says, "her family has money, and she and her estranged husband weren't divorced yet. So he's fighting over who's claiming the body. They're fighting over everything because she was real young and there's no will, no nothing, and then the kicker? They fired the first funeral home they picked, so we can't exactly be releasing her to anyone yet anyway."

"It's just as well, fortuitous in fact, because there may be other problems," I reply as I hear the sound of the elevator doors opening. "I don't want her released until I say. I want to check on a few things," I add as Bryce appears, and he's changed his clothes since we talked by phone in the trailer what seems an eternity ago.

"Who aren't we releasing?" my chief of staff says, and his blue eyes look a little bleary, maybe from hard cider.

He has on tight stovepipe jeans, a T-shirt and lots of Goth jewelry, spunking himself up for the Feds. Bryce loves to flirt, and the more it's not appreciated the better.

"Molly Hinders," I inform him. "Her manner of death will be undetermined pending further investigation. I need you to let Doctor Wier know." Then I ask Bryce if there's anything new on his marijuana-tattoo mystery. "I don't suppose we've figured out how that detail ended up in a nine-one-one call." I put it to him bluntly.

"Sure. Ethan and me got to the bottom of it," he says too flippantly as his boyish face turns red. "The weirdo next door? You know our jerk-off neighbor? It had to be him paying me back."

"How'd he know what's going on inside your own house?" Georgia pipes up, and obviously she's familiar with the tattoo story.

Bryce probably couldn't wait to tell her.

"Paying you back for what?" I ask him.

"Well . . ."

"Bryce? Your face is beet red. Obviously you know. Tell me how your neighbor found out about your fake tattoo."

"Well it seems I got a little drunker than I thought on margaritas made with that to-die-for tequila your sister gave us? And apparently after our friends left I went to take the trash out, and I heard this same really weird noise and saw a strange light again. So of course I tripped on something and fell down, and then there he was trying to help me up. Only in that crazy moment it wasn't a *he*. It was this *thing*, and I really thought it had happened this time."

"What the hell?" Georgia has stopped typing, staring bug-eyed at him. "What are you talking about?"

"I really thought I was being abducted by aliens for some research project they must be doing."

"Jeeees-us." She starts shaking her head. "You sure do waste my time."

"I'm dead serious. I've been seeing weird lights in the sky at night."

"They're called stars and airplanes." Georgia just keeps shaking her head.

"Am I to assume it was your neighbor who showed up while you were out with the trash?" I ask.

"Donald the Nasty. I don't remember what happened but Ethan does because I guess he came out to look for me and heard the ugly things I apparently said. Ethan was upset, telling me to thank Donald for coming to my aid, can you imagine? And of course in my confusion I yelled, *How the frick do we know he's not the one who pushed me down?*"

"And he knew about your tattoo how?" I again ask.

"Because of his flashlight, and I had on shorts and was barefoot. So he saw it and made some crack about us being potheads, and that it figured. But I don't remember any of it."

"Marino needs to know every word," I reply. "Please call right away. Find him, and tell him we need to talk."

CHAPTER 40

I REACH THROUGH GEORGIA'S WINDOW to remove the hand-held RFID reader from its charging cradle. Walking over to Cooler number two, I lift the big steel handle, and the huge polished door opens with a quiet suck and a puff of condensation that looks like fog but smells like death.

I move through the chilled foul air inside a huge frigid space filled with steel trays bearing body-shaped mounds, each pouch tagged with a chip embedded in a plastic sticker that should match the chip in the decedent's yellow wristband. Redundancy. Because one of the worst things you can do is lose someone, and I scan with the reader, holding it like a gun until I locate Molly Hinders.

My breath smokes out as I unzip her pouch, and the sound of blowing air is loud. I grab a pair of gloves from the box on a gurney, and momentarily I'm working my purple-sheathed fingers through her short curly black hair. Everywhere I touch is refrigerated cold as I feel around the sutured autopsy incision that follows her hairline, over her ears and around the back of her head, where I find the small gaping wound in her scalp.

Dr. Lee Wier did exactly what she was trained to do and what I recommended to her when we discussed this case. She made sure to surgically remove the burned tissue so we could have Ernie check it for microscopic particles of metals or other materials that might have been transferred to the wounds. She should have sent these samples to the histology lab days ago, and I walk back out of the cooler. Shutting the heavy door, I hope for a good signal on my phone as I try Paula in the histology lab.

"I finished up everything on that yesterday afternoon," she says in my earpiece after I ask how the case is coming. "Doctor Wier had asked me to get on it as soon as I could because of the prep time involved, so that's what I did."

"She specifically asked you to prepare wet samples for Ernie."

"Absolutely. I prepped four separate specimens from the burn on the victim's head."

"I'm very happy to hear it," I reply because the burned tissue would have to be dehydrated with acetone before it could be placed inside the vacuum chamber of an electron microscope, and this can take days.

Had Dr. Wier and Paula not been fast acting, there might not be anything to analyze until the weekend, and waiting couldn't be a worse idea. Depending on what we're dealing with, someone else might die, and up ahead I see the open door as I follow the empty corridor, passing labs and other work spaces that are dark at this early hour.

Inside the large-scale X-ray control room Anne's desk is empty, her pocketbook and keys on top of it. Through a leaded-glass window I can see her in the room on the other side, standing at the creamy-white large-bore CT scanner, a lab coat on over her jeans, talking to Luke Zenner, who's changed into scrubs. On the table in front of them is Elisa Vandersteel's pouched body, and I open the door connecting the control and scan rooms.

"You're just who I need to see," I say to Luke as I walk in.

I explain it's possible that Molly Hinders and Elisa Vandersteel aren't accidental deaths. They may be homicides that are connected, and I also let them know about Briggs. Luke and Anne begin asking questions I can't answer. They get increasingly upset.

"We can't get into it now," I finally tell them because we really can't. "We need to save our feelings for later. We have to focus and find out what's killing these people, and if it's electrical malfunctions, flukes or deliberate, such as some weapon we've not seen before."

"It's hard to imagine everything suddenly happening is coincidental," Luke says, and his eyes are hard and he's clenching his jaw.

"When you're done," I continue, "photograph the burns before excising them, and the tissue goes straight to Paula. Of primary interest are the very fine linear whitish leathery burns on her upper back and lower posterior neck, and also the top of her right hand and wrist."

"I'll need to take off the paper bags anyway," Luke says. "So I'll just do all of it in here, get everything ready for the labs. Then I'll have her moved into the decomp room."

"I'm going upstairs to clean up," I reply.

"Now that's an idea. Nothing like cleaning up before you do an autopsy in the decomp room," Anne says drolly, and she gives me an idea.

"I understand there have been some problems with the ventilation in there," I point out, and Anne gets a blank look on her plain but pleasant face, then she frowns, and then she gets it.

"Oh *that*," she says as if she suddenly remembers. "You must be talking about the downdraft table in there," she recalls, but she's making it up. "The airflow wasn't pulling odors down and venting them away from people working, I believe that was the problem the other day, and I heard the stench was so bad it had legs," she improvs. "So I hope for the sake of our guests that we don't have a problem this morning."

"That would be too bad," I agree.

THIRTY MINUTES LATER, UPSTAIRS inside my office suite, I emerge from the bathroom drying my hair with a towel.

Dressed in clean blue scrubs and black rubber surgical clogs, I walk through my sitting area of leather furniture in soothing earth tones, a conference table, and my personal collection of anatomical drawings by Max Brödel, Edwin Landseer, Frank Netter, in addition to eighteenth-century prints of William Hogarth's *Four Stages of Cruelty*.

Near my desk the data wall displays the time and other information in bright digits against glassy blackness. 3:08.45 AM EST . . . 3:09.50 . . . 3:10.00 . . . I watch the seconds silently advance as I select an app on my phone that offers a menu of CFC zones inside and out that are constantly monitored by security cameras. The data wall splits into screens that display live feeds, and my back parking lot has filled up considerably since I last checked.

There are several dark blue and black sedans and SUVs, and I pan and tilt, checking other zones and discovering the black Tahoe inside the bay where only Lucy is cheeky enough to leave her cars. Roger Mahant is already back, and he's come with quite a posse, it seems. I wonder why Georgia didn't let me know. Maybe she tried and I was in the shower.

I call her desk extension and it begins to ring as I watch digital seconds tick past. Ringing and ringing. 3:12.11 . . . 3:13.10 . . . 3:14.00 . . . Oddly there's no answer downstairs at her desk, and then my phone rings.

"What's going on?" I assume it's Georgia.

"Hello?" Ernie Koppel says. "Kay?"

"I'm sorry. I was trying to call downstairs . . ."

"Can you drop by?" he asks. "I don't usually say something's urgent but you need to see this before anybody else does. I'm waiting for a confirmation but if you've got a minute I think I've found something that's a first. At least for a crime lab."

He tells me where he is, which electron microscope, and I grab my lab coat off the back of my desk chair, hurrying out the door. I decide to avoid the elevator. Not only is it notoriously slow in my state-of-the-art biotech headquarters but I intend to duck and dodge the FBI every chance I get. A good way to start is by using the emergency stairs. While anyone can take them to exit the building, you can't access our floors without an ID badge or a code.

So I'm not likely to run into anyone, and my clogs echo on the metal-edged concrete steps as I descend to the lower level. It's as quiet as a bomb shelter in the stairwell as I go down and down, unlocking the door at the bottom. It opens into our evidence bay, where we process large items, typically cars and trucks, but we've also recovered evidence from supercars, motorcycles, Jet Skis, and even a homebuilt hang glider that obviously didn't work very well or it and its owner wouldn't have ended up here.

The lights are on a low, energy-saving setting, and I briskly walk through the gloom, passing exam spaces occupied by current cases. A boat under a tent will be fumed with superglue to develop possible latent prints, and two spaces down from that is the camper where a suspected murder-suicide occurred. Next to that, a stand-alone bay is covered in blood-spattered-and-streaked white paper from ceiling to floor to reconstruct a stabbing.

I head toward an illuminated red IN USE sign above the concrete bunker housing the transmission electron microscope, the TEM. Scanning my thumbprint on the biometric reader, I pass through the stainless-steel door as it slides open with a swoosh that always reminds me of *Star Trek*. I'm greeted by the familiar rush of positive-pressure air blowing my hair as I step inside, and the door whispers shut behind me.

"Howdy. Come on in and take a load off," Ernie says in the near dark from the console of the half-ton microscope. "Because you're going to want to sit down for this."

My top trace-evidence examiner always reminds me of a submarine pilot as he sits in front of a periscope-like thick metal tube that rises nearly to the ceiling and is topped by the assembly of the cathode, what most people call an electron gun but I tend to think of as more like a lightbulb. Its simple hairpin-shaped tungsten wire fires thermo-ionic emissions at whatever we decide to analyze, and I always find it cavelike in here, stuffy and claustrophobic.

The thick concrete walls are acoustically dead, and the dark fabric-covered fiberglass insulation seems to suck in all light. I have the sensation of being at the bottom of the sea, underground or lost in the cosmos. I always feel as if I'm passing into the unknown like Alice through the looking glass. And in a way I am because the world Ernie navigates can't be managed without instruments capable of de-tecting particles as small as one-billionth of a meter or seventy-five-thousandth the diameter of a human hair.

I could fit thousands of skin cells and specks of dust on such minus-cule and ubiquitous evidence, what I think of as the universal detritus shed by negativity and bad karma. People leave all sorts of seemingly undetectable trash in their wake, and it's constantly recycled. It can end up in the damnedest places as we track the tiniest tattletales in and out, passing them from one person or object to another, from one continent to the next.

I think back to when I saw Ernie last, maybe a month ago, and since then his blond-streaked graying hair has gotten longer. I notice that peeking out under his lab coat are a black suit and a bolo tie with a silver-and-turquoise arrowhead slide. He has on a black lizard belt, matching black cowboy boots, and I'm betting his black Stetson with its gambler crease is in his office. He must have court later today, a deposition or some other reason to dress up, and I ask him that.

"Nope." His blue eyes sparkle in his weathered face. "Something much more important. I was planning on heading over to the Kennedy School after work to hear your talk. I doubt I'll have time to go home first. A bunch of us are going from here."

I'm touched and overwhelmed by sadness as I sit down. I tell him about Briggs.

"Goddamn," Ernie swears under his breath as I brief him on what I fear we might be dealing with.

"Energy or electricity that's been weaponized somehow," I tell him what Benton suggested.

"Well in a bizarre way that would make sense," Ernie says.

"You've found something that might hint at such a thing?"

"Not exactly and maybe. I actually got onto this yesterday before I left," he refers to the Molly Hinders case as I continue scanning the bank of monitors overhead, not making much sense of what I'm seeing.

Displayed are peculiar shapes illuminated in black and white, some in the nano range and magnified two hundred thousand times. I'm confronted by spectra that are puzzling as I recognize the atomic symbols for nickel and aluminum recovered from the burn on the scalp, and also the presence of silica and iron.

I'm not sure why titanium would show up, and I'm baffled by the presence of zirconium and scandium. They aren't everyday metals. One is commonly used in nuclear reactors, the other in the aerospace industry.

"I didn't want to tell you what I'd found," Ernie says, "until I'd verified it with a buddy of mine at ORNL."

Oak Ridge National Laboratory in Tennessee is one place we turn when we have extraordinarily unusual questions in the field of materials science. In other words, if we can't figure out what something is made of and why, then we reach out to ORNL, MIT, Caltech, even NASA. A good example is the very thing I'm supposed to talk about tonight—the *Columbia* space shuttle tragedy. A typical crime lab wasn't going to determine why a heat shield failed.

"And he literally just called me as you were on your way down to see me," Ernie is saying. "You've heard me mention Bill. He works in the superconductor lab they've got down there and sleeps about as much as you do," he adds because it's not even four in the morning. Do you know what panguite is?"

"I don't think so," I reply. "In fact, I don't believe I know what you're talking about."

"This." He indicates a black-and-white image on a monitor that at 500X looks white and lumpy like misshapen molars.

CHAPTER 41

Panguite was discovered several years ago when geologists at Caltech were analyzing pieces of a meteorite that fell in northern Mexico in 1969." Ernie leans over to pull up a sock that's been eaten by his cowboy boot.

"I've never heard of a mineral called panguite," I reply.

"Named after Pangu, the god that split Ying from Yang or something," he says as my incredulity grows. "And what Bill says is just because panguite was recently discovered doesn't mean it's not present in other meteorites that have struck the earth. You'd have to go around testing space rocks in every museum in the world to know."

"How can you tell we're talking about a meteorite?" I indicate the monitors across the top of the room. "And you do realize how completely illogical this is? Molly Hinders certainly wasn't struck by a meteorite while she was watering her yard on Labor Day. Not that there's a case on record of anyone being struck by a meteorite but had she been? I would expect a lot more than a small burn on her scalp, and she certainly didn't die of blunt-force trauma. She's clearly an electrical death."

"The metals we're seeing are significant," Ernic points out. "Especially zirconium and scandium, but also iron, titanium et cetera."

"But there could be other explanations for finding them."

"But not for panguite. It doesn't naturally exist on earth." He points out peaks for Ti^{4+}, Sc, Al, Mg, Zr, Ca—the elemental components of what he goes on to explain is a new form of titania.

It occurs as fine crystals that at a magnification of 200,000X are reminiscent of pitted white bone or coral. I can see strange areas of red patina, and also irregular surface features including cracks, pits and crystal inclusions mixed with shiny fibers, what Ernie informs me are bundles of single-walled carbon nanotubes.

"Now you see our problem," he says.

"I certainly do."

"Mother Nature has been tampered with."

"You're thinking someone has built a weapon from a meteorite and carbon nanotubes?"

"Possibly."

Nanotubes are lightweight, incredibly strong, and structures made of these extremely fine fibers can be superfast and efficient at conducting electricity and heat. It's believed and feared that molecular nanotechnology is the future of everything, including war.

"Imagine making a small powerful bomb out of nanothermite or super-thermite?" Ernie is saying. "Or how about mini-nukes? Or God forbid bioterrorism delivered in the nano range? Scary shit."

"Yes it is, and I understand the utility of building something out of nanotubes, but what would anyone use panguite for?"

"That was my question too. And the possibility Bill came up with is if it's like titanium then maybe it's an undercoating, some sort of thermal protection."

"Then why not use titanium? And where might someone get hold of a meteorite, assuming the person doesn't work with them?"

"That's not hard," Ernie says. "You can buy all sorts of pieces and parts of meteorites off the Internet."

"But would they have panguite in them?"

"That's what I'm saying. We don't know. We can't know if they've not been analyzed. But I'm going to assume that this is rare." He means finding panguite is rare. "If the mineral was only recently discovered, it's hard for me to believe it's turned up often in the past or you might think it would have been discovered a long time ago."

"We're also talking about someone familiar with nanotechnology," I reply. "And if this person is actually modifying materials at the atomic level? Then we're not talking about the average bear."

"What do I say if the FBI wanders in here and starts asking me what I'm doing?" Ernie asks.

"Keep your door locked and they won't be wandering in. If you're quiet they'll never find you down here."

"Because if something like this got out, Kay? It would create a panic if the public thinks meteorites are killing people or some new death-ray-like weapon is."

"Discretion is imperative right now." I get up from my chair.

AFTER I LEAVE ERNIE, I return to the CT-scan room but it's empty now. I head back to the receiving area, where two FBI agents are drinking coffee near the door that leads out to the bay.

"I tried to call you," I say to Georgia as I pause by her desk.

"I bet you did right about the time I was out in the bay telling them they can't park in there. You see how much good it did. That big-ass SUV's still sitting in there, isn't it?"

"If it gets scraped by a stretcher they have no one to blame but themselves." I'm always warning Lucy about that.

She doesn't listen and nobody dings or sideswipes her cars. It hasn't happened once. But there's always a first time for everything, and I head in the direction of the autopsy room, which is dark and silent as

I walk past its shut door. Beyond it is another autopsy room, what's really an isolation area for badly decomposed or possibly infected cases, and the two agents on either side of the steel door leading inside don't look happy to be here.

Using my elbow, I press a hands-free steel button on the wall and the door automatically swings open on a cloud of stench that sends both agents scurrying out of the way.

"How are we doing in here?" I ask cheerfully as I take my time holding the door open wide, and the foulness is thick and bristles like something alive.

Mahant, Anne, Harold and Luke are swathed in protective clothing and clustered around the only table in a room with a thirty-foot ceiling and banks of high-intensity lights, and I note that the observation window in the upper wall is empty and dark. Anne didn't think to tell our FBI visitors that they could sit behind glass in a teaching lab and avoid unnecessary unpleasantness if they preferred. They could drink coffee up there and monitor everything we're doing on a live audio-video feed. But Anne accidentally on purpose forgot to mention it, I guess.

Luke snaps a new blade into a scalpel. The paper bags have been removed from Elisa Vandersteel's hands, feet and head, and her sports bra, blue shorts, and socks are off and spread out on a white-paper-covered countertop. He begins to run the blade through her flesh, from clavicle to clavicle, then down her torso.

"It's looking like she has cardiac damage, possibly a torn posterior pericardium, and hemorrhage in the area of the left myocardium," he tells me what he observed on the CT scan. "Plus what looks like suffusion of blood in the interventricular septum."

"What about her head injury?" I reach for rib cutters on the nearby surgical cart, and situate myself across the table from Luke.

I'm shoulder to shoulder with Mahant.

"No skull fracture," Luke says as I cut through ribs, removing the breastplate, exposing the thoracic organs, and the putrid odor blooms up our nostrils like a dark deadly flower.

Mahant's face shield isn't going to save him, and I watch as he turns a tint of grayish green. Luke lifts the bloc of organs out of the chest cavity and sets it on a big cutting board with a wet heavy sound.

"Is something wrong with the air in here?" Mahant has inched back from the table, and he's staring at me without blinking.

"Too cold? Too hot?" Anne innocently inquires.

"I mean the ventilation." He swallows hard.

"It could be worse. We had a floater in here the other day." She looks at me as I snip open the stomach with surgical scissors. "In fact that's when the ventilation didn't seem to be working all that well."

"It's the heat wave," Luke says.

"How would that affect the ventilation?"

"It affects everything."

"You can imagine how hard our air-handling system has to work in this weather." I dribble the gastric contents into a plastic carton, and I'm surprised to find undigested peanuts and raisins.

"Obviously she had a snack not long before she died," I show Mahant the palm of my glove as he backs up another several inches.

"Maybe a trail mix or something like that?" Anne suggests as I snip through the connective tissue of the bowels, dropping sections into a plastic bucket on the floor while Luke removes a kidney from the scale.

"You might want to find out about that," I say to Mahant as Luke begins sectioning the kidney and Harold makes an incision around the top of the skull.

Then Bryce walks in, and he couldn't be more oblivious to what's normal for him and for all of us.

"Taking breakfast orders," he announces cheerily, and I resist looking at Anne, who clearly has gotten to him with her evil plan. "How many takers do we have for pizza?"

"Jesus," Mahant stares wide-eyed at him, and Harold pulls the body's face down like a collapsed rubber mask so he can access the top of the skull, gleaming white and round like an egg.

"Meat or veggie?" Bryce asks as Harold plugs the Stryker saw into an overhead cord reel. "And we have gluten-free." Bryce raises his voice over the loud whining of the oscillating blade cutting through bone. "But nothing *glutton*-free," he can't resist his favorite pun. "Because you can't stop eating it," he says.

Harold picks up a chisel to pop off the skullcap.

"The trick is to cut a little notch right here," he shows Mahant, who isn't blinking and hardly breathing anymore. "Then I insert the chisel and give it a little quick turn like a skate key." Harold does it as he talks, and then he's catching the ASAC as he topples like a tree to the tile floor.

"Oh dear. Let's get him some air." Harold holds him up and walks him to the door, and he's done this quite a lot in his career. "Here." He opens it and leads him out. "Let's find you a chair," he says in his best funeral-director voice. "Can one of you gentlemen please find a chair? He just needs a little air," he says to the agents in the corridor, and I must be a bad person.

I stay inside the decomp room and do nothing to help Mahant. As long as he doesn't throw up on the body or crack his head on the floor, I don't care if he's faint or queasy. I pretend I do but I know it's not true, and maybe he and his merry band of agents will leave and not come back.

"Take a look." Luke is slicing the heart on the cutting board.

He uses a towel to pat dry a section, and the fresh myocardial contusion is a tiny bluish-black spot on the pale heart muscle.

"Basically the electrical current walloped her heart and stopped it," he says.

"Do you think the injury to her head would have knocked her out?" Anne asks. "On CT she definitely has subarachnoid hemorrhage."

"It might have," I reply, "but it doesn't matter because the head injury didn't contribute to her death. Maybe it would have but there wasn't a chance. She was already dying when she hit the ground."

"Taking everything into account?" Luke adds as he takes photographs. "Death resulted from respiratory arrest due to electrocution. She probably didn't survive longer than several minutes, and I doubt she knew what hit her."

CHAPTER 42

ACROSS THE RIVER THE rooftops of Boston are a gray dragon's back of slate tiles and chimney pots. I watch the darkness lifting on the horizon, the sun rising before my eyes.

From my office with a view I witness dawn touch the new day, the river turning variegated shades of blue with greenish hues. Iron lamps blink off along the pale gash of the fitness path where people are out riding bikes and jogging. The world is waking up as usual, as if nothing at all happened last night not even a mile downriver from here. The death in John F. Kennedy Park has hit the news but you'd never know it to look out my windows.

I walk across the carpet carrying a large very strong coffee I just made at the espresso bar. I sit down at my U-shaped desk with its bunker of large computer monitors, and I've been translating and transcribing for the better part of an hour.

I've decided spacing and line breaks based on cadence and pauses, doing my best to infer format from what I listened to in the Tailend Charlie audio clip e-mailed to me early last night:

> *Back again, K.S.—*
>   *(By popular request, no less!)*

What's next
  will be worse
  than what was first.
    (Face it Florida cracker
    you were cursed at birth.)

Chaos is coming
  in a stinging swarm,
  a death airborne.
    (Remember Sister Twister?
    Bet you won't miss her!)

Interpreting meanings in cryptic messages and symbolism is like reading tea leaves, but what strikes me most about this last communication isn't the mentions of Florida cracker and Sister Twister. Lucy had told me about these when we talked in the trailer, and I don't care about insults right now. It's the threat that we need to pay attention to, and Lucy probably missed it because her Italian is inadequate.

What's next will be worse than what was first.

Was Molly Hinders first? Is this who Tailend Charlie is alluding to? And what's next? Would that have been Elisa Vandersteel? Or maybe he's talking about something or someone else entirely, and I wonder how much personal information about me came from years of Carrie spying on Janet's sister Natalie.

Carrie could have learned all sorts of things if she put her mind to it, and she could have passed on these details to an accomplice who's now using them to taunt and belittle. Someone brilliant but deranged, it enters my mind because that's the feeling I get when I'm subjected to his communications.

But why? There are so many things one might mock me about. Why pick silly names I was called as a child? Why not pick the much worse ones I'm called now? It's childish. In fact it reminds me of the way my sister used to fight with me when we were little kids. I decide it must be Carrie's new sidekick who's having such juvenile fun with verse recited in synthesized Italian that's supposed to be my father berating and disgracing me. I try Benton again. The call goes to voice mail again, and I leave another message:

Hey, it's me. I sent you my best effort with the latest troll-ish communication. Without being too specific, I think certain phrases in it might be of interest, and while I'm not the expert, it seems to promise something disastrous. The word aerotrasportato *or "airborne" was used, and I checked multiple times to make sure I heard the canned Italian word right. Call when you're able.*

It's almost seven A.M. here or about one P.M. in France, and I remember the last time I stayed at La Tour Rose in Lyon. It's hard to believe it's been six years since I last visited Interpol's headquarters, what looks like an intergalactic space station clandestinely situated out in the middle of nowhere along the River Rhône.

The secretary-general will be eating lunch because one thing I know about Tom Perry is he never turns down a civilized meal. So I'm not likely to get him but I try his office anyway, and his assistant Marie answers the phone.

"I'm sure he's at lunch," I say by way of an apology after we exchange pleasantries.

"He is," she replies in her heavy French accent. "But he happens to be eating at his desk as he finishes a long call."

"I want to pass on information and I could use his help with something."

"Hold on, please. And it's very nice to talk to you again, Madame Scarpetta. You must come back and visit soon."

I can hear her talking to the secretary-general in French but I have no idea what they're saying. Then he's on the line, and I know instantly by the tone of his voice that he's in the middle of something that is indeed serious. More serious than usual, at any rate.

"I wouldn't bother you, Tom," I say right off, "but I think it's time we talk about what's happening in Cambridge."

"And also in Bethesda, it seems," he says, and as I suspected he knows about Briggs.

Obviously Benton or one of his colleagues with the FBI has been in communication with Interpol, and I wonder who Perry was having the long phone conversation with right before I called. I wonder if it might have been Benton. His phone goes straight to voice mail every time I try him, and I would expect him to be informing the secretary-general of what's going on since some murderous miscreant is using Interpol's esteemed name in vain, basically spoofing the agency.

Possibly Carrie Grethen is. Possibly her accomplice is. Maybe both of them together are responsible for everything, but Interpol is more than a little familiar with her at least, I remind Perry as I explain why I'm reaching out to him. They got a bellyful of Carrie long years ago, and then like the rest of us believed she was dead until she decided to show us that she's not.

"I haven't had much sleep, so I hope I'm not rambling," I add. "But you know very well how dangerous she is, and I don't have an idea what the ultimate goal is but I know she has one."

"Why do you know that, Kay?"

"Because she always does, and I feel this is something really bad, that she's looking to make a statement."

"Certainly you know her better than I do," he says, and I don't like the way it feels when anybody points out that I know her at all.

"Based on information I've gotten from Lucy, it seems Carrie has been laying the groundwork for some sort of coup," I explain. "She's been planning something for years, and I'm concerned about more people being hurt or killed. I'm concerned about a lot of things."

"Well I'm glad you reached out to me, and I'm always grateful for your input, especially about a matter you've had so much personal experience with. What did you want my help with specifically?" The secretary-general has a Connecticut accent, and he doesn't sound surprised or impressed by anything I've said.

"Last time I visited you in Lyon we had a conversation over a very nice Bordeaux, and you made the comment that anything can be weaponized, and of course that includes fear."

"Which is the point of terror."

"If you can create a weapon that causes enough fear," I explain, "the fear itself can cause damage that's as paralyzing and destructive as any physical device like a bomb or a laser gun. Fear can make decent people behave irrationally and violently. And imagine suddenly worrying that something airborne might kill you as you ride your bike or swim in your pool."

"Yes, I agree," he says. "That would be extremely bad, especially if there really is a weapon involved. I understand your office is doing the autopsy this morning in the Vandersteel case."

"We're done," I reply. "By the time we got to it we already had a pretty good idea that she's an electrocution and most likely is a homicide. But what's new and somewhat of a surprise is there may have been an earlier victim."

"Where and how recently?"

"In Cambridge at the beginning of the week. In fact I'm fairly certain of it now, and that leads to my next question. Could there be others, including in places outside the United States? Cases of presumed lightning strikes or weird electrocutions, particularly if the person is around water and out in the open. It's also possible there are victims who survived. I'm not sure Elisa Vandersteel would have died had the electrical current not hit a metal necklace she was wearing."

"We're thinking the same way," Perry says. "You and I both know that things start small but the problem is, by the time we recognize these things, they're no longer small."

"If we're not careful."

"That's right. And we must be very careful because local terror in Massachusetts or the U.S. can be a proving ground for something international," he adds, and I tell him about Molly Hinders.

I DESCRIBE HER INJURIES, explaining that she was killed in Cambridge near the Charles River and so was Elisa Vandersteel.

Both of them were attacked as it was getting dark, meaning the visibility would have been poor, and moisture was a factor in each case. Molly was standing in wet grass as she sprayed a hose, and Elisa would have been sweaty. Moisture and electricity like each other.

"But it's curious. Why would Carrie Grethen be interested in either of the women?" Perry wonders over the phone.

"If you want my opinion? Carrie wouldn't be," and it's amazing how much I resist saying her name.

But I'm thinking of what Lucy said. If I make no effort to understand Carrie Grethen, I'll never have a hope of stopping her. And I do know her. I know her far better than I let on to anyone, including myself.

"Carrie would be interested in Briggs," I explain. "I can understand her targeting him, and mostly the choice is personal for her. Benton and I had worked with him for decades. You know how close I was to him. She's paying us back. Mostly she's paying me back."

"For what?"

I start to give him my stock flip answer of *who knows?* But I do know what Carrie will never forgive, and it's not really about Lucy or any of us. It's about Temple Gault. I killed him in a confrontation, stabbed a knife in his thigh and severed his femoral artery. I knew exactly what I was doing, and he gave me no choice. Carrie's never gotten over it, and according to Benton she's never gotten over him.

"But there's nothing personal about the victim selection with the other two," Perry says.

"There probably is but probably not for Carrie Grethen," I reply. "The more we're seeing, the less likely it is that she's working alone. So maybe her accomplice, her new Temple Gault, is killing the women while Carrie is on to bigger game like John Briggs or who knows who might be next."

"You know the problem with accomplices, don't you? They don't always do what they're told."

"Suggesting Carrie might not have anything to do with the Vandersteel and Hinders cases."

"If someone goes rogue."

"That would make her very angry."

"And her partners always go rogue. But let me ask you this first," Perry says over the phone. "From an evidence standpoint what justifies your deciding these cases are homicides? Has something turned up that I wouldn't know about?"

He wouldn't know about certain developments because the FBI doesn't yet, and I'm in no hurry to share the information. If the secretary-general of Interpol tells them, that's his business.

"Something has turned up, and you're about to be the only person I've told," I reply as I watch the sun peek above the horizon, painting streaks of orange across Prussian blue. "I've not told the FBI or anyone what I'm about to say to you. We need to be extremely strategic about how the information is shared because it appears we're dealing with a weapon that at least in part has been fashioned from a meteorite—"

"All right, hold on," he interrupts me. "Say that again."

I tell him about panguite as I keep thinking about what Ernie said.

You'd have to go around testing space rocks in every museum in the world . . .

Before he mentioned that, I wasn't thinking about museums. But now I am.

"Of course someone could have bought pieces of meteorites on the Internet but they wouldn't necessarily contain panguite. So we need to consider how someone acquired it and then had the ability to engineer it into something dangerous," I'm explaining to Tom Perry. "For example, was it stolen from a collection somewhere? Just as priceless art can be heisted from museums, so can rare rocks."

"Obviously you've not talked to Benton yet," Perry says, and I imagine the secretary-general's smiling eyes and easygoing manner.

No matter how busy he is, he never acts like he's in a hurry. Some of the nicest, longest business lunches I've ever had have been with him in Lyon, and he knows French wines dangerously well for an American.

"Obviously you've talked to Benton if you're asking me that. I've not talked to him since he left here with Lucy, headed to Maryland," I reply as light flares mirror bright on the surrounding Harvard and MIT apartment and academic buildings.

CHAPTER 43

Sʜᴀᴅᴏᴡs ᴍᴏᴠᴇ ᴏᴠᴇʀ ʙʀɪᴄᴋ and granite. In the distance the skyline of downtown Boston is more sharply outlined and begins to glitter as the sun rises higher in the cloudless sky.

"Do you know who William Portison is?" Tom Perry says, and I'm betting Benton has talked to the man Elisa Vandersteel once worked for.

"Lucy says he's a tech CEO in London, clearly very wealthy," I reply. "The address for their Mayfair house is what Elisa had on her driver's license. We found it near her body."

"He's an alum of MIT, and so is his ne'er-do-well brother, both of them British. One is a mega-success worth billions and the other just as smart but missing a few wires or they're crossed or something. I'd call Theo in the spectrum, a whack-job genius."

"Theo?" I look out at pastel streaks changing in shape and intensity as sunlight flickers like shiny fish in the slow-moving current of the river across the street.

"Theodore Portison. He goes by Theo when he's not using an alias."

Rowers in colorful racing shells slice through the water, and rush-hour traffic sounds like a faraway train, a strong wind, a steady rain.

"Why would he use an alias?" I ask.

"He's paranoid people are out to get him. So he runs and hides, this is according to the brother," Perry says, and I feel sure the information actually came from Benton.

I seriously doubt the secretary-general of Interpol talked to William Portison himself, and my husband can get the most sensitive information from a stone.

"How old is the brother?" I ask.

"Theo Portison is forty-seven, single, never married. He taught quantum physics at MIT until he was fired about twenty years ago, and this has been checked out and verified."

He means that Benton has checked it out.

"Theo moved back to Cambridge about a year ago, and in fact I'm guessing that even as we speak he's either been visited by the FBI or is about to be," Perry lets me know, and I wonder where Marino is as all this is going on.

"Why was Theo fired?" I inquire, and I glance at new messages, and there's still nothing from Benton or Lucy.

"The short answer again is he's crazy," Perry says as I look out at the sunrise. "The long one is he was causing problems with female students. Apparently he would be overly attentive and then he'd start stalking them. Specifically what got him fired is he planted surveillance devices in one girl's dorm room. If you're going to spy? Maybe don't pick someone at MIT who's as smart as you are. He got caught."

"And what has he been doing for the past twenty years?" I ask.

"I don't think he has to do anything. His wealthy brother takes care of him, and in many ways always has. For a long time Theo lived with their mother in London but she died a few years back. As you're probably gathering, he has an adjustment disorder, to put it kindly."

"Would it be fair to say that the authorities have had their eye on Theo Portison for a while? I'm wondering if he has terrorist or radicalized leanings and it was brought to someone's attention?" After a long empty pause I ask, "Tom? Hello? Are you still there?"

"Yes."

"Yes what?"

"Yes it would be fair," and that's as far as he'll go in letting me know that the Portisons aren't a new problem.

What they are is a different one. Especially Theo.

"Is there a reason Theo would be in possession of panguite or have access to it?" I ask the secretary-general, bringing us back to the traces of meteorite Ernie found.

"Well that's interesting because William Portison's business is aerospace technologies, and they build rockets among other things," Perry says. "He's into cars, space travel, timepieces, all sorts of things including rocks, and has his own museum, and guess who helped him with it? His limited brother. I think Theo is William's *Rain Man* aide-de-camp."

"Then it's likely Theo was acquainted with Elisa Vandersteel since she was living with his brother's family for the past two or so years. Is the rock collection in the house?" I ask, and there's much more to what Perry is saying than meets the eye.

"He keeps his collection in a safe room with a gun vault door."

"Someone needs to find out if anything is missing," I reply. "Specifically if any type of space rock is missing, and if so, what it is and most importantly what is the provenance. Where did he get it?" I explain what we need to be finding out. "The mineral fingerprint of the meteorite might be the only real evidence in this case. We can match it if it turns up again."

"But wouldn't Theo know that if he used to help with the museum?"

"It depends on whether his brother knows the details of what he bought or was given. William Portison might have acquired part of a meteorite and not known its precise elemental composition," as I hear the lock buzz free in my office door.

"Scotland Yard will be interested in all this, I'm sure," Perry says, adding to my suspicions that the authorities have more than one fish to fry.

I END THE CALL as Marino walks in, and I'm reminded of his privileged character.

I haven't gotten around to deleting his fingerprint from certain biometric locks, including the one to the parking-lot gate, the pedestrian door that leads into the building and also the door to my office. It's been years since he headed investigations here. But I can't bring myself to eradicate all traces of him, and as I watch him walk in, I notice he's still in his same sweaty clothes he was working in earlier although he got rid of the navy jacket long ago.

He hasn't showered. That's apparent as he hovers by my desk like a predatory bird. On a scale of one to ten with ten the highest, I'd rate Marino's anger right now at a hundred. He's in what I think of as a white rage, his face livid, his eyes granite as he clenches his jaw muscles.

"You look about as pissed as I've ever seen you, and I hope it's not at me," I start to say.

"The fuckers," he growls, and I can see the pulse in his temple as a reddish-purple thrush creeps up his neck. "I'm sitting down with the guy and really getting somewhere, and the assholes showed up in fucking SWAT gear and had the mother-effing helicopter thundering over the damn house. When they realize it's just me and some local nutjob they call off the dogs, and then Mahant walks in like the new sheriff's come to town." Marino dusts off his hands. "The end."

"What do you mean *the end*? And who are you talking about?"

"Bryce's cranky next-door neighbor," Marino says to my shock. "I was just getting to the bottom of why he made the bogus nine-one-one call about you."

"Marino . . . ?" as I think of what Tom Perry just told me about Theo Portison.

He's either been visited by the FBI or is about to be.

"It was exactly what Bryce said," Marino is talking fast and without pause. "To get him back for insulting him, and what better way to hurt him than to drag the big chief Doctor Scarpetta into the mix so maybe he gets fired—"

"What did you just call me?"

"Big chief?" Marino shrugs. "It's what he called you, not me."

"That's what Tailend Charlie calls me in some of the mocking audio clips."

"Well you can tell the FBI that but I'm not helping them a damn bit."

"Are you saying that they just showed up at Theo Portison's door while you were sitting in the living room with him?" I then ask.

"Who the hell's Theo Portison?" Marino scowls, looming over me. "Bryce's neighbor is John Smyth with a *y*, the English spelling. And I guess it's not enough for the Feds to take over the Vandersteel and Briggs cases but now they're looking into crank nine-one-one calls? I mean what the hell?"

"Did Mahant or someone tell you why they were there?"

"When do they ever tell us anything?"

"His name is Theodore Portison, and apparently he's known for having aliases because he gets paranoid." I push back my chair from my desk. "He was fired by MIT twenty years ago, and he knew Elisa Vandersteel. It's quite possible he's Tailend Charlie." I get up and take off my lab coat. "We'll see if I get any more audio files after this."

"Well they grabbed him," Marino says as we walk to my door. "They ended up arresting him."

"For what?"

"Hell if I know. But they've been digging through his landfill of a place. Shit. It's my case, Doc."

"The important thing is he was caught."

"But Carrie hasn't been."

"One down is better than nothing. Assuming he's Tailend Charlie, that he's the one who killed these two women."

"And has been harassing you, me, Benton. Using voice-altering software or whatever? Why?"

"Ask Benton," I reply. "But I'm betting it has to do with fantasies and power, and maybe the delusional thinking of a damaged brain mixed in. Does Theo Portison by chance have a drone?"

"He's got shit all over the place including what look like robot parts. The inside of his house looks like *Sanford and Son*. Think crazy-ass inventor meets homeless person, and it looks like his kitchen is also a lab, and part of it was under a plastic tent like he was making crystal meth or something."

"Does he have a cough?" I ask, and we're following my curved corridor to the elevator.

"He says he's got chronic lung disease, and I can't remember whose fault he said it was. He's one of those people who pretty much blames everyone for everything."

"I'm not surprised he has lung disease."

"Why?" Marino looks at me. "Just because of a cough?"

"If he works with nanotubes and doesn't do it in an appropriate clean room or under a HEPA-rated local capture hood—in other words a protected environment—he could have a serious respiratory problem from inhaling fibers and particles too small to see. And as you may remember, the phony Interpol investigator who called you had a cough. That's what you said. And maybe not so coincidentally, so did the phony Interpol investigator who called Benton."

"Nanotubes?"

I tell Marino about that next, and we're in the elevator now, the building restored to its usual sanctity and rhythm. People are coming in to work, and the FBI is no longer here. I'm sure Theodore Portison will keep them busy for a while, and Mahant may decide never to watch an autopsy again.

"I never did have any pizza," Marino says as the elevator slowly descends.

"That was a long time ago and you weren't here. How did you know about it?" I ask.

"Oh, I know your little tricks," he says. "I heard about the ventilation system and that you grossed out Mahant so bad he hit the deck."

"*Almost* hit it." I wave at Georgia as Marino and I pass through the receiving area, headed to the parking lot.

CHAPTER 44

THE LIMITATIONS OF HUMAN flesh, and I should know better than to think I can ignore them.

Driving home is an effort, and I find myself struggling to stay awake as I ease to a halt at a stop sign near the Harvard Divinity School in our Cambridge neighborhood. My blood sugar is low, and I'm feeling the crushing letdown that's a given after I've been fueled by nothing but high-octane adrenaline for hours.

Thankfully I live not even fifteen minutes away from the CFC, and I blast cold air on my face, listening to music, doing whatever I can to stay awake. It's a few minutes past nine, and the morning sun is bright overhead as I pull into the narrow brick driveway of our nineteenth-century timber-sided house, painted smoky blue with gray shutters and doors. There are tall chimneys at either end of the slate roof, and sunlight blanks out the upstairs windows as I park behind Janet's green Land Rover.

It has half of the detached garage blocked, and when Page returns from taking the dogs to the groomer, her pickup truck will block the other half. Good luck getting Benton's or my personal cars out should I need them for some reason.

Everybody's here, I think dismally, and then I feel selfish. As much as I love my family, what I'd like right now is privacy in my own home. And I need to give that up and get over myself. I need to be a good sport and remember not everything in life is about solving crime. Climbing out with my messenger-bag briefcase, I lock my CFC SUV that I wasn't going to leave at the office this time. Following pavers through the wooded front yard, I take the brick steps, aware of the early morning heating up. But by all accounts it's not supposed to reach ninety today. This weekend it's going to rain, and my garden and lawn could use it.

There's a lot of cooking I need to do, and I'm not prepared. Had I known this many people including Dorothy would be staying here I would have done major shopping, and maybe I'll find time this afternoon to get to the store before I have to get ready for the Kennedy School. Maybe I'll throw together something easy like lasagna that we can heat up after the event is over.

We'll open a few bottles of a nice Pinot Noir and drink a toast to Briggs, I decide as I stand on the front porch with keys in hand, looking around and listening. I hear a light breeze stir the old hardwood trees in the front yard, and I detect the earthy fragrances of loamy soil and mulch. A car drives by, one of our neighbors, and she waves.

Benton and I live on the northeastern border of the Harvard campus, across the street from the Academy of Arts and Sciences, and around us on all sides are lovely antique homes that are manifestations of enlightenment. I love it here. I love fooling myself into believing I'm safe as long as I'm surrounded by smart people, and I look around some more, my hand on the door handle.

I don't hear anyone, and the dogs aren't here. But I detect a distant noise, a faint high-pitched whine like a table saw, and there's a house being renovated two doors down. Another car goes by, another neighbor, and I open the front door, noticing that the alarm isn't set. That doesn't make me happy. Stepping into the foyer of dark-paneled walls arranged with Victorian etchings I pause to listen, but I don't hear anyone, and it occurs to me that Janet, Desi and my sister might be in the backyard. In fact that sounds like a very nice plan. Maybe I'll drink coffee with them for a while. Then I'll try to sleep for a few hours.

At some point this afternoon I'll need to go over my talk for tonight because I've confirmed with my contact at the Kennedy School that I'm not going to cancel. I'm going to do this for Briggs. In spirit he'll be with me as I address policy makers about the dangerous planet we live on and why it's imperative to incorporate science and the highest level of training into everything we do if we're to expand our frontiers and protect ourselves.

Inside the kitchen I see used coffee pods on the counter near the Keurig, and someone had cheddar-cheese toast. Probably Desi, as he's become a big fan of Vermont cheddar since moving here and is quite particular about what color wrapper the block of cheese comes in. For him extra sharp is synonymous with purple, and in the mornings he asks for purple cheese toast, I'm told.

I set my briefcase on the breakfast table near a window, and I head to the back door, where Desi has parked the fishing pole, the baseball bat and glove Marino gave him for his birthday. The pole has a hard rubber casting sinker attached to a long sturdy leader line that's tied to the monofilament, and he's been teaching Desi how to cast the same way he once taught me. The nine-year-old is learning patience and precision, and not to muscle his way through life.

It's fine except for how it makes Benton feel, and as sorry as I might be about that, we have to do what's best for the child. Marino is good for Desi, and I don't mind them using the backyard as long as no one tramples my roses, and the rule is when the line gets tangled in trees, no one is climbing anything.

Safety first, and I begin to open the oak door leading outside. Then I stop because I don't understand what I'm seeing.

CHAPTER 45

Lucy is in khaki cargo pants, a CFC polo shirt, a baseball cap and dark glasses. She's near the big magnolia tree with its circular bench, and Desi is standing woodenly next to her. He's holding what looks like an iPad, barefoot and in Miami Dolphins shorts and T-shirt, and he's wearing something blue around his neck.

I duck back into the quiet gloom of the hallway as I realize it can't be Lucy who's with Desi, and my heart lurches as if I almost stepped on a snake. She's in Maryland, and even if she magically were back this soon, the androgynous-looking person with short strawberry-blond hair is too thin to be my niece. I realize who I must be looking at as my heart pounds out of my chest, and I go to an app on my phone, turning the cameras on for the house and the property.

I duck into the pantry, where there's a flat-screen monitor on the butcher block. I zoom in on the backyard, tilting and panning, hoping Carrie Grethen doesn't know what I'm doing. She should have heard me drive up but maybe she didn't. Maybe she knows someone is inside the house watching but she might not, and I check every zone monitored by cameras, making sure I don't see anyone else on the property.

So far it seems Carrie is here alone, and I think of what I assumed was a white construction van parked on the side of the road just past our driveway. I saw it when I was pulling in, and I'm on edge, worried that any second Carrie's going to notice the cameras move. But she isn't looking. Her attention is all over the place. On Desi and also straight up at the sky and down at the tabletlike device he's holding, and across at my sister and Janet, who are out of frame but I know they must be sitting there. I just heard Dorothy's voice but I didn't catch what she said.

I turn up the audio on the HD cameras as high as it will go.

". . . I don't want to," Desi tells Carrie as he shakes his head no. "I don't want to sting anyone."

"Of course you do."

"It's bad to hurt people."

"Let me show you how much fun it is. Just click on that arrow key pointing at the word *enable*. It's in green on the display, and when you touch the key the color turns red because the TC is armed. A Tailend Charlie. Do you know what that is, son?"

"I don't want to play with you anymore. And I'm not your son," he says, and Carrie smiles radiantly.

"When you find out who you are it will be like discovering you're royalty. Prince Desi." She places a hand on his shoulder.

"You're scaring me," he says.

"But why are you doing this?" It's Dorothy talking again, and I try to find her with the cameras. "I thought we were friends."

It would be like her to think she could persuade Carrie Grethen to cease and desist, to give up and go away or even more preposterous to believe that Carrie would like her and want to be friends. Of course my narcissistic sister would assume she's a match for someone who has caused misery and destruction for decades.

I lock in a camera on Dorothy and Janet sitting tensely in chairs some twenty feet from the magnolia tree. A small table with their coffees and bottles of water is between them. Both of them are in scrubs that they probably got from me, and neither of them moves. Their hands are in their laps, but I don't see any sign of restraints. Dorothy's eyes are wide, and the morning light isn't kind on her overfilled Botoxed face while Janet is quiet and steady.

I already know Janet doesn't have a gun. If she did she would have handled Carrie by now, and all of us have had to develop new habits with firearms now that a child is in the mix. I manipulate the cameras some more and I see the drone, what looks like a big black whirling spider with eight rotor blades hovering at the top of the magnolia tree. That's the high-pitched whining I was hearing. It's not construction at the neighbor's house.

I send Marino a text:

MAYDAY. She's at my house in backyard. Hostage sit & drone.

I don't call 911. I can't have regular patrol cars roar up. That's not how one deals with something like this, and it's sneaking up on me what Carrie is doing. She wants Desi to be inducted into her infernal family. She wants him to hurt someone, to kill someone with her weaponized drone.

Remember Sister Twister? Bet you won't miss her.

Carrie is going to kill Dorothy, and then she'll get rid of Janet. That leaves only Desi, and it's clear to me what she's planned to do as I think of her spying on Natalie. I wonder if Carrie was really spying on the boy.

"But why?" My sister never does know when to shut up, and Desi is a small statue holding the flight controller. "I don't understand. We had such a nice conversation on the plane," she foolishly says, and now I know.

Carrie must have orchestrated it so that she would be with my sister on the flight from Fort Lauderdale last night. No doubt she was sitting right next to her in first class, and that's probably why the alarm is off in the house and Carrie is in my backyard. Dorothy probably let her in just like she would some other new friend she's made, and my sister never meets a stranger.

She'll bring anybody home and did all the time when we were growing up. She never asked. It's always been her right to do whatever she wants, and this time it might cost her and all of us. My mind races crazily as I try to figure out what to do.

"I just can't understand why you're here being so awful, and after several drinks and our lovely conversation? I thought I had a new girlfriend, one who reminds me so much of my daughter, which is why we were so instantly taken with each other. And here I thought it was going to be such fun when I came north to see my grandson." My sister is crying. "Desi? Come over here right now and let's all go into the house like this never happened. And you just go on and leave us alone, do it now while you can," she warns Carrie, whose answer is to take the flight controller out of Desi's hands.

She moves the drone directly over my sister's head, approximately six feet above her, and the flying blades stir her dyed blond hair, which is long and makes her look harsh.

"Just touch where it says *enable*," Carrie says to Desi, and she holds the flight controller close to show him.

"Don't do anything she says!" Dorothy cries.

"Shut up. Please," Janet says to her while not taking her eyes off Carrie.

But Janet has no weapon. If she did, she'd know exactly how to use it, and even as I'm thinking this I don't see a way out. Not in the usual sense of what one does in a dire emergency. It's very hard to shoot a drone. They're filled with empty spaces and even if you take out several rotor blades that doesn't mean you're going to stop it in time.

You'd need to take out the power source the same way you would an explosive device. But I don't have a water cannon handy, and taking the lock off the pistol I keep out of reach on a top shelf of a kitchen cabinet isn't going to help. Spraying bullets in a residential neighborhood is out of the question.

PAGE AND THE DOGS are nowhere to be seen or heard. I hope they don't return from the groomer anytime soon, and my attention continues to land on the sports equipment rather sloppily tucked in the corner to the left of the door.

I see the fishing pole, and the baseball bat is wooden not metal. The baseball mitt is leather, and it, like wood and dry skin, is a good insulation against electricity. I also notice the empty hooks where Sock and Tesla's leashes hang, and it prompts me to send a text to Page:

DO NOT return home until U hear from me.

Carrie wouldn't hesitate to hurt anything we care about, including Page, including our pets.

"I'm going to show you," Carrie is saying to Desi as I continue to monitor the backyard with the cameras.

I watch the spinning drone hovering over my sister's head, and Carrie touches the display of the flight controller. The drone makes a vertical assent, and at the same time I see the conductors lowering, four of them so fine they're barely visible, like thin gray pencil lines with something round and dark weighting each at the end.

Eerily the conductors vanish from view on and off. All I see are the round weights floating in space like tiny dark planets, and I think of the round burn on the back of Briggs's neck.

"I'm going to show you something cool," Carrie says to Desi, returning the flight controller to his unwilling hands. "But first you need to do something for me. An experiment. See the bottle of water on the table? Go pour it on Granny Dorothy's head."

"No."

"Do it."

"No."

I pick up the fishing pole.

"You need to learn how to be brave. What's wrong with you? It looks like I'm going to have to toughen you up." Carrie's face is transformed by anger. "See what happens when you're raised by inferiors? Well that's all about to change, Desi."

I've been fishing a few times in my life, mostly with Marino, who went to great lengths teaching me how to cast. I'm pretty good with my hands, and I flip back the bail on the spinning reel as I walk out the back door. There's a chance the spinning blades will cut the leader and the line but I also know that even helicopters avoid monofilament. Lucy is careful flying low over beaches because of kites and helium balloons attached to hundreds of feet of fishing line.

Carrie stops me as her face turns murderous and at the same time pleased. I pull back the graceful long pole and snap it forward with just the right flick of my wrist, I hope, and the rubber sinker sails up in an arc toward the top of the magnolia tree. Sunlight catches the graceful monofilament line as it rises high and bends, falling over the whirling dervish, and I wait for the spinning blades to cut the line.

But they don't, and the drone jerks. At least one of the blades has stopped, and the sudden tugging cues me to start reeling as Carrie yells obscenities, the flight controller unable to override the lowest technology of modern time, a simple fishing pole.

"Run! Run!" Desi is yelling, and Janet is on her feet.

The drone careens like a wounded bird, and I reel and reel as Carrie's furious strides close in on me. Reeling furiously, and the drone is no more than ten feet away, loud like a whirling fan, the conductors dangling not far over her head.

I tug down hard on the fishing pole at the same moment Carrie pulls out a big stiletto and the long blade hisses out. Then blood is flying everywhere. I hear someone screaming and what sounds like a transformer blowing, and then I'm on the ground. I smell burned flesh.

CHAPTER 46

For AN INSTANT I was Elisa Vandersteel sailing through empty space and landing on my back, remembering nothing. Except I came to in the emergency room. I'm not dead, not even close, and I sit up in bed to the sound of heavy rain.

It dully beats the slate roof and spatters the windows when the wind blasts, and Sock and Tesla are wedged warmly on either side of me. I hear their breathing, and then it's drowned out by howling gusts that just now whistled and moaned, and water thrashes and drums in different intensities and tempos. The early morning sounds moody and wounded. Or maybe it's me who feels like that.

The event at the Kennedy School night before last wasn't canceled but postponed, and that not only was wise but unavoidable. One speaker was dead, the other in the hospital. Whatever the drone's conductors came in contact with in addition to Carrie Grethen and her stiletto caused me to be thrown and knocked unconscious. I spent the next day and a half being tested, prodded, probed and scanned, finally coming home last night.

So I didn't give my presentation to influential people, and here I am resting peacefully in bed with two dogs. I can't think of anything much better than that. Janet and Desi have been kind and thoughtful about looking after me, and Dorothy is around somewhere. Benton and Lucy should be home any minute, having left the helicopter behind in D.C. because of the weather. We'll have a wonderful brunch in a little while. I should get going, and I feel strangely lightweight as if someone turned down gravity.

It's as if the reign of terror has been lifted with the dry spell, the heat wave, as if the balance of life has been restored, and I feel happy in a way I've not been in a long while. Carrie Grethen was badly sliced up and burned, her skull fractured by the mechanical monster of her own design. When she's sufficiently recovered she'll be held in isolation at the local state psychiatric hospital, in a maximum security forensic unit for the criminally insane. She can't hurt anyone now, and her partner Theo Portison is in jail, neither going anywhere except to trial.

Meanwhile the police and FBI will continue their search for any other foot soldiers she may have recruited here or abroad. Lucy suspects Carrie can operate her drones remotely the same way military operators do. She could have had one docked in the Bethesda area and piloted it from South Florida to fly to Briggs's house and kill him. After that Carrie boarded the plane in Fort Lauderdale and enjoyed her friendly flight with my sister. I can't wait to hear what Dorothy has to say about that. Since I got shocked unconscious, I've not talked to her much.

I check my e-mail. My office is working overtime, and another note from Ernie confirms what we suspected, that the same panguite fingerprint we found in the Molly Hinders case was also present in the whitish linear burns on Elisa Vandersteel's body. Both women were electrocuted by carbon nanotube conductors that were retracted by spools into a monster drone powered by capacitors and coated in a thermal protective paint that includes panguite. The weights at the ends of the conductors, what resemble sinkers, also contain panguite.

Benton says making a weapon out of something stolen from his powerful brother was Theo's way of appropriating what he perceives as rightfully his. "Sort of like Jacob stealing Esau's birthright," my husband said, and he also believes that the murders in Cambridge were target practice, in a sense, except the selection of the women was emotionally driven by Theo's tendency toward erotomania and sexual violence.

Based on further information Benton has gotten from the brother William, it would seem that Elisa was friendly with Theo and likely had no idea that he was obsessed with her. Apparently after he returned to Cambridge a year ago he suggested that she should come here and try to get her foot in the door as an actress. She could stay with him while she interned, and she did for several weeks, living in a back room and helping with cooking and other chores.

Then she met Chris Peabody and soon after moved in with him, in part to get away from Theo, who by all accounts she was fond of but found increasingly annoying and overbearing. She thought him peculiar but likely never imagined that he was spying on her, stalking her, becoming increasingly enraged when he saw her with the young man she'd met and was falling for.

It's occurred to me that Theo may have been watching when Elisa rode her bicycle to the Faculty Club. I remember her kissing Chris Peabody on the sidewalk while Benton and I were there. It may very well be that Theo had been engaging in dry runs, practicing his drone maneuvers with her being none the wiser, and as she was riding through the park he may have decided to scare her. Maybe he didn't mean to kill her. But he did.

He wouldn't have shown up at the scene and taken the neckerchief or anything else from her body if he hadn't intended to kill her. The blue paisley-printed bit of cloth was a souvenir. Maybe Theo would have taken other items had Anya and Enya not appeared, and I wonder how long he might have hidden in the bushes watching them. It wasn't a deer that startled the twins. That's not what they heard running away in the dark.

There's much we'll never know unless Theo tells all. Or maybe his many recordings will offer an explanation. Benton believes the former MIT professor had been following Elisa and Molly remotely with his airborne camera. If so, there should be graphic proof of his voyeurism, dry runs, his kills. We'll get a peephole view into his violent sexual fantasies.

Benton and his colleagues will spend a lot of time going through boxes of carefully labeled audio-video storage devices. Apparently there are years and years of them inside Theo's landfill of a house, and it's a good thing he can't resist his compulsions. That may seem strange to say since people are dead, but many more would be had he been more disciplined.

The plan very well may have been to have these airborne directed-energy weapons stationed all over the place, and eventually Carrie would have an army of her own human drones operating mechanical ones. We may not know what she had in mind, and I suspect Benton won't find out no matter how much time he spends questioning her eventually.

Carrie isn't going to talk. If she does, nothing will be truthful. Or even if it is, it won't be helpful. Not to us.

I'M STARTLED AWAKE WHEN Tesla suddenly sits up and barks, and I realize I must have drifted back to sleep. I fluff pillows behind me to prop myself up, and I pet her head as she barks again and Sock barely stirs.

"Yes, I know you've learned a big dog trick but please be quiet." I pet the small white bulldog with her brown-masked eyes as she barks and barks, her sides heaving in and out like bellows.

Woof—woof—woof—woof . . . !

"Okay, that's enough. What is it you think you hear?" I throw back the covers, and she won't stop.

I get up and pad barefoot to the curtained window across from the bed, and peeking out, I don't see anything except the rain lashing and flooding the driveway two stories down. The wind howls again, and Tesla barks more frantically as our brindle greyhound Sock continues to snooze.

"All right. Shhhh." I stroke Tesla gently, talking very soothingly, and it makes me feel better too. "It's just a storm." I rub her speckled ears, and the door to the bedroom opens.

"Rise and shine," Dorothy sings out as she enters, and now I know why Tesla was barking.

It was my sister she was hearing, and Dorothy is wearing a large T-shirt and nothing else as she carries two coffees.

"Mind if I come in?" as she hands me a steaming mug and sits on the bed. "Hush Tesla. I can't stand a yippy dog."

"I wouldn't exactly call her yippy. She sounds rather fierce."

"Well it's an irony, right? She's named for a car that's supposed to be quiet."

"Actually it's Lucy's joke. For someone with the biggest carbon footprint on the planet? Now she can tell people she has a Tesla."

"How do you feel? I've heard stories about people who get shocked almost to death or struck by lightning and suddenly they can play the piano or their IQ goes up ten points."

"I'll let you know. I've always wanted to play the piano."

"Did you have unusual dreams?"

"Not yet."

"Listen, Kay. I need to explain better what happened," my sister starts to say, and I stop her.

"How is Desi doing?" I ask because all of us should worry about how traumatized he might be.

"I'm telling you!" Dorothy brags as if she had something to do with it. "What a trouper that boy is! He seems fine."

"He's had plenty of practice putting on the brave front, Dorothy. That doesn't mean he's fine."

"You know? One of the things I've learned after writing how many children's books?" She smiles at her rhetorical question. "Plenty, right? The point is, I know kids. And I'm always amazed at how we're bothered by a lot of things that don't bother them in the least."

"Just because he's not showing something doesn't mean he's not bothered. It will be good for Benton to talk to him when he and Lucy get home."

"Look." Dorothy sips her coffee. "That evil woman came up to me, and of course I did a double take because at first I thought she was Lucy."

"Stop."

"I was waiting at the gate, and she started talking to me, and what a coincidence our seats were next to each other—"

"Stop right there." I hold up a hand, and shake my head.

"But I need to explain what happened. You need to let me—"

"So far you've not explained it at all," I interrupt, "and we need to leave it that way, Dorothy."

"But I just said—"

"You've explained nothing. Period. We can't discuss what went on with you and Carrie at the airport, on the plane, or when she showed up here at the house after you invited her here and then let her in. Okay?"

"But I—"

"No."

"It's just that you must think I'm really stupid but it's not like anyone ever told me about her—"

"I'm a witness in the case the same way you are. Now not another word. Thanks for the coffee. It tastes sweet. Did you put sugar in it?"

"Agave nectar, just the way you like it."

"I don't take sweetener."

"Since when?"

"Since ever, Dorothy." And I have to laugh because the more things supposedly change the more they don't. "You were always the caretaker," I tease.

"I've never been one of those," she says sullenly, and she doesn't seem to be such a good one for herself either.

My sister's hair is too long and too blond, and whoever she's paying a fortune to for aesthetic work ought to be locked up. Her unnaturally round cheeks crowd her eyes when she smiles, her lower jaw is too heavy, and she couldn't frown if she tried, making it slightly more challenging to read her discontent and underlying chronic boredom.

"You have to understand this is the biggest thing I've ever done." Dorothy's over-enhanced breasts are on high alert, and it would suit me if her T-shirt were about ten inches longer.

"What's the biggest thing you've ever done?" I inquire. "I'm afraid I don't know what you're referring to."

"I helped catch someone. You've always been the crime buster, Kay.

And I'm just this overblown pretty woman who's doing the best she can to keep her shit together while I just get damn older all the time. I mean look at me. No matter what I do."

I start to tell her to cut out the tanning booths. Her skin looks spray-painted tan, but I don't go there. She doesn't need my criticism, and maybe I'm not the only one who's pathologically insecure but doesn't show it most of the time.

"I'll tell you what's missing." I set down my coffee on the bedside table. "If you go into the closet and open the first cabinet on the left, you'll find something special I keep down here for rainy mornings just like this one."

"A joint would be nice," she says.

"A very nice Irish whiskey," I reply. "Go on in there and pour us two shots. Then we'll talk as long as you don't ask me anything you shouldn't."

I watch my sister walk into the big cedar-lined closet, and I hear her going into the cabinet and pulling the cork out of the bottle.

"We should get Mom on the phone this morning. Both of us," I say as Dorothy returns.

"Not unless she puts her hearing aids in. I'm tired of yelling." She sets the shot of whiskey by my coffee. "You're never around. In fact you never have been ever since you left for college. So I've been on my own with her. And now I'm the one she picks on."

"I'm very sorry to hear that."

"The book business not being what it was? Kids don't want to read what I write, not this day and age."

"I don't believe that."

"I mean let's face it. I'm not going to be invited to Comic Con." My sister looks rather crushed.

"Never say never." I taste the whiskey and it's warm going down, warmer than the hot coffee but in a different way. "We spend our lives reinventing ourselves, Dorothy. I never knew that until I got a little older and wiser."

"Well our mother's decided I'm the failed one. It used to be you because of your divorce and no kids, and then you decided to be a doctor to dead people so you don't have to worry about losing patients, about them dying on you."

"I'm sure that's what mother says." I reach for my coffee.

"That and getting involved with a married man."

"Mom has to say we've failed because she feels she has," I reply. "She never had a chance to do any of the things we can, and maybe she questions what her purpose on this earth has been. If so, that's not a good way to feel when you're almost eighty years old."

"Well look." Dorothy throws back the whiskey as if she needs courage, which she doesn't. "We're the only sisters we've got, right? So we're in this together, and mainly I wanted to make sure you're okay with Pete and me."

"I don't really know much about Pete and you," I reply as I feel indignant inside when I have no right to feel that.

"It's the real thing, and one favor you could do me is make it sound like I did something helpful at least in catching that monster. What's her name? Carrie Gretchen."

"Grethen. And you were helpful," I reply, and it's true but not the way my sister would have intended.

She was helpful because she single-handedly brought Carrie to my door. It was Dorothy who began answering Facebook postings from someone who claimed to be a childhood friend from our early days in Miami. My sister bought into Carrie's traps hook, line and sinker, and began a correspondence that supplied more information to Carrie than she already had.

Dorothy happily volunteered nasty nicknames, and that my father had recorded a radio commercial for his small grocery store. Carrie must have gotten her hands on it or maybe Theo Portison did. There's nothing good to come of my rubbing it in that Dorothy engaged in a long conversation with a perfect stranger on a flight, and then invited this person to my house and almost got all of us killed and Desi abducted. Dorothy is no match for Carrie's machinations.

But then none of us really are or it wouldn't have taken this many years and destroyed lives to catch her.

CHAPTER 47

A MINUTE PLEASE TO WASH my face and grab my robe." I walk away from the bed, heading to the bathroom. "Then we'll get Tesla and Sock downstairs and you can help me in the kitchen. What's Desi doing? Is he up yet?" I call out to Dorothy.

"He slept with Janet," I hear her say. "I think they're getting started on brunch. They wanted to surprise you by helping."

I smell sausage cooking. And Desi's quite the meat-eater in our midst, he and Marino.

"Why did she want him, Kay? Why would anyone go to such lengths to kidnap a nine-year-old child?"

I stop outside the bathroom door and look at her, wondering if she's serious, and sadly she is. "People have gone to much more extreme lengths than Carrie did," I reply, and my sister doesn't want to know some of the horrors I've seen.

"Well I honestly don't get it." Dorothy wouldn't get it because she couldn't be bothered with Lucy, and that's another thing I need to let go of.

We head downstairs, a rambunctious puppy bulldog and slow old greyhound at our heels, and in the kitchen Janet has the window open over the sink. The sound and smell of the rain is carried in on warm steamy air, and my thoughts are pulled away, outside into the storm. Desi is setting the table in the dining room while Dorothy makes more coffee but I'm not in here in my head.

I'm back in my Miami neighborhood, and I see the child I once was, small and slight with white-blond hair, light blue eyes and cheap clothes. I see my yellow shoe box of a house and the scraps of overgrown yard with sagging chain-link fencing on three sides that kept nothing out including local cats and dogs and an occasional escaped parrot. I see all of it as if I'm watching a movie or back in time, and then thunder splits the air and lightning illuminates the windows.

"Uh-oh," Desi says as he walks back into the kitchen, and the power has gone out. "The lights in the dining room don't work all of a sudden."

The backup generator has kicked in. But only certain areas of the house will have power. Fortunately the kitchen does, and then someone is pounding on the back door.

"It's Marino," Janet is looking at her phone. "I'm just seeing his text. He was at the front door, now he's in back and needs to see you, Kay."

"I didn't hear him pull up."

"The rain's too loud to hear much of anything," Janet says as I follow the hallway past the pantry, to the back of the house.

When I open the door Marino is standing hunched over in a yellow slicker with the hood up, and he says, "We need someplace private to talk. The doorbell in front is broke. I rang it trying to be polite for once."

"The doorbell you pressed is original to the house and not connected to anything. Didn't you see the modern little box with the lighted button that's been there as long as we've lived here?"

"It's dark as shit. What about you grab an umbrella or something and we'll talk out here."

"In the pouring rain with thunder and lightning? How about you come inside and I'll pour you a coffee?"

"Nope. Right here." He points next to him. "Really, Doc? I'm not kidding," and I can tell he's not as I grab a waterproof jacket off the coatrack.

I put it on, pulling up the hood, tightening the drawstring. Stepping outside, I close the door and face him in the splashing downpour.

"What is it, Marino? Are you afraid there might be surveillance devices in the house? Is that what the problem is?" I ask because there could be for all I know. "I'm going to have to talk to Page and make sure she's not let someone in, perhaps someone masquerading as a service person."

It's the sort of thing Carrie would do, I explain as the rain coolly taps the top of my covered head. But Marino's hardly listening, and I'm beginning to sense bigger trouble.

"I'm not taking any damn chances, Doc."

"Why are you here? What is it?"

"I don't know how to tell you this," he says, and I feel instantly sick.

"Are Benton and Lucy all right?" I can barely speak as I think of them flying and driving in this weather.

"Huh? I don't know. I guess." Marino's eyes are wild, and he couldn't be more distracted.

"What's the matter with you?" I raise my voice above water spattering pavers and the sound of the wind-rocked canopies of old trees.

Beaten-down flower petals litter the back lawn like tatters of pastel tissue paper, and puddles sizzle as rain splashes the grass and mulch.

"That blue paisley bandanna Desi had on?" Marino says loudly, water streaming down from the peak of his hood. "The DNA's a problem. It's worse than a problem."

Carrie came to my door like anybody else would, standing there smiling, I can only imagine, and Dorothy led her through the house.

Then Carrie and the drone appeared in the backyard at precisely the same time, robbing Janet of any opportunity to defend herself or anyone. I realize this probably is why Marino is insisting we talk outside in the middle of a rainstorm.

Carrie Grethen has been inside my house. It's possible she may have planted a device or two as she walked through. Dorothy would have been none the wiser. Apparently she didn't begin to think anything was off until Carrie gave Desi the blue paisley-printed neckerchief, ordering him to put it on and stand by her side as she operated the flight control before turning it over to him so he could destroy his own adopted family.

"Did anyone from the DNA lab call you?" Marino is asking, and I bolster myself for the rest of his bad news.

"Not yet."

"Well I just found out. And maybe they don't want to bother you right now after being in the hospital. But you need to know the truth, and that's why I'm here standing outside in the damn rain with you," as distant thunder cracks.

"Who found out what?" Water is splashing over my bedroom slippers, and the hem of my pajamas and robe is already soaked.

"Elisa Vandersteel's DNA is on the neckerchief, which makes sense since it was hers. And we got Carrie's DNA on it and also Temple Gault's."

I'm certain I didn't hear that right. It's so loud and volatile out here, and a part of my brain knows what's coming even as I deny it.

"I'm sorry . . ." I start to say.

"I know what you're thinking. But you heard me," Marino says. "We got a hit on Gault's DNA in the database because he's never been purged due to open cases the Feds are still trying to tie to him. And of course we got a hit on Carrie because she sure as hell's in there."

"This is impossible. How would Temple Gault's DNA get on the neckerchief unless Carrie has some source of it and deliberately con-taminated—"

"No." Marino is slowly shaking his head side to side, water drip-ping, his eyes wide. "No, no, you aren't getting it, Doc."

"What am I supposed to be getting, Marino?" I don't want to be-lieve what he's about to say.

"At first we didn't understand why Desi's DNA wasn't on the bandanna, the neckerchief, whatever you want to call what was tied around his neck. His DNA should be on it," he begins to explain as I get an incredible feeling.

It's like condensation clearing from a window and finally I see what's on the other side. Little Desi with his angular face and mes-meric blue eyes.

"His DNA was on the bandanna after all . . ."

No one is a better fisherman than Carrie. She knows what to do. She knows how to wait and when to tug the line. Gotcha.

"Do you understand what I'm saying?" Marino asks, and the rain has turned into a roar as I remember what Lucy told me about Na-talie's pregnancy.

SHE USED A SPERM donor and a surrogate mother she'd carefully selected, but the fact is the process could have been tampered with.

That would be child's play to Carrie, and there would be no reason for Natalie knowing the truth about Desi's DNA. It would have to be run through a criminal database to get a hit on his biological parents, and that wasn't likely to happen. But Carrie has forced the matter to a conclusion, and it's one that I never anticipated.

"She must have saved Temple Gault's sperm, frozen it or what-ever." Marino turns as the wind blows, keeping the rain off his face.

"You know like these military wives do when their husbands go off to war . . . ?"

"I know what she must have done, and I can see her doing it," I reply. "Have we confirmed this with Desi's DNA? He was swabbed for exclusionary purposes."

"Yeah. It's confirmed. Carrie is Desi's mother. Temple's the father."

"Biologically only."

"She was going to take him, Doc. Carrie was going to raise him to be the next monster. A hybrid of her and Gault. Holy shit. How lucky for her that Natalie died and Carrie could then kick her plan into gear," Marino goes on.

He has it all figured out.

"She creates an incident in Maryland, and you, Lucy and Benton haul ass there," he's saying as a gust of wind sweeps a sheet of rain across the yard. "Or she assumed you'd hightail it out of town, leaving only Dorothy, Janet and Desi all by their lonesome. Only you threw a monkey wrench into things by staying here, and then the attack had to be changed to your house . . ."

"I have no idea what was planned or why," I reply. "Only that it's over and all of us are safe."

"Except for Desi. What are we going to tell Lucy and Janet?"

"We'll tell them the truth. Desi can't help who his biological parents are. It's no different than if he'd been adopted and we had no idea who or where he came from. There's no guarantee what anyone gets, Marino. Not even when it's your own biological child."

"But what if he's like them? I mean really. Think about it. He's right here with us. What if he grows up to be like them? I mean as great as the kid is? What if . . . ?"

"He won't be raised by them," I reply. "He'll be raised by us. Now let's go inside. Let's get brunch going, and I was thinking of making a pitcher of my bloody marys."

We walk back into the house, taking off our raincoats, and water drips on the mat and the hardwood floor. I kick off my drenched bedroom slippers, and step into a bathroom.

"I think I have what I need in the house to make peanut butter pie." I toss him a towel.

"Since when do you make that?" Marino looks as if he's seen a ghost, and in a way he has.

"It seems like a good day for it with Dorothy here, and she loves peanut butter and chocolate, has quite the sweet tooth." I reset the alarm. "But then you probably know that about her," as we return to the kitchen, where Desi is on a footstool getting plates out of a cabinet.

I look at his thin broad-shouldered frame in the Celtics warm-up suit Marino gave him. Desi isn't going to be very big or tall but already he's graceful and lithe, and he's getting strong. He fixes his wide blue eyes on me as he steps down from the stool with an armload of plates, and I've not really talked to him since it all happened. I take the plates from him.

"I think you know where the napkins are," I say to him.

"Yes, ma'am."

"If you want to get them, please, and I'll help you set the table."

"I already did the mats. I hope the ones I picked out are okay." He grabs my hand.

"As long as they match."

We walk out of the kitchen hand in hand, and take the first left into the dining room.

"How did you learn to fish, Kay-Kay?"

That's what Desi calls me.

"Why do you ask?" I turn on the alabaster chandelier.

"I wondered why you thought of my fishing pole when the bad lady was trying to hurt us with the drone."

382

I open the side draperies to watch the rain pound the side yard in the early-morning billowing fog. Wind shakes the spruce trees and rhododendrons, and intermittently rain smacks the glass.

"I didn't think of it," Desi then says before I can answer him. "When she kept trying to make me do things, I didn't think of doing what you did. I should have caught it with my fishing pole and stomped it to death."

"It would have been much too dangerous to stomp on it."

"I could have hit it with my baseball bat."

"You wouldn't want to get that close. Think of it as a huge Portuguese man-of-war you see on the beach with its long tentacles. What do you do?"

"Stay far away!"

"That's right."

He follows me around the table, setting down a napkin to the left of each plate I place on a mat.

"But what made you think of my fishing pole?" He's not going to let me evade the question.

"Truthfully? Because I couldn't think of anything else." I open a drawer in the breakfront, and silverware clinks as we gather that next. "When I saw what she was doing I had to do something. I was lucky."

"Why did that lady want to hurt us?"

"There are some people who aren't happy unless they do bad things to others."

"I know, I know. My moms are always telling me that," Desi says, and of late he's started calling Lucy and Janet his moms.

Specifically Mom and Moms. Lucy is the latter.

"But why did she come here and make me try to hurt someone?"

"What matters is that you didn't." I stop and look at him. "You told her no and you wouldn't do what she said. And that makes you the good person, the strong person."

"I guess so," he says, and then he scampers out of the dining room.

I hear the door open that leads into the basement, and his quick feet on the stairs. When I return to the kitchen he's standing near the breakfast table with a fishing pole. Not his because that's been taken by the police as evidence, but he's fetched mine from the basement, and he looks very serious. I recognize the old spinning reel with its graphite-black telescopic rod, and everything is coated in dust.

"Will you show me how you did it?" He offers me the pole.

"I'm not an expert and we can't really do it inside the house." I hold the rod with the reel foot between the middle and ring fingers of my left hand. "But I let out about six inches of line from the tip of the rod just like this. And I tighten it slowly under my index finger."

I show him, and the reel *click-clicks*.

"Then I hold the line and open the bail, and do you know what the most important part is after that?" I ask.

"What?" he says.

"You aim, pointing the rod at where you want to cast. You point at your target. You've got to know what it is. Then bring up the rod and load it using your elbow and wrist. And let her rip," I explain. "Like most things in life, it's all about timing."

"And it's time to make drinks." Marino walks in, and Benton and Lucy are right behind him.

"Tito's, V8, fresh limes. Who's going to help me?" I walk straight to Benton and hug and kiss him.

"I will!" Desi dashes to the pantry where we keep the liquor.

"I've got the V8 and limes." Janet opens a refrigerator.

"Where do you keep your pitchers and glasses?" Dorothy opens cabinets as she asks.

"I'm so glad both of you are back safely in this awful weather." I hug Lucy too, and I can't tell if she knows about Desi.

But I don't intend to get into the discussion now. It shouldn't be important, and if we discover it is, then we'll figure out something.

"Worcestershire, Tabasco, my special seasonings? Who's helping?" I take the bottle of vodka from Desi and tell him he's going to help me wash celery.

"I break off the stalks like this." I show him in the sink as he stands next to me on his stool. "Now we rinse them under cold water, and we pull off the fibers because they're tough and nobody wants to eat them."

"They're like dental floss."

"And all of them come off. Very good. Right there in the garbage disposal."

"Like this?" His hands are in mine as we rinse a stalk under the running water.

"Exactly like that," and we wash celery together, getting every speck of dirt.